# AN ALIEN ABROAD

## SCIENCE FICTION COLUMNS FROM <u>INTERZONE</u>

## ALSO BY GARY WESTFAHL

*A Sense-of-Wonderful Century: Explorations of Science Fiction and Fantasy Films*

*Islands in the Sky: The Space Station Theme in Science Fiction Literature* [Second Edition]

*The Other Side of the Sky: An Annotated Bibliography of Space Stations in Science Fiction, 1869-1993*

# AN ALIEN ABROAD

## SCIENCE FICTION COLUMNS FROM <u>INTERZONE</u>

### GARY WESTFAHL

**WILDSIDE PRESS**

To David Pringle,
Who kindly gave me the opportunity
to write all of these columns

Published by Wildside Press LLC.
www.wildsidebooks.com

# CONTENTS

# INTRODUCTION

This book, for the first time, makes available a body of my work that has long remained inaccessible and largely unknown to American readers: the thirty-seven bimonthly columns that I contributed to the British science fiction magazine *Interzone* from 1998 to 2004. For while it has long been respected as the best (and at times, the only) British science fiction magazine, *Interzone* has historically attracted few American subscribers, and it is never found in the university libraries or library databases that include most of my other publications. Only five of these columns may be familiar to American readers: the third column was extensively reworked to serve as a chapter in *Hugo Gernsback and the Century of Science Fiction* (2007), though it appears here in its original form; I posted three columns to my World of Westfahl website; and the piece that was submitted to become my thirty-eight column, included here in its original form, was revised to appear as a commentary for the website Locus Online. The other thirty-three columns are being republished for the first time, and as a bonus for those few readers who have read all of my columns, the book concludes with a brand-new, thirty-ninth column, never published before.

It is easy to describe how these columns came to be, but harder to pin down precisely why they ended. *Interzone* had maintained a tradition of sorts of featuring an American columnist, and after Charles Platt and Bruce Sterling drifted away, its editor and publisher David Pringle was looking for a new one. Upon reading a 1997 essay I had written for *Foundation: The International Review of Science Fiction*, "The Quintessence of Science Fiction, Forged in Brunner's *The Crucible of Time*," he decided that I would make a good choice, and while he was attending the 1997 Science Fiction Research Association/J. Lloyd Eaton Conference in Long Beach, California, he personally offered me the job. Thereafter, for over six years, I dutifully provided him with a new column, every two months or so, until the magazine began to encounter financial difficulties around 2004, leading Pringle to sell the magazine to Andy Cox.

Here is where matters get murky. Pringle reports that he sent Cox a number of unpublished manuscripts to appear in his early issues, including my thirty-eighth column; yet Cox informed me during our brief correspondence that he had never received my column. Cox further suggested he had no idea that I had been employed as *Interzone*'s regular columnist, presumably imagining that I had independently submitted thirty-seven articles to the magazine that had each been separately accepted for publication, and hence he had never contacted me about continuing my work. However, this explanation probably represented his polite way of conveying that he was not interested in retaining me as the magazine's regular columnist, a decision he was certainly entitled to make.

Perhaps, if I had aggressively pursued the issue by writing and sending him additional columns specifically designed to appeal to Cox's tastes, I might have retained a place in *Interzone*; however, by this time I was increasingly preoccupied by the need to work intensively on two massive editing projects that I had imprudently agreed to complete more or less simultaneously, *Science Fiction Quotations: From the Inner Mind to the Outer Limits* (2005) and *The Greenwood Encyclopedia of Science Fiction and Fantasy* (2005). For that reason, no longer having to write columns for *Interzone* seemed more a blessing than a curse, and so I abandoned the British magazine and, amidst other projects, increasingly settled into a new form of regular employment as a film reviewer for Locus Online.

* * * *

While I deemed it an honor to become an *Interzone* columnist, it was also a responsibility that generated a considerable amount of tension. It might seem a simple assignment—every two months, write about something interesting that is related to science fiction—but anyone who has been in such a position recognizes that this can be far more difficult than it sounds. One goes through life evaluating virtually every experience as the possible premise for a column: current events, a recently read novel or story, a panel discussion at a science fiction convention, an email message from a stranger .... all of these, and other random events, led to columns. Toward the end, perhaps reflecting a growing sense of desperation, I cannibalized some jottings from David Pringle to function as a column and even transformed a family vacation into a research project for a column. Such is the life of a columnist.

I was also keenly aware that I was writing for an unfamiliar audience—British science fiction fans—and so I very much felt, as my title indicates, like "an alien abroad," uncertain about what these foreigners might be interested in and what might please them or offend them. And I was taking on an entirely new role: previously, I had primarily written as a science fiction scholar; now, my job was to be an entertainer—a way of characterizing myself that I am now comfortable with, but it was a new experience at the time. While columns occasionally refer to ideas from previous columns, there is no overarching argument or general theme to these columns; still, they might be viewed collectively as the journal of a worried commentator constantly striving to come up with one more unexpected idea to make a discussion particularly memorable.

\* \* \* \*

The chapters you will be reading are basically identical to the columns that were published in *Interzone*, though I exclude the rare irruptions from Pringle's assistant Paul Brazier, and for the formal occasion of publication in book form, I now cite all quotations by source and page number and include a bibliography. Freed from the constraints of a 2000-word limit (which I routinely exceeded in any event), I have slightly lengthened some passages and quotations, and in the course of editing I was inevitably inspired to change a word here and a phrase there.

As I worked to polish up these columns, and recalled the experiences of writing them, I began to wonder: could I still do this, after all these years? And so, giving myself the usual two-month deadline, I undertook to produce one more column—not as any sort of grand summation or rousing conclusion, but merely as just another column that I might have submitted in the face of a looming deadline. For the record, it was duly received and approved by David Pringle, just as all of the other thirty-eight were. And it is high time that I stopped talking, and let you read them.

# WHY THE STARS ARE SILENT: THE DECLINE AND FALL OF THE SCIENCE FICTION MONOMYTH (AND, INCIDENTALLY, THE HUMAN RACE)

I believe that science fiction today is approaching a crisis of enormous proportions, one that has nothing to do with evil publishing empires, declining literacy, a dearth of new ideas, or any other problems that have been or could be cited. Rather, it is the monomyth at the foundation of science fiction itself that is gravely threatened.

Donald A. Wollheim's *The Universe Makers* (1971) tells the story as well as anyone: after enduring a near future filled with disasters, humanity will rise above its problems, establish a benevolent world government, and proceed wholeheartedly to the business of conquering space. Humans will spread through the Solar System, then the Galaxy, by means of faster-than-light travel, teleportation, or some other marvelous method. Intelligent aliens will be encountered, sometimes peacefully, sometimes aggressively, but eventually humans and aliens will learn to cooperate. Soon an interstellar government, a Galactic Empire or Federation of Planets, will be in place, and its sentient citizens will move onward to greater triumphs, perhaps even a meeting with God Herself.

This scenario underlies thousands of science fiction stories and novels by authors ranging from E. E. "Doc" Smith to Ursula K. Le Guin. It is the basis of *Star Trek*, *Star Wars*, and the other franchised universes that increasingly dominate bookstores, a common thread that unites almost all the otherwise disparate texts labelled science fiction.

And, we can now be reasonably sure, it is all a lie.

It will not happen that way. Human beings will not travel to thousands of planets in outer space, will not fight wars with implacable aliens, and will not build a complex bureaucracy to govern a million worlds.

And the reason we know this will not happen is simple enough: because it has not already happened.

That is, given that everything about humans, from our star to our chemistry, is unremarkable, and given that we are a young species in an old galaxy, surely another intelligent race, or dozens of such races, should have emerged long ago, should have embarked upon the program of space exploration and settlement that seems logical to us, and should have found and contacted humans by now. Since we have not heard from, and have no evidence of, these starfaring races, the best explanation is that there are no starfaring races. Intelligent species may exist, but conquering the universe and setting up Galactic Empires is apparently not their characteristic behavior.

Of course, other explanations for the Great Silence have been advanced, and, at the risk of conveying old news, I will briefly describe and discount them before proposing another hypothesis. Perhaps other intelligent lifeforms do not exist; perhaps they are roaming through the cosmos but accidentally or deliberately failing to contact us; or perhaps they have found something better to do.

The notion that our intelligent species represents a one-in-a-trillion chance, an occurrence so incredibly unlikely that we may be the first or only one, is improbable, and not only because of what Brian W. Aldiss described as the problem of extrapolating from a single example, namely ourselves. Rather, it is that, as noted, everything about our situation is so ordinary: the sun is a typical, run-of-the-mill star, mounting evidence shows that planet formation occurs frequently, we observe complex organic molecules in space, and the physical laws that governed our development are the same throughout the universe. Almost certainly, other stars have formed small rocky planets similar to Earth that happen to orbit at a distance creating a surface temperature conducive to liquid water—and that should be enough to set the processes of life and evolution in motion. Perhaps, as Robert T. Rood and James S. Trefil have argued in their book *Are We Alone?* (1981), certain key stages in the formation of life are unlikely, but even they accept the possibility of a few other intelligent races in the Galaxy; and even one would be enough to conquer space and, not incidentally, to come and say hello to us.

The argument that other races searching the Galaxy just haven't stumbled upon us yet has been unpersuasive to me since I learned about Von Neumann machines. In a century or so, we will be able to build space probes that can replicate themselves using materials from asteroids or meteoroids. We could build ten of them, loaded with sensing and signaling devices, and send them to nearby stars with instructions to look around, build ten duplicates of themselves, and send the duplicates to slightly farther stars. Even if they moved very slowly, we could fill the entire Galaxy with our probes in a few million years, an eyeblink of cosmic time. And what we will soon be able to do, another intelligent race could have done long ago. With radio and television signals, we have been announcing our existence to the universe for a century or so; anyone who wanted to find us would have found us by now.

Perhaps they *have* found us, but are not revealing their existence to us: malevolently, they may be plotting to exploit or conquer us, or benignly, they may be following some sort of Prime Directive to leave nascent or immature civilizations alone. Call me naïve, but I just can't believe in evil aliens: surely, a race advanced enough to cross interstellar space could develop more sensible solutions to its problems than conquering other planets—terraforming nearby planets for colonization, breeding their own life forms for food. (Still, Clifford D. Simak's *Our Children's Children* [1974] does plausibly depict an alien race imbued with a primal hunting instinct that drives it to senseless invasions.) The idea that we are a well-known, but Not Ready for Prime Time species is more palatable, but humanity has already achieved the two things that science fiction writers were traditionally sure would make the aliens take notice: atomic energy and space travel. What other hurdles must we clear before we are deemed sufficiently advanced to join the Galactic Council?

I speak only of hidden aliens, or alien probes, that might be watching us from afar; the belief among UFO enthusiasts that aliens are actually visiting Earth, but contriving to conceal all evidence of their presence, seems utterly impossible, since it demands the existence of a Perfect Conspiracy. It is hard to generalize about intelligent species (with only one example), but inevitably, any intelligent race will have a tendency to make mistakes built into its programming. Creatures that do not make mistakes have no reason to change what they are doing, and hence can never evolve or improve. At some point, a careless alien tourist would drop a ray gun where it could be picked up by a local constable, or a rookie pilot would accidentally turn off the cloaking device, momentarily revealing an alien dreadnought in the Earth's upper atmosphere. As for the theory that massive amounts of such evidence exist but are being rigorously concealed by the American government: for heaven's sake, a government that could not conceal its leader's involvement in a criminal conspiracy for two years could hardly conceal its knowledge of alien visitations for fifty years.

That leaves the theory that intelligent civilizations, for various reasons, simply never choose to venture into interstellar space. As has been often suggested, alien intelligences may invariably commit suicide by using advanced weaponry, or may invariably develop a preference for Virtual Reality, or navel contemplation, instead of space travel. Perhaps they invariably find better places to go: if they learn how to create their own pocket universes, travel through time, or travel into parallel worlds or other dimensions, the time-consuming and energy-intensive business of space exploration may be deemed unnecessary or unattractive. These are all things that many alien civilizations may end up doing; yet I find it difficult to believe that *all* alien civilizations will invariably follow one particular pattern of behavior, given the amazing differences in behavior we observe in different human societies: anthropologists have studied pacifistic cultures, militaristic cultures, puritanical cultures, promiscuous cultures, nomadic cultures, sedentary cultures, and so on. Since human civilizations resist falling into one pattern of behavior, how can one imagine that all alien civilizations will always follow one pattern of behavior? No matter how likely or appealing these other options might be, surely a few alien species would manage to escape destruction, would tire of philosophy, or would eschew the allure of other universes to explore their own universe.

Without any evidence, none of these explanations can be dismissed, and my misgivings about them might be challenged. Still, since no explanation to date is compelling, there can be no objection to placing another idea in the hopper.

\* \* \* \*

A while ago, scientist and science fiction writer Vernor Vinge created a stir with an article noting that we are approaching a "singularity" in human history, perhaps in the next thirty years: the emergence of computers more intelligent than we are. As Vinge says, we can have no idea what those machines will do, or how humans will interact with them, because our experiences provide absolutely no information about intelligences greater than our own. But critics rush in where scientists fear to tread, and the crude analogies I can devise suggests two possible outcomes.

The first scenario is that machine intelligence will be different in degree, but not in kind, from human intelligence. Machines would be like the class brains, and humans would be like the class dunces. This would not necessarily be disastrous: class brains and class dunces can be friends, can cooperate as equals to accomplish common goals, and can even help each other in various ways. Thus, humans and computers may become partners, working together to achieve further progress and expand throughout the Galaxy.

The second scenario, which strikes me as far more likely, is that machine intelligence will be different from human intelligence in both degree and kind. Machines would be like human beings, and humans would be like dogs. Or, if it bothers some people to envision humans as similar to servile and obedient dogs, they might pictures humans in the role of cats—feisty and independent, but still subordinate creatures. Now, humans and their pets can enjoy warm relationships, and pets can be helpful to humans in some situations, but humans and pets can never be equal partners. Thus, humans may be reduced to the status of pets or servants, while computers take control of civilization and direct its further progress and expansion through space entirely on their own.

From the standpoint of an evolutionary biologist like Michael Rose, of course, this would never happen, as humans would swiftly take decisive action to eliminate any threat to their hegemony. (When we served on a panel together, and someone mentioned the chance that computers would try to take over, Rose responded that, if that happened, humans would merely pull the plugs and thus win the struggle for dominance.) However, this reassuring thought assumes the sudden appearance of a huge power-mad computer that announces its intent to take over the world, the way it was usually envisioned in science fiction stories like D. F. Jones's *Colossus* (1966). But the transition to computer rule may have little to do with megalomania: when people work together on a project, power flows naturally to the most intelligent and capable person, and the computer takeover of Earth may be a similarly gradual, even invisible process. Already, today's idiot-savant computers are gaining increasing control over humans, as anyone who has watched a business grind to a halt when the computer crashes can attest; and, as more and more computers, and more and more intelligent computers, are increasingly employed in innumerable situations, humans may literally wake up one day and realize that, without their even noticing it, the new, superintelligent computers have become masters of the Earth.

If this is what will happen to humans, it will happen to all intelligent races. Sentient beings, we can confidently predict, will master technology and will, like humans, develop machines to augment their natural abilities: humans built plows and looms to augment their hands, carriages and bicycles to augment their feet, telescopes and cameras to augment their eyes, and calculators and computers to augment their brains. Whatever other qualities they may have, all intelligent species will have brains; so they will develop thinking machines, will improve those machines, and will eventually create machines that are intelligent enough to take control of their societies.

My explanation for the Great Silence, then, is this: any number of intelligent species have emerged in the Galaxy, but all of them came to be dominated by their own thinking machines. It is those machines that have expanded into interstellar space, trying to find others of their own kind. They have heard the radio transmissions of humans, but have not bothered to respond. Consider: if someone today announced the discovery, in some remote part of the world, of a hitherto unknown species of humans, that would be headline news around the world, and a small army of scientists, journalists, and tourists would rush to the scene to observe our strange new relatives. In contrast, if someone announced the discovery of a hitherto unknown species of dogs or cats, that would be at best filler material; perhaps, in a few years, some zoologist or veterinarian might scrounge up a research grant and go to study them, but neither they nor anyone else would consider it very important. Similarly, no matter how highly we value our own abilities and accomplishments, they may be of little or no importance to intelligences far superior to our own.

Uniquely, this explanation is, or soon will be, a testable hypothesis.

Research into Artificial Intelligence has not advanced as spectacularly as advocates predicted, but progress is being made; I recall watching a documentary that showed two computers trying to carry on a conversation with each other. Someday soon, computer scientists may be able to assign this task to their brightest machines: devise a message that could be understood by, and would elicit a response from, an unknown computer of unknown origin and design. And the messages they create could be broadcast out into space.

If my hypothesis is correct, a computer-crafted Von Neumann machine may already be in our Solar System, listening to our news reports and situation comedies, but with little interest in the barking of dogs. But when it hears a message from a computer, it may detect some quality therein, perhaps one imperceptible to humans, identifying its sender as an intelligent machine; then, the probe will quickly send to its control center the happy news that another intelligent race has been located, and it will immediately send a welcoming message to that new member of the galactic family.

And when the message arrives, what many thought would be the happiest day in human history will instead be our most depressing day: for while we will finally know we are not alone in the universe, we will also know it is a universe controlled by machines, a universe we will never master, a universe where we will always be subservient.

* * * *

More than a few times, I have been in the company of someone I knew was more intelligent than I was, and it was disheartening to look at a person who knew more than I would ever know, who had skills I would never have, who could do things that I would never be able to do. But evolution has endowed humans with hardy psyches, and I could eventually console myself: there were still some things I could do that the other person could not do, or would not want to do; there were still meaningful goals I could accomplish; and I could return to work and continue to enjoy my little triumphs.

Similarly, humanity will overcome its initial melancholy after realizing its universal and perpetual inferiority. Humans will think about all the things they can still do and will soon be doing them with renewed enthusiasm. Research, business, sports, arts, music, literature—these activities will be carried on as before.

Except for science fiction.

Because science fiction, at least the modern tradition that began in American pulp magazines, has always been more than another form of imaginative literature. Readers and writers believed that the genre, if lacking the power of specific prediction, was still somehow better aware of, or more attuned to, the future, and that its enthusiasts were better prepared for the future than the mundanes. Coupled with this belief was not blind technophilia, as some charge, but a gentle optimism that, with a little luck and perseverance, humanity might gradually overcome its problems, move to other worlds, make wonderful new discoveries, accomplish more and more great things, and continue progressing without the burden of old bugaboos about hubris getting clobbered by nemesis.

These are, of course, the sorts of feelings that are belittled and ridiculed by people like Brian W. Aldiss. But these feelings are real, they are palpable; innumerable people have felt them. There exists a documentary record stretching back seventy years of people expressing exactly that excitement about a literature that offered a sense of the future and intimations of awesome prospects to come. These feelings explain why a community of fans coalesced around the term "science fiction," why the genre became well-known and popular, why conferences and magazines devoted to science fiction exist, and why Aldiss's *Trillion Year Spree: The History of Science Fiction* (1986) was published. Aldiss lacks the power to erase those feelings, and lacks the authority to forbid them.

But such feelings could not survive news of a superintelligent alien machine welcoming our own superintelligent machines to the community of galactic civilizations. For the belief system behind modern science fiction would then be exposed as not only false—there is no human-directed expansion into space in our future—but impossible—the achievements of humans will forever be limited in contrast to the more limitless possibilities of computers.

At that moment, then, science fiction would become what many have always wished it to be: fantasy. Space fortresses and ray guns would be just as likely as magic carpets and magic wands; the universes of Isaac Asimov's Foundation and Frank Herbert's Dune would be just as likely as J. R. R. Tolkien's Middle-earth and Stephen R. Donaldson's Land. Stories involving the accoutrements of science fiction might endure, but its essence would be lost: even if Captain Kirk led the *Enterprise* on another million missions, the stories would only be diverting adventures, and could not function as a meaningful and inspirational message for their audience.

Signs of this coming collapse of science fiction are already visible. Vinge, who is perhaps best aware of the consequences of advanced machine intelligence, has reported that he simply can no longer write the traditional kinds of science fiction stories, with humans racing out to the stars, meeting aliens, and building galactic empires, because he no longer believes that any of these things will ever happen. That is exactly the problem I describe: science fiction writers, unlike fantasy writers, often feel the need to *believe* in their own constructed worlds—not as predictions, but at least as possibilities. Hard science fiction writers, in particular, will probably find that they cannot write about worlds they believe to be impossible, and hence, like Vinge, will not be able to write the sorts of stories traditionally regarded as science fiction.

Of course, some people like Aldiss, perhaps with the gleeful nastiness of a child telling her friend that there is no Santa Claus, will be pleased to see the foolish dreams of science fiction shattered, so that writers can focus their attention on the serious business of creating gaudy new technological disguises for tired old cautionary tales. But I wonder. A man who can see that Edgar Rice Burroughs's *Pellucidar* (1923) is a much better novel than H. G. Wells's *Men like Gods* (1923) has not entirely lost his appreciation for the zest, the joy, the giddy, adolescent energy of limitless ambitions that drives so much of the genre. And watching nemesis clobber hubris again and again can get a little boring. After reading the sophisticatedly skeptical science fiction stories in John Kessel's *Meeting in Infinity* (1992), Brian Stableford reported in his review that "I never fully understood, until I read John Kessel, how much I sympathise, in the deepest layers of my problematic psyche, with Hugo Gernsback" (128). So, when a message of bad news from outer space signals that the dreams of science fiction are only illusions, when science fiction becomes just another option for writers seeking to metaphorically describe the human condition, many may discover that they deeply regret the loss of a type of literature they had once so zealously condemned.

Contemplating an event that would be a devastating blow to humanity and all its strivings, it may seem peculiar to worry about the fate of science fiction. However, when a woman realizes that her house is burning down, she often focuses attention on small, insignificant items of great sentimental value. Having devoted my career to science fiction, I will be forgiven my special concern for the genre and not for the larger implications of the news I anticipate, which I will leave for others to explore.

Still, there is an irony here that might be of interest even to those with no commitment to science fiction. Of all the distinct forms of literature recognized by humanity, science fiction may be the newest; yet it may also be the first to die. Future historians, then, may study the field as a quaint curiosity, the one form of literature doomed to extinction because it happened to embody the only set of aspirations that humanity could never fulfill.

* * * *

After I first presented this column as a paper during the 1997 Science Fiction Research Association/Eaton Conference, David Pringle told me that it might work well for *Interzone* except for one problem: that the argument would be regarded as "typical British gloom-and-doom." Well. As a lifelong American, I hardly want my ideas to be regarded as "typically British," and thinking it over today, I am not wholly convinced that the possibility I envisioned is as gloomy as my rhetoric might have suggested.

It is characteristic of children that they express many grand and glorious ambitions. A boy might say at various times that he wishes to be President of the United States, an astronaut, a police officer, or a pop singer. Confronted with his contradictory goals, a boy might even suggest some implausible combination of careers, aspiring to become an All-Star baseball player for half the year and a veterinarian during the off-season. Yet parents and other adults will be unfailingly supportive of these virtually impossible dreams: yes, son, they will say, you can do whatever you want to do.

However, as children grow older, they typically learn, through research or some peripheral experience, that their youthful dreams simply do not correspond to their true abilities and desires, so they develop other, more modest, and more suitable goals. And those who do not do this spontaneously will be prodded by others to be more realistic: a college counselor advising graduating seniors, unlike a child's doting parent, will have no patience with someone babbling on about becoming a world-famous movie star while conducting ground-breaking cancer research in her spare time.

Abandoning these grand ambitions, I submit, usually results not in lifelong regret but quiet pleasure. For example, I now know that I will never be President of the United States, I will never be the astronomer assigned to the first Mars expedition, and I will never be the keyboard player for the Grateful Dead. Yet I spend no time lamenting those lost opportunities: rather, I realize that it is all for the best, for I would not enjoy, or be very good at, the typical activities of a political leader, scientist, or rock musician. I still have ambitions, but they are more practically and palatably centered on what I might achieve while typing on a keyboard.

Now, for the past seventy years or so, many science fiction writers have relentlessly argued that the proper goal of the human race is to conquer the universe. However, even if the particular nightmare scenario above turns out to be incorrect, the logic of this ambition is seriously open to question. Let's face it: the universe is really, really big, it is really, really old, and, except for a few rare places, it is really, really inhospitable. And any sane being interviewing species applying for the job of Universe Conqueror would quickly conclude that humans are just too tiny, too short-lived, and too fragile to plausibly take on that assignment. To be sure, humans someday might evolve into, or turn themselves into, beings that were capable of conquering the universe (perhaps by becoming machines of a sort themselves), but then they would no longer be recognizably human at all—which is, I believe, both the point of George Zebrowski's *Macrolife* (1979) and the reason why many readers find it unsatisfactory as a novel. Most humans, given the choice, would prefer to remain human, and would prefer to believe that the human race will and should always remain human—which is to say, remain beings that cannot and should not aspire to conquer the universe. And, if they perversely continue to insist upon this goal, such creatures would only be setting themselves up for future failure, and future sadness.

Arguably, at least, the human race has grown and matured a great deal in recent decades. Perhaps, then, it is time for science fiction to abandon the role of supportive parent, urging its readers to go out and conquer the universe, and instead take on the role of college counselor, seriously pondering what sorts of worthwhile ambitions the human race might more reasonably, and more happily, pursue.

# GRAYER LENSMEN, OR, LOOKING BACKWARD IN ANGER

On this side of the Atlantic at least, there has been a tremendous amount of recent concern about the so-called "graying of fandom." Old fogies attend science fiction conventions and, looking around, seem to see nothing but other old fogies. And they ask, where on Earth are the youngsters? Why aren't fresh young newcomers getting involved with the fanzines, the letter-writing, the organizations, the conventions, and so on? Panelists and chatroom participants bemoan the problem and suggest vigorous new programs and crusades to attract more young people to the noble enterprise of science fiction fandom.

Actually, this phenomenon is not really surprising, because it is always hard to recruit soldiers to fight the good fight when the battle has already been won.

\* \* \* \*

Consider the situation in the 1930s, when fandom first emerged as a visible entity. At that time, "science fiction" as a recognized genre was exhibited and celebrated only within the pages of a few, struggling, largely unknown magazines. The likelihood of its continued existence was very much in doubt; and practitioners of the subgenre of alternate history (about which more later!) could easily construct a scenario in which Hugo Gernsback decides to cut his losses and abandon his science fiction magazines a few years earlier, the elderly editor T. O'Conor Sloane dies suddenly and brings *Amazing Stories* to a halt, and Street & Smith opts not to revive *Astounding Stories*—resulting in the disappearance of all the magazines publishing "science fiction," and indeed the disappearance of the entire genre known by that name (though it undoubtedly would have later reconstituted itself and re-emerged under another name and, perhaps, with a different governing ideology).

In this dire situation, science fiction fandom as a united force was desperately *needed* to keep the genre alive. Their letters and subscriptions encouraged publishers to keep the magazines going; their vocal support boosted the egos of writers who otherwise might have fled from a field offering little in the way of reimbursement; their organizations began to collect and publish science fiction works, bringing some attention to writers that larger publishers were ignoring; they gathered and preserved magazines, manuscripts, and memorabilia that no one else seemed to care about; and in some cases, fan groups functioned as true charities, dispersing the money they gathered to help out writers and fans with major financial problems. Today, it is easy to ridicule the rhetoric of the Science Fiction League and the early fanzines, but the hard work and enthusiasm of those pioneering zealots may have been largely, if not entirely, responsible for the endurance and eventual triumph, for better or worse, of the peculiar American vision of "science fiction" as a distinct literary genre.

Supported by fandom, science fiction grew larger and better, and major companies soon began to publish science fiction books, first as small subsidiary operations, later as major sources of income. Magazine rates went up, and films and television plunged into the production of science fiction, providing profitable work for some writers and increased prominence for their genre. Writing science fiction was finally becoming rewarding, and things have continued to progress in that direction. However, even as the *financial* problems of science fiction were receding, fandom remained an important force in addressing its *aesthetic* problems. Insightful reviewers like Damon Knight and James Blish in the 1950s, and Algis Budrys in the 1960s, castigated inferior work, praised superior work, and provided expert instruction on how to avoid the former and produce the latter. Increasingly numerous and voluminous fanzines presented more and more critical commentaries on contemporary works, and fan scholars like Sam Moskowitz and Alexei Panshin schooled new readers in the history of the genre. Prestigious awards—the fans' Hugos and the writers' Nebulas—commemorated and brought attention to noteworthy stories and novels. Collections of essays about the art of science fiction writing inspired professionals to improve their writing, while manuals like L. Sprague de Camp's *Science Fiction Handbook* (1953) offered guidance to neophytes.

Prodded and pushed to meet higher literary standards, many science fiction writers responded, often impressively; and, as one result, a growing number of academic scholars turned their attention to the genre—a development that has now made the aesthetic guidance of fandom just as superfluous as its other assistance. Yes, literary critics have more than their share of flaws, and I have chronicled many of them at length. But these scholars have been consistently interested in noticing, analyzing, and supporting literary quality in science fiction, and their track record in choosing authors to focus their energies on is, on the whole, reasonably good, including such undeniable talents as Philip K. Dick, J. G. Ballard, Ursula K. Le Guin, Samuel R. Delany, Octavia E. Butler, William

Gibson, and Kim Stanley Robinson. And university-based scholars, in addition to their not entirely unhelpful training in literary research and analysis, have at their disposal a number of impressive weapons in promoting superior science fiction: some clout in getting good books back into print; university libraries to collect and preserve science fiction books and writers' manuscripts; journals and scholarly studies regularly published by university presses; massive purchases of novels for use as textbooks in college classes; sums of money to pay science fiction writers to attend conferences or serve as visiting professors; and organizations to support the "literature of the fantastic," "literary fantasy," or another buzzword designed to disguise an enthusiasm for science fiction from some of these scholars' stuffier colleagues. In contrast to all this, the egoboo of a favorable review in a fanzine or *Analog* seems like weak tea indeed.

I would never argue that science fiction fandom has become *useless*. It is still a wonderful way to come into contact with some highly interesting and usually well-educated people, a slightly weirder version of MENSA; the vast amounts of books, magazines, and memorabilia held by fans remain priceless treasures awaiting further exploration; the achievements of fan scholars in the area of bibliography at least are unsurpassed elsewhere; the science fiction conventions that earn a profit carry on good work by regularly making charitable contributions to worthwhile genre-related causes; and the research and commentaries of many non-academic critics continue to be salutary and properly appreciated in all circles. (Given a choice between Darko Suvin and John Clute, who could possibly opt for Suvin?) But science fiction fandom is no longer *essential* to the financial or aesthetic survival of the genre. In the 1930s, if fandom had vanished, the genre of science fiction might have vanished as well; today, if fandom were to vanish, the genre of science fiction would keep on trucking, probably not as good as it would have been, but viable and valuable nonetheless.

In essence, therefore, fandom is "graying" because it *succeeded*: coming upon a neglected waif named science fiction, fandom nurtured the child, helped it grow, watched it settle into mature productivity within a supportive environment, and thus, like any effective parent, made itself superfluous. Observing this situation, young people have no reason to believe that the current activities of fandom are vitally important to the genre, and hence are disinclined to commit many hours of labor to activities that are not vitally important in that way. If they do have free time, they would rather strive to save the whales, feed the homeless, or bring health care to the underprivileged—and who, in the final analysis, can blame them? For that, unlike fandom, unquestionably remains vitally important work.

* * * *

Now, if the graying of *fandom* is an inevitable development which cannot be redressed by energetic outreach programs and PR campaigns, there is another related but different concern about the potential graying of the entire science fiction *readership*, which is and always has been much vaster, and more difficult to characterize, than active fandom. Available evidence, while by no means definitive, does indicate that the average age of the science fiction reader is slowly but steadily increasing, suggesting that the genre is attracting fewer young readers than before. Such statistics may only reflect the fact that, in general, young people are reading less than they used to, chiefly because there are so many other forms of narrative entertainment available, such as films, television, video and computer games, role-playing games, music videos, and so on. And, since many works in these other forms also fall into the categories of science fiction or fantasy, it may well be that the total number of young people who are *experiencing* science fiction—not simply those who are *reading* it—is at an all-time high, and hence that there is no real cause for alarm in their seemingly smaller numbers in the limited area of linear prose narrative.

This may well be the case; but I fear there is another explanation for the advancing age of science fiction readers, a matter of graver import than a burgeoning profusion of potbellies at science fiction conventions. A disturbing process may be in motion: the average audience ages slightly, so that writers adjust and write stories for a slightly older audience; this shift in focus causes the average audience to age a bit more, inspiring writers to move a bit more in that direction; and the cycle continues onward towards senescence, if not senility.

As evidence for this chilling scenario, consider the recently prominent subgenre of alternate history.

* * * *

A few months ago, when I turned in an entry on Kim Newman for *The St. James Guide to Horror, Ghost, and Gothic Writers* (1998), editor David Pringle remarked that he found the entry "perhaps a bit lacking in praise." Well, one might say, when struggling to quickly finish one's last four assigned entries in order to be only one month late in meeting the Absolutely, Positively Final Deadline, one might well neglect a few of the niceties of form, such as the inclusion of the proper proportion of complimentary language. But such an explanation would be disingenuous, for I will admit that I did feel a growing irritation as I read several of Newman's works, and that, I must assume, subliminally surfaced while I was writing his entry. Why, I wondered, was an author with such obvious talents increasingly wasting his energies in the puerile and pointless subgenre of alternate history?

There are, after all, certain expectations long associated with science fiction. Hugo Gernsback quaintly believed that its stories could teach people about science and give inventors useful ideas; a bit more maturely, John W. Campbell, Jr. maintained that science fiction could illustrate the process of scientific thinking and provide some helpful guidance regarding whether, or how, to cope with potential scientific or social developments. The erudite readers of *Interzone* might smile at these fanciful aspirations, but underlying and unifying these dubious arguments is a more general and more admirable ideology: the idea that science fiction is, or should be, a literature focused on the *future*, a literature which might educate people about possible futures, help them come to grips with imminent future breakthroughs, and perhaps inspire people to change or improve the future by means of Awful Warnings or utopian visions.

In contrast, the subgenre of alternate history is obsessively focused on the *past*. Utterly unconcerned with changing or improving the future, the authors of alternate histories dedicate themselves to the impossible and fruitless task of changing and improving the past. Essentially an extended version of the Hypothesis Contrary to Fact, an alternate history may at times be a tempting device to illustrate a point (see above!), but such a scenario cannot persuasively support any thesis worthy of attention. True, these stories can "instruct and entertain" in the time-honored fashion of any literary work, but they might only in the most tangential or serendipitous way be useful in anticipating or dealing with the problems and possibilities of today and tomorrow.

More to the point here, alternate history is unmistakably an old man's literature, studiously ignoring the unsettling present and even more unsettling future to wallow in nostalgia about the Good Old Days, albeit observed through a distorting lens. To me, its writers sound like garrulous old veterans who, having told their war stories dozens of times, are driven to intermingle some whimsical speculations in a desperate effort to maintain the interest of their bored listeners: "Let me tell you, sonny boy, if it had been flying saucers bombing Pearl Harbor, instead of Japanese airplanes, well, that would have been a different story, yes-sirree ...." In harmony with the reduced energies of most senior citizens, alternate history is also a lazy man's literature: if writers want to invent some new characters, or come up with some new stories, that's fine, but if their imaginations are flagging when it comes to characters or plot, they can always drag familiar icons like Benjamin Franklin or Marie Antoinette onto the stage, or they can retell the story of storming the Bastille with a few minimal variations. And coming up with new ideas for stories is as easy, as endless, and as profitless as a running game of shuffleboard: what if space aliens had invaded ancient Greece? What if Charles Manson had secretly replaced Buzz Aldrin on the Apollo 11 moon flight? What if Abraham Lincoln had moved to the South, failed to prosper, and become an embittered drifter driven to assassinate that surprising actor-turned-politician, President John Wilkes Booth?

What if, what if, what if .... to which the only rational response is, who cares? who cares? who cares? I live in an ever-changing world, and I am concerned about what is happening now and what may happen tomorrow; I simply have no time to sit around and wonder, "What would have happened if William Shakespeare had been a werewolf?" But, my personal objections notwithstanding, the broader problem is that, given that modern young people are keenly worried about today and tomorrow, and given that they usually know little and care nothing about yester-day's history, a genre fixated on that subject, even as seen in a funhouse mirror, will surely not be greatly interesting to them. Thus, the growing numbers of alternate history stories testify to a genre with a growing desire to appeal to older readers, and a growing disinclination to appeal to younger readers.

To explain the puzzling popularity of alternate histories, two other points must be pondered. First, the phenomenon to date is effectively limited to prose narrative, since few if any examples come to mind in other media (except for the marginal cases of video and computer games set in the past, like Castle Wolfenstein, where an expedition into a vast Nazi castle eventually leads successful players to an obviously ahistorical confrontation with Adolf Hitler himself). Second, while it is not surprising that prominent strangers to the field ranging from Win-ston Churchill to Newt Gingrich and Richard Dreyfuss might gravitate to an unchallenging form of fictional speculation unrelated to the historic goals of science fiction, one observes a growing number of major writers seemingly steeped in all the traditions of the genre unaccount-ably playing this frivolous game. I mean, it's easy enough to dump on Harry Turtledove and Robert Forstchen, but Brian Stableford's entry on "Alternate Worlds" in *The Encyclopedia of Science Fiction* (1993) also cites recent works by Harry Harrison, S. P. Somtow, William Gibson and Bruce Sterling, James P. Hogan, Kim Stanley Robinson, and Stableford himself, all writers demonstrably attuned to the *Zeitgeist* of true science fiction and fully capable of thoughtfully probing into the possible future of the human race. So, why are they participating in this shuffleboard tournament?

\* \* \* \*

With one chain of thought to unfold, the explanatory matrix will be complete.

While many forms of science fiction have been designed to appeal to juvenile readers, the standard, and seemingly most powerful, approach is to provide exciting stories of exploration and adventure in outer space. This was how Hugo Gernsback attracted younger readers in the 1930s, how the publishers of Winston juveniles attracted younger readers in the 1950s, and how David Brin currently hopes to attract a new generation of younger readers with a forthcoming series of juvenile science fiction novels he is sponsoring and supervising. And clearly, much recent science fiction in prose, film, and television indicates that these space stories continue to be popular with young people.

Now, as I have previously suggested in *Science Fiction Studies*, and in *Interzone*, there are now good reasons to suspect that the traditional picture of near-future human expansion into space permeating modern science fiction is at best an attractive myth and at worst a pernicious falsehood.

The writers of prose science fiction, more knowledgeable and more perceptive than the people who create films, television shows, video games, and the like, are most likely to harbor deep suspicions about the validity of this predicted future, and hence are most likely to feel inclined, or even compelled, to avoid writing stories that occur in such a predicted future. Not wishing to tell lies in order to appeal to younger readers, they instead choose to address older readers with alternate histories, where all of the problematic issues raised by futuristic space fiction are conveniently avoided. And younger people, in response, drift away from prose fiction to the visual media, where creators with less insight and fewer scruples are more than happy to continue dishing out the potted pablum of The Future According to *Star Trek* and *Star Wars*.

If this is in fact the bind that modern prose writers are finding themselves in, there is a possible ameliorative solution, albeit a narrow and limited one: to write alternate histories *about the space program*, drawing upon the allure of space adventure while still avoiding all consideration of any actual futures humanity might encounter. Interestingly, both Allan Steele and Stephen Baxter have recently published novels exactly along these lines. (Also, currently stored in the directory of one inept, would-be science fiction writer happens to be a novelette entitled "Charles A. Lindbergh's Flight to the Moon.")

For the most part, however, I can now envision a bleak and bifurcated future for science fiction: on one side, ongoing media or media-derived blatherings about Boldly Going Where No One Has Gone Before into outer space, which will attract only the young and the gullible, and on the other side, unending and increasingly silly prose revisions of human history, which will attract only the old and the jaded.

And it doesn't have to be this way.

To say that humanity may have no future in exploring space is not necessarily to say that humanity has no future at all. Perhaps the long-standing dreams embedded in science fiction can now be exposed as fallacious, but it is still possible to imagine that the human race, with the assistance of science fiction, might soon discover and embrace new and different dreams which might be just as appealing and stimulating as the old goal of conquering the universe. Of course, the despair about finding such comparable dreams I previously conveyed may ultimately be validated, but it is nonetheless disheartening to see a growing number of writers already preparing to forever abandon the pursuit of futuristic dreams in order to live in an old folks' home, frittering away their time examining past impossibilities in order to amuse other senior citizens who have resolved to have nothing further to do with either the present or the future.

So you see, I don't worry at all about the graying of science fiction fandom, and I worry only a little about the graying of the science fiction readership; what I deeply worry about, however, is the graying of science fiction itself.

# CREATORS OF SCIENCE FICTION, 1 AND 2: BRIAN STABLEFORD AND JOHN CLUTE

Today, Brian Stableford and John Clute are properly regarded as two of our most erudite and insightful commentators on science fiction. For years, Stableford has produced books, articles, and reviews that are widely appreciated as valuable sources of information and ideas, while Clute, long renowned for excellent reviews, has earned new prominence as a co-editor or author of definitive reference works. When virtuosos like these are observed speaking foolishly, as occurred in the December, 1997 issue of *Interzone*, that is cause for concern—and some discussion.

Although the knowledgeable Mike Ashley has already criticized "Creators of Science Fiction, 10: Hugo Gernsback" in a letter published in the February, 1998 issue of *Interzone*, he was too kind to mention that the article, as is uncharacteristic of Stableford, included several factual errors. Gernsback's Menograph was a thought-recording device, not a "thought-reading device" (47). Clement Fezandié was not the only writer who contributed new stories to both *Science and Invention* and *Amazing Stories*; G. Peyton Wertenbaker did so as well. Gernsback never intended to make *Amazing Stories* an all-reprint magazine, since he announced plans to publish new stories in the first issue and stated the same more emphatically in a special announcement in the second issue (which also featured a new story). E. E. "Doc" Smith, Stanton A. Coblentz, and John Taine all published in the 1920s, though Stableford asserts that they "found no market for their extravagant imaginative fiction" until "the early 1930s" (49), and the first two began their careers in Gernsback-edited magazines. Gernsback sold *Wonder Stories* in 1936, not 1933. There are other errors, none grievous, but the impression cumulatively imparted is that Stableford does not know very much about Gernsback and lacks any desire to learn more about him—an odd stance for someone presenting a purportedly authoritative article about Gernsback.

Yet any distress about incidental mistakes fades in the face of the egregious inaccuracy of the overall argument. Here is what Stableford would have you believe: Hugo Gernsback was a conniving scoundrel who wrote or published science fiction solely as another way to garner profits. At the instant when science fiction ceased to be lucrative, he immediately abandoned the field to focus on other larcenous schemes and, indeed, forgot about its very existence. Then, one day, he happened to meet Sam Moskowitz, who told him, "Hey, you're the father of science fiction"—in response to which Gernsback scratched his head and replied, "Well, if you say so, I guess I am."

There is regrettably no polite way to characterize this account, because it is simply not true. One could write a book presenting mountains of evidence to disprove it; indeed, both Ashley and I have done exactly that. Here are some facts: during every decade of his life in America, Gernsback wrote science fiction, wrote about science fiction, and published science fiction—usually extensively. Between 1926 and 1936, he launched six science fiction magazines and wrote two dozen editorials and one article focused on the topic of science fiction. And what about the two decades when Stableford says he "showed not the slightest interest in science fiction" (49)? In 1940, he began publishing a science fiction comic book, *Superworld Comics* (not the late 1950s, as Stableford implies); he began to privately publish annual magazine parodies, mailed out as Christmas cards, featuring what Stableford described as his "pseudo-journalistic exercise[s] in futurology" (49), several of which were later republished in his magazine *Science-Fiction Plus*; and in 1950, he revised the text of *Ralph 124C 41+: A Romance of the Year 2660* for its Second Edition (it was not merely "reprinted" [47], as Stableford asserts), also writing a new "Preface."

Particularly objectionable is the hypothesis, stated as fact, that Moskowitz first identified Gernsback as "the father of science fiction" in the 1950s and gave Gernsback the idea. Throughout his career, Gernsback repeatedly and proudly praised himself as a pioneer in the field: in 1929, he wrote, "I started the movement of science fiction in America in 1908 through my first magazine, 'MODERN ELECTRICS'" ("Science Wonder Stories" 5). In 1934, he chose a later starting date but still labelled himself the instigator of the "movement": "Not until 1926, when I launched my first Science Fiction magazine, was any concerted movement possible .... The movement since 1926, has grown by leaps and bounds until today there are literally hundreds of thousands of adherents of Science Fiction ...." ("The Science Fiction League" 1061). By 1943, when reporters from *Time* and *Newsweek* magazine interviewed Gernsback about his first magazine parody, he surely identified himself as the father of science fiction, since both magazines printed versions of the claim: Gernsback "is also generally credited with being the father of the modern science-fiction pulps" ("Greetings, Electronitwits!" 54) and is

"The father of pseudo-scientific fiction" ("Gernsback, the Amazing" 40). One need search no further for evidence to contradict Stableford's thesis; these are smoking guns.

To be sure, Gernsback was an unscrupulous businessman and was hardly adverse to profiting from his predilection for science fiction; but data confirming some underlying sincerity in his interest is overwhelming, and the many readers of *Amazing Stories* and its successors perceived that interest as sincere and responded accordingly. It is hard to believe that Gernsback could have had such an undeniable and profound impact on people like Moskowitz, Donald A. Wollheim, and John W. Campbell, Jr. if he had been doing it only for the money, if he had really thought of science fiction only as a "contemptible bastard" (50).

So, why would the normally reliable and judicious Stableford produce such a sloppy and slanderous diatribe? Demonstrably, Stableford has an agenda, one with no place for Gernsback. As a champion of the "scientific romance," a tradition he observes in Britain from 1888 to 1950, he must discern a lamentable error of judgment in most histories of science fiction: after H. G. Wells, they unaccountably abandon the Mother Country, nodding only in the direction of Olaf Stapleton and C. S. Lewis, and rather than discussing major writers like John Gloag and S. Fowler Wright, they lavish attention on a grubby American and his loathsome magazines. Perhaps, then, by casting him only as an avaricious charlatan falsely elevated in importance by the myth-making Moskowitz, Stableford can persuade historians to de-emphasize this rude upstart and the literature he engendered. But it is a hard road to travel, with too many facts in the way.

However, while erasing a person from the history books by rewriting the past is problematic, another method is available: rewriting the future. That is, examining someone of conspicuous accomplishments, one can confidently predict that everything the person achieved will soon wither and fade away, so future historians will most likely ignore the person. Do you dislike Bill Gates? Well, you might concoct a scandalous "unauthorized biography" charging that Gates is merely an opportunistic crook who swindled his way to the top by stealing other people's ideas, or you could gather any available evidence of nascent weaknesses in the Microsoft empire to contend that the company will soon collapse, with all of its products forgotten. Either way, you are striving to reduce Gates to insignificance; and it is by following the latter sort of strategy that my friend John Clute wages his own subtle campaign against Gernsback and his legacy.

* * * *

Recently, whenever someone of importance in the field of science fiction dies, Clute seems driven to interpret that death as another portentous sign of the impending death of science fiction itself. After Moskowitz died, Clute (in "Mantra, Tantra, and Specklebang") called science fiction "a genre intimately tied to the lives of those who created it as a literature and as a subculture, and who are dying now or dead," and went on to say, "I personally find myself thinking—as I thought when Isaac Asimov died—that the genre is, inevitably, losing its default voices. That...sf had become far too amorphous to know long before Sam Moskowitz ceased his acts of knowing .... That he carried the template of his era down with him when he died." Now, in the column "Been Bondage," he again sounds this elegiac note, describing the deaths of Judith Merril and George Hay as "a warning shot at the heart of genre" and asserting that the literature they championed is now "mostly history," "a bondage of the been" (52).

Fresh Clute is delightful; stale Clute, much less so. Someday soon, another science fiction giant is going to perish, and I do not want Clute to prepare another funeral oration for the premature burial of science fiction; so, a few words of gentle protest might forestall another descent into the rut.

The last time I saw Clute was at the 1996 World Science Fiction Convention in Los Angeles, in a large auditorium crowded with people, many of them far from elderly. That evening, Clute was handed a Hugo Award, in the form of a costly and beautiful statuette, for the Best Nonfiction Book of 1995, his popular *SF: The Illustrated Encyclopedia*. And at that time, taking part in a lavish, videotaped presentation amidst throngs of enthusiasts, he said nothing about participating in the death throes of a doomed and inexorably declining movement; in that setting at least, it would have been a difficult argument to make.

The problem with Clute's position is that he espouses a Great Man (or Great Person) theory of science fiction history: for decades, the genre was held together by its Great People; now, one by one, those Great People are dying; and when they are gone, the genre itself will lose its "shape" and quickly disintegrate. However, science fiction is better regarded as a successful institution, and one characteristic of such institutions is that they continue to survive even after the deaths of prominent constituents. The United States endured after the deaths of George Washington, John Adams, and Thomas Jefferson; science fiction endured after the deaths of Gernsback, Campbell, and Wollheim, and it will endure after the deaths of Moskowitz, Merril, and Hay. It is incongruous to hear Clute lamenting the loss of science fiction's "default voices" because he himself (like Stableford, to a lesser extent) has now *become* one of those voices, with a prose style—highly literate, bordering on the pretentious, but always motivated by an urgent desire to *communicate*, not merely play with words—that ideally reflects some current attitudes towards science fiction.

That is how institutions work: one figure dies, but another takes her place, doing the same job in a different but equally suitable way. The Book Review Department, first headed by Damon Knight, is now run by John Clute. Judith Merril capably led the Annual Anthologies Division, but Gardner Dozois is currently in charge. Special Research Projects were long supervised by Sam Moskowitz, but Mike Ashley has taken control. Some members of the Default Voices Committee departed, so new members have been recruited.

Science fiction is a successful institution, in large part, because Gernsback ably supervised its initial construction. He established the first international organization of fans, the Science Fiction League, in 1934 (which Stableford somehow neglected to mention); and though he may have done so, as Frederik Pohl maintained in *The Way the Future Was* (1978), primarily as a "plain buck-hustle" (18), he still beat the drum for that organization with remarkable vigor, featuring lengthy reports on League activities in every remaining issue of *Wonder Stories* that he edited. Even as the League itself faded away, the organizational impulse remained, expressed in various successor associations, and science fiction soon became an established genre bolstered by a well-organized and energetic support group. And, several decades later, science fiction is still functioning pretty well, with more than enough talented writers producing original and memorable work, and fandom carrying on all its traditional enterprises.

Because no institution lasts forever (except, perhaps, the Catholic Church), one can legitimately worry about the long-term viability of both the literature and the community of science fiction, and I have myself speculated about one possible scenario for its eventual demise. But the beast remains alive and kicking today, and it seems indefensible, and even a bit rude, to seize upon every one of its personal tragedies as ineluctable evidence of its imminent death. Science fiction will perish only in response to a body blow, not a glancing wound. It will not die because a few beloved old people pass away, and it will not die because John Clute announces that it must.

\* \* \* \*

When the perspicacious Clute repeatedly proclaims that science fiction is about to die, based on at best insufficient evidence, the unavoidable speculation is that Clute actually *wishes* science fiction as we know it to die; but why? The problem for the Canadian Clute, like the British Stableford, may be that the institution of science fiction was originally an *American* institution, and both fandom and the literature it espoused have retained a strong American flavor even as Gernsback's "movement" expanded to other nations and continents. (George Hay, for example, was undeniably British, but he was also a devotee of Campbell and a one-time follower of L. Ron Hubbard.) So, if the institution, the genre, even the *idea* of science fiction fades away, there may ensue a regrettable absence of large and vibrant organizations dispensing attractive awards, but authors and readers would otherwise be free to create and enjoy imaginative literature without the oppressive atmosphere of American-ness associated with the term "science fiction." And this is, perhaps, the utopia that Stableford and Clute dream of, explaining why Stableford endeavors to remove America from the past of science fiction, while Clute endeavors to remove America from its future.

Now, I fully realize that there are sensitive issues of national pride involved here. The panoply of American culture, much of it lacking in artistry or appeal, has spread—some might say like a disease—throughout the world. People in many countries may justifiably believe that their distinctive native cultures are being overwhelmed by an ugly tsunami of jeans, Coca Cola, and MTV. In the case of science fiction, commentators may resent, and seek to resist, the excessive influence of American authors and approaches, and rewriting history or redacting the future so as to minimize the American presence may seem an appropriate procedure to liberate their worlds from suffocating cultural oppression. And it was undoubtedly emotions like these that inspired Stableford to dismiss my first defense of Gernsback and his centrality (in *Foundation: The Review of Science Fiction* No. 47) with the comment, "Mr Westfahl has all the charm and sensitivity of the typical American tourist, and thus knows exactly how to put the British and Europeans firmly in their place" (29).

Still, one must note, resentment about cultural oppression can go both ways. Reflecting habits that centuries of independence have not erased, numerous Americans continue to display a deferential attitude towards the Mother Country and all of its works. For decades, Sunday nights on American public television have featured a procession of dull, mediocre BBC dramas, under the infuriating umbrella title of *Masterpiece Theatre*, which find a large and loyal audience of American viewers who evidently believe that celluloid was invented primarily for the purpose of recording actors with British accents dressed in impeccable period costumes delivering speeches to each other; and every year, an insufferably tedious movie of similar ilk invariably garners widespread critical acclaim and several Oscar nominations.

American commercials selling pricey or supposedly upscale products habitually employ British performers and British settings to communicate the high status of persons using the product; an extremely expensive but otherwise unremarkable car called the Rolls Royce remains an American icon of automotive superiority. Devotion to the Royal Family is as strong in America as it is in Britain, amply evidenced by the unrelenting American media coverage of Princess Diana's death and the endless stream of tacky Diana "souvenirs" still being advertised and purchased by American consumers. And though it would be rash to discuss the extraordinarily controversial case of Louise Woodward, I will venture one opinion: if this had been the case of Louise Sanchez, imported from Mexico to work as a nanny, the young woman would now be in prison, serving a long sentence; it was undoubtedly the charming cadences of that British accent that inspired a New England judge, deferentially, to be unprecedentedly lenient in sentencing her to no further imprisonment while simultaneously agreeing that she was guilty of a crime that normally mandates a prison term of three to five years.

Do I sound rabidly anti-British? Nothing could be farther from the truth; why, some of my best friends are British .... really. But there is a point to be made: back at the time when Americans were generally content to mind their own business, it was the British who were brutally and peremptorily imposing their own culture on countries throughout the world, implanting a residual belief in British superiority that is still held by some residents of its former colonies and correspondingly resented by other residents of those nations. Thus, when critics born in or residing in Britain begin to belittle major figures in American science fiction, implicitly promoting the superiority of their British counterparts, or when they visibly long for the end to an American-dominated science fiction tradition, presumably in order to engender a literature that might be .... well, a bit more British in its tone and timbre, then many Americans may start to feel that the British have once again come to put the Americans firmly in their place.

Yet all of these essentially irrelevant emotions about national cultures need to be removed from the picture, so we can dispassionately confront the narrow questions of the origins and status of modern science fiction. Making absolutely no general claims about the superiority or inferiority of things American or British, I do not find it culturally chauvinistic to assert that Americans, led by Gernsback, were the first people to truly recognize what science fiction was and how important it was, and were the first people to forge the field into a genre with recognized attributes and an effective support system, so that the triumph of the American model of science fiction was not merely a side effect of American postcolonial hegemony, but was rather a triumph richly earned. Furthermore, I do not find it unreasonable to ask commentators to discuss the founder of that tradition in a reasonably thorough and accurate manner, or to ask them to display some respect for the power and durability of his work and the work of his many successors. It is, one might say, what the default voices of science fiction should be doing.

# POINT AND CRINGE: A NON-INNOVATIVE, NON-INTERACTIVE COLUMN

In one respect at least, Geoff Ryman has achieved the ultimate goal of any writer: he has changed the life of one of his readers.

That is, after reading his remarkable story "Family, or, The Nativity and Flight into Egypt Considered as Episodes of *I Love Lucy*" (1998), I repeatedly find myself, at odd moments, pondering how one might recast famous stories as episodes of situation comedies. For example, Samuel Taylor Coleridge's "The Rime of the Ancient Mariner" (1798) considered as episodes of *Gilligan's Island*:

> *It is a first mate Gilligan,*
> *And he stoppeth one of three;*
> *"By thy clean-shav'd face and unzipper'd fly*
> *Now wherefore stopp'st thou me?"*
>
> *He slipp'd on a banana peel*
> *The Guest can't help but grin*
> *And listens like a three years' child:*
> *The tale just right for him.*
>
> *"The Minnow cheered, the harbour cleared,*
> *The guests had paid their dues;*
> *The Sun not dark, we did embark*
> *Upon our three-hour cruise ...."*

Or, the resurrection of Jesus Christ considered as episodes of *Amos and Andy*:

> KINGFISH: Now dat dat Jesus fella be gone, I gonna be moneylendin' in dah temple agin, and ain't nobody gonna knock over mah table.
> AMOS: But I be tellin' yah, Kingfish, he done *come back*.
> KINGFISH: He done come back .... *from dah dead*?
> AMOS: Thassa truth, bruthah.

KINGFISH: Lordamercy! Feets don't fail me now!

The open question, of course, is whether Ryman has changed my life *for the better*.

To be perfectly honest, I have another reason to be peeved with Geoff Ryman. Last October, I argued in a speech that science fiction was a naturally conservative genre in matters of narrative style, so it was only to be expected that its writers have tended to avoid new, experimental forms of writing. Then, it was embarrassing when a questioner from the audience pointed out that Ryman, a certified science fiction writer, had done exactly that by writing *253*, his interactive "novel for the Internet." (It really is a shame how so many wonderful arguments are undone simply because of a few *facts*.)

* * * *

On a broader level, though, I am troubled by the whole idea of writing, as Ryman suggests, over a million words so that an idle reader at a keyboard might someday request and examine, say, several thousand words. Now, this sort of multiple-choice narrative might be defended as an exciting opportunity for *readers*, though I expressed skepticism about the idea in my speech. (I think most readers want to write their own stories as much as most homeowners want to do their own plumbing.) But producing "interactive fiction" appears almost impossible to defend from the perspective of *writers*.

In the first place, and as seems only natural, when I write for publication, I want people to read *every single word* I've written. Right now, I can't *prevent* you from throwing away this magazine in disgust or turning to another page, but I'm certainly not going to *encourage* you to do so. ("IF YOU ARE TIRED OF READING THIS COLUMN, AND WOULD PREFER TO READ AN INTERESTING BOOK REVIEW, PLEASE TURN TO PAGE xx.") Yet an author of interactive fiction is doing exactly that, announcing to readers, "While pressing this button or starting to read this book grants you potential access to millions of words I have written, I will give you a series of choices so you only have to read a few thousand of them." In effect, she is criticizing her own work, telling members of her audience that they are likely to value only a small fraction of what she has produced. Further, she is making it maddeningly difficult—almost impossible—for even a stubborn and dedicated reader to read everything she wrote, since that will demand repeated journeys through well-traveled prose to reach points where unexplored options remain available. Once I tried to read every possible version of a Choose Your Own Adventure book, but finally abandoned the attempt; it was so *boring* to return to that same old haunted house again and again, changing one decision each time. As for *253*, I've attempted several times to sample all of its pleasures, but I invariably get tired of doing all that pointing and clicking, and the labor is unimproved by the occasional cheery rhetoric conveying to me how much jolly good fun it all is. (Memo to Ryman: it isn't.)

Accompanying the problems of overproduction, implicit self-criticism, and nearly inaccessible prose is that the author of interactive fiction effectively surrenders control of her work to others, and I can't imagine a writer *wanting* to do that. When it comes to writing, I'm a total control freak: I want to control the horizontal of my prose, I want to control the vertical, I want to change its focus to a soft blur or sharpen it to crystal clarity. (And Lord help the proofreader who tampers with my words without my permission or a very good reason! Paul Brazier, are you listening?) Right now, I'm striving to write in a manner that is occasionally silly without obscuring a serious argument, not always an easy trick to pull off, and I may end up missing the mark entirely; but I want that to be *my* decision, thank you; I don't want this column preceded by instructions that let *you* determine its tone. ("BEFORE READING THIS COLUMN, PLEASE SELECT A SILLINESS FACTOR OF 1 THROUGH 10. IF YOU CHOOSE 1, THE COLUMN WILL BE ENTIRELY SERIOUS. IF YOU CHOOSE 10, THE COLUMN WILL BE ENTIRELY SILLY.") When Ryman invites me to read his online novel, making my own choices as to which character to read about and so on, he in effect makes me his collaborator. But why on Earth would someone like Ryman want *me* as a collaborator? And, not to get personal, but why on Earth would he want *you*? I mean, works like *Was* (1992) and "Family" persuasively demonstrate that Ryman writes more than capably when he is completely in charge of things.

This leads to a final, and central, objection to interactive fiction: it is manifestly the strategy of the totally incompetent, totally stupid writer. An experienced, effective storyteller knows what sort of stories readers will like, knows how to keep the plot moving to hold their interest, knows what characters they will find involving, knows how much information they will want or need to enjoy the story. Following their instincts, talented storytellers throughout history have done pretty well. But suppose you are an inexperienced, ineffective storyteller, utterly clueless about how to construct an appealing narrative. Well, there is one approach that is extremely time-consuming but certain to succeed: prepare every conceivable option for your readers, and keep asking them what they want. Instead of following your instincts, you constantly solicit advice: what kind of story would you like? What would you like to happen now? Which character do you want to follow now? Do you want to know about this, or about that? Such a storyteller would be literally following an ancient dictum of popular entertainment: always give the public what it wants. But talented writers should *know* what the public wants without having to keep *asking* them what they want, for heaven's sake; all of this please-choose-A-or-choose-B stuff makes the writer seem like an idiot, like a stand-up comedian who keeps interrupting his routine to ask, "Okay, would you like to hear a joke about women drivers, or about President Clinton? Show of hands, please ..... Hmmmmm, looks like Clinton in a landslide. Now, do you want to hear the joke with dirty words, or without them?"

And, having identified interactive fiction as the appropriate strategy for a diligent, energetic moron, I naturally return to a subject I have previously considered, the development of computer intelligence.

* * * *

That is, there are clear analogies between the way that the computer Deep Blue plays chess and the way that the author of interactive fiction tries to achieve a satisfactory story. As Greg Egan noted in a letter (in *Interzone* No. 130), Deep Blue's approach is the essence of sheer plodding stupidity: having been informed that its goal is to successfully attack the opponent's king, or achieve a material advantage or favorable position most likely to lead to such an attack, the computer examines every single possible move, considers every possible consequence of each move for several moves in advance, and chooses the move that offers the best chance for a favorable outcome regardless of how the opponent moves. Thus, after moving the king pawn two spaces for its first move, the computer, planning its second move, considers what would happen if it moved the king one space forward, compiles the data showing that all possible consequences of the move are ruinous, and goes on to consider the next possible move—wasting its computational energies on any number of potential moves that a human chess player would instantly reject as senseless. However, if the computer has the capacity and speed to go through this monotonous procedure accurately and quickly, it will almost always hit upon a suitable move.

Now, suppose a more advanced version of Deep Blue were assigned the task of creating a story for a particular reader. While thoroughly informed about all possible narrative elements, it would have no idea about how to go about pleasing that reader. Would A or B be a more appealing protagonist? Should event C occur, or event D? Should the action move to locale E, or locale F? Somewhere in the multiple choices would lie the best possible story, but Deep Blue Two would have no way of knowing which choices to make. And so, just as the chess-playing computer constantly examines every single possible move, the storytelling computer would constantly offer its reader every single possible story development; and, just as Deep Blue kept managing to find the best move, Deep Blue Two would keep managing to find the best development for its reader.

Although I'm tempted by Egan's vision of humans and computers harmoniously blending together into unified beings, thus avoiding scenarios of conflict or conquest, it cannot be denied that, at least today, humans and computers think differently, a gap that may always create divisions. The human brain is tremendously good at finding shortcuts, making intuitive leaps, and reaching sound decisions quickly; the computer brain, lacking these abilities, must consider every single option before reaching a decision. But that seeming liability may in many cases yield superior results. While humans still beat computers in most thinking competitions, the rapid-fire cybernetic plodding of Deep Blue can already outshine the chess-playing instincts of Gary Kasparov; and, while no human topologist was able to prove the Four-Color Theorem, a computer quickly but carefully considering 50,000 or so possible cases churned out a proof. In the future, then, a computer may be able to absorb the language and background of William Shakespeare, consider all possible plot developments in *Hamlet*, and generate innumerable different versions of the play—even including, I suppose, the *I Love Lucy* version. ("Hey, Ophelia, I'm home!") But seriously, amidst the thousands and thousands of results, we may find that a version in which Hamlet promptly kills Claudius and ascends to a troubled kingship strikes most readers as a better play—a deeper *Macbeth*, as it were. Sure, Shakespeare had darn good instincts as a storyteller, but good instincts may not matter when your competition can consider and develop every possible option. Just ask Kasparov.

And so, at a near-future time when computers are not yet ready to take over the world, they may signal their imminent ascendancy by taking over the task of storytelling, making human writers as obsolete as slide rules, by rapidly grinding out every single variation on a story idea and allowing you to Choose Your Own Masterpiece. Storytelling machines have long been predicted in fiction—in Isaac Asimov's "Someday" (1956), R. K. Narayan's *The Vendor of Sweets* (1967), and elsewhere— and writing a good novel can't be that much more difficult than playing a good game of chess or executing a topological proof. However, in the meantime, just as I'd rather see Kasparov beat the computer, I would rather read the works of a human storyteller—and a human storyteller who writes like a human, not one perversely endeavoring to imitate an *idiot-savant* machine.

Thus, to conclude what is undoubtedly the last and longest response to Geoff Ryman's request for reader feedback at the end of "Family," my advice to Ryman is: instead of struggling to devise multitudinous variations on classic stories and situation comedies, why not do something wild and crazy like, say, writing a novel? I'll trust you to make all the best decisions, and I promise to read every word of what you write. Really, now, doesn't that make you feel better?

# THE SKY IS APPALLING, OR, GO TO BED, JEREMY, AN ASTEROID ISN'T GOING TO LAND ON OUR HOUSE TONIGHT

So, have you bought *your* asteroid-impact insurance yet?

I mean, to judge from the recent flurry of films, news reports, and documentaries, one should apparently expect the event to occur in a matter of years, if not weeks or days. Last March, a few astronomers made the electrifying announcement that a roving asteroid was going to come *within 30,000 miles* of Earth in the year 2002. However, even as television news directors were arguing about which title to employ for their special coverage of the impending catastrophe ("Death from the Sky"? "Lethal Impact"? "Disasteroid?"), other astronomers recalculated the orbit and quickly declared that the object would actually come only within 600,000 miles of Earth—though we were warned that this was "still a near-miss, by astronomical standards."

While that particular fear has subsided, asteroids and comets will remain highly visible in 1998, with two major films about calamitous collisions, *Deep Impact* and *Armageddon*, following on the heels of two television movies and innumerable documentaries with computer-generated images of gigantic objects crashing into the Earth and unleashing firestorms, darkening clouds of debris, and devastating tidal waves. And this steady stream of ominous warnings is having some effect: a while ago, after my son Jeremy watched one of these documentaries, he had trouble sleeping that night, worried about a big rock falling from the sky and hitting our house.

Coincidentally, this all reminds me of a story that I often heard as a child: "Chicken Little," about some silly animals running around screaming "The sky is falling!" and working themselves into a panic for no reason.

\* \* \* \*

Shall we consider the true dimensions of the horrifying threat we were recently presented with? The earth has a diameter of about 8000 miles. On a piece of paper, draw a small circle with a one-inch diameter to represent the earth. Measure a distance of four inches from the circumference of the circle; at that point, draw the tiniest little dot you can possibly draw. Now you have a scale diagram of the posited close encounter that briefly panicked the world.

Are you terrified yet?

Next, to represent where this object will actually be in 2002, place your paper on the floor, measure 80 inches away from the circle, or over two yards, and place your tiniest dot there. That's a scale drawing of a "near-miss, by astronomical standards"—which is, as some may not realize, analogous to saying that ten million years is "a short time, by geological standards."

(By the way, despite governmental diktats, I trust that English readers can still understand and employ their own, user-friendly units of measurements instead of the arbitrary standards foisted upon the world by eighteenth-century French revolutionaries; but that is of course a topic for another column ....)

Well, if that one asteroid will, by some remarkable luck, avoid a ruinous rendezvous with the Earth, what about the thousands of other known and predicted "Earth-orbit-crossing" asteroids and comets out there? Even ignoring the fact that most of these objects have very eccentric orbits that only rarely bring them anywhere near Earth's orbit, we must recall that Earth's orbit is about 300,000,000 million miles long, and Earth's diameter is about 8000 miles, so the odds of an impact would seem comfortably minuscule.

Lacking proper credentials, though, I will defer to expert testimony regarding the actual odds of a devastating celestial visitor. One astronomer interviewed for a sleazy, sensational documentary called something like *Impact: Could It Happen?* interrupted his familiar doomsday rhetoric to mention in passing that, of course, the odds of a really large asteroid hitting the Earth, causing cataclysmic destruction and a possible end to life on Earth, were about one hundred million to one.

Stop. Pause. Rewind. Replay. *One hundred million to one?* These are the odds that we are panicking about?

Anyone with an elementary knowledge of statistics realizes that when the odds of something happening are one hundred million to one, you have nothing to worry about. It simply isn't going to happen, at least in your lifetime or your grandchildren's lifetime. And the people involved in these films, documentaries, and news reports know that very well.

* * * *

Still, while readers may be anticipating fiery denunciation of these modern-day prophets of doom, I discern no villains here. Filmmakers are in the business of providing entertainment, and as long as their stories do not incorporate, or do not arrive accompanied by, pious rhetoric about the significance and relevance of their films' messages, they cannot plausibly be charged with misrepresentation or deceit. In less obvious ways, broadcast journalists are also in the entertainment business, limited only by the stipulation that their reports have some slender basis in fact; and, if obsessively focusing on colorful but unlikely cosmic disasters at the expense of other, more meaningful problems does not seem like responsible journalism, we must remember that, at any given time, "responsible journalism" can be conveniently defined as the sort of journalism that purportedly flourished about thirty years prior to laments about its contemporary absence.

And I find it hard to condemn the astronomers who keep testifying on television about the likelihood of these events, even as they knowingly shade the truth in addressing an audience whose understanding of phrases like "it's possible" or "it could happen" is far different than a professional's. It's nice to be noticed; it's fun to appear on television. And astronomers interviewed for a documentary about asteroid impacts know the rules. If they say, "This is all nonsense—there are no killer asteroids heading for Earth," their footage will end up on the cutting-room floor. If they cautiously concede, "It's very, very unlikely, but yes, it could happen," they may earn thirty seconds of air time. And if they ominously intone, "It's happened before, and it's going to happen again—and when it does, it could mean the end of life on Earth as we know it," they will be the stars of the show.

(I can relate to the desire to appear on television since I have succumbed to it. Devotees of sleazy, sensational documentaries may someday hear a certain has-been actor reduced to narrating these travesties introducing "Professor Gary Westfahl" to discuss the imminent development of functional time machines. I can honestly say that I was not properly informed about the contents of this documentary, that I was prodded by inane questions, and that my statements were misleadingly edited to remove important qualifying language—but if the producer called me to do the talking-head routine again, I probably would. Alas, appearing on national television is more impressive to family and friends than publishing in *Interzone*.)

Rather than indignation, then, watching noted astronomers pontificate on the impending extinction of humanity should inspire a feeling of sadness; for I remember the time when noted astronomers could attract the public's attention without having to tell scary stories to frighten children. That time, evidently, has passed.

* * * *

Recently, while looking up page numbers for an essay I am editing, I read an undistinguished 1935 space opera from *Amazing Stories*, Leslie F. Stone's "The Fall of Mercury," filled with humanoid aliens of various sizes and colors befriending or fighting each other. And I recalled that outer space was once depicted as a familiar, even friendly place. The other planets in the Solar System were exotic and sometimes inhospitable, but they were not unlike good old Earth. The sentient beings encountered there may have been larger or smaller, or they may have resembled some terrestrial animal (like "Lizard Men from Pluto"), but they otherwise looked like us and acted like us to a remarkable extent. This was the space of Percival Lowell's Mars and Edgar Rice Burroughs's Barsoom—a solar system that represented a picturesque new venue for re-enactments of inspiring sagas of the past, a new frontier for America to conquer, a new empire for Great Britain to forge. And it was a craving for this outer space that animated the science fiction writers who dreamed about a manned space program and the scientists who made it happen; think of young Carl Sagan, standing under the stars at night, yearning that he too, like Burroughs's John Carter, could be instantly teleported to Barsoom.

Well, a century of research has persuasively demonstrated that this vision of space was only a fantasy. Except for Earth, there is no place in the solar system where a human can survive for an instant without a bulky spacesuit; and, except perhaps for a few microorganisms buried deep in the Martian soil, or some fishlike creatures swimming in the icy oceans of Europa, there aren't any signs of life either. The young Sagan who longed for Barsoom lamentably became the old Sagan obliged to gibber excitedly about meager evidence suggesting the possible existence of planets that might engender life. The scientists who once hoped for photographs of sentient Martians could now only study Pathfinder pictures of Martian rocks, which were playfully named for popular cartoon characters like Yogi Bear and Boo Boo in a gesture both poignant and stupid.

And, despite the sounds of excitement in the astronomers' voices, the public has not failed to notice that the real outer space seems much less interesting, and much less attractive, than the phony outer space once featured in popular science and science fiction. Let's face it: compared to a Martian, a Martian rock is really, really boring, even if you call it Yogi Bear. (And especially if the rock turns out to be, to the astonishment of scientists, remarkable similar to an ordinary Earth rock.) No bizarre aliens, no landscapes of virgin land for farms or settlements, not much of anything at all except for rocks, vacuum, and freezing cold—who can possibly be surprised to find that public interest in space exploration is at an all-time low?

As it happens, I personally find the austere beauty of the actual solar system more interesting and attractive than the plastic playgrounds of space operas, and a documentary filled with photographs and computer graphics of its many wonders will always catch my attention. But this isn't exactly what Lowell, Burroughs, and Stone promised, is it? And this isn't the sort of display one would expect to attract widespread public admiration and support.

And so, when we see astronomical dramas and documentaries increasingly focus on the implausible scenario of a huge comet or asteroid striking the Earth, we confront a stark and unpleasant truth: today, the only way you can get people interested in space is to tell them that a big chunk of it is about to fall in their backyards.

* * * *

Now, I am not *entirely* dismissive of the dangers of debris from the sky. I approve of the sorts of modest steps long advocated by Arthur C. Clarke, and now being undertaken, to thoroughly examine nearby space to locate and track every object that ever approaches our planet, though I support this work more because of the increased scientific knowledge we will incidentally gain than because of any genuine anxiety that an emissary of doom will be observed heading straight for Earth.

However, every new film and documentary on this topic does in fact fill me with fear—though not of a wayward asteroid. This is the scenario that frightens me: suppose a comet or asteroid is detected that will come perilously close to the planet Earth—perhaps, within 30,000 miles. Preconditioned to panic by years of bad movies and dubious documentaries, and ignoring the sedate astronomers who note that the chances of a collision are extraordinarily small, the American government decides to eliminate the threat by improvising a space mission, led by an heroic astronaut resembling Robert Duvall or Bruce Willis, to rendezvous with and either destroy or deflect the invader. And this mission disastrously fails, either splitting the object into several smaller objects—a few of which strike the Earth—or deflecting the asteroid in the direction of, say, New York City.

(The problem is, cosmic billiards is a lot more difficult than the tabletop variety. Suppose you have an approaching asteroid shaped like a big, lumpy peanut, of unknown composition and density, rotating head over heel at a 25-degree angle to its axis of rotation; now, if you want to change its course in a certain way, exactly where do you plant the bomb, and when do you set it off? Put a team of physicists to work on the problem, and you'll still get an answer which begins, "Our best guess is ...." For now, I'll take my chances with the way nature runs the Solar System, but I get a bit nervous at the thought of human beings taking the controls.)

Even this, however, is a minor fear, compared to the genuine dangers that humanity currently faces. During the week I wrote this column, there were two starkly contrasting news events. First, NASA revealed that it was hard at work devising procedures for informing the world about impending asteroid collisions—an activity that seems just as vital as drafting protocols for our first meeting with alien visitors. (How should we address the first alien who steps out of the flying saucer? "Distinguished Emissary from Space"? "Your Exalted Alienness"?) Second, India exploded three atomic bombs as part of an accelerated program to build a nuclear arsenal, which inspired its neighbor Pakistan to announce its own plans for atomic weapons. Thus, for the first time in history, two nations which have hated each other for fifty years, which share a long common border, and which claim the same large territory will both be armed with nuclear weapons. Factor in the data that India is historically an ally of Russia, and Pakistan is historically an ally of the United States—the nations that lead the world in nuclear armaments—and it's clear that the *Bulletin of the Atomic Scientists* needs to move its doomsday clock a bit closer to midnight again.

This worries me a great deal more than the slim prospect of an asteroid hitting the Earth.

And one cannot forget the ongoing threats of nuclear proliferation elsewhere in the world, the development and stockpiling of biological and chemical weapons, and eventually ruinous environmental changes due to massive deforestation, ozone-layer depletion, and global warming—among other things.

In sum, it's foolish to worry about cosmic murder when the gravest danger facing humanity has been, and continues to be, suicide.

# DID ALIEN ASTRONAUTS MAKE THE SHROUD OF TURIN?

Like most readers of *Interzone*, no doubt, I own many science fiction novels that I've never read, but I try to catch up whenever I can. Recently, I finally read a 1983 paperback, *The Mansions of Space* by John Morressy, that I purchased long ago solely because the cover announced it was about the Shroud of Turin. And, while not exactly a religious person, I have long been fascinated with the Shroud because its existence proves one of two interesting things.

The first, obviously, is that a man who lived 2000 years ago miraculously returned from the dead, in the process emitting mysterious radiation that seared his image onto a burial shroud. Such physical evidence to support Christian doctrine would be astounding, and until 1988, one could cogently argue that the Shroud was authentic.

What happened then was that radioactive carbon dating, meticulously executed by independent laboratories, showed that the Shroud was only 700 years ago, about the time that it first surfaced in medieval Italy. For those who appreciate the science of carbon dating, this conclusively demonstrated that the Shroud had been created at that time, not in ancient Palestine.

(For those who do not appreciate the science, a review: on Earth, carbon overwhelmingly consists of stable carbon-12, atoms with 6 protons and 6 neutrons, though every trillionth atom or so is radioactive carbon-14, with 6 protons and 8 neutrons. When living organisms, mostly made of carbon, are alive, they constantly exude old carbon and absorb new carbon, so the ratio of carbon-14 to carbon-12 in their bodies remains $1/10^{12}$. When they die, the exchange process stops, and the radioactive carbon-14 atoms steadily decay, so the ratio of carbon-14 to carbon-12 gets smaller and smaller. Measure that ratio, and you roughly determine how old a piece of organic material is.)

Although believers in the Shroud devised various theories to account for the carbon dating—fire damage, unnoticed repairs to the cloth, even an extra dose of radioactivity from Jesus's resurrected body—only one seemed logical: that undetected microorganisms infesting the Shroud distorted the dating process. For if living material were mixed with 2000-year-old material, the result could be a date somewhere in between, say, 700 years ago. One can raise serious questions about the nature of these microorganisms, their ability to survive indefinitely without visible sustenance, and the remarkable coincidence that they attained by the twentieth century the precise amount of growth needed to generate an incorrect date which coincided with the Shroud's first known appearance. Still, one cannot immediately say that the theory is impossible.

One can, though, quantitatively analyze the theory, and since I have long bedeviled my Precalculus students with carbon-dating word problems, I can walk you through the math.

If $t$ is the number of years, the formula for carbon-dating from my *Precalculus* textbook is

$$\frac{\text{carbon-14}}{\text{carbon-14}} = \frac{1}{1{,}000{,}000{,}000{,}000} \times 2^{-t/5700}$$

If $t$ equals 0 (the organism is alive), the ratio is simply one-trillionth, or $1 \times 10^{-12}$; if $t = 2000$, the ratio is $7.8411 \times 10^{-13}$; and if $t = 700$, the ratio is $9.184 \times 10^{-13}$. For any amount of Shroud material tested, let $M$ equal the proportion of microorganisms, so $(1 - M)$ equals the proportion of genuine Shroud. We set up a mixture problem: $M$ times the living ratio, plus $(1 - M)$ times the 2000-year ratio, equals 1 times the 700-year ratio. Or, $M \times (1 \times 10^{-12}) + (1 - M) \times (7.8411 \times 10^{-13}) = 9.184 \times 10^{-13}$. And the answer is: $M = 0.622$.

In other words, for the theory to be correct, about 62% of the material believed to be the Shroud actually consists of microorganisms. If this is true, one cannot say that the Shroud of Turin is infested with microorganisms; the Shroud, basically, *is* microorganisms. The Shroud of Turin is *alive*—and perhaps poised to crawl out of its case and smother the next scientist who questions its authenticity.

\* \* \* \*

If, however, one accepts that the Shroud cannot possibly be authentic, its existence proves a second interesting thing: that about 700 years ago, there existed a really smart person who was capable of creating a convincing forgery using methods that modern researchers still do not understand and cannot duplicate.

Though the notion is apparently plausible, many who study the Shroud simply can't accept it. To suggest the impossibility of fraud, believers in the Shroud ask: how could someone in (presumably primitive) medieval Italy know enough to make a burial shroud similar to those actually used in the era of Jesus? How could this (presumably simple-minded) person invent a way to cover the Shroud with an image so persuasive that it looks better as a photographic negative? Even those who agree it's a forgery can't quite believe that someone living at the time could have pulled it off. Consider the absurd theory, now widely discussed, that Leonardo da Vinci made the Shroud of Turin, despite the inconvenient fact that the Shroud was already reported to exist about a century before he was born. Yet the reasoning underlying the idea is clear: since it is such a good forgery, a really smart person must have created the Shroud; the only really smart person in Italy around this time was Leonardo da Vinci; therefore, da Vinci must have created the Shroud.

However, we know that human anatomy and cranial capacity have not changed measurably throughout history. At any given time in the past, there must have existed a small percentage of highly intelligent people, even if we don't know their names. These people were certainly *ignorant* by modern standards, but they were not *stupid*. Today, smart people do remarkable things with plastics and microchips; centuries ago, smart people could do remarkable things with cloth and stone. A fourteenth-century Italian woman may well have been resourceful and intelligent enough to research ancient burial practices and devise an ingenious way to place a convincing image of Jesus on a correctly-proportioned shroud.

Of course, a refusal to accept the intelligence of our ancestors is not limited to Shroud fanatics, as I was reminded one recent evening when I ended up watching a dull documentary about the Shroud of Turin—Ian Johnson, pontificating about his pet microorganisms—primarily to avoid watching another documentary featuring a man who I thought had been permanently laughed off the stage: Erich von Däniken.

\* \* \* \*

In the early 1970s, like many people, I read von Däniken's *Chariots of the Gods?* (1968) and was almost persuaded by its argument that alien astronauts had often contacted ancient civilizations. I started to become skeptical when, in his second book *Gods from Outer Space* (1970), he preposterously asserted that the biblical story of the creation of Adam and Eve represented a garbled account of alien bioengineering. By the time he descended to obvious lies in *The Gold of the Gods* (1973), describing personal visits to alleged hordes of secret alien treasures, I was no longer paying attention, and everyone else stopped paying attention as well. But you can't keep a bad man down, I guess, because there he was, right before my disbelieving eyes, hosting a new documentary featuring the same old ideas.

There is no need to argue against the illogic and dubious evidence of the Von Däniken Hypothesis, since many others have done that work, but the key objection was well expressed by John Sladek in *The Science*

*Fiction Encyclopedia* (1979): "It is central to his thesis that all ancient peoples were moronic, unable to invent or imagine, capable only of copying what the spacemen showed them" ("Erich von Däniken" 635). Thus, every time a civilization accomplished something significant, like building pyramids or creating an accurate calendar, it must be because aliens were helping them every step of the way.

In the new, improved, made-for-television version of the Von Däniken Hypothesis (which I witnessed only fleetingly, unable to watch for long), he claims that ancient people employed amazing alien machines, though they were too stupid to record, or pass on knowledge of, their existence in any way other than ambiguous artworks. To correct the historical record, von Däniken constructs working devices resembling these artworks to "prove" that they really existed. He displayed an Egyptian wall carving featuring something that, by desperate contortions of the imagination, looked like an elongated light bulb. Then he had an artisan construct an incandescent light bulb in exactly the same shape. He flipped the switch and, lo and behold, the bulb lit up! Thus proving that aliens taught the Egyptians how to build light bulbs! Then, he built a larger model of a tiny trinket vaguely resembling an airplane, and discovered that it could fly! Thus proving that aliens taught the ancients how to build airplanes! Still, while von Däniken's archaeological acumen and reasoning ability have not improved with age, he is developing a definite flair for showmanship, so it is only appropriate that he now plans to build a German amusement park, a Von Dänikenland, devoted to his theories, which have value only as entertainment.

Of course, it remains *possible* that aliens once visited Earth, and several science fiction works have explored the idea. Arthur C. Clarke intelligently speculated in *2001: A Space Odyssey* (1968) that aliens may have been responsible for humanity's ascent to intelligence; others, less intelligently, speculated that the gods of Greek mythology were really aliens (an idea that I first encountered in an old *Rip Hunter, Time Master* comic book story, "The Secret of Mount Olympus" [1962], and later figured in the *Star Trek* episode "Who Mourns for Adonais?" [1967]); and *The X-Files* (1993-2002) seems poised to argue that secret aliens have long been resident on Earth, pulling the strings of our civilization. The common theme is that our ancestors were manifestly too witless to develop tools or invent imaginative stories about gods or keep a society functioning without extraterrestrial assistance.

But my favorite story about archaic aliens, Poul Anderson's *The High Crusade* (1960), offers an opposing viewpoint: here, medieval knights in shining armor quickly thwart an alien invasion, master their technology, and proceed to conquer the universe. An unlikely scenario?

Probably. But if someone at that time was clever enough to outwit intelligent twentieth-century people with a piece of cloth, others from that era may have been clever enough to outwit advanced aliens.

(Maybe, the logic of von Däniken whispers, something like that *really happened*; maybe the Bayeux Tapestry, reputed to depict Halley's Comet, is actually a picture of an alien spaceship .... However, while he has not entirely ignored phenomena like Stonehenge and French cave drawings, the Swiss-born von Däniken generally declines to attribute the creations of ancient Europeans to altruistic aliens—presumably because only the non-white peoples of the world were entirely incapable of genuine achievement—which adds an unattractive tinge of racism to his already risible theory. It's a shame, though, since one could neatly account for the mysteries involving the Shroud of Turin by hypothesizing that it was crafted by advanced aliens, easily capable of technological tricks we cannot fathom.)

\* \* \* \*

And what about Morressy's *The Mansions of Space*, the novel that provoked these musings? Well, I can't say the book is an undiscovered masterpiece, but it's regrettable that this sort of novel is overlooked. It is unusually a kinder, gentler space opera, in which even the villains are nicer than the heroes of your average cyberpunk novel, and while never rising above competence in its execution, the novel ultimately earns your respect in a way that many flashier novels do not.

The story begins on Peter's Rock, a distant planet colonized by a remnant of the Catholic Church which left Earth carrying the Shroud of Turin, encased in a priceless reliquary, though it was later removed to parts unknown by a dissident sect. When they are visited by a free trader, the abbot does not care about finding the Shroud, but he does want to spread his faith to other worlds; and the trader agrees to transport missionaries. Against all odds, they soon recruit many alien and human converts, including the once-skeptical trader himself.

While absolutely silent about the authenticity of the Shroud—which never appears in the novel—and about the truth of Christianity itself, *The Mansions of Space does* argue that a belief system perfected centuries ago by human beings may continue to be worthwhile in improving the lives of spacefaring humans, and even the lives of strange headless aliens. It is, like *The High Crusade*, one of the rare science fiction novels about our descendants that acknowledges and venerates the intelligence of our ancestors.

The scarcity of such stories, while deplorable, should not be surprising. As individuals, we typically go through three stages in characterizing our parents: as children, we are awed by their abilities and behave deferentially; as adolescents, we realize that our parents are really stupid and become rebellious; and in adulthood, as the saying goes, the older we get, the smarter our parents get. Civilizations undoubtedly experience a similar cycle; while older cultures rigidly adhere to tradition and worship their ancestors, our modern civilization, now in its giddy adolescence, happily ignores all of the lessons of history as worthless irrelevancies and welcomes arguments that our ancestors were really congenital idiots secretly depending on divine or alien intervention to accomplish anything. Like the famous tantrum at the end of Robert A. Heinlein's *Have Space Suit—Will Travel* (1958), it is an attitude both embarrassing and endearing.

So, instead of condemning our current disrespect for ancient peoples, perhaps we should cherish it while it lasts; for when our ancestors start getting smarter, it will mean that we as a species are getting older.

# UNLUCKY STARR AND THE OMISSION OF VENUS

So, I confessed to David Pringle that I wasn't sure I would meet my next deadline, one reason being the ongoing distraction of America's constitutional crisis, and he responded, "Why not try to take some kind of science-fiction angle on the Clinton thing?"

Though one should be attentive to editorial suggestions, taking a "science-fiction angle" on this business first brought to mind a traditional, and dreary, approach: the critic says, "Ho hum. You see, we science fiction readers are entirely bored by this Clinton business, because science fiction long ago predicted the emergence of a relentlessly intrusive, media-dominated, scandal-driven society." And a few texts are trotted out—here, Norman Spinrad's *Bug Jack Barron* (1969) is the first that comes to mind—to cite as uncannily accurate anticipations of the event.

One problem with such arguments is that they reveal a longstanding contradiction in science fiction commentaries. On one hand, whenever somebody criticizes science fiction for failing to predict some obvious development, the aficionado sniffs and answers, "That's irrelevant. Science fiction is not a literature of prediction." On the other hand, whenever a prediction from science fiction is spectacularly realized, the aficionado smugly smiles and says, "Hey, we predicted that. Aren't we smart?" And science fiction cannot have it both ways, refusing to accept blame for its long record of predictive failures while trying to capitalize upon its shorter record of predictive successes. The larger problem is that these claims depend on an audience of people who have not read the cited predictive texts, and hence will not recognize that their prophetic elements were heavily intermixed with irrelevancies and prophetic blunders.

If there is a defensible "science-fiction angle on the Clinton thing," it rather involves a Brobdingnagian failure of science fiction prediction; Spinrad *et al.* notwithstanding, we are today *not* living in the world that science fiction almost universally predicted, and all the attention now being given to Bill and Monica is arguably one consequence of that.

* * * *

As an example of typical science fiction visions of our future, consider Arthur C. Clarke's *The Lost Worlds of 2001* (1972), which included background information about the whereabouts of the *Discovery* crew in the year 2001, not too distant from today, when they were summoned to join the mission. David Bowman, anchored at Phobos, observing Mars. Peter Whitehead, working on the surface of Mercury. Victor Kaminski, orbiting a thousand miles above Venus. William Hunter, riding an experimental boat near the Great Barrier Reef. Jack Kimball, in geosynchronous orbit above the Earth. Kelvin Poole, in an underwater lab near Bimini.

This was the world we were promised, thirty years after reaching the Moon: humans in outer space, on other planets, deep below the sea, all living and working in strange new worlds. Had these predictions come true, our daily lives would now be different in innumerable ways. Of course, there would be news reports about striking new discoveries or technological breakthroughs, but there would be much more than that: human interest stories about the first grandmother on the Moon, universities adding Space Science majors to prepare students for new professions, soap opera subplots about dejected ex-lovers applying to work in Space Station One as a new device to explain the absence of departing actors, the insufferable lady boring her neighbors with scrapbooks of photographs of her nephew on Mars, giant tomatoes grown in microgravity as the newest delicacy in supermarkets, and so on. In many obvious and subtle ways, the vastly expanded range of human environments would significantly alter all aspects of daily life.

As we know, predictions like Clarke's of life in 2001 can now be regarded, at best, as a strong possibility for life in 2101; yet the human race is not visibly suffering from its lack of progress in conquering the universe. This undermines the contention of some space advocates that a desire to travel is a fundamental human drive, so that our failure to vigorously move into space represents a shameful betrayal of our human nature. I have elsewhere argued, however, that no such drive exists, given the relentlessly sedentary habits of most humans throughout most of human history; and the fact that there now exists no great clamoring for human expansion into space would seem to support my thesis. Sure, hundreds of thousands of Americans have signed up for the first commercial flight into outer space, but that leaves two hundred and fifty million Americans who have expressed no interest in catching that flight.

Still, I have agreed that there is a fundamental human desire for new *information*, and that travel often stems from that desire. And the real problem caused by our arrested advance into space is our thwarted curiosity: lacking new environments to inhabit, we are lacking new information.

Nonsense!, one might retort: due to our ongoing inhabitation of near-orbital space, camera-laden space probes to various regions of the solar system, and the powers of the Hubble Space Telescope, we have gained more new information about the universe in the last thirty years than in the last three thousand years. That's true. But our human desire for new information has a parochial tinge: as people, we are especially interested in other people, and we like our new information to involve, or somehow relate to, other people. Thomas Jefferson could have commissioned some research to find out about the Louisiana Territory he had purchased; but he wanted to send two people he knew, Meriwether Lewis and William Clark, who could conduct a personal investigation and provide a personal report. Traveling through Europe, my parents did not merely wish to photograph every single one of its famous sights; they wanted to photograph every single sight with their children in the foreground, engendering my lifelong antipathy to being photographed. Among extinct creatures, dinosaurs receive an inordinate amount of attention because they are the only creatures in Earth's history who might have given the human race some real competition, and both our nonfictional and fictional speculations inexorably focus on imagined juxtapositions of dinosaurs and people.

So, there is a simple reason why Pathfinder photographs of Mars, or Hubble pictures of strange phenomena in space, do not attract much public attention: they include no images of dear old Aunt Bertha, waving at us in the foreground.

* * * *

However impressive our burgeoning knowledge of space may be, therefore, it manifestly lacks the human touch; and so, the public turns elsewhere to satisfy its curiosity. If there are no new sorts of people to examine—aquanauts, Martians, whatever—people will stare more intently at old sorts of people, seeking new information there. Attempting to explain the Clinton-Lewinsky scandal, I think not about any science fiction story but Alfred Hitchcock's film *Rear Window* (1954). Originally, the photographer played by James Stewart was probably an ordinary sort of person with an ordinary sort of curiosity; but, once confined to his apartment by a serious injury and unable to leave, he began to constantly and obsessively observe all his neighbors, trying to find out as much as he could about their private lives.

That is our situation: first promised unlimited access to new environments, but finding ourselves indefinitely confined to planet Earth after all, we are beginning to constantly and obsessively observe all our neighbors, trying to find out as much we can about them. Unable to explore the cosmos, we poke around in closets. Human curiosity, even if misdirected, must be satisfied somehow; new information, even if inconsequential, must be obtained.

And information is a powerful addictive drug; once we are hooked on a certain stream of data, we never want it to be cut off. Long ago, an American candidate for political office made his income tax returns public, to show that he had nothing to hide; at the time, such voluntary revelations of legally private personal information were unprecedented. But once the pattern was established, all candidates were increasingly *expected* to release their returns, so the inquisitive public could find out how much money they had made, how much they had contributed to charity, and so on; now, the rare candidate who resists public pressure to release his returns engenders dark suspicions that he has something to hide. So it is absurd to hope, like some idealistic commentators, that the American media and public, repulsed by the unprecedented disclosures about the sex lives of Clinton and his adversaries, will henceforth resolve to rebuild the firewall between private life and public life to prevent embarrassing personal information from reaching the public eye. Rather, the pattern has been established, and journalists and the media are now prepared to investigate and publicize the private lives of errant politicians, and the public is prepared to absorb each new sordid detail.

It is not only politicians who will have to deal with assaults on their privacy: unidentified Clinton allies have hinted that the journalists now chastising the President for his behavior may see their own scandalous pasts revealed; the role of the *paparazzi* and tabloid reporters in hounding and tormenting celebrities hardly needs mention; and American businesses, with the general support of the courts, have become increasingly nosy in seeking and demanding personal information about the people they interview and hire. Everybody wants to know more about everybody else, and they will increasingly be able to do exactly that.

However, this can lead to other problems. Longstanding tradition indicates that if we observe something carefully enough, and intently enough, we can learn absolutely everything about it. In the words of Jack Webb playing Joe Friday, often cited by his modern disciple Kenneth Starr, determined investigation will always lead us to "just the facts." Yet twentieth-century science tells us this simply isn't so. Given our innate propensity to observe patterns, we may detect nonexistent patterns in random occurrences. Some desired information may be flatly unobtainable. Fuzzy lines, examined more and more closely, may become fuzzier and fuzzier instead of clearer and clearer. After relentless, exhaustive examination, then, the examiner may be just as uncertain as she was at the beginning, or even more uncertain. The Clinton scandal seem to hinge upon perpetually unanswerable questions: at what point does giving a young woman gifts become an attempt to influence her possible future testimony? What exactly is the difference between making misleading statements to a grand jury and committing perjury? In these cases, the line between stupidity and criminality may be as complex and infinitely convoluted as the Mandelbrot Set.

When thwarted in an effort to obtain complete, definite truth, investigators may refuse to accept the fact that some key questions are essential irresolvable and reach a different conclusion: that something or somebody is deliberately trying to *prevent* them from finding the truth. As best I can determine, Starr did not begin his work as a rabidly partisan Republican determined to drive a Democratic president from office; however, from the data he gathered he discerned a pattern of criminal behavior on the part of the Clintons, he found himself unable to prove this was true, and he finally became enraged upon deciding that his inability to obtain proof stemmed from a deliberate effort on the Clintons' part to obstruct his justice. Starr thus epitomizes the potentially unhappy results of efforts to obsessively observe our fellow humans: we can see patterns that aren't really there, fail in our efforts to get definite answers, and come to suspect that unseen evil forces are at work preventing us from getting definite answers. In a word, we become *paranoid*.

* * * *

While a reference to *The X-Files* (1993-2002) might provide proof enough of an embryonic problem, that program at least ventures far enough into the fantastic that no one can reasonably construe its wild stories as a serious attempt to explain the world's mysteries as the work of malevolent aliens allied with chain-smoking quislings secretly controlling the government. But real-world examples are readily available. I recently watched a documentary about Princess Diana's death featuring an animated recreation of the fateful drive into the tunnel with the deadly columns—and it looked strangely familiar. Then it hit me: I had often seen similar animated sequences recreating the final drive of President John F. Kennedy down that freeway, through that tunnel, beneath that Book Depository, and past that infamous Grassy Knoll. For thirty-five years, a legion of obsessed investigators have endeavored to prove that the Kennedy assassination was the work of a vast conspiracy; however, while they have developed some intriguing theories and have turned up tons of suggestive data, they have failed to bring to light anything resembling definite proof of their theories. But they're still trying today, working harder than ever. Now, with the death of Princess Diana—which apparently occurred suspiciously only days before her engagement announcement, and which prominently featured a mysterious chauffeur purportedly linked to networks of international spies—Britain may have its own version of the Kennedy assassination, an event to suck up decades of investigative energy without any prospect of definitive results.

Paranoia also infests the fringes of the Clinton investigation: an e-mail message now circulating throughout cyberspace lists numerous friends and associates of Clinton who all committed suicide or died in car accidents, sometimes just before they were reportedly ready to talk to the authorities. The implication is that the Clintons have assembled a team of assassins to eliminate anyone who might expose their criminal deeds. However, even ignoring the fact that this imagined conspiracy inexplicably failed to properly deal with such obvious Clinton enemies as Starr, Newt Gingrich, Linda Tripp, and Monica Lewinsky, we must realize that the Clintons, in twenty years of public life, have had thousands and thousands of friends and associates, the vast majority of whom died peacefully in the sleep or survived to the present day. Perhaps the percentage of people connected to Clinton who died violent deaths is slightly higher than average, and that might seem suspicious, but it doesn't *prove* anything. Examined intently enough, *anything* can look suspicious. The next time you are in a grocery store, round up everyone in the store and do some investigating. You'll uncover astounding facts: some 34% of the people in the store had last names beginning with L! Seven people in that store all had the same fourth-grade teacher! Over 53% of the people had the same frozen dinner in their carts! These improbable departures from statistical norms can't be accidents, for heaven's sake; there must have been a plan, some *reason* why these particular people were all shopping in that particular place at that particular time. In the deaths of Kennedy, Princess Diana, and Clinton aide Vincent Foster, there were simply too many suspicious circumstances—something sinister must have been going on. Or so people unfamiliar with the principles of modern science might suppose.

Overall, it is not a pretty picture: frustrated by our inability to enter new frontiers and learn about new sorts of personal experiences, we turn our insatiable curiosity on the people around us, determined to learn more and more about them; we learn some things, probably things that were better left unknown; and when we cannot learn everything we want to learn, we invent something even more unflattering than what we have learned. No doubt there are many reasons for our increasing descent into this world of mutual prying, probing, and paranoia, and as one aspect of the obsessive media coverage of the Clinton-Lewinsky affair (of which this column is one minuscule part), each and every one of those reasons will be brought to light and earnestly discussed. But I cannot help feeling that if the predictions of science fiction had come true, and if people were now inhabiting all parts of the inner solar system, engaged in the greatest expansion of the human environment ever effected, we would all be paying a little less attention to a semen-stained dress.

# JANEWAYS AND THANEWAYS: THE BETTER HALF, AND WORSE HALF, OF SCIENCE FICTION TELEVISION

Consumer warning: this column will present, in a näive and explor-atory manner, observations and hypotheses that some may regard as sexist—though I will limit myself to the form of sexism occasionally acceptable to the politically correct, that which validates and celebrates women.

A while ago, when I attempted to write a column about science fiction television, the project collapsed for one reason: despite the in-arguable quantity and arguable quality of contemporary science fiction programs, I rarely if ever could bring myself to watch them, and, given my lifelong enthusiasm for the genre, I could not begin to understand why. (And for that reason, I might add, I represent absolutely no threat to *Interzone*'s television reviewer Wendy Bradley—despite this one-time incursion into her territory—since I watch so little science fiction televi-sion that I could never make commentaries thereupon my avocation.)

It was therefore strange and fortuitous when organizers of the 1998 Loscon (Los Angeles Science Fiction and Fantasy Convention) for some reason assigned me to a panel on "Nineties Science Fiction on TV—Trend or Menace?" I expected only to make a brief opening statement about my inexplicable lack of interest in the field, hear a few dissenting words from passionate defenders of one program or another, and yield the microphone to the other loudmouths on the panel, who might say something enlightening.

There were, as it turns out, no other loudmouths on the panel—in fact, there was only one additional panelist, who didn't seem anxious to say very much at all. Without very much to say myself, I opened up the discussion to an audience that was eager to talk about science fiction television and, surprisingly, often seemed to dislike it more than I did.

A sampling of their disparaging comments: science fiction television is not really science fiction, displays no intelligence, doesn't make you think, ignores modern scientific ideas, is negative and fearful rather than positive and hopeful, reflects the short-sighted stupidity of television executives, and now serves only as an expression of popular mythology and "family values." The most striking criticism: whereas older shows like *Star Trek* (1966-1969) attracted young people to science fiction fandom, modern programs have their own support groups to draw in their devoted viewers; instead of strengthening fandom, then, science fiction television now weakens fandom. As my guest Paul Barnett laughingly observed, the complaint was absurdly parochial—but also keenly revelatory, as it allowed me to epitomize all of these fans' grievances in one sentence:

Science fiction television is not *ours*.

Science fiction television is not driven by the principles and conventions of written science fiction, is not influenced by the science fiction community, is not created by science fiction writers, and is not produced for science fiction readers. Science fiction television thrives in its own universe, increasingly dominating the scene and drawing attention away from written science fiction. And members of traditional fandom can do nothing about it except to resent it.

As today's scholars endlessly note, wherever there are issues of power and powerlessness, of dominance and subservience, another issue is usually involved, that of gender.

\* \* \* \*

When first pondering my reactions to science fiction television, I considered one clue: there was one program which, if I stumbled onto it, usually kept my fingers off the remote control—*Star Trek: Voyager* (1994-2000). Why did this program, and this program alone, appeal to me? The flippant explanation was that I found it enjoyable, for the first time since the 1960s, to see a *Star Trek* starship under capable feminine control—because I have argued in print, undoubtedly like many others, that the original *Star Trek* was structured like a romance novel, with Captain Kirk playing the willful, impetuous heroine torn between the comforting boy next door (Dr. McCoy) and the dark, mysterious stranger (Mr. Spock).

Even putting this particular theory aside, one can discern something archetypically *feminine* in the priorities that Kirk consistently displayed: he wanted to *communicate* with all alien races in the galaxy, to *share his feelings* with them, as it were; he wanted to *explain what "love" is* to baffled aliens; he argued with Spock about the primacy of *emotion* over *logic*; and he repeatedly violated the sacrosanct "Prime Directive" because he felt compelled to *help others in distress*. Traveling through unexplored regions of space, he always sought to interact with newly discovered races in an egalitarian, non-hierarchical, and reassuring fashion; "let's be friends" was his message, even to the aliens who greeted him with threats or violence. And Captain Janeway, in her lonely quest through sectors of space far from the Federation, visibly shares these admirable tendencies.

In contrast, the other two *Star Trek* series—*Star Trek: The Next Generation* (1987-1994) and *Star Trek: Deep Space Nine* (1993-1999)—had male, and thoroughly masculine, captains manifesting radically different priorities. Operating in realms dominated by their ubiquitous Federation, Captains Picard and Sisko functioned as middle-level managers in the grand, hierarchical Federation bureaucracy, charged with carrying out its policies and imposing its will upon any recalcitrant pockets of space resisting its benevolent wisdom. "Exploring strange new worlds," whenever they were obliged to do so, was typically regarded only as a nuisance, something disturbing their orderly routines; in response to unusual situations, they sat in their peripatetic offices, consulted the regulations, or contacted a higher-up for guidance. Then, with humorless pomposity, these men in their gray flannel spacesuits dutifully implemented the mandated solution, only rarely exhibiting any passion or personality.

If you question my description of the essential femininity of Kirk, watch the episode "Turnabout Intruder" (1969), in which Kirk's body is taken over by the mind of a vengeful woman, and notice that, portraying this emotionally volatile female, *William Shatner acts exactly the same way that he always does*. Similarly, if you disagree with my description of the dull, domineering masculinity of Picard, watch the episode "The Best of Both Worlds" (1990), observe him absorbed by and carrying out the commands of the collective alien Borg, and notice that, portraying this soulless bureaucratic minion, *Patrick Stewart acts exactly the same way that he always does*.

So, as the governing presence in science fiction television shifted from female to male, from Jane to thane, the fans who had previously embraced the reassuringly familiar, feminine aura of *Star Trek* grew alienated by the burgeoning masculinity of more recent programs.

\* \* \* \*

What's this, you say, about "the reassuringly familiar, feminine aura" of science fiction? After all, isn't science fiction regularly condemned as the quintessentially masculine genre, long written almost exclusively by and for young men, filled with muscle-bound macho heroes swaggering and bullying their way through the galaxy?

Actually, for those who can look beyond the predominantly male casts and purportedly phallic spaceships, this is not what earlier science fiction was like at all.

The argument resists rigorous proof, but I am currently reading through E. F. Bleiler and Richard Bleiler's massive *Science-Fiction: The Gernsback Years* (1998), which summarizes every science fiction story published in a genre magazine between 1926 and 1936, and I suspect you will find therein more soulmates to warm, empathetic Captain Kirk than to John Wayne or Rambo. Spacemen progressing through the cosmos were more likely to form alliances with other races than battle them, unless of course they attacked us first; concerns about communicating with and understanding aliens were just as common as the us-versus-them mentality; strong female characters were not unusual; and there were even a few women writers, like Leslie F. Stone, churning out space operas with the best of them.

Why should this be, given the undeniable fact that most of the writers and readers were male? Well, the young nerds attracted to science fiction may have shared the gender and skin color of the era's dominant class, but in every other way they were alienated and marginalized members of society, dreaming of domed cities and Martian canals when most people longed for an idealized domestic past and idolized Gene Autry and Andy Hardy. If, at that time, you read magazines with pictures of squid-like monsters and built miniature rockets in your backyard, you undoubtedly felt rejected, ridiculed, and out of place. Such people often bond with, and adopt the attitudes of, other members of society who feel rejected, ridiculed, and out of place. By this logic, one would expect to find in early science fiction stories passionate arguments against prejudice and racism, celebrations of oppressed workers struggling against evil bosses, and proto-feminist tracts applauding the abilities and sentiments of women. And if you look carefully, you will find, in the science fiction of the 1930s and thereafter, numerous examples of all of the above.

\* \* \* \*

So it was that science fiction fans, representing a literature born from and still reflecting the philosophy of society's downtrodden classes, including women, responded so strongly to the original *Star Trek*, part of what was then another genre of the oppressed, science fiction television. In the 1950s and 1960s, programs in that category were viewed solely as fodder for children or evanescent novelties; in such an atmosphere, Gene Roddenberry dared dream only that his genuinely science-fictional *Star Trek* might last as long as five years. Unwanted, misunderstood, and constantly on the verge of cancellation, *Star Trek* naturally became a program that sided with the oppressed, espoused alliances with other outsiders, and came to embody attitudes traditionally associated with women. Then, science fiction fans previously repelled by the robotic masculine hubris of travesties like Irwin Allen's *Voyage to the Bottom of the Sea* (1964-1968) found the feminine sensibility of *Star Trek* uniquely recognizable and appealing.

Unfortunately, *Star Trek* eventually became popular, far more popular than written science fiction, and success often makes you smug and self-satisfied, inclined to sympathize more with your fellow millionaires than the bohemians you once befriended, more like one of the boys than one of the girls. Hence, asked to create a new *Star Trek* after twenty years of adulation and swelling profits, Roddenberry crafted *Star Trek: The Next Generation* which, despite its cosmetic gestures towards feminist concerns (changing "no man" to "no one" in the opening narration, replacing mini-skirts with pants), soon evolved into an odiously arrogant and thoroughly masculine program (and it was odiously racist as well, far more than the original series, but a scholar named Daniel Bernardi, in *Star Trek and History: Race-ing Toward a White Future* [1998], has already argued that case). And one can make similar claims about *Star Trek: Deep Space Nine* and other science fiction television programs of the 1990s.

How did *Star Trek: Voyager* escape this fate? Surely, the fortuitous tokenism of its female commander, and the influence of its female co-creator and executive producer Jeri Taylor, helped to steer the show in a better direction. Also, unlike the other second-generation *Star Trek* series, independent kingdoms in the syndication market, the fortunes of *Star Trek: Voyager* were from the onset tied to those of the tiny, upstart UPN network, continually struggling to compete against the larger American networks, so that the program may have instinctively resisted the bourgeois complacency of its compatriots and instead aligned itself with society's marginalized classes.

(The irony here is that *Star Trek: Voyager*, an overt expression of the wise and nurturing feminine approach, has been attacked as "sexist" because of one addition to the cast, the ex-Borg Seven of Nine, a curvaceous blonde bombshell attired in a skin-tight jumpsuit. But such expressions of feminist outrage are baffling to me. Never mind that the brusque, brilliant Seven of Nine is about as far away from the stereotype of the "dumb blonde" as one could imagine, or that the character replaced another female cast member who actually was, in fact, a dumb blonde; if people sincerely believe that unattractive women in dowdy uniforms represent respect for women, whereas attractive women in attractive outfits represent exploitation of women, then they are several generations behind the times in their understanding of feminism, a field of scholarship where paeans to Madonna are now almost *de rigueur*.

Ignore the surface features; episode after episode, *Star Trek: Voyager* reveals itself as feminist, and thus science-fictional, to the core.)

\* \* \* \*

While one might hope that *Star Trek: Voyager* would lead the secret masters of the *Star Trek* universe to rediscover the spirit that energized the original series, the onward plodding of *Star Trek: The Next Generation* through movie theatres suggests that Captain Janeway may be an anachronism more than a trend-setter, and that the institutionalization and masculinization of American science fiction television will continue. It all seems another instance of an unfortunately familiar story: an appealing underdog (science fiction television) achieves deserved success, adopts an new, upper-class lifestyle, grows self-righteous and haughty, and forgets her old friends (science fiction fans). But such stories usually end with a final comeuppance, and there is reason to suspect that will be the case here.

Today, televised science fiction enjoys a position roughly comparable to that of the televised western in the 1950s, another genre that shifted from sympathizing with the outcast to endorsing the status quo and grew to dominate the airwaves—before vanishing with surprising speed. Inevitably, the mighty empires of syndication, spinoffery, and sycophantism that have encrusted around the paternalism of *Star Trek: The Next Generation*, the power politics of *Babylon 5* (1994-1999), and the paranoia of *The X-Files* (1993-2002) will disintegrate, and to entertain genuine hopes for the future of science fiction television, as audience members suggested in the panel's final moments, one must look away from the dominant American networks and studios—to those recent British and Australian series that never reach North America (with the lamentable exception of, God help us, *Space Precinct* [1994-1995]), to Japanese *anime*, to the cheap original programs on the Sci-Fi Channel. Only in such places, perhaps, can one still find that spirit of alienation, disempowerment, and femininity that has long animated the best of science fiction literature.

# THE NINE BILLION NAMES OF FANTASY...AND AN ENCYCLOPEDIA OF OTHER CONCERNS

*The Encyclopedia of Fantasy* (1997), edited by John Clute and John Grant, has won several awards, and at the 1999 Eaton Conference on Science Fiction and Fantasy Literature, I had the privilege of accepting one of them—the Eaton Award, honoring the outstanding critical work on science fiction or fantasy published in 1997 and 1998. Before reading an acceptance speech from Clute and Grant, I remarked that I might properly claim a few splinters from the plaque myself, in recognition of my small contributions to the volume as a Consultant Editor.

Even since the book appeared with a title page listing four Contributing Editors and two Consultant Editors, everyone has surely wondered, "Exactly what does a Consultant Editor *do*?" While I can't say how David Hartwell earned his billing, I might summarize my role by stating, less than illuminatingly, that a Consultant Editor sits around and waits to be consulted. Yet, to satisfy a waiting world's desperate curiosity, I can be somewhat more specific about how I affected—or tried to affect—the final product.

In the beginning, years ago, I spent a considerable amount of time, along with several others, going through a massive computer file, entitled (for some reason) "EXP.TRE," that listed all proposed topical entries in the volume. Each reader was asked to add her own comments about issues to raise, or important works to mention, in the entry; this would presumably be helpful to those assigned to write the entries. So, under ACHILLES, I noted the interesting appearance of Achilles in Dave Duncan's *A Rose-Red City* (1987), and under BOOKS, I described the talking book that uniquely functioned as the villain in *The Care Bears Movie* (1985).

Other comments similarly ranged from the useful to the moronic; under RINGS, for instance, someone felt the need to mention J. R. R. Tolkien ....

Three times, I recall, I received this file, made additions, and returned it to Clute. However, reading the volume, I discern no evidence that any contributors actually consulted this file before writing their entries. My theory is that the vaunted EXP.TRE file was basically busywork, provided for the people besieging the editors with eager offers to help, giving them something to do while Clute, Grant and the Contributing Editors did the real work of preparing the volume.

My other "small contributions"? I later received from Clute some draft entries to review, edited or reworked a few of them, and wrote eleven entries on my own. After the book was published, I read through the entire text, line by line, and produced a massive compilation of notes ranging from spelling and punctuation errors to impassioned complaints about omitted, superfluous, or misguided entries; some of this material, edited and toned down, will appear, along other people's comments and corrections, as an addendum to the forthcoming paperback edition. But my greatest, and most fruitless, energies were devoted to correspondence with Clute about the overall theory and methodology of the volume.

* * * *

Before *The Encyclopedia of Fantasy* materialized, Clute had already spoken about his proposed "model of fantasy" that would serve as the book's foundation. In this fundamental sentence of fantasy narrative, an idyllic world is first disturbed by a sense of Wrongness, corresponding to supernatural fiction; then, wrongness erupts into the widespread devastation of Thinning, corresponding to horror; finally, the evil is dispelled and the world proceeds to Healing, corresponding to pastoral literature. While I thought "Thinning" a poor choice of words, I liked the model, but found it crucially incomplete.

That is, in fantasy, evil is not defeated rapidly and effortlessly, leading immediately to Healing; such quick reversals are more characteristic of horror, where youthful protagonists may at the last minute fortuitously stumble upon just the right talisman or magic formula that disintegrates the vampire or sends the demons back to Hell. For a fantasy hero, more work is involved. After the hero has educated and improved himself to the point when he is ready to confront the opponent, there typically follows a long and sustained struggle which, I maintained, constituted the third narrative stage of Agon, or Contest, in the master narrative of fantasy. In this grand confrontation, both hero and villain have become so powerful that they may seem possessed by, or infused with the spirit of, powers greater than themselves; thus, this stage evokes a correspondence with myth. Only after this epic battle, when the evil is destroyed and the hero reverts to humble ordinariness, does a spirit of pastoral Healing prevail.

I labored to persuade Clute to add this fourth stage to his model, which I had grown fond of. It would neatly express the key difference between fantasy, which includes this stage, and horror, which lacks it. It would provide the model with evocative seasonal imagery—Wrongness, autumn; Thinning, winter; Contest, spring; Healing, summer—and effectively resonate with, without duplicating, the master narrative of Northrop Frye's *The Anatomy of Criticism* (1957). (There is, though, one intriguing divergence: Frye's monomyth begins in spring, but fantasy begins in autumn.) And it would elevate fantasy above other forms of fantastic literature—supernatural fiction, horror, myth, pastoral—as the one grand narrative that incorporated and harmonized them all (with science fiction intriguingly positioned as one significant effort to contradict or challenge the pattern, but that's a story for another day).

Yet Clute seemed skeptical. He once floated a sort of three-part/ five-part model—his three stages, with two transitional phases between Wrongness and Thinning and between Thinning and Healing—but as I tactfully noted, this only made matters worse. Although something first called Knot, and later renamed Recognition, was finally presented as a key "moment" between Thinning and Healing, it never emerged as the complete fourth stage I envisioned. While others certainly influenced his thinking, my objections may have been one reason why Clute presented the model in more muted tones than originally projected; in the volume, I was struck by the relative brevity of the entry on FANTASY explaining the model—two pages—especially when compared to other bloated monstrosities like Mike Ashley's ten pages on ANTHOLOGIES, Grant's eleven pages on TARZAN MOVIES, and everyone's favorite bloated monstrosity, Hugh Davies's twenty-five-page list of OPERAS.

Still, my most vociferous complaints about the embryonic volume involved its occasional tendency to avoid using the English language.

\* \* \* \*

In one early letter, Clute declared, with apparent excitement, that while planning the book, he and his colleagues had discovered that there did not exist a suitable critical vocabulary to describe all aspects of fantasy; thus, the editors would have to unearth, or invent, the required terms. Looking through the EXP.TRE file, with numerous words and phrases unknown to me or anybody else, I became concerned. The English language, I argued, is naturally conservative; innumerable new words are proposed every year, but only a few are deemed truly necessary and used often enough to enter the dictionary. If a word doesn't exist to describe a given phenomenon, the odds are excellent that it is simply because there is no *need* for the term.

Consider examples from science fiction: we all know stories in which aliens that look like human beings live on Earth as unobtrusive observers; but what is the *name* for such stories? What about people whose minds are taken over by evil aliens? What is the *name* for such possessed people? The answer is that there aren't any names for these things, because we don't need them; on the rare occasions when the matters are discussed, a brief description is not troublesome. Yet *The Encyclopedia of Fantasy* at times seemed engaged in an endless quest to identify virtually every possible feature in fantasy and provide it with a special name.

Although many proposed terms did not made the final cut (thank goodness!), possibly in response to my criticisms, enough of them did to occasionally result in obfuscation. In extreme cases, statements in the encyclopedia are little more than strings of neologisms: a RITE OF PAS-SAGE, Clute's entry intones, "may be undertaken by a CHILDE protagonist without benefit of counsel; or by a person who wanders INTO THE WOODS of a GODGAME from which s/he returns wiser, with gifts, and perhaps married; or by a figure who, in order to LEARN BETTER, must undertake a NIGHT JOURNEY ..." (813) To say the least, such rhetoric can be murky unless one has already mastered the vocabulary; if the purpose of encyclopedias is to communicate information, these outpourings of neologisms are manifestly counterproductive. Further, with the vast majority of the proposed coinages certain to be rejected, like the vast majority of coinages are always rejected, authors of such prose risk sounding foolish to posterity.

I'm not sure why crafting *The Encyclopedia of Fantasy* came to involve so much creative vocabulary. In some cases, people may have sincerely believed they were devising urgently needed terms that would be ecstatically embraced by fantasy commentators, though I personally have not seen much evidence of that. In a few cases, people may have dreamed of securing a modicum of immortality by inventing a word that ended up in *The Oxford English Dictionary*; however, words do not enter the language accompanied by credits, and the people who invent successful words generally remain just as obscure as the people who don't. The most provocative theory would be that these terms were employed, consciously or subconsciously, in order to convey contempt for the genre of fantasy.

* * * *

Consider: if a person seeks to name and categorize every single possible element or aspect of fantasy, she implicitly asserts that fantasy narratives are not only governed by one underlying pattern but, in fact, are nothing more than mechanical assemblages of pre-fabricated elements. Do you want to write a fantasy? First, you choose an overall pattern:

ANIMAL FANTASY, DYNASTIC FANTASY, URBAN FANTASY... Next, choose a protagonist: BRAVE LITTLE TAILOR, JACK, UGLY DUCKLING... Then choose a setting: ARCADIA, FOREST, LABY-RINTH... And so on. Choose one from column A, one from column B, one from column C, put the pieces together, and you have a fantasy.

Could the distinguished editors of this encyclopedia actually entertain such a reductionist vision of fantasy literature? Yes, they do, *but only in some cases*, as Grant explains in his entry on GENRE FANTASY, where he says,

> its main distinguishing characteristic is that, on being confronted by an unread GF book, one *recognizes* it...the territory into which the book takes one is familiar—it is FANTASYLAND. The characters, too, are likely to be familiar: HIDDEN MONARCHS, UGLY DUCKLINGS, DWARFS, ELVES, DRAGONS... In short, GF is not at heart fantasy at all, but a comforting revisitation of cosy venues. (396).

Thus, Grant agrees, innumerable texts published under the aegis of fantasy are indeed "mechanical assemblages of pre-fabricated elements"; yet his disdain for them doesn't matter, because such books are "not at heart fantasy at all." Here, the logic of the argument escapes me: on one hand, the volume identifies things like "HIDDEN MONARCHS, UGLY DUCKLINGS, DWARFS, ELVES, [and] DRAGONS" as common elements of fantasy; on the other hand, if authors put these elements together with insufficient imagination and originality, the resulting stories are not really fantasies. To me, this represents wordplay of another, more dangerous sort, renaming and removing what doesn't like in a genre in order to make it prettier.

Then, if one eliminates works of "genre fantasy" that are only iterative shufflings of a well-worn deck of cards, what about the remaining fresh and stimulating texts that Grant would endorse as *genuine* fantasy? *The Encyclopedia of Fantasy* has a special name for the good ones too: INSTAURATION FANTASY—the coinage that is undoubtedly nearest and dearest to Clute's heart, and also the term that I, with characteristic charm and grace, assailed with the greatest vehemence.

I dislike the term in part because I know something about the person who promulgated the term "instauration," Francis Bacon, and I know Clute is misappropriating the word (as he all but acknowledges); yet I also question whether this subgenre truly exists. To quickly simplify Clute's discussion (I'm already over my word limit—again!), an INSTAURATION FANTASY ends with not the restoration of the old order, but the birth of a distinctive new order. To convey the difference, he cites exemplary texts like John Crowley's *Little, Big* (1981), Gene Wolfe's *The Book of the New Sun* (1980-1983), and Grant's *The World* (1992). However, any fantasy written from a reasonably adult perspective for a reasonably adult audience will impart an understanding that the end can never be exactly like the beginning, that no realm ravaged by relentless evil can be perfectly restored to previous conditions, that building a new castle on the ruins of the old or placing a dead king's son on the throne cannot engender a future that will precisely replicate the past. Since any thoughtful fantasy will color its concluding triumph with such recognition of irretrievable loss, any thoughtful fantasy might qualify as "instauration fantasy."

The distinction Clute is making, then, is one of degree, not of kind: when the recognition of irretrievable loss is especially profound, and the ending aura of newness especially strong, one has an "instauration fantasy." The meaning of "instauration fantasy," then, is perilously close to "really good fantasy," so that vocabulary is again being deployed to segregate favored texts from unfavored texts. Indeed, since Clute's descriptions virtually preclude the possibility of there being a *really bad* "instauration fantasy," the term functions only as a novel way for Clute to salute the books he especially admires.

Within *The Encyclopedia of Fantasy*—an extraordinary reference work, I should add, that I am proud to be associated with, despite my complaints—one finally uncovers a clear and valuable argument: when one writes fantasy in a perfunctory, mindless manner, the result is terrible fantasy ("genre fantasy"); when one write fantasy in a creative, reflective manner, the result is magnificent fantasy ("instauration fantasy"). I can't see why the point must be shrouded with word games; and sometime in the future, if invited to join the SECRET MASTERS of this encyclopedia in planning its Second Edition, I will raise the issue again, though I may be tilting at windmills. But what else can a KNIGHT OF THE DOLEFUL COUNTENANCE do?

# PASTWONDER: THE REDEMPTION OF ORSON SCOTT CARD

For the record, I don't spend all my time devising new ways to ir-
ritate *Interzone* readers: I teach college classes, struggle to function as a
proper husband and father, and work on other writing projects that usually demand reading and research. Some tasks provide only the satisfaction of publication or a free book in exchange for a review; others offer
payments ranging from the inconsequential to the almost-consequential.

So it was that my reading during one recent month was limited to
two areas: Everett F. Bleiler and Richard Bleiler's massive reference
book, *Science-Fiction: The Gernsback Years* (1998), summarizing every
single story published in a science fiction magazine between 1926 and
1936, which I'm reviewing for the journal *Extrapolation*; and the science
fiction novels and stories of Orson Scott Card, which I read in order
to write an essay for another massive reference book, Richard Bleiler's
second edition of *Science Fiction Writers* (1999).

Other than the distinguished Bleiler family connection (son Richard was taking over for his father in editing *Science Fiction Writers*),
the two projects apparently had little in common; yet I sensed a strange
symmetry in my reading assignments. Examining Everett Bleiler's extraordinary compilation, I could observe the beginnings of an interesting
process; analyzing the storytelling genius of Orson Scott Card, I could
observe signs of its conclusion.

\* \* \* \*

Generally, *Science-Fiction: The Gernsback Years* confirmed my
impression of the often-misrepresented formative years of magazine science fiction: asked to characterize that era in one word, I would be torn
between "diversity" and "monotony."

Diversity? While there were, predictably, space operas of the "Doc"
Smith variety, these did not entirely dominate the magazines. Rather, almost every type of story imaginable appeared: utopias and dystopias following the classic models; stories of exotic lost races recalling H. Rider
Haggard, still sometimes located in remote terrestrial realms but now
more frequently inside the Earth or on other planets; future-war stories
of the sort perfected by George Griffith, typically involving obsessed

scientists bent upon world conquest employing astounding inventions; other stories of powerful inventions deliberately or accidentally misused, with disastrous results; stories about adventurous aviators sprinkled with some advanced technology (an unfortunate specialty of *Scoops*, the sole British magazine represented in the book); oddities like tales of personified antibodies in the bloodstream battling invasive bacteria; and mundane stories of "scientific detectives" in contemporary society with few speculative elements.

Monotony? As is apparent, all these sorts of stories tended to follow particular patterns that usually had existed for decades before Hugo Gernsback started publishing science fiction magazines. The same formulas occur again and again: the story opens with an elderly scientist ushering friends into the laboratory to admire his latest invention, and if a young hero is among them, you can be sure the scientist has a lovely daughter ready for wooing. If the invention proves dangerous, some concluding contrivance—the death of the only man who understood its operation, destruction of essential notes, or exhaustion of a required rare ingredient—removes the invention from the scene to restore the status quo. Every lost race is governed by a beautiful princess with a predilection for falling madly in love with the first handsome stranger who penetrates her realm. Space travelers are precisely analogous to cowboys or soldiers, with humanoid aliens standing in for the Native Americans or Germans.

What authors failed to recognize was that science fiction was best created not by fitting superficial oddities into familiar patterns, but by *thinking* about potential oddities in a logical manner, extrapolating from the present to the future and considering the long-range effects of innovations that spread throughout society (as opposed to the brief disruptive effects of one evanescent invention). Some writers well before Gernsback, most notably H. G. Wells, had achieved their own understanding of the concept; a few writers who worked for Gernsback, most notably Stanley G. Weinbaum, also figured it out; a few years later, Robert A. Heinlein and other newcomers demonstrated their own mastery of the process; and John W. Campbell, Jr. noticed what they were doing and explained their methods to everyone. The result was a tremendous increase in the production of superior science fiction, beginning in the 1940s and continuing into the present.

However, we cannot be sure that this production will always continue. As David Brin has noted, the number of interesting ideas for science fiction stories is not necessarily infinite. Some of the genre's stalwart tropes—like human expansion into space to build empires and encounter aliens—have been drained of all vitality and seem increasingly incongruous in the context of our burgeoning awareness of the realities of space travel. When new concepts like cloning or space elevators do become available, they may be seized upon, exploited, and exhausted with amazing rapidity; while other new concepts—like visions of a ten-dimensional universe folding into a semblance of three dimensions a few microseconds after the Big Bang—do not lend themselves to involving, character-driven narratives. A few contemporary writers can still hit upon genuinely novel ideas that lead to imaginative stories, but these seem increasingly rare. What writers do instead, and what they do very well, is retelling old stories better than they have been told before, but examining superbly crafted redactions of familiar ideas inspires little optimism about the future of science fiction.

Enter Orson Scott Card.

\* \* \* \*

Say what you will about Card, but he has always been scrupulously honest in describing why he became a science fiction writer. He grew up with no special fondness for or commitment to the genre; he read some science fiction, but mostly read other stuff. He began writing science fiction not due to any interest in scientific speculation, but because he concluded, after surveying the options, that science fiction offered the best opportunities for new writers.

Oddly, Card was first pigeonholed as an *Analog* writer specializing in hard science fiction, though his novelties stemmed more from inspired cleverness than from scientific acumen. While some intriguing concepts surfaced in his first two Ender novels, *Ender's Game* (1985) and *Speaker for the Dead* (1986), he was visibly reduced to moving chess pieces around the board while churning out the next two installments, *Xenocide* (1991) and *Children of the Mind* (1996). Worse yet, one day, when he couldn't think of an idea for a science fiction novel, he picked up his trusty Book of Mormon and realized that, with some jazzy substitutions, he could turn the story into a five-volume, far-future epic, and that's exactly what he did in his Homecoming saga, surely the low point of his career. It was almost a relief to observe Card turning his attention to fantasies and mildly horrific "mainstream" novels like *Lost Boys* (1992).

No one can deny that Card is a masterful storyteller and writer, but in terms of what Wells and Heinlein achieved, it became increasingly hard to regard him as a true *science fiction writer*. He was simply telling stories that had been told before, better than they had been told before, and the stories occasionally took the form of science fiction. So, by 1998, I had long ago given up on Card and hence had not read *Pastwatch: The Redemption of Christopher Columbus* (1996).

However, one reason writing for reference books can be fun is that it forces you to read books you might not have otherwise read, often with pleasing results—as *Pastwatch* surprisingly demonstrated.

* * * *

To summarize the story not as it is told, but from a fifth-dimensional chronological perspective: in the earliest version of history referenced, Christopher Columbus is obsessed not with sailing to the West but with leading a new Crusade, and his advocacy leads to a ruinous campaign that drains Europe of resources and manpower. Meanwhile, a rapidly developing Meso-American civilization masters shipbuilding, sails East, and conquers a weakened Europe, imposing a brutal dictatorship founded on human sacrifice and engendering centuries of misery. Eventually, to improve their own history, scientists invent time travel and send a projector into the past showing Columbus a vision urging him to abandon dreams of a Crusade and sail to the West instead. This intervention erases Earth's barbaric history and leads to our own history of Europe conquering America, with its own unfortunate results—slavery, exploitation, and widespread environmental damage still threatening humanity in the future. When members of Pastwatch, a team of scientists using special devices to observe the past, deduce what has occurred, they resolve to use their own, newly developed form of time travel to change, and improve, history again: three people return to the past and persuade Columbus to remain in the New World as the leader of a new, enlightened American nation that will prevent mistreatment of both people and the environment.

The novel can be read metaphorically: people continually seek to improve their history by rediscovering forgotten figures and reinterpreting familiar icons. Contemporary history books feature more women and persons of color, rescued from obscurity by diligent research, and we eagerly embrace the notion that Columbus, instead of being an avatar of European paternalism, was really someone who, with a little nudging, might have established a non-racist, non-sexist society in the fifteenth century. While villains and shameful events cannot be entirely removed from the picture, we strive in every conceivable way to make our history seem more humane, more congruent with contemporary values, than it has been previously portrayed. The intervention of Card's time travelers to upgrade their own history, then, might be viewed as a science-fictional metaphor for what historians and commentators do all the time.

Still, the book more disquietingly invites a literal reading, because erasing old history and creating new history is something that may actually be feasible in the future. Working within the confines of general relativity, physicists have designed time machines; the last model I heard of required the energy of an entire galaxy to funnel a few muons through time, but such technical problems may be overcome, perhaps sooner than we think. And if we could entirely eliminate our undesirable past, is this something we would really want to do?

* * * *

What distinguishes *Pastwatch* from the other "alternate histories" it is associated with is, first, its chilling recognition that changing human history will involve changing absolutely everything. Given the premise of *Pastwatch*, someone like Harry Turtledove might work up the story of King James's ambassador to America, John Smith, summoning William Shakespeare out of retirement to write a play for the visiting American ruler, Pocahantas—the sort of "comfy manipulation of the familiar," to use Darrell Schweitzer's phrase, that so often characterizes the subgenre (Letter, *Interzone* No. 131 4). Yet Card's protagonists realize quite well that a major change in one moment of time will eliminate every person born afterwards: keep Columbus in America, and King James, Smith, Shakespeare, and Pocahantas will never exist. Changing history does not mean playfully shuffling the deck of humanity, but entirely throwing it away. The major weakness in *Pastwatch* is that this awesome decision to erase billions of human lives to produce a history with less injustice and suffering seems to occur with insufficient deliberation; they are eliminating the evils of slavery and colonialism, true, but they are also eliminating Ludwig von Beethoven and Pablo Picasso—perhaps to replace them with other, equally wonderful talents, but there are no guarantees of that.

The fact that *Pastwatch*'s tinkering with history is debated, planned, and meticulously carried out represents the second feature distinguishing *Pastwatch* from other alternate histories. The subgenre's tangled permutations of reality usually just *happen*, either with no explanation at all or as an unforeseen accident—as in Ward Moore's *Bring the Jubilee* (1953), wherein the accidental death of a general changes the outcome of the battle of Gettysburg and, hence, the Civil War. However, remember that, as writers of Gernsback's era did not understand, the best and most interesting sort of science fiction depicts not mysterious one-time marvels, but thoroughly understood and institutionalized marvels. *Pastwatch* almost uniquely presents a future society that has the power, as may someday be the case, to deliberately and intelligently create an alternate history, and that provides far more for readers to chew on than the cute twists and role reversals that otherwise permeate the subgenre. In this respect, *Pastwatch* recalls another classic novel, Gregory Benford's *Timescape* (1980), that also depicts scientists thoughtfully seeking to change the past to avoid their disastrous present. And, since Benford's final creation of two distinct timelines seems a more comforting result than Card's erasure of the old timeline, one can argue that Card is being especially courageous by defying conventional human desires—the goal of science fiction as Campbell once articulated it—to interpret the cold equations in the coldest possible manner.

Further, Card ups the ante by indicating that humans may be able to do this more than once. In the world of *Pastwatch*, perhaps they have and perhaps they will: the ill-advised crusade that leads to Europe's brutal subjugation may itself represent some prior civilization's improvement upon an even more dismal history; descendants of the superior culture emerging from Columbus's new America may eventually resolve to change the past again and achieve an even better world. A vision emerges of a future society, having mastered time travel, that sets out to constantly improve its history through innumerable changes in its past, eventually creating a utopia not only in its present, but throughout its entire history—big thoughts, awe-inspiring thoughts, but not entirely impossible thoughts, and that is, after all, what science fiction is supposed to provide.

It's easy to foresee the demise of science fiction, and I've done a bit of that myself. But to discover a disturbing and genuine science fiction novel emerging from a source as unlikely as Orson Scott Card is enough to inspire momentary optimism. If such miracles can occur, maybe the genre isn't dead just yet.

# "'SCUSE ME WHILE I KISS THE SKY": AN OPEN LETTER TO A YOUNG SCIENCE FICTION SCHOLAR

Believe it or not, my works are not generated in a mad frenzy and rushed into print; rather, I do pause to reflect, reconsider, and revise before submitting anything, though the process may result in the calm decision to emulate the tone of a frenzied madman. At times, when discussing matters beyond my usual areas of expertise, I may even e-mail a draft to a colleague to get some feedback before proceeding. If the piece involves science fiction and children's literature, I may run it past my friend Andy Sawyer; if it involves science fiction cinema, I may bother a certain graduate student who has written about science fiction films.

Recently, then, after completing a pithy, 10,000-word exegesis of one of my favorite science fiction films, *This Island Earth* (1955), for my book *Science Fiction, Children's Literature, and Popular Culture* (2000), I sent the draft to this student; and, while the response inspired a few minor revisions, it was more impressive for what it revealed about the radically different conceptual universes we inhabit. Suddenly, I felt oddly tempted to play the graybeard (having now been active in the field for more than a decade!) and offer some sage advice to the neophyte on the business of analyzing and writing about science fiction.

\* \* \* \*

First, in the section of the paper where I catalogued the charming idiocies that permeate *This Island Earth*, I touched upon the scientist's purported research into the "conversion of lead into uranium," noting that the only ways to transmute heavy elements were radioactive decay and nuclear fission, both of which must begin with radioactive elements and must end with elements of a lower atomic number; thus, proposing to convert a heavy element with no radioactive isotopes into a radioactive element with a higher atomic number made no sense. I considered adding a discussion of the possibility—rather, the impossibility—of somehow duplicating the extraordinarily high temperature and pressure within a supergiant star to achieve some sort of fusion between lead atoms and other atoms to create uranium atoms, but felt no need for belabored scientific explanations in order to establish the film's quintessential stupidity in this area.

Surprisingly, you found this excursion into elementary physics revelatory and impressive, and speculated that I might have some sort of concealed scientific background. Far from it! I do not and cannot claim any special expertise in scientific matters; all I know about science is what should be common knowledge to anyone who studies science fiction.

For better or worse, science fiction is a genre founded upon, and sometimes claiming to derive authority from, a commitment to scientific accuracy, making this a relevant area of inquiry. This doesn't mean that scientific accuracy is the most important thing in science fiction—it isn't. This doesn't mean that scientifically inaccurate texts are necessarily bad—some of the science fiction works I most admire have little to do with science, or are riddled with errors. All this means is that, in order to properly evaluate a work of science fiction, one of the many qualities you must possess is sufficient scientific awareness to assess its scientific accuracy. I'm sorry to be blunt, but in my view, if the phrase "conversion of lead into uranium" doesn't immediately make you giggle, you should either brush up on your science or find another area of literature to study.

* * * *

I was also bemused by your relentless determination to discern references to contemporary events in both the film and the original novel by Raymond F. Jones (1952). In your eyes, these works appear to comment on such matters as the Korean War, President Truman's seizure of the steel industry, debates over American atomic policy, and the rise of the "organization man." As it happens, I believe these spontaneous theories about the novel and film are fanciful, but I am more disturbed by the critical mindset they represent: the notion that all creative writers are robotic recorders of current events, consciously or subconsciously awaiting the arrival of the newspaper every morning so they can thrust the headlines into their latest story. Sure, people are influenced by, and comment on, their times, but if we have any respect for the human intellect, we must grant the possibility that people can also be influenced by, and comment on, things other than their immediate present. As I am writing this, Americans are still debating the implications of the Columbine High School shootings while NATO bombs are falling on Yugoslavia. And what does this column have to do with these developments? Next to nothing, obviously. And if writers of nonfiction have the power to wrest themselves away from the concerns of the moment, writers of fiction must enjoy the same power.

Further, though commentators of all sorts can get absurdly carried away when detecting references to current politics or culture in literature and film, I feel this is an especially infelicitous approach to science fiction. For one of the unique strengths of the genre is its ability to address, in a direct and literal fashion, the grandest of cosmic questions: what is this vast, uncaring universe all about? Why are we here? Are there other beings like us? Science fiction does not always deal with these issues, and rarely does so with great artistic success, but the impulse to do so is strong and pervasive. The genre also includes satirical or allegorical representations of contemporary persons and events, but just as a cigar is sometimes only a cigar, in science fiction, sometimes the universe is only the universe, eternity is only eternity, and aliens are only aliens.

Some seemingly astute observers, of course, have argued the contrary. Since science fiction is written by humans, all of its characters are necessarily humans in disguise, and all its perspectives are necessarily human. Since science fiction is written in the present, all its stories are necessarily about the present, not the future. In other words, despite pretensions to the contrary, the writing of science fiction involves nothing more than the production of colorful self-portraits and journalism as seen in a funhouse mirror.

Which is to say, it is impossible to dream.

I will not debate the logic behind these positions, but I feel a deep sense of gratitude because my innumerable ancestors who aspired to look beyond their immediate environment, improve their lives, and broaden their understanding of the cosmos did not embrace such pernicious nonsense.

To be sure, science fiction films, as collectively crafted enterprises of popular culture, may be less visionary than science fiction literature and more plausibly read as disguised reflections of contemporary events and concerns. But the spirit of written science fiction can infect its celluloid cousins as well. The creators of *This Island Earth* had read Jones's novel and, as their statements suggest, were definitely inspired by its cosmic perspective and were interested more in exploring the sobering implications of the phrase "this island Earth" than in, say, working a reference to the Army-McCarthy hearings into the story.

Reading over your message, then, I feel sorry for you; because, if you watch science fiction films of the 1950s solely in order to detect Communists or Native Americans in alien disguise, you will miss everything that is profound and magical about them. You will never fully appreciate the poignancy of *The Man from Planet X* (1951), the inspiring altruism of *It Came from Outer Space* (1953), the befuddled awe of *This Island Earth*, or the crazed affirmation of the human condition in *The*

*Incredible Shrinking Man* (1957). You will instead transform a fascinating and multifaceted body of works into a dull, reductive history lesson.

\* \* \* \*

Of course, for graduate students of literature, dull reductionism is often the name of the game. Young scholars writing dissertations may be expected to construct their own critical machines to eviscerate whichever texts happen to lie in their way. There is nothing inherently wrong with this: theoretical models as a basis for interpretation can be useful, and aspiring commentators should learn how to build them. For my own dissertation, I constructed—more accurately, I unearthed, oiled, and polished—the Hugo Gernsback/John W. Campbell machine, and over the years I have found it helpful in analyzing many science fiction works.

However—and here is my final lesson for the apprentice—science fiction is a large and variegated field, and no single machine will work in every case. A while back, when I struggled to determine why John Brunner's *The Crucible of Time* (1983) was one of my favorite science fiction novels, the Gernsback/Campbell machine was no help at all; instead, I had to build a new machine on the spot. And to figure out why *This Island Earth* was one of my favorite movies, I surprisingly needed to activate the Olaf Stapledon machine—to recognize that the peculiar appeal of the film derived from its determination to convey, in a manner all the more powerful because of its ineptitude, the futility and insignificance of human activity in the humbling context of a limitless universe.

My conclusion is that a science fiction commentator must begin with the text and only the text, must allow the text to sing its own song, and only then should determine which machine is required to illuminate and elucidate that particular song.

So, while this may seem to contradict everything I have said, the critical approach you espouse is perfectly appropriate when analyzing *some* science fiction films of the 1950s. If, for example, you elect to revisit the most overpraised and overanalyzed film of that decade, *Invasion of the Body Snatchers* (1956), you will undoubtedly be driven, like other commentators, to a political/cultural/sociological/psychological interpretation, because nothing about the film is science-fictional in the ways I describe—though if you feel compelled to deal with the so-called "paranoia" of the 1950s (as if the era's fears of communist invasion and nuclear annihilation were entirely irrational), I'd recommend *Quatermass II* (aka *Enemy from Space*) (1957) as a refreshing alternative. *I Married a Monster from Outer Space* (1958) invites analysis as a parable about suppressed male homosexuality, with homosexuality quaintly represented by periodic donning of a grotesque rubber mask. And what on Earth is going on in *The Monolith Monsters* (1957)? I wish I knew. I would love to engage in an extended study of the science fiction films of the 1950s, but I can't imagine cramming them all into the same Procrustean bed.

\* \* \* \*

When the genre was younger, the only people who wrote about science fiction were people who loved science fiction, and while the results of their labors varied in quality, the sincerity of their interest and devotion was unquestionable. Today, however, science fiction commentary faces its own invasion of the pod people, tenure-seeking academics who seize upon science fiction works as new pieces of meat to send through their grinders to make some tired point about man's inhumanity to woman, the insidious persistence of postcolonialist thought, or the impossibility of crafting coherent narratives in our postmodern world. And this may represent your wisest career move: determine what sorts of interpretative contortions are currently fashionable, grab some science fiction texts, submit them to the regimen, and generate mounds of polysyllabic discourse which will lead to a college teaching position and promotions while needlessly wasting valuable trees and computer memory before your words drift into well-deserved oblivion.

Or, as the alternative, stupidest career move, you can dedicate yourself to the unending challenge of thoughtfully analyzing science fiction, employ only the tools that are appropriate for the task at hand, and wrestle with the bewildering variety of issues raised by its innumerable texts, including the foundational questions raised by humanity's existence in an immense and incomprehensible universe that will always remain important, no matter how naïvely they are expressed or how clumsily they are confronted. And, if you follow that course while struggling to stay afloat and pay the bills, you just might write something that will be worth reading. This is what I foolishly persist in attempting to do, and I wish you luck should you be foolish enough to do the same.

# A MODEM UTOPIA, OR, WHY ALLISON'S BORING DADDY HOPES THE MACHINE DOESN'T STOP

Now that I have made my e-mail address (Gwwestfahl@yahoo.com) available to *Interzone* readers, and thus have invited you all into my home, I suppose I should say a few words about myself.

Not—you'll be thankful to hear—that there is much to say. As my fourteen-year-old daughter Allison perceptively notes, "Daddy, you have no life." During the daytime, twelve months a year, I teach credit and non-credit classes for two universities. At night, after a hard day, I simply veg out in front of the television watching baseball games or documentaries, refusing even to engage in conversation; after a not-so-hard day, I talk with my wife and children or do some reading and writing. On weekends, when I am usually relieved of other responsibilities, I work on future publications such as *Interzone* columns, this one being drafted on Saturday, August 7, 1999.

Visibly absent in my ongoing routine is anything resembling a social life, other than rare trips to the movies or the beach: I do not spend time with friends, I do not know my neighbors, I do not exercise, I do not go to restaurants or bars or sporting events, I appear to be completely alienated from my environment. As such, I exemplify what many regard as a growing societal problem.

For increasing numbers of Americans, like me, are avoiding the traditional social activities that long seemed essential to a functional community. As one indicator of this alarming trend, a Harvard professor named Robert D. Putnam, in the essay "Bowling Alone: America's Declining Social Capital" (1995), studied the sharp decline in bowling leagues throughout the United States, concluding that this was evidence of a grave situation urgently demanding attention. Americans are devoting insufficient amounts of their free time to communal bowling! Can the Republic survive?

\* \* \* \*

As my tone suggests, I was not inspired by Putnam to rush out and join a bowling league to help repair America's tattered social fabric. Once, while working at a credit union, I actually joined its bowling team; and to me, the iterative experience of rolling a large ball down an alley again and again, and watching it roll back to you every time, is entertaining only momentarily as a technologically streamlined realization of the mythological torments of Sisyphus.

Bowling leagues? Sorry, I have better things to do with my time—which leads to my defense of an apparently sociopathic lifestyle.

Despite all appearances, you see, I don't *feel* as if I have a sociopathic lifestyle, entirely cut off from the world. On the job, I interact normally with colleagues and students; at home, I interact with family members and their friends. More to the point, there are many people that I socialize with *from a distance*—sometimes by letters or phone, but mostly by e-mail. A few of them are well known to *Interzone* readers. While my cybernetic correspondence with David Pringle typically focuses on business matters (such as, "Dear David, What is the last possible moment that I can send you my next column and have it published on time?"), we sometimes have more substantive conversations. John Clute checks in every few months or so with a question or news, and Paul Barnett (John Grant) has been talkative of late. But I don't wish to imply that I am particularly close to these luminaries, or that my correspondence exclusively involves luminaries; it is mostly people who are unknown to you but well worth knowing—professors and students and others devoted to science fiction—that I stay in touch with.

From my perspective, then, I am not anti-social at all; rather, I have found people to be sociable with who are more stimulating than those in my immediate vicinity.

Yet concerned professors, viewing my hours at the computer as a disturbing rejection of society, want to tear me away from the internet and bring me into personal contact with people in my neighborhood, to recreate an idealized American past of community barn-raisings, square dances, and quilting bees by means of contemporary equivalents like bowling leagues.

Well. Let's consider one of my neighbors, a man I can castigate without concern because there is not the slightest chance that he will ever learn of the existence of *Interzone*, let alone read an issue. As far as I can tell, the primary obsession of his life is washing his car. Every weekend, he stands in his driveway, spending hours devotedly scrubbing and polishing his car to a state of pristine beauty. When his teenage sons were part of the household, they were in the driveway too, washing their own cars, as the father schooled his sons in the proud family tradition of automotive cleanliness. And sometimes, no doubt, they would scorn-fully look across the street at my conspicuously filthy car, a sure sign of wrongheadedness and rampant moral decay.

So, what I am supposed to do? To bond with this man, should I spend my weekends washing my car too? As we both washed our cars, would he wander over to engage in engrossing discussions about the best products and techniques to make one's car most immaculate? Would the conversation then drift into other exciting areas, like current weather conditions or the changing fortunes of the local baseball teams? To fur-ther expand our hours for social contact, would we resolve to launch a bowling league?

* * * *

Let's face it; neighborhoods are random collections of people whom we may—or more likely, may not—particularly care for. Our ancestors built barns and danced and quilted with their neighbors not because they loved each other, but because they had no choice: they needed each other's labor, and they had no one else to socialize with. Today, we can earn money to have somebody else build our houses and sew our quilts; we no longer require volunteers from across the glen to assemble basic necessities. Today, we can use communication networks to search the world to find the best possible people to socialize with; we no longer have to settle for the people who happen to live nearby.

Thus, it's not that I am *alienated* from my car-washing neighbor, my neighbor who belongs to the National Rifle Association, or my neighbor who cannot speak English; I am *liberated* from them. Instead of enduring the neighborhood I happened into, I am allowed by modern technology to construct my own virtual neighborhood, filled with far more interest-ing people than I can find by walking down the street. If you say that I am "cocooning"—prognosticator Faith Popcorn's term for people who spend all their time at home, surrounded by electronic devices—let's remember that there's a reason why caterpillars go into cocoons: to turn into butterflies. Had I remained solely in the company of the people that life threw in my path, I might have devolved into a beer-drinking cretin fuming about the lousy pitching of the Los Angeles Dodgers, and why can't Shaquille O'Neal learn how to make a free throw? Instead, in part because of the people I have chosen to read and have chosen to com-municate with, I developed into the erudite and fascinating irritant that I am today.

Of course, while science fiction friends constitute my most impor-tant virtual community, they are not the only one. Recently, I have been playing bridge online, anonymously interacting with players all over the world who enter and withdraw from games at any time as the mood strikes them. Less frequently, I consult with colleagues about teaching remedial math and English. No matter what you care about today, you can find a listserv devoted to it or can assemble your own circle of scattered companions.

And in this way, we have realized in an unexpected but spectacular fashion one of the dreams of science fiction.

* * * *

When space habitats first became prominent, they were presented as a perfect solution to all social problems. To avoid conflicts with others, like-minded individuals could settle in their very own habitat, to be happily isolated from potentially irritating outsiders. There could be separate habitats for dedicated nudists, fanatical bridge-players, or hard-core Marxists. William Forstchen's *Into the Sea of Stars* (1986) envisioned 700 of these harmonious, homogenous enclaves, which leave the solar system to enjoy a peaceful existence far from Earth.

However, there was one problem with this plan, which is that people rarely fit comfortably into one group, and one group alone. Under the Forstchen system, what happens if you are a bridge-playing Marxist? You choose the bridge habitat, but the first time a partner trumps your ace, you start longing for some intellectual arguments with your Marxist friends; unfortunately, they are now heading for the Galactic Center while you are drifting towards the Lesser Magellanic Cloud. Even if you can make the switch, discovering that most Marxists don't know how to finesse gives you second thoughts once again.

Now, with the internet, you can join a community of bridge players *and* a community of Marxists, and you can alternately interact with each of them anytime you wish, which provides much more flexibility than an array of space habitats. And what about those potentially irritating outsiders you'd like to avoid? Well, you can't put millions of miles of vacuum between you and them, but passing by their offices or occasionally seeing them in the supermarket isn't that troubling, and soon, with the growth of online employment and shopping, you may even eliminate that incidental contact.

In sum, free from the necessity of interacting only with those around us, free to seek out desirable people all over the world and craft our own cybernetic communities, contemporary people enjoy unprecedented opportunities to bond together in innumerable ways for mutual enrichment and enjoyment—a veritable virtual utopia. One prescient writer predicted all of this ninety years ago; strangely enough, he despised it.

* * * *

In 1909, as a jaundiced response to H. G. Wells's *A Modern Utopia* (1905), E. M. Forster published "The Machine Stops," which envisioned a future Earth governed by a vast Machine that delivers all of life's necessities to citizens living in private underground chambers and thus eliminates the need for travel or personal contacts between people:

> For a moment Vashti felt lonely.
>
> Then she generated the light, and the sight of her room, flooded with radiance and studded with electric buttons, revived her. There were buttons and switches everywhere—buttons to call for food[,] for music, for clothing. There was the hot-bath button, by pressure of which a basin of (imitation) marble rose out of the floor, filled to the brim with a warm deodorized liquid. There was the cold-bath button. There was the button that produced literature. And there were of course the buttons by which she communicated with her friends. The room, though it contained nothing, was in touch with all that she cared for in the world. (53-54)

Sounds good to me. But to Forster, this paradisal existence represented despicable decadence, as humanity had lost contact with the real world and real people, and he gleefully describes the gradual cessation of the Machine's activities, which drives Vashti and her compatriots to the harsh environment on the surface where they can no longer survive—leaving Earth to be inherited by the hearty "Homeless" people who had previously escaped from the Machine and adapted to the rugged outdoor life.

Forster's prophecy was flawed because he anticipated a Machine that would *force* people to remain indoors and become dependent upon its contrivances for life support and communication, so that rebels like Vashti's son must surreptitiously struggle to regain access to athleticism and adventure. In fact, we now have a Machine which simply *allows* people to do these things. So, if the personal lifestyle I've described strikes you, like my daughter, as sterile and stifling, if you believe that networks of virtual comrades are shabby, ersatz substitutes for the energizing warmth of genuine personal contact, you remain perfectly free to spend your days hiking through the mountains with friends or bowling with your neighbors. All the activities and experiences ever known to humanity remain available to us today; what is different now is that we have the option of refusing to engage in them and the ability to succeed, and even prosper, while refusing to engage in them. And this is driving some people crazy.

\* \* \* \*

Today, the internet and other technological advances can empower talented individuals who happen to lack social or physical skills while disempowering individuals whose exclusive talents in social or physical skills make them less and less important in an online world. Since it is disheartening to be disempowered, the affected individuals may indulge in fantasies of worldwide destruction and degeneration that will confound all the pampered sissies now lording it over their betters and return control to the resourceful he-men who can take care of business in an unforgiving wilderness. Since the long-awaited nuclear holocaust of survivalist fiction now appears unlikely, these persons are focusing their hopes on the Y2K problem, dreaming that on January 1, 2000, our technological civilization will grind to a complete halt and force people like me under the thumb of people like my gun-toting neighbor, who will emerge as the natural masters of their reprimitivized environment.

Fortunately, I very much doubt this will occur. In the course of human history, progress has sometimes come to a standstill, but it rarely goes in reverse. If the Machine does stop, we will have the knowledge and equipment to quickly rebuild it, and few will endorse Forster's call for its permanent destruction.

In the meantime, while the Machine is still running smoothly, it is time for me to push a button and instantly send these thoughts to a distant friend, thousands of miles away, and carry on with my blissfully boring life.

# BIG DUMB OPTICALS: FILM CONSIDERED
# AS THE MOTION PYRAMID

*The Biographical Encyclopedia of Science Fiction Film*—the work
in progress now sprouting in the *Interzone* website that I feel obliged
to explain—was my first project inspired by greed. Years ago, at a time
when I felt especially impoverished, I resolved to create a book that
might interest a major publisher, make its way to bookstores, and earn
money for its author. Such a book, I realized immediately, would have to
be about science fiction film, not science fiction literature.

This was hardly a stretch, because like everyone else I had long been
fascinated by movies and found it easy to discuss them. But *why* are we
so fascinated by movies? It has little to do with aesthetically satisfying storytelling, as was apparent after the mind-numbing experience of
watching *The Mummy* (1999). How, I wondered, did a movie that is so
manifestly awful, so deficient in all aspects of capable filmmaking covered in introductory cinema classes, become so popular?

At first, the movie brought to mind the pyramid-shaped Luxor Hotel
in Las Vegas, which features three thrill rides linked by some senseless
plot about uncovering ancient superscience in an Egyptian archaeological site and observing its effects on humanity's future. On one ride, like
Disneyland's Star Tours, you sat in synchronized moving chairs while a
television screen displayed your enclosure's purported flight through a
cavern. So, I thought, *The Mummy* might be considered an amusement
park ride without moving chairs.

From that perspective, traditional expectations of narrative logic
are irrelevant. One can protest that the film's idiot plot rests upon not
a single group of idiots but upon generation after generation of idiots;
that if ancient Egyptians had actually possessed the magical abilities displayed in the picture, they would now be enjoying their fifth millennium
of world domination; that the Israelites were slaves in Egypt a thousand
years after the pyramids were built and spoke a language unlike modern
Hebrew, so an Egyptian from that era wouldn't recognize Hebrew as
"the language of the slaves"; that a resurrected mummy savvy enough to

adjust to twentieth-century Cairo would figure out that he didn't need to be afraid of a house cat. But this would be like critiquing a roller coaster. ("For what *reason* does this vehicle slowly climb to a great height, then abruptly veer downward and to the right?")

Then, recognizing that not all popular films recall thrill rides, I hit upon another reason for the appeal of contemporary movies, also suggested by *The Mummy*, that has nothing to do with skillful narrative: movies are fascinating because they are *big*. Specifically, they are *monumental*.

\* \* \* \*

The impulse to construct and admire huge monuments is ancient, and Egyptian pyramids were only one early expression of that impulse. Other Mediterranean civilizations constructed less enduring Wonders of the World, remembered now only as evocative names and imaginative drawings. Rome built the Colisseum, China the Great Wall, India the Taj Mahal; Meso-America created its own pyramids, medieval Europe erected cathedrals, Easter Island raised gigantic statues. In the last two centuries, new materials and techniques brought more monumental marvels like the Eiffel Tower, the Statue of Liberty, and the Golden Gate Bridge. To impress the world and attract spectators, it seemed, you needed something huge and striking; and if you built it, they would come.

In recent decades, though, massive monuments have been less attractive. A sign of changing attitudes came in the 1960s, when the city of St. Louis unveiled, with great fanfare, its own answer to the Washington Monument and Arc de Triomphe, the Gateway Arch, expressly designed to become a major tourist attraction. It didn't. While older icons like Big Ben and the Empire State Building continued to draw crowds, other massive new projects, like Seattle's Space Needle and the Sydney Opera House, also did not garner much notice. If there was a fundamental human desire to gaze in awe at bigness, big buildings no longer satisfied it.

Enter Hollywood.

From the beginning, films often aspired to largeness, as demonstrated by epic fossils like *Intolerance* (1916) and *Napoleon* (1927). But it was in the 1950s that the American industry, threatened by something very small—television—responded by visibly striving to be Big. Some innovations, like Cinemascope, 3-D, and Cinerama, were efforts to *literally* make films bigger, and in other ways—extreme length, lavish spending, huge sets, all-star casts, and special effects—Hollywood struggled to lure audiences with the sheer, egregious hugeness of its products.

As *Interzone*'s film reviewer Nick Lowe has suggested, bigness temporarily went out of style in the 1960s, since big films of that era, mostly biblical epics and sentimental musicals, kept bombing. Instead of being bigger than television, Hollywood resolved to be more naked, more foul-mouthed, and more violent than television. But bigness roared back a decade later in several forms, including the big disaster movie (*Earthquake* [1974], *The Towering Inferno* [1974]), the big horror movie (*The Exorcist* [1973], *The Omen* [1976]), and the big science fiction movie (*Star Wars* [1977], *Star Trek: The Motion Picture* [1979]). And, as the films got bigger and bigger, people started paying more and more attention.

* * * *

After moving to the Los Angeles area in the 1970s, I was amazed by how extensively the local media covered the movie industry: every new film was reported on and reviewed, and there was a constant flood of news about planned and forthcoming films. I seemed in a privileged position, close to the center of film production and privy to insider information. Today, I am privileged no more: thanks to *Entertainment Tonight*, the E Channel, *Premiere* magazine, websites, and countless other resources, people in Montana or Manchester can learn just as much about movies as people in Burbank. Each weekend, all of America watches film openings like the Super Bowl, anxiously waiting to see if *Stir of Echoes* (1999) can top *The Sixth Sense* (1999) in the Friday box office receipts. During the week, everyone checks out the latest on the on-again, off-again James Cameron-Arnold Schwarzenegger *Terminator 3* project. (News flash: as of last week, it looks to be On again.)

All this attention surely reflects, in part, an understanding that building a modern motion picture is far more difficult and complex than building a pyramid. At first, equipped only with a script or scenario that can be epitomized in a catchy sales pitch ("It's *Godzilla* Meets *The English Patient*!!"), an enterprising player with clout essentially must create an entire company devoted exclusively to making the proposed film; persuade a few "bankable" performers to front the project; attract financial support in the neighborhood of a hundred million dollars or more; recruit a small army of talented craftspeople; work out dozens of deals for merchandising, novelizations, promotional tie-ins, world rights, video rights, and television rights; plan the entire filmmaking process in the manner of General Dwight D. Eisenhower preparing for D-Day; and shepherd the film to completion while coping with daily disruptions that threaten to bring the campaign to a dead halt. Films like *Titanic* (1997) are precise analogues of the Egyptian pyramids: on the one hand, they represent the collective labors of thousands of diligent workers; on the other hand, they embody the vision of one domineering individual determined to immortalize his personal obsessions.

(This is, by the way, why Warren Beatty is a credible presidential candidate—not because he is an actor, but because he is an experienced *producer*. Anybody who can keep launching and completing film projects under current conditions undoubtedly can effectively manage a large, pre-existing bureaucracy.)

To appreciate movies as the modern equivalents of monuments, remain in the theatre after the film ends, as I do, and watch all the credits. First, you can hear some excellent music through a sound system better than anything available for the home. Second, the credits may provide surprising information: at the end of *The American President* (1995), for example, I stared incredulously at dozens of credits for special effects (not recalling any explosions, spaceships, or monsters in the film) until I realized that all the crowd scenes—the President at the ball, the President addressing Congress—must have been filmed in front of a blue screen. Finally, the endless credits persuasively communicate just how massive an accomplishment you have witnessed; true, a few names don't really belong in the credits (does providing sandwiches for the cast and crew really make you a co-creator of the film?), but the vast majority of the people listed are essential to the film's completion. Even a stinker like *Lake Placid* (1999), which invites consideration as a rejected script for the old *Outer Limits* modernized and padded out to pass for a film, culminates with ten minutes of credits, proudly recognizing the thousands of people who conspired to ruin your Saturday afternoon.

So, following the modern blueprint for successful filmmaking, Stephen Sommers takes his 115 million dollars, hires a few performers and legions of talented technicians, and resurrects an ancient *Mummy*. Its inadequacies as narrative don't matter; the film is Big, accompanied by trailers and commercials promising a frenzied grandeur, and strategically unveiled a few weeks before the summer's most celebrated pyramid, *Star Wars: The Phantom Menace* (1999), is available for viewing, this lesser edifice manages to attract an impressive number of awestruck observers.

I am describing a pattern, not a rule, and occasional "little" films like *The Blair Witch Project* (1999), lacking big stars, big budgets, and big effects, may be unexpected hits. But like *Marty* (1955) or *David and Lisa* (1962), such films never start any trends. Hollywood keeps returning to the safest strategy to attract audiences, namely giganticism. So, if *The Blair Witch Project Part Two* gets made for under twenty million dollars, I will be very surprised.

* * * *

And what does all this have to do with science fiction?

An obvious answer is that the genres of fantasy and science fiction may be particularly well suited for full-scale monumental filmmaking. Realistic films must spend some time in realistic settings, too familiar to be truly impressive. Non-realistic films can economically construct, with computer graphics, any sort of spectacular world the director may envision. Realistic films may be limited in their extra-cinematic extensions: Cameron couldn't copyright the name "Titanic" and couldn't interest toymakers in selling little Titanic boats that would split apart and sink in your very own bathtub. Non-realistic films can be entirely owned by their creators, and stories can be specifically shaped to enhance marketing possibilities—remember George Lucas's animated stuffed animals, the Ewoks? And building and inhabiting you own world may especially appeal to the egomaniac star or director often required to actually get a movie project off the ground: think *Judge Dredd* (1995). Think *The Postman* (1997). Or think (but don't get me started on) *Star Wars: The Phantom Menace*.

Still, contemporary films may be best seen as a replacement for, not an expression of, science fiction.

An essay by Peter Nicholls, "Big Dumb Objects and Cosmic Enigmas: The Love Affair between Space Fiction and the Transcendental" (2000), offers the argument suggested by its title. He finds a characteristic "sense of wonder, the sublime, the transcendent, or the romantic" in science fiction and adds that "one rather mechanical way of creating this effect is for the storyteller to imagine something very, very big and mysterious, like the spaceship *Rama*, or like Larry Niven's *Ringworld*" (12). For the less imaginative, I submit, large and distinctive monuments long served to inspire similar emotions; what happened in the 1960s to diminish their impact may have been the newly available photographs of Earth from orbital space. From that cosmic vantage point, we were repeatedly informed, only one human artifact could be seen, the Great Wall of China; even that, it turned out, was undetectable. Suddenly, the monuments of Earth were diminished in stature; if the vaunted Gateway Arch could not be observed from space, was it really important at all?

Now, perhaps, only the artificial and natural wonders of space would suffice to impress the masses, so images of the Saturn V rocket and close-up photographs of the Moon and Mars were proffered to the public. A few films also endeavored to be conspicuously Big in this respect, most notably *2001: A Space Odyssey* (1968), with depictions of planetary alignments, the spaceship *Discovery*, and the immense monolith orbiting Jupiter. But usually this sort of Bigness proved more alienating than inspiring. Consider that uneasy blend of *2001* and *Star Trek*, *Star Trek:*

*The Motion Picture*, a film driven from the start by the studio's insistence upon making it "big." The result was a dull, lifeless epic, with the *Enterprise* crew doing little more than gazing in awe at cosmic immensities. A livelier space film, *Star Wars*, gave viewers touches of such majesty— an opening shot of a huge imperial dreadnought, brilliantly parodied in *Spaceballs* (1987)—but otherwise entertained audiences with other sorts of spectacle—exotic aliens, zooming spaceships, big explosions.

Gradually, the films themselves, as well as what they displayed, came to play the role of contemporary monuments, as people grew equally fascinated by the stories behind the screen—the huge budgets, huge egos, huge lawsuits, and so on. And why not? Whether it's pyramids, cathedrals, or films, monuments can always be criticized as criminal wastes of a civilization's resources, particularly when they seem tacky or tasteless. However, people always feel compelled to build them, and it would be churlish to condemn such a characteristic human activity. We have devised an interesting new sort of monument to construct, and in a world cluttered with massive structures, there is something appealing about a monument that can be preserved in a roll of celluloid or a computer. So, with no aspirations to become a regular film reviewer, I will keep gazing in awe as new monuments are erected, and occasionally record my frank opinions about the modern-day equivalents of Cheops who create them.

# A CHRISTMAS CAVIL, OR, IT'S A PLUNDERFUL LIFE

If we seek to define those works belonging to the genre of the Christmas story—and surely, such stories are numerous and distinctive enough to warrant the term "genre"—there are two obvious characteristics: the story takes place on or around Christmas, and the story is promulgated, absorbed, and revived only during the Christmas season.

However, while these are *necessary* conditions for texts in the genre, they are not *sufficient* conditions. Consider the films *Holiday Inn* (1942) and *Home Alone* (1990). Both stories take place primarily or exclusively at Christmas time, both were released during the holiday season, and both appear on television every year around December. Yet it is difficult to regard these films as Christmas stories; somehow, there is something insufficiently *Christmassy* about them.

For a work to truly be a Christmas story, another condition must be met: the story is *about* Christmas; it takes the holiday itself as its main subject (as *Holiday Inn* and *Home Alone* do not). One can go further: the story is a *defense* of Christmas, of the spirit of kindness and generosity associated with the holiday. So the Christmas story will often involve a characteristic plot: someone who is not being nice enough during the Christmas season learns his lesson and starts behaving like a fine fellow.

As another distinguishing trait, the Christmas story frequently approaches or intersects with fantasy. While ghosts, as in Charles Dickens's *A Christmas Carol* (1843), are uncommon, celebrating a Christian holiday invites the appearance of angels, and the figure of Santa Claus, with his elves and flying reindeer, may also move the story into the realm of fantasy. Even Christmas stories without fantastic elements can mimic the structure and atmosphere of fairy tales, as numerous examples illustrate.

If Christmas stories are defined as defenses of the Christmas spirit, a surprising corollary emerges: stories about the first Christmas, when Jesus was born, are not true Christmas stories—because, whatever worthwhile messages are conveyed, these stories rarely focus specifically on the need to be kind and generous. The origins of the Christmas genre lie in more recent times. A naïve person would start the search in the era when the custom of Christmas gift-giving first became ubiquitous; a

cynical person would begin when there first emerged businesses dependent upon holiday purchases motivated by this generosity and thus interested in promoting a form of literature to stimulate such purchases. Both
searchers would end up in nineteenth-century Europe; and while other
works from that era might be advanced as generic prototypes, the story
that most served to define and establish the form is *A Christmas Carol*.

\* \* \* \*

Dickens's story can be interpreted as an extended response to the
question, "Why should people be kind to each other?" The four ghosts
each provide a different answer to the question, in increasing order of
importance.

Marley's Ghost reminds people that kindness to others may be mandated by both law and custom, and Scrooge violated British law and
custom in his shameful treatment of a business partner. But this message,
like Marley's Ghost himself, is merely an introductory flourish, a point
that should be made but one not important to Dickens. His substantive
defenses of Christmas will invoke more universal principles.

The Ghost of Christmas Past presents the *genetic defense* of altruism:
human beings are born naturally kind, so kindness is our characteristic
behavior. But some people, due to unfortunate experiences, have been
driven away from their true nature. The Ghost of Christmas Past drives
the message home by forcing Scrooge to examine his younger self: look,
you weren't always this mean person; in fact, you were once rather nice.
That's the way you were born, and that's the way you should be.

The Ghost of Christmas Present offers the *therapeutic defense* of
altruism: being nice to other people makes you *feel good*; improving others' lives improves your own life. Scrooge learns this by observing the
family of Bob Cratchit: according to the precepts of capitalism, Scrooge
should be happy, since he has plenty of money, while the Cratchits
should be miserable, since they have little money. But Scrooge notes
that the Cratchits are a pretty contented bunch—and crippled Tiny Tim,
who should be the most miserable, curiously is the happiest of them all,
because he is the kindest person in a family of kind people.

While these episodes begin to melt Scrooge's cold heart, he changes
his selfish ways only after the visit of the Ghost of Christmas Future,
who unveils Dickens's final defense of altruism, the *immortality defense*:
humans live on after death only in the minds of their compatriots; if you
are not nice to other people, they will not remember you, and you will
be erased from the pages of history. To endure, you must be kind, so
your contemporaries and descendants will remember you. This is what
Scrooge learns from contemplating his unattended funeral and ignored

grave; and it is to avoid this fate that he becomes a profligate philanthropist, smiling at everyone while purchasing that goose for a generous Christmas feast.

If this brilliant story is rarely appreciated, it is a matter of inappropriate context: placed next to Dickens's longer novels or other classics of British literature, *A Christmas Carol* indeed seems puerile. However, considered in the context of a genre which necessarily presents a puerile message about the need for kindness, *A Christmas Carol* emerges as not only the template of the Christmas story but its most comprehensive and profound exemplar. While many successors crudely parrot its appeals to human nature and therapeutic benefits in defending altruism, few venture as close to the grave as Dickens does, and the electrifying chill of that visit to Scrooge's dismal future gives his Christmas story unparalleled depth and substance.

In the century following *A Christmas Carol*, the story of the mean person who learns better at Christmas time became ubiquitous, but one memorable Christmas story, O'Henry's "The Gift of the Magi" (1905), strikingly inverts the formula. Two people, already generous to a fault, learn the necessity of selfishness: if either or both had acted selfishly, they would have been better off; their simultaneous decision to be generous beyond measure led to their ruin. The lingering prominence of the story suggests some subterranean dissatisfaction with Dickens's message, a sense that boundless generosity is perhaps not the panacea proffered by the relentless promoters of Christmas. But the clearest rebuttal to Dickens comes in the only story that approaches *A Christmas Carol* in stature and profundity, and that is a film entitled *It's a Wonderful Life* (1946).

\* \* \* \*

Others have noted a relationship between Dickens's novel and Frank Capra's movie, but it is far from derivative; in fact, *It's a Wonderful Life* is stunningly original because it simultaneously incorporates, expands upon, and refutes *A Christmas Carol*, along with all other Christmas stories.

The parallels between Dickens and Capra can be stated as follows: both stories feature a man who, on Christmas Eve, vocally challenges the true meaning of Christmas. He receives a supernatural visitor intent upon changing his attitude. To demonstrate that the man has gone astray, the story examines his past, his present predicament, and a possible situation. Anxious to prevent the possible situation from occurring, the man returns to present-day reality as an enthusiastic proponent of the Christmas spirit. This artfully worded summary conceals a few differences in the stories, but the overall similarities are inarguable.

The film significantly departs from Dickens's story in two major respects. First, while Dickens links Scrooge and Cratchit only when the Ghost of Christmas Present visits, contrasting Cratchit's contented family with Scrooge's loneliness, *It's a Wonderful Life* maintains a connection throughout its story between its malignant Scrooge figure, Potter, and its likable Cratchit figure, George Bailey. Second, Capra makes Cratchit the main character, an amicable person driven by desperation to question everything he values in life. This makes the challenge to Christmas more threatening, since denunciations of the holiday are now attributed to a character we love and admire, but the full, devastating impact of this shift on any effort to uphold Christmas values cannot be appreciated until the film ends.

Despite Cratchit's enlarged role, *It's a Wonderful Life* remains Scrooge's story as well—and, considered as such, the film's darkness becomes apparent, since it is nothing less than the unsettling saga of a triumphantly unrepentant Scrooge.

* * * *

In the beginning, like Scrooge, Potter commits a crime—grand larceny, no less—by seizing and concealing the $8000 that he knows belongs to Bailey's bank. Though Scrooge goes unpunished for cheating Marley, at least Marley's Ghost appears to upbraid him and make him feel a little guilty. But nobody upbraids Potter, and he never displays any guilt about his theft. So, while *A Christmas Carol* presents kindness as something that law and custom endeavor to enforce, that notion here is even more powerfully brushed aside as idealistic and irrelevant; instead, *It's a Wonderful Life* shows that rich people can get away with cruel crimes without fear of punishment. In the meantime, it is gentle, law-abiding Bailey who faces possible imprisonment because of Potter's crime, further demonstrating that law and custom don't support kindness very well.

During Bailey's past, Potter is always the same—mean, manipulative, avaricious. Bailey's father explains him as a "sick man," but Potter surely makes it hard to contend that people are naturally kindhearted. Bailey's history undermines the argument more subtly: yes, he does kind deeds, but it is always something he feels *obliged* to do, not something he *wants* to do, and it is usually something that harms him—due to his kindness, he loses his hearing, his college education, and his honeymoon. Bailey suggests not that humans are intrinsically generous, but that they are indoctrinated by society to act generously, even when it is contrary to their own desires and interests. This is not exactly a ringing endorsement of the quintessential love in everyone's hearts that Christmas is supposed to bring out.

In Bailey's present, Potter is sitting pretty, since the stolen $8000 may finally allow him to crush Bailey's competing bank and control the entire town. If he feels sad about his lonely, unfulfilled life, there is not an instant in the film that conveys that. Rather, the unfailingly generous George Bailey is angry and bitter; though surrounded by his family on Christmas Eve, like Cratchit, the presence of his family is only irksome. Cruelty is making Potter happy, while kindness is making Bailey miserable.

The alternate world to which Bailey is taken by his guardian angel, where he was never born, is also a world without Potter; although Gloria Grahame ad-libbed the line "I know Potter" while being arrested, the script doesn't mention him at all, and it is entirely possible that screenwriters Frances Goodrich, Albert Hackett, Capra, and Jo Sterling intended to convey that Potter has died, or that he has departed to find new towns to conquer. But unlike Scrooge, he is hardly forgotten: Bedford Falls has been renamed Pottersville in his honor, other landmarks like the housing development Potter's Field commemorate him, and the town has become precisely the sort of place that an ambitious capitalist would dream of: neon signs, thriving businesses, and frenetic commercial activity everywhere.

While Capra despises, and wishes audiences to despise, Pottersville and everything it represents, that city clearly represented, even in 1946, what the Western world was inexorably becoming, thanks to the greed and ambition of businessmen like Potter. In the context of American history, this tableau of conquering capitalism refutes Dickens's assertion that kind people are remembered, while mean people are forgotten. Quite the contrary: the names of many wonderfully nice people in nineteenth-century America are utterly unknown, but monuments and institutions still bear the names of savagely acquisitive robber barons like Andrew Carnegie and John D. Rockefeller. Further, in the context of the film's echoes of Dickens, we are invited to view this scene not as an alternate world but as the future of Bedford Falls: eventually, Bailey's futile efforts against Potter will falter, and Potter will take over the town to remake it in his image.

Yet the film's happy ending, with Bedford Falls restored to its pastoral ambiance and Bailey rescued from disgrace by his friends' generosity, apparently indicates that the Potters of the world can be resisted and put in their place. Or does it? First consider precisely what it is that makes Bailey so happy: a growing pile of money in his house. Whatever the logic of the narrative suggests, the scene functions as a giddy visual celebration of pure, unadulterated greed.

Also consider the only thing that has really changed by the end of the film: Potter is $8000 richer, while Bailey's friends are $8000 poorer. After Christmas is over and accounts are settled, Bailey will return to the daily struggle of opposing Potter not one whit stronger than he was before. Since the film does not challenge or transform Potter, as Dickens challenged and transformed Scrooge, he remains a powerful evil force; all the film does is to needlessly reprimand an essentially good man who is experiencing an understandable temporary bout of anger and depression while ignoring the true villain of the piece. This is the masterstroke of the film's conclusion: instead of bringing Potter onstage to be chastised or punished, *It's a Wonderful Life* lets him be, suggesting that mean people like Potter can never be reformed or defeated; at best, they can be ignored and occasionally thwarted. Thus, the final scene both validates Potter's values and implicitly licenses Potter's behavior.

\* \* \* \*

So, if you watch *It's a Wonderful Life* this holiday season, enjoy it as a bracing antidote to the treacly sentiments of *Christmas Carol* adaptations and other Christmas stories; revel in its thinly veiled argument against the Christmas spirit. Kindness is not enforced by law and custom; kindness is not intrinsic to human nature; kindness does not make people happy; and kindness does not make people immortal. Go ahead and swindle your partner, steal several thousand dollars, and launch underhanded schemes to destroy your opponents. It is the way that residents of Pottersville are supposed to behave.

And have a Merry Christmas.

# THE SOUND OF THE CITY...AND THE CALL OF THE COSMOS

As those who knew me in college will attest, rock'n'roll music was once the passion of my life: I spent hours at any available piano, teaching myself to play every song on the radio and writing hundreds of my own songs. Even as I later settled into a career as a teacher and writer, I occasionally returned to the subject of rock music, as when I authored brief entries on "The Beatles" and "Rock Video" for *The Encyclopedia of Fantasy* (1997). So, after one participant in the "fictionmags" Internet discussion group raised the issue of the relationship between science fiction and rock'n'roll music, arguing that the issue had been insufficiently explored, I should have been inspired to pursue the topic at length. Strangely, I wasn't.

It is hardly difficult to compile a list of relevant works. Rock music that displays the influence of science fiction? David Bowie's "Space Oddity" (1969), "Starman" (1972), and other songs from his Ziggy Stardust phase. The Rolling Stones' "Two Thousand Light Years from Home" (1967), Elton John's "Rocket Man" (1972), and Jefferson Starship's *Blows Against the Empire* (1970). Jeff Wayne's rock-opera version of *The War of the Worlds* (1978), featuring songs by Justin Hayward of the Moody Blues. The music of Hawkwind and Klaatu. Songs from the musicals *The Rocky Horror Picture Show* (1973, 1975) and *Little Shop of Horrors* (1982, 1986). Billy Idol's *Cyberpunk* (1993).

Science fiction that displays the influence of rock music? Chester Anderson's *The Butterfly Kid* (1967). Norman Spinrad's "The Big Flash" (1969). Michael Moorcock's Jerry Cornelius stories. Gregory Benford's "Doing Lennon" (1975), Edward Bryant's "Stone" (1978), John Grant's *The Truth about the Flaming Ghoulies* (1984), and John Shirley's *Eclipse* (1985). Stories by Howard Waldrop and the early novels of Allan Steele. Further, these connections have not been entirely unnoticed by commentators and scholars: the entry on "Music" in *The Encyclopedia of Science Fiction* (1993) discusses several of these titles and others, and one critical anthology, Michael A. Morrison's *Trajectories of the Fantastic*

(1997), features a section on "Fantastic Rock" with essays about Bowie and Moorcock.

Yet I was not eager to examine any of these works; while sometimes striking, they were not interesting as a group and did not appear to be of central importance to their respective genres. To express the point as I did in my "fictionmags" response, consider creating an album of *The Best of Science Fiction Rock'n'Roll* and an anthology of *The Best of Rock'n'Roll Science Fiction*. These would be easy to assemble, but no one would ever mistake them for *The Best of Rock'n'Roll* or *The Best of Science Fiction*; with rare exceptions, these compilations would exclude the works that a scholar of rock music and a scholar of science fiction would need to discuss in order to convey the essence of their subjects.

* * * *

To explain why this may be true will require some generalizations easily open to challenge, but being challenged is not, after all, a novel experience for me at this point. First, let us accept the position of *Time* magazine, in choosing Albert Einstein as its Person of the Century, that the tremendous progress of science has been the most important development of the last hundred years. In at least three respects, its multitudinous advances are profoundly challenging our understanding of what it means to be human. New technologies like automobiles, airplanes, atomic energy, satellite communication, and computers are significantly altering all aspects of human existence, from daily routines to global politics. An improved understanding of genetics and biotechnology is providing us with the power to change the human mind and body in previously unthinkable fashions, perhaps crafting people who are immortal, superintelligent, or augmented by mechanical organs and memory implants. Space travel and a growing knowledge of the universe engender the genuine possibility of contact with alien intelligences, which would forever alter how we see ourselves. In all these ways, then, modern science requires that we ponder the implications of forthcoming, and fundamental, changes in the human condition.

Unfortunately, early twentieth-century literature, increasingly preoccupied with character studies, stylistic experimentation, and recycling ancient mythology, could not and would not address these issues. Thus, there arose the need for a new type of narrative, science fiction, which implausibly blended the dime novel, utopia, Gothic novel, satire, travel tale, popular-science essay, and other influences as a new vehicle for explorations of diverse aspects of our potential inhumanity.

However, while it is both exciting and necessary, contemplating such prospects as revolutionary new gadgetry, the advent of *homo superior*, or the arrival of a message from Arcturus engenders a natural counterreaction: a desire to reaffirm the human condition, to delight in the most basic aspects of everyday existence, to be reinvigorated by the simple pleasures that have characterized our lives for millions of years. Yet the first part of the twentieth century also failed to provide a proper medium for these impulses: all forms of the written word were ill-suited to convey such primal emotions, and most forms of music, ranging from discordant orchestral compositions to experimental jazz and urbane Broadway show tunes, seemed too arcane or sophisticated for the task. Thus, there arose the need for a new type of music, rock'n'roll, which implausibly blended the blues, jazz, folk music, country music, Gospel music, and other influences as a new vehicle for expressions of diverse aspects of our enduring humanity.

Whenever I think of rock'n'roll music, I recall the most basic of the human senses—touch, which we share with even the most primitive microorganisms—and the four sensitivities of human touch: heat, cold, pressure, and pain. This is one way to explain what rock'n'roll is all about: the heat of sexual passion, the chill of unrequited or lost love, the pressure of trying to cope with an ever-changing technological society, and the pain of failing to do so. One could say with equal justice that rock music celebrates the direct stimulation of our pleasure centers, whether by sex, drugs, a fresh breeze while driving down the open road, or the thrill of catching a wave on a sunny beach. Conversely, rock'n'roll rejects artifice, artificiality, and any alterations in traditional human qualities; thus, when Ray Davies of the Kinks was asked to write something about organ transplants for the film *Percy* (1971), he responded with a protest song, "God's Children" (1971), singing "we are all God's children, / and they've got no right to change us, / we gotta go back the way the good Lord made us."

In *The Universe Makers* (1971), Donald A. Wollheim once discerned a vast metanarrative underlying science fiction—a near-future of disastrous problems caused by new technology, gradual human expansion into space, encounters with alien beings, and an eventual approach to God—its essence epitomized by the title of a collection of Konstantin Tsiolkovsky's works, *The Call of the Cosmos* (1960). There is also a metanarrative underlying rock'n'roll, though true experts in that music could better articulate it. The story involves the growing urbanization of American life—hence, the title of Charlie Gillett's study of rock'n'roll, *The Sound of the City* (1970)—as simple country boys like Johnny B. Goode discover the joys of city life (fast cars, loose women, electric guitars) even as they sometimes long to return to a peaceful rural existence. Young men and women encounter an increasingly restrictive civilization and cry for freedom; they observe social inequities and demand justice. Defying conventional values in their clothing and sexual preferences, they flirt with crime and violence, indulge in alcohol and drugs, look for easy money, and break all the rules. Their stirring anthems include Chuck Berry's "Roll Over Beethoven" (1956), Elvis Presley's "Jailhouse Rock" (1957), the Rolling Stones' "Satisfaction" (1965), Bob Dylan's "Like a Rolling Stone" (1965), Steppenwolf's "Born to Be Wild" (1968), the Who's "Won't Get Fooled Again" (1971), Lou Reed's "Walk on the Wild Side" (1972), Alice Cooper's "School's Out" (1972), Lynyrd Skynyrd's "Free Bird" (1973), Queen's "We Will Rock You" (1977), the Stray Cats' "Stray Cat Strut" (1982), Donna Summer's "She Works Hard for the Money" (1983), the Talking Heads' "Burning Down the House" (1983), Nirvana's "Smells Like Teen Spirit" (1991), and Alanis Morissette's "You Oughta Know" (1995). For all of rock's assertive simplicities, it projects a rich, complex, and evocative story that continues to move generation after generation of young people almost half a century after its emergence.

But it doesn't have a heck of a lot to do with science fiction.

\* \* \* \*

Clearly, I am constructing a grand conceit: ignoring new media created by technology (such as film, radio, television, and video games), I argue that two major new forms of expression emerged in the twentieth century—science fiction and rock'n'roll music—both assembled by necessity out of disparate older genres, one designed to ponder potential new realities and the other designed to validate enduring values. Like any grand conceit, it should be greeted with skepticism, and given its topics, that is only fitting—since, as forms largely created for and embraced by marginalized youth (science fiction for nerds, rock'n'roll for hoods), both encourage a healthy skepticism for recognized authority, whether it is Sir Arthur C. Clarke's skepticism about an elderly scientist announcing that something is impossible or Carl Perkins's skepticism about some nefarious individual poised to step on his Blue Suede Shoes.

One skeptical response would be based on the large numbers of related works, some listed above, that even a lethargic researcher could readily identify. If so many rock songs reference science fiction, and so many science fiction works reference rock music, doesn't there have to be some sort of affinity between the two? But this isn't necessarily true: since science fiction and rock'n'roll are both dynamic mixtures of egregiously dissimilar progenitors, they are naturally ready to combine with almost any conceivable partner. The existence of science fiction rock'n'roll, then, is not especially significant when one considers that rock'n'roll has also been blended with opera, jazz, classical music, political commentary, and comedy; and rock'n'roll science fiction also is only one of many unlikely combinations.

More to the point, I maintain that rock songs influenced by science fiction are not really that numerous and are definitely not that important. Almost invariably, science fiction in a rock star's oeuvre seems either an unfortunate phase that the artist thankfully grew out of or a disastrous career-ending move. I mean, who could sanely listen to Bowie's "Rebel, Rebel" (1974) and wax nostalgic about the good old days of "Space Oddity"? And it is perhaps not a coincidence that the Carpenters had their first big flop when they covered Klaatu's "Calling Occupants of Interplanetary Craft" (1976), or that Billy Idol's once-thriving career came to a screeching halt with the release of his *Cyberpunk* album. In the same way, rock'n'roll science fiction stories such as those listed above are generally lesser moments in their authors' careers; a genre born to wrestle with the largest implications of our ongoing confrontation with the universe and our burgeoning abilities to alter its realities can seem anemic and cramped when it focuses exclusively on mundane human drives—just as rock music can sound pretentious or nauseatingly sentimental when it addresses aliens, robots, and spaceships.

Another line of objection would focus on the fact that many people, like myself, are tremendously fond of both rock music and science fiction; doesn't that suggest that there is some strong connection between them? But this isn't necessarily true either. Here, we encounter the basic fallacy that underlies repeated efforts to relate these two contrasting forms: the idea that if I am interested in X, and if I am interested in Y, then X and Y must be related in some way. Nonsense! Human beings are, or should be, complicated and multifaceted creatures who can readily respond to the allure of contradictory forces. Someone on the "fiction-mags" list surprised me the other day by commenting on the outcome of an American football game; if he is a fan of both science fiction and football, then must we posit that there is some close relationship between science fiction and football? It makes more sense to believe that he is simply a man of variegated passions who is sometimes moved by science fiction and sometimes moved by football, and there is nothing wrong, or truly incongruous, about that.

\* \* \* \*

Therefore, I suggest that an attraction to both science fiction and rock'n'roll is simply a complete and appropriate response to contemporary times: we should sometimes be intrigued by and receptive to the possibility of revolutionary changes in the human condition, and we should sometimes be inspired and stimulated by a reaffirmation of our most ancient human urges and desires. But I submit that we cannot felicitously do these things at the same time. A friend once proposed that there were three secrets to successful cooking: everything tastes better with mushrooms; everything tastes better with peanut butter; and mushrooms and peanut butter do not go well together. Science fiction and rock music similarly strike me as experiences to be relished alternately, but not simultaneously; some things are best communicated through stories, while other things are best communicated through songs. In a sense, though, it is not surprising that so many writers and musicians keep coming up with ill-advised combinations of story and song; for as already suggested, both science fiction and rock music encourage their audiences to defy conventional wisdom, move beyond the ordinary, and attempt the impossible. And that may be the only quality that these forms have in common.

# WHAT IS A SCIENCE FICTION MAGAZINE? (AND WHY ON EARTH ARE THEY STILL AROUND?)

The first question would appear to require less than 20 words, not 2000: "A science fiction magazine is a magazine that publishes science fiction stories." Yet there must be more to it than that, since science fiction magazines do not list their contents on page one, begin the first story on page two, and carry on exclusively with fiction until the final story ends on the final page. One exception does come to mind, the short-lived magazine *Crank!* (1994-1998), but if you have never seen or heard of *Crank!*, that in a way makes my point: having a science fiction magazine that features science fiction, and only science fiction, has never been a formula for success.

Looking at the science fiction magazines that have endured, and disregarding the inevitable clutter of advertisements, one invariably finds other ingredients therein. Some of these qualify as other forms of science fiction, such as serialized novels or humorous vignettes that cannot properly be called "science fiction stories." In addition, science fiction art, ranging from lush cover paintings to dynamic interior drawings, is usually considered essential; one occasionally finds science fiction jokes, science fiction puzzles, science fiction cartoons, and (don't ask me why) science fiction poetry; there were experiments with science fiction comic strips, even a magazine with an inserted science fiction comic book; and attached CD-ROMs with science fiction computer-game demos will surely be tried someday (if they haven't been tried already).

But other common ingredients cannot qualify as science fiction by any standard definition. Science articles, sometimes including photographs, tables, and schematic diagrams. Articles about, or interviews with, noteworthy science fiction writers. Editorials, ranging from brief promotional blurbs to John W. Campbell, Jr.'s lengthy and pugnacious commentaries. Readers' letters, often followed by editors' responses. Reviews of new books, films, and television programs. Classified ads aimed exclusively at science fiction fans and collectors. News reports on the activities of the science fiction community, which started with "The

Science Fiction League" section of Hugo Gernsback's *Wonder Stories* in the 1930s and continues on in today's "Ansible Link." Even ("don't ask me why," you say?) opinionated columns.

As it happens, my own, non-standard definition of science fiction would incorporate all these materials, largely on the grounds that they seem so wedded to science fiction as to be virtually part of the genre; however, even as one of their creators, I freely acknowledge that they are only of secondary importance. The factor that unifies all readers of a science fiction magazine is their desire to read stories; only some of them want to read editorials, or reviews, or letters, or science articles. Still, though their numbers are smaller, each group of devotees is intensely loyal to their favorite feature, and if a magazine fails to provide it, editors will be bombarded with complaints. At first, even the science-obsessed Gernsback did not include science articles in his science fiction magazines, but he later relented in the face of constant requests from readers. Even the most stubborn of institutional wills may be bent by recurring reader demands for a certain feature: for over fifty years, *The Magazine of Fantasy and Science Fiction* has steadfastly refused to include a letters column, but editor Gordon Van Gelder has recently started to post some letters on his magazine's website, and one of them—from veteran author William Tenn (Philip Klass), no less—presented the predictable request: "I still think—as I always have—that it would be valuable to print a small letters department in F&SF ...."

What all these features reflect, and to an extent replicate, is the characteristic ambience of a science fiction convention, where one may find: booths or speakers representing science-oriented organizations like the L-5 Society; science fiction authors offering readings or answering fans' questions as they sign books; large exhibits of science fiction art to admire or purchase; rooms full of dealers selling science fiction books, magazines, and memorabilia; and plenty of heated arguments about science fiction during formal panel discussions and informal hotel-room parties. Like conventions, magazines have served as the waterholes of science fiction, where fans gather not only to enjoy the latest stories from old masters and rising stars, but also to sample its associated products and overhear another portion of the fascinating extended conversation that has accompanied science fiction ever since it was first recognized as a genre.

So, I will advance another answer to my first question: "Science fiction magazines are the written equivalents of science fiction conventions"—and we are well on our way to answering that second question.

\* \* \* \*

To be sure, one must acknowledge, there are many who regard the science fiction magazine as an endangered species, apparently with good reason. After all, we have just witnessed the recent death of *Science Fiction Age* (1992-2000), joining other defunct enterprises of the last decade like the aforementioned *Crank!*, *Odyssey* (1997-1998), *Tomorrow SF* (1993-2000), *Pulphouse* (1988-1995), and *Omni* (1978-1998). Others, like *Aboriginal SF* (1986-2001), are hanging on by a thread, and even the hardy perennials like *Asimov's Science Fiction* (1977- ), *The Magazine of Fantasy and Science Fiction* (1950- ), *Analog Science Fiction/Science Fact* (1930- ), and *Interzone* (1982- ) never seem to be doing quite well enough to put a smile on their editors' faces.

Still, the species stubbornly refuses to die, as old survivors and brash upstarts continue their struggle for survival. A recent issue of *The Bulletin of the Science Fiction and Fantasy Writers of America* lists almost 50 current magazines paying at least one cent a word for science fiction and fantasy stories; I can't see how some of these unknown magazines are paying the bills, but somehow, they are staying afloat. Even as I speak, some prominent figure in the field with better things to do is trying to persuade a major publisher to back her proposed new science fiction magazine, while some poor fool of lesser renown has just spent her recent inheritance producing the first issue of a brand-new science fiction magazine, hoping to find a niche and collect enough subscriptions to pay for a second issue.

It's hard to argue that all this activity reflects only a widespread desire to write and read science fiction, since there are many companies publishing tons of science fiction books, including occasional anthologies of original stories, and they are enlisting new authors all the time. The manifestos that launch new magazines may boast of a passionate desire to showcase and foster innovative, controversial, cutting-edge science fiction of the sort that a mainstream publisher would never touch, but the same worthwhile goals might logically be addressed by setting up a small press to publish innovative, controversial, cutting-edge books. Why do these noble aspirations so often manifest themselves in new magazines?

The conclusion is inescapable: publishers and readers do not simply cherish science fiction of certain sorts, but they cherish science fiction magazines. They want great stories first and foremost, but they also want the artwork, the articles, the reviews, the editorials, the letters, and so on. Publishers and editors want to play host to their own, ersatz science fiction conventions, and readers want those ersatz conventions delivered to their home on a regular basis. In defiance of economic logic, the science fiction community is engaged in an ongoing collective effort to maintain the institution of the science fiction magazine at whatever cost. Rather than extrapolating the curves to make depressing predictions about the imminent death of the science fiction magazine, then, we should rather be astounded by its stubborn vitality—especially in contrast to the near-disappearance of the other varieties of fiction magazines.

* * * *

Decades ago, there were literally hundreds, if not thousands, of magazines that specialized in or published some fiction; today, these magazines are becoming harder and harder to find. If one considers today's numbers as a percentage of yesterday's numbers, the decline in general fiction magazines surely is far more precipitous than the decline in science fiction magazines.

If asked to explain this decline, I would point to the changing nature of the typical reading experience. During the last century, reading became an ideal activity for people on the go; they read while riding to work on the bus, read while waiting in doctors' offices or airport terminals, and read while sitting on a park bench awaiting the arrival of a friend. And something portable, episodic, and disposable, like a fiction magazine or a paperback book, was ideal for this sort of peripatetic reading. Today, however, people increasingly listen to their Walkmans while on the bus, watch television in doctors' offices and airport terminals, and chatter away on cell phones while awaiting a friend's arrival.

While many people do continue to read, their reading has evolved into more of a planned, even ritualized activity. At the end of a busy day, they get a glass of wine or cup of tea, pick up their favorite reading material, and settle into their easy chairs for a few hours of quality reading. Or when they go on vacation, they take something along for long hours of reading while resting by the pool or on the beach. At these times, they don't want, or need, something portable, episodic, and disposable like a magazine; rather, they want something weightier, more unified, and more permanent—something better suited for the *gravitas* of their reading experience. In short, they want a hardcover book; and although there are other factors involved, this is surely one reason why sales of hardcover books remain strong, while sales of their more fragile cousins—like magazines, paperbacks, comic books, and newspapers—keep falling.

And why have science fiction magazines resisted this trend? I theorize that the readers of other forms of fiction historically regarded the magazines as ephemeral products to read in a casual manner and throw away after reading; now that their manner of reading has grown more controlled and more bourgeois, they no longer want to bother with such *declassé* material. But science fiction readers, as indicated, have always felt a special commitment to science fiction magazines that extends beyond their basic commitment to science fiction itself. As embodiments of the entire experience of being a part of the science fiction community, science fiction magazines have always been treasured by their purchasers; even in the 1920s and 1930s, when science fiction magazines were still in their infancy, fans were already building their private collections, buying every new magazine that appeared on the stands and searching through used book stores for the past issues they were missing. Today, all types of fiction magazines may be eagerly collected, but first-time purchasers of science fiction magazines, I submit, have always tended to save and collect their magazines more so than first-time purchasers of other fiction magazines.

In this way, science fiction magazines have escaped the tinge of proletariat disposability that has contributed to the disappearance of many other, seemingly comparable, fiction magazines in other fields. A fan of detective fiction, about to settle down for an afternoon of serious reading, may feel that a hardcover novel, not the latest issue of *Ellery Queen's Mystery Magazine* (1941- ), is the only product that suits the dignity of the occasion. But to a science fiction fan, the latest issue of *Interzone*— or *Asimov's Science Fiction, Analog*, or *The Magazine of Fantasy and Science Fiction*—is every bit as important, every bit as dignified, as a hardcover novel. The science fiction fan peruses her magazine solemnly and carefully, so as not to bend the pages or break its spine, because she views that magazine, despite its fragility and eclecticism, as a worthwhile addition to her permanent collection and a sentimentally appealing *gestalt* representing everything that she loves about the genre.

In sum, my brief answer to the second question would be: "they are still around because science fiction readers uniquely value, and uniquely seek to preserve and maintain, their written equivalents of science fiction conventions."

\* \* \* \*

At a time when the entire publishing industry is always in turmoil, and when the internet is poised to revolutionize everything about the way people read, it may seem quaint or reactionary to cling so tenaciously to an ancient medium like the magazine. Yet science fiction should be committed to progress in the truest sense of the word—which doesn't mean constantly replacing the old with the new, but rather means improving what doesn't work while holding on to what works. And, considering how the magazines have helped science fiction grow from a tiny backwater to a major force in the publishing world, and how they have helped to maintain the genre's distinctive identity in the face of innumerable threats, one is forced to conclude that the magazines represent something that works, and therefore something worth keeping.

And so, just as Harlan Ellison still chooses to communicate—and create his new worlds—by means of his old-fashioned manual type-writer, the science fiction community still chooses to communicate—and continually reaffirm, renew, and recreate itself—by means of its old-fashioned magazines. Call me a Luddite, but I can't see this as a problem.

# PREHISTORY LESSONS

I have occasionally toyed with the notion that science fiction could be profitably defined as the literature that describes those eras of human existence undocumented by eyewitness testimony. The main period examined in science fiction is the future, which no one has yet observed; in purported accounts of aliens among us, or secret societies manipulating modern civilization, one could say that science fiction endeavors to deal with unchronicled aspects of the present; and there are finally the millennia of human prehistory before the discovery of writing depicted in the subgenre of prehistoric science fiction.

The reason why science becomes involved in these stories is simple enough. Authors creating fictions about recognized events of the past five thousand years or the present can draw upon written accounts (or unwritten accounts preserved by oral tradition) produced by the people who were actually there to give their works an air of authenticity; no other research is necessary. When such accounts are not available, however, authors must base their stories on known scientific findings or their own scientific speculations. As they construct imaginary futures, physics provides accurate projections of future conditions on Earth and in space, while biology and sociology offer less certain grounds for informed guesses about the future of humanity. Authors crafting secret histories of our historical past or present must gather what data they can, from UFO sightings to analyses of anomalies in fiscal policy, to make their vast conspiracies seem plausible (though I will henceforth abandon efforts to include this minor category on the grounds that the vast majority of science fiction deals either with the distant past or the future, whether it is the day after tomorrow or millions of years from now). And authors telling stories about human prehistory must depend upon the evidence and conclusions of anthropology and paleontology.

\* \* \* \*

This is one way to explain why stories about prehistoric humans, in defiance of most standard definitions, have always been accepted as science fiction. H. G. Wells, who originated or popularized most of the characteristic tropes of the genre, wrote "A Story of the Stone

Age" (1897) which Hugo Gernsback republished in *Amazing Stories*, officially blessing it as "science fiction." Thoughtful novels like Jack London's *Before Adam* (1906), J. H. Rosny Aîné's *La Guerre de Feu* (1909), and William Golding's *The Inheritors* (1955) are discussed in histories of science fiction literature, and even preposterous films along similar lines like *One Million B.C.* (1940), *When Dinosaurs Ruled the Earth* (1969), and *Caveman* (1980) are cited in histories of science fiction film. Why not? Everything we know about our prehistoric ancestors, ranging from the sometimes-ignored absence of dinosaurs in their vicinity to the clothes they wore and animals they hunted, stems from scientific investigations of available evidence; we have never listened to actual cavemen and cavewomen describing their lives, and barring some scientific breakthrough enabling us to travel through time or revive a long-frozen corpse—science fiction scenarios that seem unlikely—we never will. So, we must depend upon fossils to imaginatively reconstruct fossil behavior.

Another way to defend such stories as science fiction would appeal to a definition of science fiction that I have criticized: Brian W. Aldiss's "search for a definition of mankind" (*Trillion Year Spree* 25). One problem is that this search is endemic to all literature and hardly serves to distinguish science fiction as a genre. Still, stories about humanity's distant past or far future might be an unusually effective means of achieving such a "definition of mankind." There are two ways that we naturally define people as individuals, illustrated by the two questions inevitably asked by arriving college students when meeting new peers: "Where are you from?" And "What's your major?," a specialized version of "Where are you going?" In similar fashion, to properly define humanity, we must ask: where are we from? And where are we going? Prehistoric science fiction wrestles with the former question, while futuristic science fiction wrestles with the latter.

This brings to mind another claim I usually have no patience with—that science fiction represents the contemporary equivalent of ancient mythology, ignoring their innumerable dissimilarities. However, one service that religions past and present have always provided is answers to otherwise unanswerable questions about humanity's origins in the past (the Garden of Eden, Pandora's Box) and destiny in the future (Armageddon, Ragnarok). So, when people grow skeptical about religious answers, science must step forward to provide its own speculative answers, often presented in narrative fiction.

We arrive, then, at yet another reason for regarding *2001: A Space Odyssey* (1968) as the quintessential science fiction film: it singularly addresses the question from both angles, beginning with the dawn of humanity on Earth and concluding with humanity's rebirth in space. Where are we from? An ability to employ tools, bestowed upon our ancestors by unseen aliens, allowed our species to dominate the Earth, first with bones used as clubs and, more recently, with spaceships. But tool-making only takes a species so far, and the destructive rampage of humanity's newest tool, the supercomputer HAL, along with the ominous prospect of nuclear war highlighted in Arthur C. Clarke's novel, suggests that advanced tool-making might eventually threaten the survival of sentient beings. So, where are we going? As shown in the film's final scene, aliens will somehow re-create us with abilities beyond tool-making, allowing us to eliminate the danger of nuclear weapons and progress to new levels of civilization. (Interestingly, however, since Clarke's sequels recast David Bowman not as the prototype of a new human race but simply as a tool of the alien monoliths; since the homicidal HAL is repaired and again made a useful tool in *2010: Odyssey Two* [1982]; and since *3001: The Final Odyssey* [1997] suggests that the monoliths themselves are, as HAL once was, an out-of-control tool of now-absent aliens, there emerges the perhaps unintended message that tool-making actually is not something that intelligent species do or should transcend.)

\* \* \* \*

If we appreciate human prehistory as a key to understanding our true nature, we can understand our continuing fascination with *Homo neanderthal*—humanity's stillborn twin, in the news again due to DNA discoveries indicating they were less closely related to us than previously suspected. Ancient Cro-Magnons had something that ancient Neanderthals didn't, so we survived while they became extinct; but what was it? Since evidence of tool use among chimpanzees has debunked the once-popular idea employed in *2001* that tools made us what we are, four other theories can be advanced. First, and most straightforwardly, Cro-Magnons were more intelligent than Neanderthals and hence better able to survive during harsh conditions. Second, Cro-Magnons developed the innate capacity for language that we all have today, while Neanderthals did not, so Cro-Magnons could more effectively communicate and cooperate with each other for their mutual benefit. Third, Cro-Magnons had a strong family structure, while Neanderthal men and women lived apart, so Cro-Magnon men and women working together were better able to cope with adversity. Finally, Cro-Magnons were more violent and aggressive than peace-loving Neanderthals and thus were able and eager to slaughter their competitors.

Establishing one theory as true would effectively define the essence of humanity. Perhaps we truly are, as we named ourselves, the Wise

Species, *Homo sapiens*, although much human behavior, then and now, has been noticeably less than wise. Perhaps we are best regarded as the Language-Using Species, although we can now train other primates to employ basic language. Perhaps we are the especially Social Species, although many of us wouldn't exemplify that very well. Finally, and most dishearteningly, perhaps we are simply the Born-to-Raise-Hell Species, although we regularly celebrate peace, love, and understanding. My problem with the first three theories is that many mammalian species on this planet have been considerably less smart, less communicative, and less sociable than people, yet they have survived and prospered; noting the spectacular success of *Homo sapiens*, one would imagine that even half-assed, inferior versions of human beings could contrive to avoid extinction. Thus, I suspect that we are the only surviving species of the genus *Homo* principally because we didn't really enjoy the company of half-assed, inferior versions of ourselves and so wiped them off the face of the Earth.

Other theories are possible. Perhaps virulent disease decimated the Neanderthals while Cro-Magnons luckily developed a natural resistance. Or one could combine the language-ability theory and the violence-loving theory, as explained in one of John W. Campbell, Jr.'s editorials. His charming conjecture was that humans came to universally possess an aptitude for language through a rigorous policy of selective breeding: when tribes encountered a boy who couldn't talk, they slit his throat, so that only talking people grew old enough to have children who would inherit their talents. (It is only fitting that the interminably garrulous Campbell would so cheerfully envision a science-fictional world of the past where people were murdered for lacking the gift of gab.)

No matter how much our knowledge of human prehistory improves with new discoveries and techniques, it may always be impossible to say precisely why our species rose to the top—which might mean that the small and marginalized subgenre of prehistoric science fiction will eventually prove the form of science fiction with the greatest longevity. We are moving into the future that we once only envisioned: we will soon enough learn whether our species is going to exterminate itself or conquer the universe, and we will soon enough discover alien civilizations or prove that they don't exist. Some scenarios employed by science fiction writers to explore definitions of humanity, like the development of artificial intelligence or the creation of new human species, will actually occur, becoming topics for research and analysis instead of imaginative storytelling. Humans will perpetually face an unknown future, but they may not regard it as evocative or revelatory. However, alluring mysteries about the true origins of humanity may keep inspiring storytellers to offer fresh speculations about our prehistoric ancestors.

Whether future humans will always be fascinated by stories about cavemen and cavewomen is impossible to say, but I will offer one prediction with absolute confidence: certain fictions to the contrary, future humans are not going to *become* cavemen and cavewomen.

* * * *

I have neglected one other type of science fiction story involving prehistoric humans: those that depict such people as our descendants. We all know the story: a young tribesman in a fur loincloth, defying the old taboos, ventures into "The Forbidden Zone" and discovers the ruins of a long-vanished civilization—*our* civilization, destroyed by nuclear war or a similar disaster. Noteworthy versions of the story include Stephen Vincent Benet's "By the Waters of Babylon" (1937), Andre Norton's *Star Man's Son* (1952), and the film *Teenage Caveman* (1958). Without envisioning such extreme cultural amnesia and barbarism, other post-holocaust stories posit a devastated future humanity reverting to the habits and customs of Native Americans, medieval knights, or cowboys. And, like other ideas from science fiction, such scenarios are beginning to influence policymakers: in one section of Gregory Benford's fascinating *Deep Time* (1999), he describes serving on a government commission charged with devising a lasting and universally recognizable warning to keep future citizens away from stored nuclear wastes, as if bureaucrats really feared that, someday, marauders out of a *Mad Max* movie might cross the New Mexico desert and stupidly storm into radioactive caves in search of plunder unless they observe some iconic equivalent of the Skull and Crossbones to persuade them to depart.

It is better to be safe than sorry, and one cannot wholly discount Benford's intelligent speculations about possible future societies that forget or don't care about our great accomplishments and irresponsible actions. However, we must base projections of humanity's future on the patterns of humanity's past, and both prehistory and history demonstrate that humans are collectively very good at *remembering* things. Ancient humans learned to make and use various tools, knowledge that was invariably passed down from generation to generation. Throughout history, a few people have always been dedicated to preserving the memories and wisdom of their precursors; when information has been lost, later scholars have struggled to devise new methods to retrieve it. Today, out of the six billion people on the planet, surely at least one billion of them possess—in the forms of books, manuscripts, recordings, artworks, computer files, or sharp memories—some substantive portion of the accumulated knowledge of our species. The notion that a nuclear war, lethal plague, or asteroid impact will somehow erase all of this, condemning our descendants to ignorance and primitivism, is implausible in the extreme. If global disasters do occur, it will take us some time to recover; but eventually, thanks to everything we have learned, the human race will begin again—from where we left off, not the very beginning.

As children naturally love their parents, we are naturally fond of our prehistoric ancestors: we dream that a few of them may have survived as the legendary Yeti or Bigfoot; we symbolically draw them into our own worlds in films like *Iceman* (1984) and *Encino Man* (1992); we welcome news that a "caveman diet" of meat and vegetables might represent the healthiest possible regimen; in wilderness outings, we briefly reenact the hunting and gathering activities of prehistory; and we contemplate with concealed elation a projected future when, coming full circle, humans might return to the simple, invigorating lifestyle of our earliest days. But in this respect as in others, we cannot, and should not, go home again— except, of course, while reading science fiction, the form of literature that uniquely allows us to imaginatively visit not only our future but also our distant past.

# THE ANTHOLOGY ON THE EDGE OF FOREVER

After reading the magazine's recent interview with Harlan Ellison, some readers of *Interzone* were upset because he was not asked about *The Last Dangerous Visions*—his famous, long-delayed anthology of original science fiction stories. As it happens, at the 1997 Science Fiction Research Association/Eaton Conference, I attended a question-and-answer session with Ellison when precisely that question came up, and I can describe how he responds. First, he looks *very, very* displeased; then, in a tone of voice that noticeably fails to inspire confidence, he sighs and says, "Well, maybe the first volume will come out next year."

Needless to say, the first volume of *The Last Dangerous Visions* did not appear in 1998, just as it has failed to appear in every year since 1973, its original announced date of publication. Most people have understandably come to believe that *The Last Dangerous Visions* will never be published, although an occasional report surfaces about the book, and although Ellison has never publicly acknowledged that the project is dead.

Now, when a highly publicized and eagerly anticipated book fails to appear, one would expect extensive discussions about its unexpected absence; yet people in the science fiction community have been strangely reluctant to talk about *The Last Dangerous Visions*. It has been intimated that any criticism of Ellison for failing to publish a book promised to readers almost thirty years ago will result in angry phone calls, threats, and/or lawsuits. But I cannot take these reports seriously, because expressing a personal opinion about matters of public record is a protected constitutional right in America, and no one as savvy as Harlan Ellison would be foolish enough to undertake or sanction any actions against someone who is only exercising a protected constitutional right. (Still, I must add that after the publication of this column, I did in fact receive an angry phone call from Ellison, but I shrugged it off, having received similar phone calls from him in the past.)

Before expressing a personal opinion about *The Last Dangerous Visions*, however, I must emphasize the following, just to make everything perfectly clear: I have no information about this book and its contents beyond what is in published reports; what I will say is purely a matter of idle speculation, from which no rational person could draw firm conclusions; and I commit these speculations to print with no malicious intent, but only because I regularly publish commentaries on science fiction, and I can't think of anything else to write about at the moment.

* * * *

So, let us confront the blindingly obvious question: why hasn't *The Last Dangerous Visions* appeared in print? We know, from various accounts, that Ellison long ago assembled more than enough stories to fill a hefty volume. The authors said to be represented include luminaries like Alfred Bester, Michael Bishop, Anthony Boucher, Octavia E. Butler, Orson Scott Card, Jack Dann, Avram Davidson, Gordon R. Dickson, George Alec Effinger, Edmond Hamilton and Leigh Brackett, Harry Harrison, Frank Herbert, Anne McCaffrey, Vonda N. McIntyre, Michael Moorcock, Robert Sheckley, Clifford D. Simak, Bruce Sterling, A. E. van Vogt, Ian Watson, and Jack Williamson. Several publishers have committed to publishing the volume, only to withdraw after endless delays.

Christopher Priest, in his self-published commentary *The Last Deadloss Visions* (aka *The Book on the Edge of Forever*, which inspired this column's title) (1993), leans toward the theory that Ellison, having established the policy of writing lengthy introductions to every story he publishes, can never quite manage to finish the innumerable introductions that *The Last Dangerous Visions* would require and/or can never quite manage to rewrite all of the already-written introductions that have become hopelessly outdated. The evidence for this theory is that in the 1970s, whenever Ellison announced the impending publication of the volume, he always declared that the only task remaining before putting the manuscript in the mail was finishing the introductions. So, Priest suggests, the volume never appeared because Ellison never completed the introductions. A second, related theory is that Ellison is too much of a perfectionist: determined to make *The Last Dangerous Visions* the greatest science fiction anthology ever published, he keeps delaying the project in order to add one more telling insight to an introduction, to eliminate one irritating flaw in an otherwise excellent story, or to find the one additional masterpiece that will permanently enshrine the collection as a major event in the history of science fiction.

As noted, I have no facts upon which to base an opinion, but neither theory really accords with what I know about writers.

Regarding the first theory: to any experienced writer, writing an introduction isn't difficult at all, compared to the genuine agony of writing a story; it is simply a chore. One can follow a formula: in Ellison's case, he typically begins by discussing personal experiences (if any) with the author in question, provides some basic biographical data (or quotes from the biographical data provided by the author), and concludes with a few remarks about the story that follows. A passable introduction along these lines could be churned out in less than an hour. Given Ellison's indisputable energy and productivity, it is hard to believe that this project has been left in limbo for decades because he can't finish writing some introductions.

Regarding the second theory: if I were an editor who had gathered a group of superlative stories inarguably demonstrating my editorial talents, I would want to rush them into print as quickly as possible, to immediately garner all the praise I was due. I couldn't stand the thought of waiting twenty years, or thirty years, to proudly show the world the fruits of my labors, even if there were a few rough edges here and there. Ellison's authors would feel the same way: if I had given him one of my best stories in 1970, and he still hadn't published it ten years later, I would remove the story from Ellison's control and publish it elsewhere, no matter how difficult the process of disentanglement proved and no matter how angrily Ellison reacted.

In fact, when prominent authors included in *The Last Dangerous Visions* are asked about their contributions, they typically respond that they consider the story in question to be one of their lesser efforts; more than one author has said that if their story was actually about to be published, they would take steps to prevent its appearance. And this suggests a third theory about *The Last Dangerous Visions*, which should have been the first theory considered.

After all, when a manuscript isn't published, there are many possible reasons, but any inquiry would always begin by pondering the most logical explanation, the most likely explanation, the default explanation, which is that the manuscript isn't worth publishing.

* * * *

Perhaps, in other words, what Ellison has been withholding for decades is not a collection of masterpieces, but a big pile of crap. That would certainly explain why Ellison doesn't want to publish it, why most participating authors have complacently accepted its non-appearance, and why publishers keep abandoning the project. Of course, given the stellar line-up of authors known to be contributors to Ellison's volume, many will find this theory laughable; yet in my opinion, it is the theory that best fits the available information.

As an imaginative exercise, I will speculate as to how this situation might have developed. First, let us return to the year 1968, when Larry Ashmead of Doubleday first persuaded, or pressured, Harlan Ellison to produce a sequel to the award-winning and much-lauded *Dangerous Visions* anthology. Blessed with a huge advance, and anxious to make this second volume bigger and better than the first, Ellison begins to collect stories. In an exuberant mood, let us suppose, he buys some excellent stories, some not-so-excellent stories, and more than a few out-and-out stinkers. He buys mediocre stories from well-known writers because he wants their names for their marquee value; he buys mediocre stories from unknown writers because he wants to encourage new talent. He buys all the stories that we have heard of, and large numbers of stories that we have never heard of. He buys far more stories than he is budgeted for, and far more stories than he could possibly publish.

Eventually, after another nagging phone call from Ashmead, he concludes that he really must put something together. So, he gathers together most of the excellent stories, salted with a few of the not-so-excellent stories and stinkers, and presents the world with *Again, Dangerous Visions* (1972), which is received favorably, though not quite as enthusiastically as its predecessor.

Now, as this hypothesized scenario continues, Ellison faces the task of assembling a third anthology from a generally unimpressive stack of leftovers, and he knows that what he has to offer cannot begin to match the high expectations created by the previous two volumes and his own celebratory hype. So, he hesitates. He contacts more authors, and purchases more stories, in an effort to bolster the overall quality of his material. He lets the other manuscripts sit, hoping against hope that the lousy stories he wishes he had never bought will somehow start to look better with time, or that he will suddenly figure out how to revise a loser into a winner, or that some pretext will emerge for jettisoning some of the weaker items in his collection. Yet the delays only make matters worse, as most of the remaining stories that Ellison truly cherishes gradually drift away. So, this proud man hesitates some more, enduring the irksome and ever-increasing grumbling about the volume's absence because the alternative—publishing an anthology that is embarrassingly inferior to his previous efforts—is even worse.

All of this, I emphasize yet again, is only speculation, but in the absence of definitive data, critics must be forgiven if they prefer the explanation that provides the best story. And the story I have just outlined strikes me as far more satisfying, and far more poignant, than the story of an obsessed perfectionist, or the story of an anthologist who just can't bring himself to finish writing a few introductions.

* * * *

There is a broader lesson here. During their lifetimes, all authors choose to publish certain of their works, and choose to leave certain of their works unpublished. In a few prominent cases, they have chosen not to publish some excellent stuff: Emily Dickinson wrote wonderful poetry that she inexplicably kept to herself, and E. M. Forster suppressed an accomplished novel, *Maurice* (1971), because of its explicit homosexual content. In the vast majority of cases, however, we find that major authors who have chosen to keep certain works from appearing in print have chosen wisely, as evidenced by dreary streams of inferior posthumous publications foisted upon a gullible public by greedy heirs or misguided scholars. So, when we hear about the unpublished manuscripts of our favorite authors, it would be foolish to demand their immediate publication when the most likely result would be extreme disillusionment. Did you know that Robert A. Heinlein completed a novel in the early 1970s, decided that it wasn't worth publishing, and put it back in his trunk? I do, but despite my fondness for Heinlein, based on the quality of a few of the later novels that he did publish, I have absolutely no desire to read the novel that he could not bear to publish.

So, unlike other commentators who have addressed this topic, I will not conclude by calling upon Ellison to finally complete and publish *The Last Dangerous Visions*. The non-appearance of this volume should not be attributed to Ellison's irresponsibility or lassitude; rather, it is simply his *choice*. Harlan Ellison has *chosen* not to publish this volume; and, since he is an intelligent man, we should surmise that he has chosen wisely, and we should respect his decision. I have absolutely no desire to read the anthology that Ellison cannot bear to publish.

Instead of chastising the man, then, we should perhaps be praising Ellison for the tremendous services he has performed for the science fiction community. First, he has possibly seized some inferior stories by noteworthy writers and kept them out of sight, so as to prevent their many fans from being disillusioned. Second, rather than wasting his time vainly struggling to make a probable sow's ear into a silk purse, he has wisely devoted himself to producing a steady stream of memorable new stories and articles, overseeing the republication of his classic works, providing provocative commentaries at scores of conventions, and offering his behind-the-scenes guidance to the creators of two worthwhile television series, the revived *Twilight Zone* (1985-1989) and *Babylon 5* (1994-1999). So the best way to answer my initial question—why hasn't *The Last Dangerous Visions* appeared in print?—may be: because Harlan Ellison has had better things to do with his time.

# AMERICA'S DUMBEST COLUMNIST, OR, THE REMARKING MORON

Of late, an increasingly common topic in American public discourse has been the amusing exploits of stupid criminals. While such stories were occasionally covered by local news programs to add some levity to the proceedings, there is now an entire television show devoted to the subject—*America's Dumbest Criminals* (1996-2000)—featuring chortling co-hosts who regale their studio audience with videotapes, reports, and reenactments of various idiocies perpetrated by inept thieves, con artists, and felons. Anecdotes of this kind also percolate through the modern medium of urban folklore, endlessly forwarded e-mail messages.

A typical story: a would-be bank robber entered a Bank of America, wrote "This iz a stik-up" on a deposit slip, and stood in line to confront a teller. Suddenly worried that someone may have seen him writing the note, he left the bank and went across the street to a Wells Fargo Bank to stand in its line. When he handed the note to the Wells Fargo teller, she sensed his probable low intelligence and informed him, with a straight face, that she could not accept his hold-up note because it was written on a Bank of America deposit slip; he would have to leave the window, write his message on a Wells Fargo deposit slip, and get back in line. In response, the man meekly returned to the Bank of America with his note and again stood in its line, where he was identified and apprehended.

While such stories make the audience erupt with laughter, I never find them funny at all.

\* \* \* \*

One problem is that I have spent many years teaching college classes in California prisons, so I have a first-hand awareness of the true punchline to these stories: "And so this poor doofus was arrested, tried, convicted, and sentenced to spend the next twenty-five years of his life in a hellhole." That, I think, rather spoils the joke.

While such sentiments might be dismissed as the idealistic blatherings of a soft-on-crime, bleeding-heart liberal, another disturbing question is raised by these reports: just *why* is America apparently suffering from a growing epidemic of moronic, incompetent criminals? Decades ago, when I was growing up, I recall hearing no stories of this kind. Indeed, the criminals in nonfiction and fiction, ranging from Al Capone to Lex Luthor, were usually portrayed as brilliant masterminds. Stupid criminals could be observed in some films and cartoons, but these were only the henchmen of evil geniuses, included as plot devices to provide the hero with a foe he could easily outwit to escape certain doom. No one imagined that these dimwitted flunkies would ever attempt to set up their own operations.

Crime, in other words, was once recognized as what it is: a difficult and demanding occupation. Ignore any legal or ethical concerns and consider crime only as a potential career. A successful criminal, like any self-employed businessperson, must be highly motivated, efficient, and well-organized. Depending on his criminal specialty, he must master complex skills like safecracking, using firearms, laundering money, and setting up front organizations. He must have both the ability to meticulously plan his crimes and the improvisational intelligence to instantly devise and implement alternate plans when everything goes wrong. As anyone can see, crime isn't a job for dummies.

Then why are so many dummies embarking upon criminal careers? Well, there are positive aspects of this chosen occupation: no application form, letter of recommendation, interview, experience, or education is required. Anyone and everyone can become a criminal. So, one may assume, many of these hapless felons were people who needed good jobs, couldn't find good jobs, and so were obliged to take the one good job they could find, being a criminal. And the results are not always funny. Television news programs in Los Angeles covered the story, strangely ignored by the producers of *America's Dumbest Criminals*, of a seventy-year-old woman, unable to pay her bills with her meager pension and Social Security checks, who bought a gun and attempted to hold up a nearby gas station. She was so terrible at it that the poor woman ended up leaving without taking the proffered money, though she was later identified and arrested. Does anyone feel like laughing at her?

* * * *

At this point, non-American readers may wish to draw a polemical contrast between a senseless American system that drives the impoverished and the incapable into lives of crime, and sensible European systems that offer numerous programs and benefits to assist the needy and the unemployed. And they will hear no arguments from me. The point to make is that we are talking about two different kinds of welfare programs: the reprehensible, expensive, and inefficient American program of lifelong incarceration for millions of its citizens, and the benign, expensive, and inefficient European program of expansive, cradle-to-grave welfare for millions of its citizens. One is better than the other, but neither is really desirable; an ideal society would have the vast majority of its citizens supporting themselves by gainful employment. My concern is whether, in an advanced technological society such as ours, this is still possible.

A century ago, any American or European man with a few years of basic education and a willingness to work could find a job that provided sufficient income to purchase a home and support a wife and family. Now, according to one recent survey, over 70% of the jobs in America require a college degree, and many of the remaining jobs demand extensive training and specialized skills (such as car repair, which now involves some knowledge of computers). The situation in Europe is surely similar. And, if many good, decent people aren't quite capable of completing college or years of vocational education, what are they supposed to do, to keep themselves alive?

I am reminded of one of the most celebrated, and criticized, stories in the history of science fiction: C. M. Kornbluth's "The Marching Morons" (1951). Its premise is that, since stupid people tend to have more children than smart people, we will end up with a future society mostly consisting of imbeciles, with a few intelligent people forced to work incessantly to keep all the morons alive. But Kornbluth's premise is incorrect: the correlation between a parent's intelligence and a child's intelligence is actually inconsequential, meaning that, in the long run, the descendants of people perceived to be stupid will be just as intelligent as the descendants of people perceived to be smart. Still, this fallacy fueled an outpouring of racist and anti-immigrant hysteria in early twentieth-century America, with effects that are still felt today, transforming this otherwise-amusing story into unpleasant reading.

There is, however, another way to realize Kornbluth's future society that does not invoke pseudoscience. Suppose that we simply raise our standards. If we define normal intelligence as an IQ of 100, then only a small minority of people can be classified as stupid. But if we redefine normal intelligence as an IQ of 120, then larger numbers of people will be reclassified as stupid. And if we redefine normal intelligence as an IQ of 150, then the vast majority of people will be reclassified as stupid.

This is what I fear may be happening in contemporary societies: as typical jobs demand more and more knowledge, more and more qualifications, more and more skills, fewer and fewer people will be able to handle them. So far, by completing intensive educational programs and stressing themselves out, most citizens are keeping up with the ever-increasing demands of remunerative employment. Yet certain signs, like the noted increase in incompetent criminals and unemployment rates held steady by growing numbers of persons who have stopped looking for jobs, suggest that many are not keeping up, and their numbers are sure to grow. If the trend continues, the majority of good jobs in the future will call for geniuses, and in the context of such expectations, most people will indeed be marching morons.

*  *  *  *

While Kornbluth's story invites readers to arrogantly identify with the intelligent elite who will emerge as society's secret masters, I am, nowadays, more likely to cast myself as a moron. For our advancing civilization requires more and more knowledge and skills not only at the workplace, but in all aspects of life. It is in this respect that I often feel overwhelmed; I simply do not know many things that ordinary citizens are expected to know. So while I may, unlike others, have education and wit enough to remain profitably employed until I retire, I lack the increasingly numerous ancillary skills that everyday life now requires.

That is: as a homeowner, I should be able to deal capably with plumbing and electrical problems, do basic carpentry and masonry, and keep my lawn and its plants vibrant and healthy. As a purchaser and user of appliances that require assembly, I should be able to assemble them, and later, to replace their faulty parts. As a regular commuter, I should be able to maintain and repair my car. As a writer who depends on a computer, I should be able to diagnose and correct any flaws in its hardware or software. Yet, with rare exceptions, I can't do any of these things. Of course, as my wife reminds me, some men in this world are still masters of many skills who productively spend their weekends rewiring lamps, planting trees, constructing patios, and rebuilding carburetors while I fritter away my energies on writing. Yet even these purported polymaths, I suspect, sometimes face tasks that they hesitate to attempt, and the variety and difficulty of societally mandated skills will surely keep increasing.

In my own case, I try to cope in various ways. If the household problem is minor, my family and I simply adjust to it; so, for several years, my front doorknob hasn't worked properly, a hallway light has been broken, and one of the toilets needs to be flushed just right. With my computer, I have so far handled all difficulties by following my three basic steps of computer repair: 1) turn the computer off and turn it on again; 2) turn the computer off, wait a few minutes, and turn it on again; 3) turn the computer off, wait *a really long time*, and turn it on again. To solve other problems, I must call upon a series of repairmen and craftsmen (and such individuals, in my experience, are invariably male, for whatever reason). I have given up promising myself that I will someday buy a few books, engage in some practice, and learn these skills. Instead, I continue to endure the gut-wrenching feelings of utter helplessness and stupidity whenever I take my car to the shop or listen to a plumber explaining what new parts must be installed in my shower, and I have accepted the fact that I must keep working, as much and as hard as I can, to pay for the expensive help I need.

* * * *

I have hit upon another, frequently noted, contemporary trend: while some unqualified people cannot work at all, many qualified people are constantly working overtime or are holding two or three different jobs. Social commentators repeatedly wonder: why are so many people working so much? It may be because even the brightest and most talented persons cannot possibly master all of the skills that contemporary life demands, requiring that they work especially hard at what they do best to afford capable assistance or to compensate for its absence (like eating at restaurants because they cannot cook, or buying a new television set because they cannot repair their present set).

This represents the second of two respects in which the old predictions of science fiction have proven most spectacularly inaccurate. First, science fiction writers worried that advanced technology would lead to totalitarian superstates, like that of George Orwell's Big Brother, which monitored and controlled all aspects of their citizens' lives. Instead, recent decades have seen a growing trend towards democracy, as the world's Big Brothers have been falling one by one. Second, writers worried that advanced technology would eliminate the need for human employment, forcing citizens into dull and unfulfilling lives of enforced leisure. Instead, while a minority of citizens, due to disability or incompetence, enjoy leisurely lives at government expense, either in prison cells or at home receiving welfare checks, most people are working harder than ever, with little relief in sight.

The fallacy behind both fears is that advanced technology would empower the state, making ordinary citizens powerless or useless. In fact, as Alvin Toffler and others have noted, advanced technology empowers the individual. In industrial societies, we have all become our own Big Brothers, controlling our own lives to an unprecedented extent. With proper credentials and training, we can enjoy any number of stimulating, challenging jobs, along with tremendous freedom in our leisure time. The trouble is, being your own Big Brother is hard work; there is so much to know, so many tasks to perform, so many decisions to make, and every new option, every new "labor-saving" device, demands a new body of knowledge. Facing the burden of being their own one-person governments, many people unsurprisingly are barely hanging on, while others give up the game and surrender to lives to dependency—on relatives, charities, or the government—or foolishly embark upon ill-advised criminal careers that also lead to lives of dependency, sitting in prison cells.

Forgive me if this column seems less polished than others, but I have been working hard all year, and I currently feel overwhelmed by the many things that I still must accomplish. Perhaps you have been feeling the same way.

# ROBERT A. HEINLEIN'S 2001: A SPACE ODYSSEY

As we enter the year 2001—the true beginning of the third millennium—a natural topic for discussion would be the landmark film and novel *2001: A Space Odyssey* (1968), perhaps drawing a contrast between Arthur C. Clarke's glorious predictions about 2001 and the dismal reality of the actual 2001. And, if I read my e-mail correctly, editor David Pringle is suggesting that I provide exactly such a discussion.

Unfortunately, I strive to avoid the obvious, and Clarke's world of 2001 is a topic that has already been discussed many times, and hence a topic that is unlikely to inspire striking new insights. So, with David's indulgence, I will address an entirely different question: what did Robert A. Heinlein, the other giant of twentieth-century science fiction, have to say about the year 2001, and what lessons lie in his vision? The question will launch a journey with a modest beginning, standing on a ledge with a kitten, but will later take us back to Clarke and even to the start of the fourth millennium in 3001.

\* \* \* \*

If you examine the chart of Heinlein's Future History, once a standard feature of his books, you find precisely one story that occurred around the year 2001: "Ordeal in Space," originally published in *Town and Country* in 1948. It is one of the most obscure Heinlein stories, rarely discussed or even mentioned in the critical literature; even Alexei Panshin's *Heinlein in Dimension* (1968) and H. Bruce Franklin's *Robert A. Heinlein: America as Science Fiction* (1980), which undertake to analyze all of Heinlein's novels and stories, simply summarize the story in one paragraph virtually without comment. To the extent that "Ordeal in Space" is known at all, it is thought of only as one of the sloppily sentimental stories that Heinlein cynically peddled to the slick magazines after World War II, most of them later republished in the collection *The Green Hills of Earth* (1951).

Yet, when I finished rereading it, I sensed that this may have been a story with special meaning for its author. For one thing, its central plot device is the rescue of a kitten, and reverence for cats is an absolutely central aspect of Heinlein's world view, expressed most vividly in his masterpiece *The Door into Summer* (1956). Second, when protagonist Bill Cole adopts a pseudonym, he chooses the name "William Saunders"—but Saunders is also a pseudonym that Heinlein chose for himself, first publishing his 1941 story "Elsewhen" under the name "Caleb Saunders."

Looking at its plot, one does detect autobiographical resonances. Spaceman Cole ventures out onto the surface of his rotating spaceship to replace a broken radar antenna that must function properly for the ship to land safely. Unable to reach his lifeline, he finds himself clinging to a handhold on the spaceship, gazing down into the endless depths of deep space for over two hours, until he finally loses his grip and falls into the abyss. Even though another spaceship saves him, he develops a severe case of acrophobia that requires him to quit space travel and take a menial job in New York under an assumed name, scrupulously avoiding all exposure to heights. Then one night, staying in a friend's apartment on the thirty-fifth floor, he hears a kitten howling on a ledge four feet below a window. Fighting off his fear of heights, he drops down onto the ledge and inches over to retrieve the kitten and carry it back to the apartment. Recognizing that he has finally conquered his acrophobia, he resolves to return to space and take the kitten along as his companion.

In Heinlein's own case, he was first obliged to retire from a promising career in the Navy because he contracted tuberculosis; he spent several years trying his hand at various professions with little success; but when he finally turned to writing science fiction, he instantly became one of the field's most popular authors. Then, after World War II began, Heinlein went back to work for the Navy, albeit as a "civilian engineer," Franklin reports, working "in the designing and testing of materials associated with naval aviation" (13-14), Having contributed to the Navy once again, and having established himself in a field that allowed him to vicariously experience military service through the heroes of his space novels, Heinlein may well have felt that, by means of grit and determination, he had effectively returned to the military career he had once been forced to abandon. From this perspective, Cole's triumph was not unlike Heinlein's own triumph.

But one trivializes "Ordeal in Space" by seeing it purely as a veiled autobiographical sketch, for it is also very much a story about the cold realities of outer space. In an era when science fiction sought to domesticate and familiarize space—an impulse still observed today in countless novels, the *Star Trek* series, and *Star Wars* films—Heinlein recognized and frankly emphasized the vastness and terror of space. When Cole is about to complete his repair job,

The wrench slipped as he finished tightening the bolt; it slipped from his grasp, fell free. He watched it go, out and out and out, down and down and down, until it was so small he could no longer see it. It made him dizzy to watch it, bright in the sunlight against the deep black of space. (290)

Then, when he lost his lifeline and found himself clinging to the hand-hold,

He looked down—and regretted it.

There was nothing below him but stars, down and down, endlessly. Stars, swinging past as the ship spun with him, emptiness of all time and blackness and cold. (290)

This is not the sort of language one normally associates with Heinlein; but he is unusually striving for effect, if not with total success, in order to communicate just how huge, how hostile, how inhuman the depths of space would seem to a single, vulnerable man in a spacesuit.

If this part of the story did not impress the readers of *Town and Country* magazine, it did impress Heinlein—because, two years later, he told the same story all over again.

\* \* \* \*

The project began when a famous filmmaker approached a famous science fiction writer and asked him to collaborate in creating the world's greatest science fiction film. The author chooses one of his stories for the film, radically revises it, and tosses in a vignette from another one of his stories. You may think that I am talking about Stanley Kubrick and Arthur C. Clarke and how they transformed Clarke's "The Sentinel" (1951) into *2001: A Space Odyssey*, including the sequence from Clarke's "The Other Side of the Sky" (1957) when an astronaut is briefly exposed to the vacuum of space. But I am actually talking about George Pal and Robert A. Heinlein and how they transformed Heinlein's juvenile novel *Rocket Ship Galileo* (1947) into the film *Destination Moon* (1950), including—as I now realize—a sequence from Heinlein's "Ordeal in Space."

For, on their way to the moon, Heinlein's astronauts encounter the same problem that Cole faced—a broken radar antenna that must be fixed by venturing out onto the surface of the spaceship. What follows, as I argue elsewhere, is one of the most memorable scenes in the cinema of space travel, a powerful illustration of the vastness and strangeness of outer space. First, the men put on their space helmets; pushing a button, one man watches as the light comes on to announce "vacuum"; then the airlock door slowly opens to reveal the starry blackness of space. Next, the camera shows the men emerging from the spacecraft *upside down*, a visual reminder that in space there is no "up" and "down" in the standard sense; and, still upside down from the audience's perspective, the three men pause to stare at the awesome immensity of space. Proceeding to work, they walk on magnetized shoes around the hull of the spaceship, gradually vanishing from view as they walk past the ship's "horizon." At this point, one astronaut bends over, his feet are no longer in contact with the spaceship hull, and he drifts into the vastness of space, just like Cole; but he doesn't go far and is quickly retrieved by an astronaut wielding an oxygen tank as a miniature rocket.

While *Destination Moon* does represent Heinlein's *2001: A Space Odyssey*, it is unquestionably a film that lacks Clarke's cosmic perspective and mythic resonances; but Heinlein valued space more as a new arena for fulfilling human activity than as a way to encounter the alien and ponder the mysteries of creation. Still, he shared with Clarke the realization that outer space represented both an awe-inspiring and a dismayingly dangerous new home for humanity, and he harkened back to "Ordeal in Space" to convey that chilling lesson. Later, Clarke himself would do the same thing.

* * * *

Reading about "Ordeal in Space" and *Destination Moon*, you might be thinking, "An astronaut goes outside his spacecraft to fix a broken antenna? Where have I seen that before?" Or perhaps you have already hit upon the answer: in *2001: A Space Odyssey* itself—because, in one of that film's several references to *Destination Moon*, it is HAL's claim of a fault in the spaceship *Discovery*'s antenna system that forces first David Bowman, and then Frank Poole, to venture into space to deal with the problem. Further, during the second trip, the maniacal HAL murders Poole and sends him hurtling into the abyss of space, visualizing Cole's fearful plight far more dramatically than *Destination Moon*. And while this homicide may seem quite unlike the accidents that befell Cole and the astronaut of *Destination Moon*, one might recall that HAL became deranged in the first place due to flawed programming, so his assault on Poole was in fact an "accident" of sorts.

The trouble with this scene, in contrast with its predecessors, is that it does not end the way we would wish, with Poole's rescue and recovery. Instead, although Bowman tries to save him, he sees that he is already dead and, needing to focus on the task of overcoming HAL, he abandons the body to drift endlessly through space. Perhaps Clarke was troubled by this downbeat turn of events, because he returned to this scene thirty years later and finished the story properly in his final *2001* novel *3001: The Final Odyssey* (1997). Here, a thousand years after the original story took place, Poole's body is finally recovered and, with the advanced medical techniques of the era, he is restored to life. Even though, like Cole, he takes a while to recover from the experience, Poole is soon back on his feet and ready for heroism again, as he takes the lead in combatting the now-malevolent alien monoliths. So, it took him rather a long time, but Clarke, like Heinlein, eventually transformed this experience into an inspirational tale of rescue and redemption.

* * * *

So, what are we to make of this seemingly inconsequential vignette that resonates through the careers of the twentieth century's greatest science fiction writers? The broken radar antenna conveys how dependent an astronaut will be on advanced technology to navigate through this new ocean; the astronaut's plunge into the depths of space conveys how helpless he may seem in venturing into this strange new environment; and the astronaut's rescue and return to space conveys how humans will nevertheless be able to adjust to and deal with the dangers and mysteries of space. It is a hopeful message, but not a naïve one, as it fully recognizes the many difficulties in the exploration of space, as well as the time and effort that may be required to accomplish the task.

Recognizing this theme in their work, we can defend Heinlein and Clarke against the charge most frequently brought against them: that they were wildly over-optimistic in predicting that humans would be traveling through and colonizing the solar system by the year 2001. Yes, they did say that conquering space would happen much more quickly than it has, but they never said conquering space would be easy. While they surely found it disappointing to see things progress so slowly, their understanding of the daunting challenges involved surely made this turn of events not entirely unexpected. In response, however, both men would urge humans to stay the course and keep struggling to overcome both the technical problems of space and their own fears. And, in defiance of all logic, it is a message that some may still find inspirational as they confront humanity's dishearteningly earthbound existence in the year 2001.

# TALKING TO ALIENS—AND TO OURSELVES

For purposes of argument, grant that extraterrestrial aliens are a centrally important feature of science fiction. Also recall a standard model of the three elements of writing: an author to write, a subject matter to write about, and an audience to read what the author has written. Then, we can deduce the existence of three possible forms of science fiction.

First, *stories in which the purported author is an alien*. Such works exist, though they aren't as numerous as one might think; I remembered only Edgar Rice Burroughs's *A Fighting Man of Mars* (1930, 1931) and H. B. Hickey's "Gone Are the Lupo" (1970), while the erudite members of the fictionmags discussion group nominated others like Fritz Leiber's "The Bump" (1972), Jody Scott's *Passing for Human* (1977), and Sheila Finch's "Nor Unbuild the Cage" (2000).

Second, *stories in which the subject matter is a purported alien or aliens*. No examples necessary!

Third, *stories in which the purported audience consists of aliens*. Here, we arrive at the peculiar form of science fiction sponsored and promoted by the United States' National Aeronautics and Space Administration (NASA).

\* \* \* \*

To understand the strange and sorry history of humanity's efforts to communicate with aliens, one must consult three texts: Carl Sagan's *The Cosmic Connection: An Extraterrestrial Perspective* (1973), which in part discusses the plaque placed on the *Pioneer 10* space probe; Carl Sagan, Frank Drake, Ann Druyan, Timothy Ferris, Jon Lomberg, and Linda Salzman Sagan's *Murmurs of Earth: The Voyager Interstellar Record* (1978), which describes the compilation of spoken words, photographs, and music attached to the *Voyager* space probes; and Gregory Benford's *Deep Time: How Humanity Communicates across Millennia* (1999), which in part chronicles an abortive attempt to attach a diamond medallion to the *Cassini* space probe. These fascinating accounts explain why these messages, properly contextualized as forms of science fiction, have been consistently unsatisfactory, even dysfunctional, in fulfilling their announced goals.

The story begins in the 1960s with Drake, who describes in *Murmurs of Earth* how he hit upon the notion of broadcasting a message to aliens by means of dots and dashes, similar to Morse code. If the total number of dots and dashes was the product of two prime numbers, like 551, aliens could figure out that this represented a rectangular gridwork of 29 by 19 units and could construct an informative picture with 551 tiny squares alternately colored black and white. The picture that Drake devised included a crude picture of a person—a figure with a head, two arms, and two legs—along with symbolic representations that aliens would recognize as the numbers one through five, our solar system, and our carbon-based biology. Or so Drake maintained. In fact, given aliens who would know absolutely nothing about the message's senders, they would be just as likely to spend years trying to interpret the figure of a person as a chemical formula and that series of numerical dots as our self-portrait—assuming that they could figure out the transformation from code to picture in the first place. Give Drake points for originality, but the approach was not promising.

Carl Sagan became involved in 1971, when he realized that the *Pioneer 10* space probe, destined to be shot into interstellar space after passing by Jupiter, could carry a physical message to aliens who might encounter the probe millions of years from now. After persuading NASA that the project was worthwhile, Sagan, Drake, and Linda Salzman Sagan designed the Pioneer 10 plaque that briefly emerged as a cultural icon. The left side of the plaque, more decipherably than Drake's coded message, showed Earth's position in space, the solar system, and some numbering and measuring conventions. The right side of the plaque, to show aliens what we looked like, famously displayed a naked man waving in greeting next to a naked woman.

At the time, Sagan undoubtedly envisioned the plaque as little more than another contribution to a long, private discussion among astronomers regarding the best ways to communicate with aliens; but it unexpectedly inspired some public debate and discussion. As Sagan said in *The Cosmic Connection,*

The golden greeting card placed aboard the *Pioneer 10* spacecraft was intended for the remote contingency that representatives of an advanced extraterrestrial civilization, some time in the distant future, might encounter this first artifact of mankind to leave the Solar System. But the message has had a more immediate impact. It has already been meticulously studied—not by extraterrestrials, but by terrestrials. Human beings all over the planet Earth have examined the message, applauded it, criticized it, interpreted it, and proposed alternative messages. (21)

Indeed, those reactions were so extensive that *The Cosmic Connection* devotes only four pages to the plaque as "A Message from Earth" (17-20) and thirteen pages to the plaque as "A Message to Earth" (21-33). Sagan concluded from this that "The greater significance of the *Pioneer 10* plaque is not as a message to out there; it is as a message to back here" (33).

And herein lies the first major problem that has consistently bedeviled this activity.

\* \* \* \*

Invariably, writers respond more to visible, vocal readers than to invisible, silent readers. An author may first resolve to write for posterity, but her work will ultimately be shaped and influenced primarily by the people around her who send letters and review her books. As long as talking to aliens was an astronomers' parlor game, the participants could focus on aliens; but as soon as the public started paying attention to the process, they became the messages' principal audience.

Thus, a significant though unheralded shift occurred in Sagan's outlook: instead of a serious scientific project to communicate with probable nonhuman civilizations, the messages were reconceived as a novel way to convey the essence of the human condition, from the vantage point of imagined aliens, for the enjoyment and enlightenment of modern humans. In other words, these messages became a different sort of science fiction, representing an old tradition of stories that brought alien visitors to Earth to react to contemporary conditions—as in works ranging from Voltaire's *Micromégas* (1752) to Gore Vidal's *Visit to a Small Planet* (1957) or even the television series *Mork and Mindy* (1978-1982). The new wrinkle here was that these aliens were asked not to visit the Earth, but only receive and respond to a message from Earth.

Viewed in this way, sending messages to aliens might seem a stimulating new subgenre emerging from an intriguing question: what is it about humanity that aliens might find most noteworthy, most surprising, most reprehensible? Voltaire and Vidal delivered effective social commentary with such a device, and one is also reminded of I. F. Stone's pugnacious response to another NASA-sponsored message to possible aliens, the statement on the plaque brought to the moon by the *Apollo 11* astronauts:

HERE MEN FROM THE PLANET EARTH
FIRST SET FOOT UPON THE MOON

JULY 1969 A.D.
WE CAME IN PEACE FOR ALL MANKIND

Stone's suggested alternative:

HERE MEN FIRST SET FOOT OUTSIDE THE EARTH
ON THEIR WAY TO THE FAR STARS. THEY SPEAK
OF PEACE BUT WHEREVER THEY GO THEY BRING
WAR. THE ROCKETS ON WHICH THEY ARRIVED
WERE DEVELOPED TO CARRY INSTANT DEATH AND
CAN WITHIN A FEW MINUTES TURN THEIR GREEN
PLANET INTO ANOTHER LIFELESS MOON. THEIR
DESTRUCTIVE INGENUITY KNOWS NO LIMITS AND
THEIR WANTON POLLUTION NO RESTRAINT.

LET THE REST OF THE UNIVERSE BEWARE
(both cited in "That Moon Plaque" 146-147)

The trouble with this potentially exciting genre is that messages to aliens on NASA space probes represent very expensive projects paid for by millions of American taxpayers, all of them easily offended or upset in innumerable ways. Under such constraints, any wit, insight, or social commentary along the lines of Voltaire, Vidal, or Stone will inexorably be stripped away.

Consider, for example, some of the negative responses to the *Pioneer 10* plaque. After a picture of it appeared in *The Los Angeles Times*, a woman wrote to complain that the images of naked people were "pornography" and "filth" inappropriately being "spread…beyond our own solar system" (cited in *The Cosmic Connection* 25); she disliked the message because she thought it communicated wantonness. One person worried that, coupled with images of World War II broadcast by television into space, aliens might interpret the man's raised hand as a Nazi salute—and as an aggressive warning (*The Cosmic Connection* 28-29); he disliked the message because he thought it communicated belligerence. Since only the man was waving, and since the woman was shorter than the man, feminists thought "the woman appears too passive" (*The Cosmic Connection* 22); the disliked the message because they thought it communicated sexism. A columnist (I cannot today track down his name) complained that NASA had effectively established an "intergalactic foreign policy" of rash openness, announcing our presence and location to potentially hostile aliens looking for new worlds to conquer; he disliked the message because he thought it communicated naïveté. And these were all responses to *unintentional* meanings in the message;

imagine the indignation that would have ensued if Sagan had tried to *deliberately* slip something less than completely complimentary to humanity into the picture.

And this is the second major problem in our efforts to communicate with aliens: envisioned not simply as messages principally for humans, but also as messages that must *please* all humans, they have become bland, unfocused, and unilluminating, resembling NASA's dull moon plaque more than Stone's ornery variation, the cosmic equivalents of airbrushed graduation pictures or encomia inscribed on tombstones.

* * * *

So it was that when Sagan, Drake, and Linda Salzman Sagan, along with new collaborators Ann Druyan, Timothy Ferris, and Jon Lomberg, began to create a more elaborate message for the *Voyager* space probes—a long-playing record with sounds and pictures—they had two principles firmly in mind. First, they would primarily speak to their fellow humans, not to aliens; *Murmurs of Earth* approvingly quotes Bernard Oliver's observation that "There is only an infinitesimal chance that [the message] will ever be seen by a single extraterrestrial, but it will certainly be seen by billions of terrestrials. Its real function, therefore, is to appeal to and expand the human spirit, and to make contact with extraterrestrial intelligence a welcome expectation of mankind" (11). Second, they would relentlessly accentuate the positive so as to offend no one; Sagan asked, "Is it a mistake to put our best face to the cosmos? .... Why not a hopeful rather than a despairing view of humanity and its possible future?" (40) These priorities must be understood to explain a project that, regarded solely as a message to aliens, is utterly senseless.

What did Sagan and his colleagues decide to include on their little record? First, as everyone knows, they compiled a collage of "Sounds of Earth" along with a selection of Earth's greatest music, ranging from aborigine songs and Johann Sebastian Bach to Louis Armstrong and Chuck Berry. This seems an odd choice for one simple reason: while it is hard to imagine a technological civilization developed by beings without a sense of sight—since that is how we obtain about 90% of our information—it is easy to imagine such a civilization developed by beings without a sense of hearing—especially if it arose on a world with a thin atmosphere where sound carried so poorly as to serve as an inconsequential source of data. In other words, Sagan and friends may have literally assembled a symphony for the deaf.

However, despite lengthy rhetoric in *Murmurs of Earth* about music as both a uniquely mathematical and a uniquely emotional form of communication, the focus on music actually reflected one simple consideration: music is the most content-free, and hence the least objectionable, form of human expression. Consider, for example, what would have happened if Sagan and his colleagues had elected to compile a portfolio of the world's greatest artworks. El Greco's *The Assumption of the Virgin*? No religious imagery. Michelangelo's *David*? No full-frontal nudity. Pablo Picasso's *Guernica*? Left-wing political propaganda. Jackson Pollack's *Convergence*? "Why, my six-year-old son can paint better than that." And so on. No, the emphasis on music was based on political expediency, not scientific logic.

Second, the *Voyager* record featured 120 photographs, including numerous diagrams of human biology and physiology and a series of random pictures of humans all over the world engaged in various activities. Yet an intelligent civilization will surely learn to associate sequence with cause-and-effect, and noticing that several brief series of photographs are clearly in chronological order, they would struggle to interpret all 120 photographs as one continuous narrative, without success. Wouldn't it have been more reasonable to employ a series of pictures depicting a typical human life from womb to tomb, showing a fetus, a baby, a small child in school, a graduating high school senior, an adult at work, a parent with children, a senior citizen, and finally a burial? But that would have meant choosing to feature a man or a woman, an American in a suit or an Amazonian in a loincloth, and any possible choice would have led to indignant criticism from those who felt they were not being represented. Thus, while the random snapshots represented a confusing injustice to alien interpreters, their deliberate avoidance of coherence and narrative served the purposes of human creators striving to avoid conflict at all costs.

Finally, the *Voyager* message featured recorded greetings from fifty-four representatives from the United Nations, all of them essentially saying "hello" to the aliens in their own languages. Now, it may or may not be possible for alien linguists to figure out how to translate and understand one of our languages, but the best way to assist them would have been to include a lengthy discourse in a single language; snippets of dozens of different languages would almost certainly be impossible to decipher, and the greetings are so consistently banal that even sophisticated aliens who figured out how to do it would probably abandon the task as a valueless exercise. However, as Linda Salzman Sagan noted in *Murmurs of Earth*, "We were principally concerned with the needs of people on Earth during this section of the recording" (132), and selecting English as the sole method of communication would have angered too many non-English speakers.

Overall, while one can readily criticize the *Voyager* record on several grounds, Sagan and his colleagues must be praised for navigating the treacherous waters of bureaucracy and public opinion to actually get their message into space. The next time a team of scientists would attempt to send a message to aliens, they would not be so successful.

\* \* \* \*

In the 1990s, Lomberg became involved in another message to aliens that seemed more sensible: a CD-ROM, to be carried on a Russian Mars mission, featuring seventy-three stories and fifty-four images conveying human impressions of Mars. This at least would give future aliens enough information to gain some significant knowledge about humanity. Unfortunately, the Russian Mars probe misfired and plunged into the Pacific Ocean, its CD-ROM perhaps destined to someday enlighten—or baffle—a future race of intelligent fish. In the meantime Lomberg, along with NASA scientist Caroline Porco and Gregory Benford, had launched another project to include a message on the *Cassini* space probe to a possible future civilization on Saturn's moon Titan, as is fully described in Benford's *Deep Time*.

They decided to create a new version of the *Pioneer 10* plaque on a small diamond medallion that could endure indefinitely in the harsh environment of Titan. One side would feature a number of astronomical diagrams and photographs to identify the origin and age of the medallion; the other side would feature a stereo photograph of several humans at a beach, ranging in age from children to senior citizens. In making their plans, they inherited the two dangerous principles developed by Sagan. First, they would primarily address other humans, not aliens; Benford said that "Perhaps the most important audience would be not distant generations, but ourselves" (93). Second, they would make the message unfailingly positive—"understandable, optimistic, and awe-inspiring" (94).

The resulting photograph, reproduced in *Deep Time* (119), gives new meaning to the phrase "political correctness." Recalling that feminists had objected to the apparent subordination of the woman on the *Pioneer 10* plaque, Porco suggested that an elderly woman serve as the central figure; recalling complaints about the nudity of the figures, they decided to have the adults and older children dressed normally, while two small children would be naked to inoffensively display human anatomy to alien viewers. (This struck me as strange; surely, if the photograph had ever reached the public, that same woman in Los Angeles might have written to complain that NASA was now dispatching "child pornography" to other worlds.) All races are represented, there are equal numbers of men and women, and everyone appears to be getting along rather splendidly.

Unfortunately, as Benford wryly notes, the people involved in this project did not get along nearly so well. First, Porco abruptly dismissed Benford from the project; later, when the diamond medallion was almost ready to go, she aggressively asserted that she should receive sole credit for the medallion even though Lomberg had done most of the creative work. As an ugly dispute erupted between Porco and Lomberg's supporters, cautious NASA administrators decided to end the controversy by removing the medallion from the *Cassini* mission.

Although one can blame the project's cancellation on Porco's blind ambition, the experience actually illustrates a third major problem in sending alien messages that has emerged only after the death of Carl Sagan. In true scientific research—which such messages supposedly represent—collaborative work followed by collaborative credit is the norm; in describing the brainstorming sessions that led to the medallion, Benford remarks that "Such free-for-alls are one of the best aspects of scientific collaboration, spirited and enjoyable. They are quite the opposite of how other creative people work, as in the classic image of solitary, agonized artists" (94). However, in the creation of science fiction—which such messages have become—there is a natural tendency for one leading agent to seek the lion's share of the credit, and a natural tendency for the public to identify one person as the principal author. In this respect, Sagan was lucky: he could frequently and effusively praise his collaborators for their contributions, in the manner of a true scientist, but he also recognized that, as the celebrity in the group, he would always be regarded as the guiding force behind the messages regardless of how much he shared the credit. After years of bureaucratic infighting within NASA, Porco may have believed that she deserved a turn in the spotlight, so that she could emerge as Sagan's successor, another prominent and effective proponent of space exploration and research. Perhaps she was not suited for the role, but creating and promoting messages to aliens may become more common in the future as scientists, like Porco, come to view the activity as a way to achieve fame and fortune.

* * * *

My overall conclusions? First, it is important to separate the tasks of sending alien messages to talk to aliens and sending alien messages to talk to ourselves. Both goals are worthwhile, but attempting to accomplish both of them at once, in a manner that is amenable to absolutely everyone, is leading to results that are unsatisfactory across the board.

When we address representatives of an extraterrestrial civilization, of course, nothing is certain, but two assumptions are reasonable: first, in order to communicate among themselves, aliens will certainly develop, and recognize, languages; second, in order to master science and technology, they will have to develop an understanding of causes leading to effects, which represent the simplest form of narrative. This suggests that aliens might most enjoy and benefit from human stories. Our experiences on Earth also support the idea: while the art, music, and dance of distant countries and cultures have penetrated western culture only fitfully, stories from all nations and all periods of human histories have found their way to every library and bookstore, so that a modern British child may grow up reading American science fiction, French picture books, adaptations of African folk tales, and stories from Greek, Norse, and Indian mythology. Thus, the best sort of message for aliens would resemble the CD-ROM that never made it to Mars: a collection of the world's greatest literature, all translated into one language chosen by the launching nation. With several million words on the disk, aliens might even be able to figure out English.

When we address ourselves while pretending to address extraterrestrials, the important thing to remember is that this is science fiction, not science, and as such will be best produced by "solitary, agonized artists" instead of committees of scientists and bureaucrats. Following up on one of Benford's ideas, NASA might invite individuals to submit their own proposals for alien messages, building and attaching the best ones to all forthcoming space probes. If NASA has the gumption to embrace the ideas in their original, idiosyncratic forms without attempting to dilute, homogenize, or prettify them, the results might be a fascinating stream of imaginative commentaries on the human condition that could enliven the pages of Sunday newspapers—and provoke letters from irate citizens.

Finally, even if we fail to clutter the heavens with both meaningful and meaningless messages to aliens, we might consider this endeavor, more modestly, simply as another fruitful type of science fiction for the printed page. Stories for aliens might be just as involving and entertaining as stories by or stories about aliens. It is an activity that everyone might be well advised to practice as often as possible in as many forms as possible—both as a way to better understand ourselves and as preparation for a possible future time when we discover actual aliens to converse with.

# THE THREE MOST IMPORTANT REASONS WHY GARY WESTFAHL DOESN'T COMPILE SCIENCE FICTION LISTS

A while ago, I was approached by a German editor who was conducting a global survey of science fiction writers and critics, asking us to list .... I wish I could recall what it was exactly. I *think* it was our choices for the ten best science fiction stories of the twentieth century, but it may well have been the ten best novels, writers, or something else. As a matter of courtesy, I probably should have responded; however, as demonstrated by my inability to even remember the assignment, I could muster no enthusiasm for the task.

I will acknowledge, right from the start, that some special circumstances in the science fiction world definitely demand list-making of some sort: anthologists of previous published stories, in assembling their collections, necessarily compile lists of "the greatest science fiction stories ever written that fit the parameters of this anthology." And college professors teaching science fiction classes, in planning their assignments, necessarily compile lists of "the ten best science fiction books to represent the genre to students."

Yet these sorts of lists have often been discussed elsewhere; so, to demonstrate the perils and pitfalls of list-making, I will consider the unique challenge that confronted the researchers of Whitehall Line when they set out to create a card game of "Science Fiction Authors." To adapt a standard deck of playing cards for this game, one selects thirteen authors (for each rank of card) and four works per author (to represent each card in each suit). Several years ago, I received "Science Fiction Authors" as a Christmas present, and since I recall no mentions of this strange artifact in print, I will list, as of 1991 (the game's copyright date), Whitehall's honor roll of the world's greatest science fiction writers and books (with titles given exactly as they appear on the cards):

| | | |
|---|---|---|
| Ace of Spades | Piers Anthony | *A Spell for Chameleon* |
| Ace of Hearts | | *Juxtaposition* |
| Ace of Diamonds | | *On a Pale Horse* |
| Ace of Clubs | | *Split Infinity* |

| | | |
|---|---|---|
| Two of Spades | Jules Verne | *20,000 Leagues under the Sea* |
| Two of Hearts | | *The Mysterious Island* |
| Two of Diamonds | | *Around the World in Eighty Days* |
| Two of Clubs | | *A Journey to the Center of the Earth* |
| Three of Spades | Ray Bradbury | *The Illustrated Man* |
| Three of Hearts | | *The Martian Chronicles* |
| Three of Diamonds | | *Fahrenheit 451* |
| Three of Clubs | | *Something Wicked This Way Comes* |
| Four of Spades | Isaac Asimov | *Foundation* |
| Four of Hearts | | *The Caves of Steel* |
| Four of Diamonds | | *The Gods Themselves* |
| Four of Clubs | | *Nightfall* |
| Five of Spades | Arthur C. Clarke | *2001: A Space Odyssey* |
| Five of Hearts | | *Against the Fall of Night* |
| Five of Diamonds | | *Rendezvous with Rama* |
| Five of Clubs | | *The Fountains of Paradise* |
| Six of Spades | H. G. Wells | *The Invisible Man* |
| Six of Hearts | | *The History of Mr. Polly* |
| Six of Diamonds | | *The War of the Worlds* |
| Six of Clubs | | *The Time Machine* |
| Seven of Spades | C. S. Lewis | *The Screwtape Letters* |
| Seven of Hearts | | *The Lion, the Witch, and the Wardrobe* |
| Seven of Diamonds | | *Perelandra* |
| Seven of Clubs | | *That Hideous Strength* |
| Eight of Spades | Robert A. Heinlein | *Stranger in a Strange Land* |
| Eight of Hearts | | *Rocket Ship Galileo* |
| Eight of Diamonds | | *The Cat Who Walks Through Walls* |
| Eight of Clubs | | *Double Star* |
| Nine of Spades | Ursula K. Le Guin | *The Left Hand of Darkness* |
| Nine of Hearts | | *The Eye of the Heron* |
| Nine of Diamonds | | *The Dispossessed* |
| Nine of Clubs | | *The Beginning Place* |
| Ten of Spades | Frank Herbert | *Dune* |
| Ten of Hearts | | *Whipping Star* |
| Ten of Diamonds | | *The Dragon in the Sea* |
| Ten of Clubs | | *The Green Brain* |
| Jack of Spades | Roger Zelazny | *This Immortal* |
| Jack of Hearts | | *Changeling* |
| Jack of Diamonds | | *Lord of Light* |
| Jack of Clubs | | *Damnation Alley* |
| Queen of Spades | Gordon R. Dickson | *Time Storm* |
| Queen of Hearts | | *Master of Everon* |
| Queen of Diamonds | | *Mutants* |

| | | |
|---|---|---|
| Queen of Clubs | | *None But Man* |
| King of Spades | J. R. R. Tolkien | *The Hobbit* |
| King of Hearts | | *The Two Towers* |
| King of Diamonds | | *The Return of the King* |
| King of Clubs | | *The Fellowship of the Ring* |

Comments, anyone?

\* \* \* \*

About the selection of authors: to be charitable, the choices reflect some knowledge of the genre, and regardless of personal tastes, almost everyone would agree that seven of them—Asimov, Bradbury, Clarke, Heinlein, Le Guin, Verne, and Wells—are indisputably credible. And, granting that the absence of a separate deck of "Fantasy Authors" mandates some representatives from science fiction's sister genre, one might also embrace the selection of Tolkien and Lewis (since I would regard Lewis primarily as a writer of fantasy, not science fiction). It is the game-maker's other four choices that strike me as questionable. Many may feel comfortable placing Herbert and Zelazny among the genre's greatest, but I personally feel that Herbert's successes with the *Dune* series, and Zelazny's brilliancies of the 1960s, do not fully qualify them for science fiction's elite class. And the final two choices—Dickson and Anthony—with all due respect to their admirers, simply must be laughed out of court.

The book selections similarly reflect both a certain degree of knowledge and a certain degree of cluelessness. While one could quibble about key omissions like Asimov's *I, Robot* (1950), Clarke's *Childhood's End* (1953), and Verne's *From the Earth to the Moon* (1865), the choices for those authors are generally reasonable (though I'm not sure whether the reference is to Asimov's collection *Nightfall and Other Stories* [1969] or the miserable Asimov/Robert Silverberg novelization *Nightfall* [1990]), as are the choices for Bradbury, Lewis, and Tolkien. But other lists resemble random gatherings of titles—as is true of Heinlein, where one finds two of his masterpieces incongruously accompanied by two of his worst clunkers—and Wells is even represented by one novel that is not science fiction by any conceivable definition (*The History of Mr. Polly* [1910]).

How, then, might one design an improved version of "Science Fiction Authors" that would better epitomize the genre's best writers and works? Having expressed concerns about at least four of the current authors, I am obliged to suggest alternatives, and that is hardly difficult. The most egregious omissions, I believe, are Olaf Stapledon, a massive and lingering influence on the entire genre, and William Gibson, still the most intriguing of our recent authors. For purely sentimental reasons, I would nominate Clifford D. Simak, and others with different sentiments could mount powerful cases for Brian W. Aldiss, J. G. Ballard, Philip K. Dick, and Harlan Ellison, to name only a few. Also, worried about the preponderance of white, male, English-speaking authors in the deck, some might prefer other credible choices like Octavia E. Butler, Samuel R. Delany, Stanislaw Lem, Mary Shelley, and Boris and Arkady Strugatsky. (If David Pringle and Paul Brazier wish to add other logical nominees that I have overlooked, they may do so here:        .) Then, once the new candidates are anointed, there remain the secondary tasks of choosing four works to represent those authors and improving the lists of works previously chosen to represent retained authors.

So, for all those who gather in pubs on Friday nights to discuss science fiction, I bequeath to you this topic for debate, which will occupy as many hours as you care to devote to it, and which is positively guaranteed to never lead to a final choice of authors and works that everyone will agree on. But you'll get no further help from me—because, barring the extraordinarily unlikely event of Whitehall Line hiring me as a paid consultant to oversee a revised edition of "Science Fiction Authors," I won't be giving this matter, or any similar question, another moment of thought.

* * * *

Why not? In the first place, as conscientious anthologists and college professors know, it's hard work, confronting a vast array of possible choices and boiling everything down to a small list of well-chosen, exemplary items. Second, in a world already plagued by disharmony and pain, generating lists of the best, the weirdest, or the whatever of anything simply inspires additional disharmony and pain, as the creation of lists may divide lifelong friends, who discover to their displeasure that they have vastly divergent opinions on previously unimagined questions, and the publication of lists may hurt the feelings of writers, who feel that their names or works have been unjustly omitted.

Still, I have demonstrated before that I am willing to work hard, and willing to inspire disharmony and pain, if I believe there is some worthwhile reason for doing so, whether it be to promulgate new ideas, draw attention to neglected issues, or (rarely, it seems) bring a smile to some reader's face. The third reason I avoid list-making is that I can discern no real purpose in the activity. Except in special circumstances such as those described above, it is only a game, a way to kill some time, and nothing more than that.

You play the game by first choosing a number—"ten" is the usual choice, but any number will do. Then, you choose a phrase describing an entirely subjective judgment: "the best," "the most overrated," "the funniest," and so on. Finally, you choose a category of science fiction items to be evaluated, such as "novels," "writers," "films," or subcategories like "women writers" or "British films." One could put lists of numbers, phrases, and categories in three columns and instruct participants to choose one from Column A, one from Column B, and one from Column C; with ten items on each list, your array would generate 1000 possible arguments: this week, "the twenty-five / most unusual / science fiction environments," next week, "the ten / most important / science fiction artists," and the week after that .... Or, if some combinations don't generate vigorous debate, you can get additional ideas by consulting two books that are stuffed with various lists: Mike Ashley's *The Illustrated Book of Science Fiction Lists* (1982) and Maxim Jakubowksi and Malcolm Edwards's *The SF Book of Lists* (1983).

\* \* \* \*

But is there is any real *reason* for these endless exercises in list-making? I can think of some possible answers, but find none of them persuasive.

To publicize significant works or writers that aren't receiving their proper share of attention? Perhaps; that is, if I offered my list of "the ten greatest science fiction movies" and included the obscure *Doin' Time on Planet Earth* (1988) alongside better- known films like *The Day the Earth Stood Still* (1951) and *2001: A Space Odyssey* (1968), that might encourage some people to seek out and view that remarkable film. Yet if that is my goal, wouldn't it be better accomplished by, say, writing a short essay on the film? Also, when people like that German editor compile the votes of many people to produce group lists, it is precisely these sorts of unexpected, idiosyncratic candidates that will be lost in a sea of routine, predictable choices.

To bolster the egos of the creative people whose names or works appear on such lists? Just possibly, but remember, we're not talking about the Pulitzer Prizes or Academy Awards here. Would it really warm the cockles of Paul Di Filippo's heart more than one or two degrees, for instance, if he happened to see his name come in at number seven on someone's list of "The Twenty Most Underrated Science Fiction Writers"?

To gather important data about the interests and opinions of various members of the science fiction community? Perhaps to a limited extent; that is, the fact that stories like Asimov's "Nightfall" (1941), Clarke's

"The Sentinel" (1951), and Bradbury's "A Sound of Thunder" (1952) regularly dominate lists of most-frequently- anthologized science fiction stories says something about what readers value in short fiction, and the fact that novels like Le Guin's *The Left Hand of Darkness* (1969), Mary Shelley's *Frankenstein* (1818), and Wells's *The Time Machine* (1895) regularly dominate lists of most-frequently-assigned texts in science fiction classes says something about how academics view science fiction. Yet these compilations never resemble a truly scientific survey, and finding out the majority opinion about some issue at a given time is not always useful in determining the best position to take. If, for example, I am choosing stories for my own anthology, or books for my own science fiction class, I shouldn't allow myself to be influenced by which works have been most often favored in the past; rather, I should make my own best choices, seeking (if only in a tiny way) to improve on the collective wisdom of the community, not merely to reflect it. In most tasks that people confront, in other words, it is not always helpful, and may even be harmful, to be overly aware of what everyone else has thought about the matter.

To assist posterity in selecting which works and writers to enshrine and which ones to abandon? We arrive, I think, at the true underlying purpose for these parlor games—to instruct future generations as to what constitutes the best and brightest of our literature—yet attempting to do this is utterly futile. For posterity is going to find its own uses for things, including science fiction, and it isn't going to give a darn about what we think. Today, someone assembling an anthology of nineteenth-century American poetry wouldn't care about the results of an 1870 survey of "The Ten Most Loved American Poems," especially when she finds out that seven of the choices were written by Henry Wadsworth Longfellow. She will instead choose the poems that most appeal to contemporary tastes—as she should.

There is, then, a very serious game going on here, which list- makers demonstrate an awareness of: all science fiction writers wish to be remembered, but only a few will succeed, and the rest will be forgotten. To those who take the genre seriously, this is perhaps the most significant game of them all. Unfortunately, we of the present day aren't allowed to play this game, and it is pointless to pretend that we can.

So, to return to the question that started all of this: what *are* the ten best science fiction stories of the twentieth century? It's not for us to say; that is something to be determined by future generations, not ourselves. We need to find more productive ways to spend our precious time.

# MARTIANS OLD AND NEW, STILL STANDING OVER US

One night, seeing that *The Day the Earth Stood Still* (1951) had just started on television, I immediately sat down to watch—because *The Day the Earth Stood Still* is one of those classic movies you should watch whenever it's available, as it always offers something new to notice and appreciate. This time, I noticed that when Klaatu describes his journey, he specifies that the distance from his home planet to Earth was "250 million of your miles." He even repeats the figure.

Since aliens are rarely so definite about such matters, I wondered where a journey of 250 million miles to Earth might have begun. There was only one answer: Mars. When Earth and Mars are in opposition, they are 234 million miles apart, close to the stated distance. Venus and Mercury are always much less distant; Jupiter and the other planets are much farther away.

Other possibilities? Klaatu couldn't come from a tiny asteroid, and the only place to conceal a nearby body of planetary dimensions is in Earth's orbit, directly opposite Earth behind the Sun—the "Counter-Earth" of John Norman's Gor series, the film *Journey to the Far Side of the Sun* (1969), and other undistinguished epics. Yet journeys from Counter-Earth to Earth, even with a generous swing around the Sun, would take little more than 200 million miles. Further, if Klaatu comes from a planet nobody on Earth has heard of, why does he bother to be so coy about his home? When asked, "where it is you come from," he answers vaguely, "From another planet. Let's just say we're neighbors." A Klaatu from an unknown world could have given a more frank but equally uncommunicative response like "I come from the planet Zahgon."

The more I pondered the issue, the clearer it seemed: though for some reason unwilling to disclose his true identity, Klaatu had to be a Martian.

* * * *

Seeking more evidence to support the idea, I read the Harry Bates story that inspired the film, "Farewell to the Master" (1940), but it provided no help, since the story's alien vessel arrives on Earth by means of teleportation, not space travel, and Klaatu and Gnut (Bates's name for Klaatu's robot companion, thankfully changed to Gort in the film) are from another solar system. Reading the film's script reminded me of other clues, including the line about neighbors (Venus and Mars are the only planets that can be termed Earth's neighbors) and the newspaper headline "'MAN FROM MARS' ESCAPES FROM ARMY HOSPITAL!" Also, while the lines aren't in the script, a radio announcer in the film speculates that Klaatu comes from either Venus or Mars, and when the film was released in Sweden, it was given the name *The Man from Mars*.

To see if the theory had emerged in the critical literature surrounding *The Day the Earth Stood Still*, I put the question to a young science fiction scholar studying 1950s films (yes, *that* young science fiction scholar, inexplicably still on speaking terms with me after reading "'Scuse Me While I Kiss the Sky"). While I was told that the idea hadn't arisen, my "scientific" evidence to support Klaatu's Martian origins wasn't necessarily strong, from that scholar's perspective, since students of these films quickly learn that the facts and figures thrown out therein are often meaningless or unreliable—which is true enough, as in the movie we argued about, *This Island Earth* (1955), with its comets turning into planets and planets turning into suns.

Still, if a lazy screenwriter was randomly concocting an impressively large number, one would expect more of a round number—"a hundred billion miles" or "a million light years." "250 million miles" wasn't a figure someone would come up with out of the blue. *The Day the Earth Stood Still* was also striving to be a class act, and though screenwriter Edmund North isn't noted for science fiction films—his only other genre credit is *Meteor* (1979)—he was manifestly a diligent craftsperson who might actually pick up a science book to strengthen his script with accurate information.

Yet if North, director Robert Wise, or others working on the film envisioned Klaatu as a Martian, why wasn't that openly acknowledged? Perhaps it seemed appropriate following the internal logic of the story. Klaatu explains that his people had learned Earth's languages by "monitoring your radio broadcasts for a good many years," so they had surely heard the 1938 radio broadcast of *The War of the Worlds* and the anti-Martian panic that ensued, making it advisable for them to avoid mentioning Mars while on Earth. Klaatu also emphasizes that he represents not just one world but a federation of worlds dedicated to suppressing interplanetary violence—"A sort of United Nations on the Planetary level." Identifying himself as a Martian might have led people to interpret his mission more narrowly, and more negatively, as Mars's effort to conquer Earth. Alternately, one might consider the external logic of film producers who wanted to market a serious science fiction film during a time when shoddy productions like *Rocketship X-M* (1950), *Flying Disc Man from Mars* (1951), and *Flight to Mars* (1951) were giving the Red Planet a bad name. Removing references to "Mars" may have seemed a necessary way to preserve one's dignity amidst the inanity.

Discounting appeals to textual evidence and logic, however, I have accepted Klaatu as a Martian, and have added *The Day the Earth Stood Still* to my bibliography of science fiction works involving Mars, primarily due to his actions: he comes to Earth, observes our behavior, and delivers a stern lecture about why we need to mend our foolish, evil ways. That is, he does what Martians generally do.

* * * *

It began with Percival Lowell, who prominently theorized in the late nineteenth century that Mars was home to an advanced civilization, much older than ours, capable of constructing innumerable and vast canals to bring water to thirsty Martians throughout a desiccating world (but not of devising more practical solutions, like relocating Martians to where the water was). As discussed in my article "Reading Mars: Changing Images of Mars in Twentieth-Century Science Fiction," Lowell's ideas engendered a rich literary tradition of Martians who act like parents—sometimes implacably evil, like H. G. Wells's invaders in *The War of the Worlds* (1898), sometimes fading into senescence and in need of energetic human assistance, like Edgar Rice Burroughs's Barsoomians—but most frequently older, wiser beings who look down on humans as childish savages. It is a ubiquitous trope in science fiction, ranging from the high-tech Martian utopia of Hugo Gernsback's *Baron Munchausen's Scientific Adventures* (1915-1917) to the virtuous, unfallen Martians of C. S. Lewis's *Out of the Silent Planet* (1938) and the enigmatically powerful Martians of Robert A. Heinlein's *Stranger in a Strange Land* (1961).

It is a tradition that Klaatu fits into quite nicely. While critics focus on Klaatu as a Christ figure (he calls himself Mr. Carpenter, he dies for our sins and is reborn, etc.), he actually seems more of a father figure: actor Michael Rennie looks the part, with his grey hair and dignified bearing, and we learn that Klaatu is rather elderly, in fact 78 years old (so he was born in 1873, around the time when Giovanni Schiaparelli's apparent discovery of Martian "canali" led to the birth of Lowell's theories—an intriguing coincidence). While Klaatu declines to romance the widowed Helen Benson to become her surrogate husband, he embraces the role of surrogate father to her son, escorting the lad around Washington D.C. and praising the words of another fatherly figure, Abraham

Lincoln, engraved in the Lincoln Memorial. But the way Klaatu discusses our backwards Earth, in contrast to his progressive home world, best reveals his Martian heritage: "I don't intend to add my contribution to your childish jealousies and suspicions." "I am impatient with stupidity. My people have learned to live without it." "Your mutual fears and suspicions are merely the normal reactions of a primitive society." It is the voice of adult experience, familiar to teenagers everywhere, hectoring heedless youth about their lamentable immaturity.

It is a voice that reverberated through science fiction for many decades, until scientific evidence demonstrated beyond doubt that Mars could not be the home of an ancient, parental civilization. Yet traditions die hard, and we may now be witnessing the rebirth of the tradition that Klaatu represents.

* * * *

Recently, during two lengthy flights across the Pacific, I finally read Kim Stanley Robinson's *Green Mars* (1994) and *Blue Mars* (1996), completing his Martian trilogy. I had earlier enjoyed *Red Mars* (1993), but was less pleased with its successors, and not simply because of the unpleasant environment where I read them.

Part of the problem is the classic sort of wheel-spinning that afflicts many trilogies: most of *Green Mars* is devoted to retelling the story of *Red Mars*—an attempted Martian revolution—with a happy ending this time; characters even remark on the similarities between unfolding events and previous events, reminding themselves (and perhaps their author) to do things differently this time. And with Martian independence established, *Blue Mars* is, despite its length, a novel without a narrative—even though Robinson keeps trying to interest himself in various people and minor crises afflicting his developing Martian utopia, without much success, as he desultorily decides to ignore this character, kill off that character, and take another look at that other character.

Also disturbing was the fact that these novels preach democracy but display a fascination with aristocracy. Even after the Martian population surpasses one billion, Robinson remains exclusively focused on the *de facto* royalty of Mars: the First Hundred colonists, along with their children and spouses, who remain alive indefinitely due to longevity treatments and keep dominating every sphere of Martian activity, whether it is the government or sporting events. The common people of Mars serve only as props, to cheer worshipfully whenever the saintly Nirgal visits their town or to be horribly misled by Jackie Boone's crude anti-immigrant rhetoric. To celebrate this elite class even more, Robinson methodically weeds out or reforms all of its bad apples: his intriguingly flawed characters, John Boone and Frank Chalmers, are killed off in *Red Mars*; his scoundrels are removed—Phyllis Boyle by assassination, second-generation Jackie by exile to another planet; and his formerly disruptive and confrontational Ann Claiborne and Maya Toitovna are allowed to mellow into pleasant, agreeable folks. To fill the void left by Boone's and Chalmers's departures, *Green Mars* adds boring new characters who are too good to be true: the second-generation Nirgal, absolutely incapable of harboring an evil thought, and Art Randolph, who is dispatched to Mars by a visionary billionaire to help the Martians solve all their problems and proceeds to do so with unfailing charm and kindness. (I longed for a plot twist that would reveal Art as an evil agent of Earth's despised multinational corporations, insinuating himself into Mars's inner circle only to betray them all; unfortunately, although that is the only logical explanation for his unbelievable benevolence, Art turns out to be what he pretends to be, eventually marrying one of the First Hundred to officially join the Elect.)

But Robinson is both an industrious and intelligent writer; why would he allow his meticulously crafted and compelling story to devolve into a dull tableau of plastic paragons? The answer, I believe, is that he was writing about Martians. And Martians, a deeply rooted tradition whispers in an author's ears, are older and wiser than mere humans. So, even though Robinson's Martians are children of Earth, he felt obliged to somehow create out of them an assemblage of beings who are preternaturally mature and sagacious—so that later, when Earth dissolves into chaos due to environmental disaster, a team of those Martians can visit Earth to offer assistance, again serving as experienced mentors and harsh critics of primitive human civilization.

It is telling that, as a trilogy that visibly struggled to be multicultural approaches its conclusion, Robinson repeatedly likens his Martian civilization to a standard Western model for idealized super-scientific cultures: ancient Greece. Buildings "devoted to the island's olympiads... had a consciously Greek look to them" (591), and marathon runners race in the nude, like Greek Olympians. Evocative Greek place names keep cropping up—Elysium, Hellas, Hellespontus, Aegean, Acheron, Olympus. There are references to a twenty-first-century "Professor Athens" (671) and statements like "as if the ancient Greeks by introspection alone had intuited the very geometry of timespace" (662) and "The island slipped under the horizon like a dream of ancient Greece" (599). Maya's theater group performs Greek tragedies, and she notices "a connection to the ancient Greeks...being made in any number of ways all around Hellas Basin...a neoclassicism that Maya felt was good for them all, as they confronted and tried to measure up to the Greeks' great honesty, their unflinching look at reality" (613). One starts to imagine Robinson's exemplary Martians wearing togas, like the magisterial Martians who greet and chastise visiting human astronauts in the 1918 Danish film *Himmelskibet*.

* * * *

Despite such infelicities, one must acknowledge Robinson's trilogy as a monumental achievement. Earlier writers, after all, could simply have people stumble upon an older, wiser Martian civilization; Robinson had to build his older, wiser Martian civilization from scratch, beginning with only a small band of settlers from Earth. And, given Robinson's familiarity with and commitment to the literature and traditions of science fiction, it is predictable that his creative energies would increasingly follow a well-trodden path.

In "Reading Mars," I posited that the new outpouring of novels about terraforming Mars might engender a third Martian paradigm, a reinhabited Mars, to replace Lowell's inhabited Mars and the uninhabited Mars of contemporary science. After reading Robinson's novels, however, I now suspect that science fiction may simply be returning to the original paradigm, the difference being that now, the awesome, parental Martians who tower over mere humans and upbraid us for our follies will be our own descendants, transformed by the experience of Martian life into superior beings. Klaatu is coming back to Earth, and this time, he will be one of us.

# GOING WHERE LOTS OF PEOPLE HAVE GONE BEFORE, OR, THE NOVELS SCIENCE FICTION READERS DON'T SEE

It is, apparently, a form of science fiction that most members of the science fiction community are determined to ignore. In listings of "Books Received," *Interzone* once exiled such items to a special section headed "Spinoffery" and now includes them only sporadically; *Locus* acknowledges them in compilations of forthcoming and published books but never reviews them. These books are never nominated for awards, never mentioned in interviews, and never analyzed by scholars, despite their wide visibility and undeniable popularity.

I became acquainted with the subgenre at its birth, when I purchased and read the first two *Star Trek* novels, Mack Reynolds's juvenile *Mission to Horatius* (1968) and James Blish's *Spock Must Die!* (1970). Both novels were the work of respected science fiction writers who had repeatedly demonstrated the ability to write involving, innovative, and at times brilliant stories. Both novels easily qualified as the worst pieces of crap that their authors had ever produced.

In the 1980s, when Pocket Books transformed *Star Trek* novels into a major industry, other examples of the form were added to my collection, almost invariably as gifts from well-meaning friends who knew that I liked science fiction and, therefore, knew that I liked *Star Trek* novels. I read several of them, but it didn't matter whether they were written by prominent award-winners, diligent craftspersons, or unknown writers; they were always terrible. Vonda N. McIntyre's *Enterprise: The First Adventure* (1986) tells the contrived, meandering story of Captain Kirk's first mission, a humiliatingly trivial chore which, of course, soon blossoms into a genuine crisis. J. M. Dillard's *Star Trek: The Lost Years* (1989), purportedly intended to describe what happened during the five years between the final episode of the original series and the beginning of the first film, moves at such a snail's pace that it ends up barely covering the first year, as if Dillard was hoping to develop her one-book deal into a tetralogy. Jean Lorrah's *The Vulcan Academy Murders* (1984) is an inept murder "mystery" in which the perpetrator of the crimes all but steps forward and confesses in the first chapter. The last one I started reading was a *Star Trek: Deep Space Nine* novel by Esther M. Friesner, *Warchild* (1994). Surely, I thought, if any writer could infuse a *Star Trek* novel with some originality and sparkle, it would be Friesner. Wrong. It was so insufferably dull that I couldn't even force myself to finish the thing.

Commentators have attempted to explain why these novels are regularly unsuccessful despite the impressive talents that sometimes labor to produce them. My personal approach to an explanation would invoke a Rule of Three. Most great works of literature are products of one author, one dominant creative force. Yet classics may also emerge from the interaction of two dominant creative forces—not only co-authors, but also an author wrestling with the legacy of some previous author or tradition, or an author with an energetic editor functioning as collaborator. But true artistic achievement becomes impossible when, as is the case with *Star Trek* novels, three creative forces are involved: first, Gene Roddenberry and all the other producers, writers, and actors who helped to develop and shape the original series and its successors; second, the editorial advisors who closely supervise today's novels to ensure that continuity and consistency are rigorously maintained; and third, the credited author, haplessly vying for some wiggle room in a doubly-binding straitjacket. Authors can work well within a preexisting narrative framework, and they can work well under tight editorial supervision, but both forces acting together are an absolutely deadening combination. The *Star Trek* universe has been compared to the collectively generated mythologies of past civilizations, which inspired many masterpieces; but, then again, no editors were telling Homer and Sophocles what they could or couldn't do with the characters of Ulysses and Oedipus.

With hundreds of *Star Trek* novels in print, and new ones appearing every week, I may be overlooking some remarkably excellent works within the subgenre. Still, based on my random samplings and other reports, my suspicion that they are uniformly execrable is reasonably well grounded, and I cannot motivate myself to further investigate these texts in my limited time for leisure reading.

* * * *

At this point, you may think you know where this argument is going, and you may be wrong. Consider precisely what I have said so far: I reporting reading several *Star Trek* novels and regarding them as awful; I described some examples in fairly scathing terms; I announced a resolve to read no additional works of this sort; and, if I am ever asked to recommend some good science fiction books, it's easy to deduce that I will not suggest any of these novels. However, consider also what I have *not* said: I have *not* said that these novels are *evil*, and I have *not* criticized or condemned the innumerable people who read and enjoy these novels.

Others have viewed the phenomenon of *Star Trek* novels with great alarm, particularly vexed by this question: why are so many people reading this *bad* science fiction, when there is so much *good* science fiction out there that cannot garner the wide audience it deserves? Two answers have been advanced: first, that these people are simply unaware that better reading material is available, leading to various proposals to educate and uplift these lost souls—perhaps we could pressure Pocket Books to staple copies of Nebula Award-winning stories in the middle of *Star Trek* novels to let readers know what they are missing. The second theory is that devotees of these novels are hopeless clods, Fans Who Aren't Slans, high school dropouts who read *Star Trek* novels while picking their noses, guzzling cheap wine, and watching wrestling matches on television. I find neither theory persuasive, largely because I have met, over the years, any number of people who admitted, with visible embarrassment, to reading *Star Trek* novels, and they generally impressed me as intelligent, literate persons, well aware that better science fiction novels exist and perfectly capable of appreciating them.

Why, then, don't these people seek out those other novels and appreciate them? Because there is no reason to expect that they should.

\* \* \* \*

Underlying the frustrations inspired by *Star Trek* novels lies, I suspect, the false belief that there exists some Royal Road to Superior Reading, and that maturing readers will naturally make their way through some neat hierarchal progression, beginning with juvenile science fiction novels, advancing to *Star Trek* novels as a key transitional phase, then continuing onward to David Weber and Lois McMaster Bujold, then to Ken MacLeod and Joan Slonczewksi, moving higher and higher up the aesthetic ladder until they finally achieve the Empyrean heights of appreciating, say, Gene Wolfe. If a number of readers are visibly stalled in their upward progress at the low rung of *Star Trek* novels, it means that something has gone horribly wrong, demanding corrective action or vigorous censure.

There are two problems with this model. First, readers never follow such rules in their evolving reading habits; over the years, they will careen from bad to good and back to bad again. The model is further based upon the hidden assumption that literature represents people's only available source of intellectual stimulation, so that if readers are settling for monotonous, formulaic fare like *Star Trek* novels, they are regrettably depriving themselves of the rewardingly complex narratives that they desperately require in order to continue growing as active, productive individuals.

But this isn't true. People can get all the intellectual stimulation they need without ever opening a book—by listening to fine music, examining outstanding works of art, watching memorable films, or attending plays, ballets, and operas. Beyond artistic genres, others may focus their energies on learning about and working with other people, who can be just as fascinating as books. Assembling an effective team to accomplish an important task, or advancing a worthwhile initiative through convoluted layers of bureaucracy, is genuinely stimulating and rewarding, just like reading Samuel R. Delany's *Dhalgren* (1975).

The larger issue is this: people should have the right to assemble the mosaics of their own life, gathering bits and pieces of disparate experiences and influences into a whole which they find satisfying, and their individual mosaics will inevitably involve certain amounts of treasure and certain amounts of trash. And we should trust people to make their own decisions about the treasures and trash they bring into their lives without passing judgment, without assuming that their failure to appreciate our favorite pastime means they are boors. In my own case, while endeavoring to display some discrimination in my reading, I hardly limit myself to the very best the world can offer in most areas of imaginative endeavor, opting instead for routine products that would appall connoisseurs in those areas as much as *Star Trek* novels appall experienced science fiction readers. Most of the music I listen to is on Top 40 radio, so I'm currently tapping my feet to Jennifer Lopez's "Play" (2001), Missy Elliott's "Get Ur Freak On" (2001), and other songs that I fully recognize are ephemera destined for well-merited oblivion. I rarely attend any of the events that should appeal to educated persons—concerts, plays, ballets, poetry readings, lectures; at the end of a busy day, I may watch baseball on television instead of more sophisticated diversions. Still, despite all the junk that I place in the mosaic of my life, my ongoing research, writing, and teaching suffice to keep me mentally alive despite these necessary pauses to wallow in mindless mediocrity.

* * * *

This is the perfectly respectable, even admirable, purpose of *Star Trek* novels. These bland, predictable narratives fit precisely into the mosaics of many people's busy lives, and their readers never advance to more demanding science fiction for the same reason that I never advance to more demanding music: the novels they read, and the music I listen to, provide exactly what we need, while superior varieties would provide different sorts of rewards that we are already receiving from other aspects of our lives.

Yet science fiction has long been associated with imaginative and literary aspirations of the grandest sort; must the genre now be homogenized and dumbed down so that its stories can serve as entertainments equivalent to pop songs and baseball games? Well, as long as other forms of science fiction remain available, why not? *Star Trek* novels arouse indignation only because science fiction readers are so often obliged to *pay attention* to them—since they are labelled science fiction, placed in the science fiction sections of bookstores, and sometimes written by established science fiction writers. If we could simply *ignore* them and go about our business—as the noted publications and people have been properly attempting—science fiction readers and *Star Trek* readers could happily co-exist in perpetually separate worlds.

After all, there now exists a popular form of science fiction that is even more objectionable, even more formulaic and uninspired, than *Star Trek* novels, but it inspires not one iota of indignation in the science fiction community because few members are aware of its existence. I refer to the "time travel romances" written by Diana Gabaldon and many others, in which beautiful heroines are transported by unspecified means into attractive past eras to engage in the familiar rolls in the hay with dark, mysterious strangers. Surely, here is science fiction homogenized and dumbed down to the nth degree. But science fiction readers remain blissfully unaware of these abominations because they are not labelled science fiction, not placed in the science fiction sections of bookstores, and not written by established science fiction writers. They are the novels that science fiction readers don't see.

Bearing in mind the old *Interzone* term for *Star Trek* novels and the like—"Spinoffery"—one might recall that the word "spinoff" originally referred to a television series created by taking a character from an existing series and placing him or her in a new milieu to develop a distinctive identity of her own. *Star Trek* novels and time travel romances might be regarded, then, not as *forms* of science fiction but as *spinoffs* of science fiction which both seized a chunk of the genre, placed it in a new milieu, and developed distinctive identities of their own. If, then, my remarks do not accurately represent the nature and benefits of *Star Trek* novels, that may be because these have evolved in isolation to the point that they are no longer usefully regarded as science fiction—so that in discussing them, I unwisely step outside of my area of expertise.

# POUL ANDERSON AND THE HUMAN CRUSADE

To be brutally honest, I was never a great admirer of the late Poul Anderson. Long ago, like any young science fiction reader emerging from David G. Hartwell's omnivore stage, I needed to make practical decisions about which authors to continue reading and which authors to stop reading, and Anderson ended up in my second category. I know that he produced respected novels in his later years demonstrating an active imagination and artistic growth, and someday I may read them. But today, I would celebrate Anderson primarily for one of his early novels, an essential text for anyone seeking to understand science fiction, and that is *The High Crusade* (1960).

To place the novel in context, one might say that science fiction has three stories to tell about humanity's future. The first is that humans of tomorrow will become extinct or insignificant, supplanted by aliens or their own intelligent creations. This bleak scenario is palatably presented in Clifford D. Simak's *City* (1952), wherein charming robots and intelligent dogs replace the humans who abandoned Earth for mindless pleasures, but conveyed more chillingly in stories like Fredric Brown's "Answer" (1954), Brian W. Aldiss's "Who Can Replace a Man?" (1958), and Mike Resnick's *Birthright: The Book of Man* (1982).

The second story is that the humans of tomorrow will survive but evolve into something superhuman or not quite human in response to changing conditions or as a way to master new environments. Versions of this scenario include some of the genre's most enduring and unsettling works, such as H. G. Wells's *The Time Machine* (1895), Olaf Stapledon's *Last and First Men* (1930), Arthur C. Clarke's *Childhood's End* (1953) and *2001: A Space Odyssey* (1968), and George Zebrowksi's *Macrolife* (1979).

The third story is that the humans of tomorrow will be precisely the same as today's humans, save that they will travel through space, encounter aliens, harness incalculable cosmic powers, and so on. Such scenarios may further claim that humans will revert to behavioral patterns of the past, like those found in the American West, medieval England, or ancient Rome. This is the future universe of space opera, *Star Trek*, *Star Wars*, and many other science fiction stories and films. Although skillful writers can produce memorable works along these lines, these stories may justifiably be seen as unadventurous, unimaginative, and—given what one might reasonably expect in the future—extremely implausible.

This is the sort of story that I came to associate with Anderson, due to the random, omnivorous reading that kept me away from innovative novels like *Brain Wave* (1954) or *Tau Zero* (1970) and instead brought me into repeated contact with Nicholas van Rijn and Ensign Flandry. And the teenage Westfahl simply wasn't impressed. I didn't know what the future would be like, but I knew that it certainly wouldn't involve savvy merchants or diplomats negotiating their way through tiny principalities on distant worlds or vast galactic empires modeled so explicitly upon European history. Authors who wrote such stories, and readers who enjoyed them, struck my snotty young self as incredibly naïve.

\* \* \* \*

That Poul Anderson was never naïve is powerfully communicated by *The High Crusade*, which seizes, literalizes, and explicitly defends the conceit that the human past is prologue to our future (and does so quite seriously, unlike the inane 1994 film version). Its main text is purportedly a document examined by spacefaring humans of the future amazed to discover an advanced human civilization speaking archaic English near the center of the galaxy. In 1345 A.D., Brother Parvus writes, an alien spaceship landed in England to begin its conquest of Earth; but its blue-skinned Wersgor occupants were attacked and defeated by English warriors led by Sir Roger de Tourneville. Planning to travel to France and the Holy Land in the huge spaceship, thousands of English men and women under Sir Roger's command were instead diverted by a duplicitous Wersgor navigator to the distant planet Tharixan; but the humans, by means of bluster, cunning, and brute force, conquered its Wersgor overlords and took over the planet. Sir Roger then returned to space, forged an alliance with other alien races, and destroyed the Wersgor empire in a great space battle. The final threat to Sir Roger's burgeoning domain came not from aliens, but from a deceitful comrade, Sir Owain, who deluded his disgruntled wife; after a spirited brawl on board the traitor's spaceship, however, his plans were thwarted.

Throughout this incredible narrative, Anderson confronts and answers all of the objections one might make to stories where replicas of ancient humans successfully master the universe. How could primitive means of fighting prevail against superscientific weaponry? "The trouble of the Wersgorix was that they had gone too far. They had made combat on the ground obsolete, and were ill trained, ill equipped, when it happened" (43). How could the experiences of European history allow humans to dominate interstellar politics? "On Earth there've been many nations and lords for many centuries, all at odds with each other .... we've perforce learned all the knavery there is to know" (118). Why might governments on other planets resemble those of medieval Europe? "Sir Roger de Tourneville established the feudal system on newly conquered worlds .... the collapse of Wersgorixan was not unlike the collapse of Rome, and similar problems found a similar answer" (157).

*The High Crusade* thus mounts a sophisticated defense of the apparently unsophisticated plot elements permeating both written and filmed space adventures. Why, in Flash Gordon serials and *Star Trek* episodes, does the fate of worlds so often depend upon who wins a chaotic fistfight? Perhaps, no matter how advanced and powerful weapons may become, hand-to-hand, or hand-to-claw, combat will always be the best strategy in some situations. Why do stories of space federations and empires so often have humans running the show? Perhaps something about Earth's tumultuous history prepared us especially well for the problems of fighting enemies and forming coalitions amidst strange alien civilizations. Why do governments on distant worlds so often resemble those of medieval Europe, with kings and princesses, scheming servants and court intrigues? Perhaps that represents the most efficient and humane way to govern isolated worlds inhabited by more than one sentient species.

To be sure, defending the future utility of time-honored patterns of behavior may lead into contentious political territory, specifically to the argument that all of humanity's contemporary history—with the organization man and keyboard-wielding nerd replacing the rugged individualist and sword-wielding warrior—represents a tragic and temporary aberration, a veneer of effete civilization that must be wiped away so that manly figures emulating the giants of the past can lead humanity to conquer the universe and fulfill our manifest destiny. Yet as earlier explained, I do not regard recent efforts to achieve an enlightened and egalitarian society as a horrible mistake; and since Anderson, rightly or wrongly, was sometimes linked to this sort of testosterone-driven libertarianism more vocally espoused by the likes of Jerry Pournelle and L. Neil Smith, that may be another reason why I devoted my time to other authors.

\* \* \* \*

Yet *The High Crusade* answers this objection as well, signaling repeatedly that its medieval heroes have, due to their unique experiences, grown wiser than their original contemporaries. After the first victory, Parvus writes, "I returned to the abbey and spent the night on my knees, praying for a sign. But the saints remained noncommittal" (18). The cynical humor initially seems a case of breaking character; yet as the story progresses with fewer and fewer references to seeking religious guidance or finding biblical interpretations for events, one realizes that the elderly Parvus writing this manuscript and his compatriots have moved beyond stolid reliance on simple doctrines to balance their faith with a determination to reach their own decisions in a bizarre environment where ancient texts and precepts offer little assistance. When Sir Roger departs to engage in interstellar diplomacy, he leaves his wife to govern the conquered planet, which she does very well, suggesting a newfound confidence in women's abilities. (She is also the person who, after belatedly recognizing Sir Owain's treachery, resolves the conflict by calmly killing him and his alien cohort.) While striving to defeat the Wersgorix, Sir Roger interacts courteously with aliens resembling cats, centaurs, and octopuses, indicating a developing respect and tolerance for beings unlike himself. Most strikingly, Parvus begins his manuscript by stating that he writes at the behest of "Archbishop William, a most learned and holy prelate" (9); at the end of the novel, we learn that "Archbishop William" is in fact Huruga, the former Wersgor governor of Tharixan who (like many of his fellow Wersgorix) converted to Christianity.

Anderson might agree, then, that we should not overly romanticize our ancestors, that they were backward and narrow-minded in many respects; but he argues that such people would inexorably progress beyond such failings as fundamentalism, sexism, and racism in response to the variegated stimuli of space travel. The universe of *The High Crusade* is not conquered simply by medieval warriors, but by medieval warriors who retained their basic character while being tempered and improved by their new circumstances—people who combine, one could maintain, the best of humanity's past and humanity's present.

It is a vision not to be lightly dismissed. Many theories have been proposed to explain why film and television science fiction is so popular nowadays, while print science fiction is so relatively unpopular, and it won't hurt to toss one more idea on the table. For the last twenty years, the predominant philosophy in written science fiction has been that the human body is obsolete; in his 1986 introduction to *Mirrorshades: The Cyberpunk Anthology*, Bruce Sterling identifies "Certain central themes that spring up repeatedly in cyberpunk": "The theme of body invasion: prosthetic limbs, implanted circuitry, cosmetic surgery, genetic alteration. The even more powerful theme of mind invasion: brain-computer interfaces, artificial intelligence, neurochemistry—techniques radically redefining the nature of humanity, the nature of the self" (xiii). His novel *Schismatrix* (1985) portrays future humans arguing not over whether to alter the human body, but only whether to alter it using machinery or genetic engineering. Works produced by the contemporary authors who garner critical respect usually follow science fiction's second story, with every future human sporting implants or body modifications, having evolved beyond the merely human to survive in some perilous underground world. Yet in media science fiction, future people are just like us; they may be surrounded by exotic aliens and high-tech gizmos, but they still look and act pretty much like people today, or even (as noted) like people of previous centuries.

Of course there are exceptions: recent films like *Gattaca* (1997) and *Johnny Mnemonic* (1995) reflect the cyberpunk embrace of transformed humanity, and descendants of Anderson's de Tourneville, van Rijn, and Flandry, like David Weber's Honor Harrington, have recently appeared in print, carrying on in a recognizably human manner. Yet science fiction film and television may have eclipsed the literature in popularity because they generally feature characters who resemble their audiences, whereas modern novels may feature characters who have elected to bear little resemblance to their audiences.

From Sterling's perspective, this might mean only that science fiction writers of his school are visionaries speaking to other visionaries, whereas the hacks working for film and television are muddled reactionaries pandering to similarly muddled viewers. Yet their seeming simplemindedness may conceal a deeper wisdom. Consider the development of humanity from our origins millions of years ago until the fifteenth century, the age before science. Humans during those times accumulated a tremendous amount of *lore*, practical skills in growing crops, forging armor, constructing windmills, and the like, but they lacked the understanding of unifying principles which marks true science, and which led to the accelerated progress of the last five centuries. Still, as demonstrated by the medieval Europeans of *The High Crusade* and, in a different way, by the achievements of medieval China, human beings armed only with the abilities and intelligence bred into them managed pretty well, all things considered. And while humanity has greatly advanced by means of science, and may advance even more by means of future science, it remains possible that the human being molded by millennia of evolution, the human being that progressed from caves to castles, just might, tempered by the enlightened attitudes of the present, represent a sturdier and more capable citizen of the future than the human being to be constructed in our laboratories.

* * * *

I'm not necessarily sure that this is true, but I cannot deny the logic and emotional appeal of the argument, which is virtually intrinsic to science fiction, in many ways a conservative genre despite its futuristic concerns. James Gunn often argues that Tom Godwin's "The Cold Equations" (1954) represents a "touchstone story" for science fiction, since only a person who understands science fiction can appreciate it; and I respectfully disagree, as someone who both understands science fiction and despises that flat, idiotic tale. Instead, I suggest *The High Crusade* is a true touchstone story to determine one's ability to appreciate science fiction. Even the most sophisticated readers of science fiction should be able to enjoy *The High Crusade*, should be moved by its energetic yet somber portrait of simple human attributes overcoming the daunting challenges of a cold, vast universe, and should fall under the spell of Anderson's craft and creativity to root for Sir Roger and his medieval comrades as they fight to conquer the stars. And if readers cannot respond at least fitfully to this intoxicating narrative, the sort of story that Poul Anderson did so well and the sort of story that reverberates so forcefully throughout the genre, then I would argue that they cannot understand science fiction.

# CLAREMONT, CALIFORNIA: NOTES FROM THE HOME FRONT

Well, what other topic could an American possibly write about, a month or so after the events of September 11, 2001?

Although there has been little else on my mind nowadays, I discuss the attacks on the World Trade Center and the Pentagon with great reluctance: it is dangerous to analyze a story before it is finished, and during the weeks between this column's completion and publication, dramatic new developments could make some comments sound laughable, irrelevant, or repugnant. And as an expert of sorts only in the field of science fiction, I freely acknowledge that I am completely unqualified to pontificate on this topic.

I also don't want to criticize others in the science fiction community who have commented on this tragedy, especially those who were close to ground zero; one deals with overwhelming disaster as best one can, and if references to familiar literature help people make it through troubling times, so be it. Still, I was disheartened by repeated observations that the scenes of destruction in New York City were "like science fiction," or "something out of science fiction." Such remarks might be attributed to the common misuse of the term "science fiction" to mean "something strange," or "something that isn't true," or they could stem from occasional images of devastated national landmarks in science fiction films like *Earth vs. the Flying Saucers* (1956) or *Independence Day* (1996). From my perspective, however, the events of September 11 bear little relationship to the central themes and texts of science fiction as I have known it for many years. If there is a literary connection to be made, it involves a related but distinct genre, once known as future-war stories before reemerging under the name of technothrillers.

\* \* \* \*

Almost everyone would agree that the future war story originated with George Tomkyns Chesney's *The Battle of Dorking* (1871), and almost everyone who has actually perused that document would agree that it was an inauspicious beginning. As novels about coming global conflicts proliferated in the decades that followed, they did display certain features that are unquestionably associated with science fiction: they took place in the future, and they usually posited either modest or spectacular new technological innovations to be employed in warfare. However, despite the energetic research of I. F. Clarke and others, these stories were and remain almost entirely forgotten, and not only because they were soon overtaken by events. Rather, to a significant degree, future-war stories were antithetical to the emerging genre of science fiction.

As eventually articulated by John W. Campbell, Jr. in the editorial "Non-Escape Literature" (1959), science fiction is a literature open to the possibility that scientific and social progress will bring far-reaching and fundamental *changes* to the human condition, in contrast to the emphasis on "Eternal Truths" in "main stream literature" (228). Yet future-war stories rarely posit any genuine *changes*: once-weak nations may rise to the status of great powers, and vast arrays of flying machines may unleash unprecedented weapons of mass destruction, but novels otherwise maintain the worldview of Klemens von Metternich, as the elite groups governing various countries keep forging and breaking alliances to gain an advantage or plot new series of advances to quickly defeat an enemy. There are some honorable exceptions, such as H. G. Wells's *The War of the Worlds* (1898), but one could generally define the future-war story as "a story of a past or present conflict somewhat distorted and projected into a flimsily futuristic context" and encounter little dissent.

Campbell also explained in various forums that science fiction was a literature that sought to explore the effects of new technological and social developments on everyday life, offering not stories of isolated inventors creating new devices that are used once and immediately suppressed, but stories of new devices that are fully integrated into human society. Yet the typical innovations of future-war stories were only superscientific *deux ex machinas* that may have turned the tide in a global struggle but otherwise had no effects on ordinary people, and stories characteristically focused only on prime ministers and generals, not citizens and foot soldiers. Future-war stories were therefore less narratives and more narrativized logistics games (which uncoincidentally emerged during the time when future-war stories enjoyed their greatest popularity) with little to say about the coming interactions of society and advanced technology.

The actual horrors of World War I, never predicted in these quaint, sanitized sagas, temporarily dissipated all interest in future-war stories, but after a decade of peace, the field reemerged in the 1930s, with a number of stories appearing in science fiction pulp magazines, like John Taine's *Twelve Eighty-Seven* (1935), and slick magazines, like Fred Allhoff's *Lightning in the Night* (1940). Positing that these stories represent a concealed yearning for renewed warfare after long periods of peace, one might have expected another burst of future-war stories in the 1960s, but the explosion of the atomic bomb irrevocably limited the author's possibilities, as it was now clear that a future conflict along the lines of World War II would immediately destroy most of the planet, a prospect not conducive to lengthy, suspenseful war novels. There could be stories about barely avoiding World War III, like Eugene Burdick and Harvey Wheeler's *Fail-Safe* (1962), or stories about the horrific aftermath of World War III, but World War III itself could not be the subject of a sustained narrative.

As the world evolved strategies to avoid such an all-out war, the literature of future war correspondingly evolved into stories of far-ranging international conflicts that stopped short of all-out war—alternately describing espionage, secret negotiations, covert operations, and scattered skirmishes, all presented as moves in a vast chess game played by powerful enemies reluctant to commit to open warfare. Like future-war stories of the past, these novels typically take place in the near future and feature modest scientific breakthroughs; also like future-war stories, their worldview is conservative, positing an indefinite continuation of current political tensions and moving toward outcomes that bring no meaningful changes to the situation, or to human civilization as a whole. In a concession to the democratic spirit of the times, these technothrillers do strive to incorporate the perspectives of both grunts and generals as the action leapfrogs across the globe, but their similarities to the future-war stories of a century ago are otherwise remarkable.

* * * *

So, I currently feel like I am living in a technothriller, not a science fiction novel. There are periodic outbursts of drama—planes crash into the World Trade Center! Anthrax outbreak in Florida!—amidst a long series of quieter developments all over the world—late-night conferences in the White House and in the hills of Afghanistan; leads investigated in Germany and in California; soldiers moving into place in Uzbekistan and in the Indian Ocean. One can almost envision the terse, geographic chapter headings: Riyadh, Saudi Arabia; Islamabad, Pakistan; Camp David, Maryland. Even the rhetoric emanating from the White House appears designed to prepare Americans to vicariously participate in a technothriller, as we are advised that the conflict will be long and variegated, with initiatives undertaken all over the world, some of them public and some of them secret. Tom Clancy has already appeared as an expert talking head on television, and if officials of the United States Defense Department are finding it helpful to talk to Hollywood writers about possible terrorist threats, they might as well seek out the advice of writers like Clancy and Dale Brown on how to put the pieces together and cope with a multifaceted world struggle.

The trouble with living in a technothriller is that I have never really cared for the genre: I have never been attracted to stories with military trappings or interested in following the parries and thrusts of determined adversaries on the contemporary global stage. More to the point, as a long-time reader of science fiction, I prefer stories that depict major innovations, paradigm shifts, in the human condition; yet the technothriller, like its literary ancestors, is mentally trapped in the past, committed to the indefinite continuation of the status quo. The fact that our newspaper headlines now recall the technothriller is not, as some would have it, a sign that our world has undergone some massive transformation, but rather a sign that our world, for the most part, remains depressingly the same.

That isn't, I know, what the smart people should be saying. Like another commentator that I'm not criticizing, I should be describing the World Trade Center disaster as unmistakable evidence that the world has been turned upside down, that everything in our lives has changed, that none of the old truths hold true anymore—which means (one must assume) that we are now forced to rely upon the guidance of those few gifted visionaries who first recognized and announced the death of the old order. But the argument doesn't bear examination. Arab and Muslim resentment of the Western world? As Osama bin Laden has so thoughtfully explained, that dates back at least eighty years. Organizations dedicated to acts of violent terrorism? These have been active for decades, killing perceived enemies or innocent bystanders with alarming regularity, especially in a few benighted regions of the world. Fears that certain nations—Iraq, China, Syria, even renegade elements in the former Soviet Union—may be covertly assisting terrorist networks? This is only evidence that the Cold War is not really over, that dangerous adversaries remain on the scene, and that even former enemies turned friends cannot yet be fully trusted. Granted, the bombings of September 11 were larger in scope than previous terrorist acts, but not that much larger; several attacks have killed hundreds of people, while this one killed thousands of people—a tenfold increase to be sure, but we are still far from talking about megadeaths.

As evidence that there was nothing significantly new or different about what happened at the World Trade Center, consider the various polemical "explanations" of the event that surfaced almost immediately. Many people instantly displayed an absolute certainty that the attack could be attributed to such things as: the evils of American foreign policy in the Middle East; the dangerous tendency toward fanaticism inherent in the Muslim faith; the just punishment of God for the sin-fulness of modern Americans in tolerating homosexuality and other of-fenses against morality; the natural, inevitable violence and irrationality of the male species. Some of these views were more risible than others, but they all had one thing in common: they had been *rehearsed*. Rather than the surprise, confusion, and incoherence one finds in reactions to truly unprecedented events, these horrific attacks, by and large, served only to trigger tape recorders in people's brains, prefabricated responses nurtured and polished to perfection by many previous occurrences.

(And my own thoughts about these events are not necessarily any better. Having ruminated in the past about the world's failure to change in the manners once foreseen in science fiction, I am naturally inclined to view this disaster as additional evidence to support my views—an observation that interestingly serves to both undermine and buttress my position that this event illustrates a continuation of, not a break from, old patterns.)

* * * *

It is arrogant to assume that reading science fiction makes one an expert on any given situation—because it doesn't. Despite extravagant claims, science fiction does not deal with all aspects of life, all possible situations, and science fiction has done nothing to prepare me for the world we now find ourselves in. And please don't tell me, like yet an-other unnamed and uncriticized commentator, that the problem lies in the genre's incurable optimism. Yes, science fiction did prepare me for a benign world government embarking upon the peaceful colonization of the cosmos, but it also prepared me to live under ruthless, oppressive totalitarian regimes, and it prepared me to painfully stagger through the ruins of a world reduced to ashes by nuclear war. Science fiction prepared me for many different future worlds transformed by scientific and social progress. What science fiction did not prepare me for, and what science fiction cannot account for, is a world that stubbornly remains the same.

So, even as I write, the technothriller continues, with familiar con-flicts and intrigues in various locations throughout the world, which will no doubt eventually lead to a tenuous resolution closely resembling the status quo. And I am reminded that, for all of the triumphs and toys that modern science has brought into our lives, the human race largely remains trapped in patterns of behavior from the past, still divided by nationalities, religions, and cultures. Americans wave their flags, Iraqis burn them; Israelis and Palestinians take turns assassinating political leaders; Protestants and Catholics in Northern Ireland cannot bring themselves to trust each other; Indians and Pakistanis skirmish over

Kashmir. I long to stop reading the newspapers and return to reading science fiction, where the events, whether transcendent or tragic, are at least occasionally novel.

# CELEBRATING A CENTURY OF SCIENCE FICTION COLUMNS WITH A TRIP TO THE MOON

As creatures with ten digits, we attach special importance to powers of ten in counting the years, so the arrival of a new decade, century, or millennium always provokes a hullabaloo. When commemorating other events, however, tenth anniversaries are too common to bother about, while one thousandth anniversaries may involve circumstances too distant in time to arouse concern. One hundredth anniversaries better command our attention.

The twentieth century, unfortunately, gave the science fiction community few causes for centennial observances, with some exceptions. If the western world in 1918 had enjoyed a proper understanding of science fiction, and had not been distracted by the Great War, they might have staged a jolly good celebration for the one hundredth anniversary of the first publication of Mary Shelley's *Frankenstein*. The centennials of the births of Jules Verne (1928), H. Rider Haggard (1956), and Hugo Gernsback (1984) might have been recognized, along with milestones like the one hundredth anniversary of the first use of the term "science fiction" (1951). Only recently have commemorations along these lines actually occurred: utopian scholars feted the one hundredth anniversary of the first publication of Edward Bellamy's *Looking Backward* in 1988, and science fiction conferences were held in honor of the one hundredth anniversaries of the first publications of H. G. Wells's *The Time Machine* (1995) and *The War of the Worlds* (1998).

Yet the twenty-first century, in contrast to the twentieth, will offer innumerable opportunities for centennial observances of important science fiction authors, texts, and events of the twentieth century, the era when the genre developed its distinctive identity, greatly expanded in size and visibility, and emerged as a dominant cultural force. Virtually every year will offer some pretext for celebration: 2012—a century of Tarzan! 2026—a century of science fiction magazines! 2038—a century of Superman! 2056—a century of J. G. Ballard! 2066—a century of *Star Trek*! 2082—a century of *Interzone*! And which celebrations actually take place, and the extent and fervor of those celebrations, will provide early clues about whether certain icons will endure through the ages. For those wondering how Robert A. Heinlein will hold up in Northrop Frye's literary stock market, for example, observing what happens in 2007, the one hundredth anniversary of his birth, should prove revelatory.

Truly, if the twentieth century was The Century of Science Fiction, the twenty-first century will be The Century of Science Fiction Centennials.

Among other effects, this will make life easier for those who write about science fiction on a regular basis. When a deadline approaches and no promising subjects are available, the desperate columnist can simply consult a reference book, find out what happened a hundred years ago, and launch into a retrospective discussion. One could generate a century of science fiction columns in this fashion.

And, as you've guessed by now, I'm about to start the ball rolling.

* * * *

Though I neglected this strategy in 2001, only two missed opportunities come to mind, the one hundredth anniversaries of the first publications of M. P. Shiel's *The Purple Cloud* and H. G. Wells's *The First Men in the Moon*. For 2002, only one topic merits discussion, the one hundredth anniversary of the first science fiction film, Georges Méliès's *Le Voyage dans la Lune* [*A Trip to the Moon*].

On the basis of this film, can we inarguably commemorate "A century of science fiction films"? Objections might be raised. Phil Hardy's *Encyclopedia of Science Fiction Films* (1984) cites some relevant films that preceded *Le Voyage dans la Lune*, though these are brief and inconsequential—like depictions of machines that transform live animals into sausages. After Méliès, critics seeking a first science fiction film with greater length and substance might look longingly at *Metropolis* (1926) or *Things to Come* (1936). And the film that established science fiction as a recognized film genre was undoubtedly *Destination Moon* (1950), which along with its sleazier sister film *Rocketship X-M* (1950) might provide excellent material for the columnist writing in *Interzone* No. 755 (May, 2050).

Despite these quibbles, if science fiction film requires a father figure, Méliès is, for all his shortcomings, the most obvious candidate. In some respects, he invites comparison to another father figure that many wish to forget, Hugo Gernsback: both came from continental Europe, both were fascinated with gadgetry, both appeared to lack vision in their artistry, and both were eventually obliged to retreat from the arena of their greatest success. Yet there are two key differences between them. First, unlike

Gernsback, Méliès was no businessman, and while Gernsback kept profiting from other publications whenever he abandoned science fiction, the collapse of Méliès's filmmaking career drove him into menial jobs and humiliating obscurity. Second, and more tellingly, Gernsback fully recognized what science fiction was and why it was important, while such insights eluded Méliès. It's hard to blame him for this, because in the early 1900s such insights eluded virtually the entire world, including Wells himself, who soon gave up science fiction to fritter away his energies on forgotten projects outside the genre. Still, in any evaluation of Méliès, his failure to understand the special value of science fiction does qualify as a darn shame.

* * * *

Despite what certain websites suggest, one should not attach too much importance to the biographies of famous filmmakers in assessing their works, and it is emphasized far too often that Méliès was originally a stage magician and thus, like a magician, was intent solely upon presenting series of impressive tricks. Yet despite its episodic qualities, *Le Voyage dans la Lune* does project some talent for sustained narrative, and it can be regarded as a shrewd combination of Jules Verne's *From the Earth to the Moon* (1865) and Wells's *The First Men in the Moon*. (Inarguably, then, 2002 at least provides reason to celebrate "A century of Jules Verne and H. G. Wells on film.") Méliès recognized what was most interesting in these novels and took the best of each in constructing his film.

Verne, one might say, was most fascinated by Process—how something gets done, how someone gets from one place to another—and *From the Earth to the Moon* offers an involving account of how scientists in the nineteenth century might have achieved space flight. Upon reaching the goal of this effort, however, Verne falls flat; unable to devise a plausible way for his voyagers to reach the lunar surface, his sequel merely sends them *Round the Moon* (1870) to observe from a distance. Wells, in contrast, was more interested in Product—what has gotten done, what one sees upon arriving at a different place—and *The First Men in the Moon* magically summons up some gravity-defying Cavorite to get explorers to the Moon as quickly as possible, so most of the novel can be devoted to portraying a singular alien civilization. Some argue that Verne's attentiveness to Process makes him the progenitor of hard science fiction, dedicated to scientifically defensible descriptions of what might be done, whereas Wells's attentiveness to Product makes him the progenitor of soft science fiction, concerned more with employing what has been done to achieve literary ends.

*Le Voyage dans la Lune* serves well as the first science fiction film because it focuses on both Process and Product. It borrows from Verne the Process of getting to the Moon, and in the context of an era when films were farcical vignettes, Méliès is reasonably accurate in adapting *From the Earth to the Moon*. Astronomers first discuss the proposed moon launch, complete with a diagram on a blackboard, anticipating many similar scenes in later films about space travel. We observe the projectile for the voyage being constructed by blacksmiths and carpenters, then being moved by comely women into a gigantic cannon for launching. Borrowed from Wells's *The First Men in the Moon*, less faithfully, is the Product of these labors—the landing on the Moon, the discovery of underground aliens resembling apes or birds, and the explorers' successful escape from the aliens and return to Earth. Méliès's film thus foreshadows other films based on Verne and Wells novels: Verne adaptations would be respectful, if sometimes slow-moving, enlivened by female characters added to Verne's all-male casts—like *Around the World in Eighty Days* (1956), *From the Earth to the Moon* (1958), and *Journey to the Center of the Earth* (1959). Wells adaptations would wildly depart from the texts to metamorphose into monster movies—like *The Island of Lost Souls* (1933), *The War of the Worlds* (1953), and *The Time Machine* (1960).

What distinguishes *Le Voyage dans la Lune* from Méliès's other fantastic films—like *Les Quatre Cents Farces du Diable* [*The Merry Frolics of Satan*] (1906) and *A la Conquête du Pôle* [*The Conquest of the Pole*] (1912)—is that it derives a genuine sense of conviction from its sources. We may laugh at the film's touches of humor and fantasy—the astronomers garbed in the star-studded robes of stereotypical astrologers, the projectile attended by bathing beauties and famously poking the eye of the Man in the Moon, the explorers walking on the Moon without spacesuits—but there remains something realistic about its Vernian spacecraft, and something credible about its Wellsian aliens, which accounts for the film's remarkable longevity.

A key moment comes when the exhausted explorers settle down for a nap after landing on the Moon. We observe an obvious dream sequence: above the astronomers' heads materialize the stars of the Big Dipper with women's faces, a goddess perched on the crescent Moon, an old man representing Saturn, and two girls holding a star. These images perfectly reflect the aura of precious, sentimental fantasy found in other silent films about space travel. But *this* voyage to the Moon is *not* a dream: the explorers wake up, enter a cavern, marvel at some giant mushrooms (borrowed from Verne's *Journey to the Center of the Earth*? [1864]), and are attacked by hostile aliens—things that might really happen to humans visiting another world.

Although *Le Voyage dans la Lune* thus decisively steps away from fantasy to follow the path of science fiction, Méliès clearly didn't comprehend his own breakthrough. In 1904, striving to match the success of *Le Voyage dans la Lune*, he employed logic worthy of a contemporary Hollywood executive—I've taken men to the Moon, so why not take them to the Sun? As even that brief synopsis suggests, *Voyage à Travers l'Impossible [An Impossible Voyage]* (1904) is unrelieved silliness, with a train flying into the Sun's mouth as part of an improvisational plot utterly lacking the relative coherence and purposefulness of *Le Voyage dans la Lune*. (In 2004, should we celebrate "A century of bad science fiction film sequels"?) Since the special effects in the two films are equally impressive, they illustrate another important principle long understood by science fiction fans, if not by Hollywood executives: the success of science fiction films depends not on the quality of their special effects, but on the thoughtfulness and integrity of their stories. That is why most great science fiction films, like *Le Voyage dans la Lune*, are based (however tenuously) on science fiction stories and novels, such as *Things to Come*, *The Day the Earth Stood Still* (1951), *2001: A Space Odyssey* (1968), *The Andromeda Strain* (1971), and *Blade Runner* (1982).

What Méliès should have done, then, was to closely base his subsequent films on other science fiction novels of his day—like *The War of the Worlds*, Verne's *Off on a Comet* (1877), or even *Looking Backward*—further developing the embryonic flair for credibly fantastic narrative displayed in *Le Voyage dans la Lune* with scenarios that would also offer opportunities for spectacular illusions. What Méliès actually did was to keep making it up as he went along in countless incohesive films until the maturation of filmmakers around him drove his old-fashioned tableaux out of the theaters.

\* \* \* \*

Still, if Méliès never fully achieved the sort of science fiction film we now admire, his influence can be felt in our era's equivalents of silent films, music videos. Peter Gabriel's "Sledgehammer" (1986), Michael Jackson's "Leave Me Alone" (1989), and Madonna's "Bedtime Story" (1995) are modern short films without dialogue featuring people traveling through strange worlds created with state-of-the-art special effects—precisely what Méliès specialized in and would have greatly appreciated had he survived to see them.

But one video in particular brings this story full circle, the Smashing Pumpkins's "Tonight, Tonight" (1995), an affectionate tribute to Méliès that meticulously recreates the plot and mood of *Le Voyage dans la Lune*: amidst footage of band members performing the song as ethereal be-ings, a man and woman travel to the Moon, confront and disintegrate its strange inhabitants, return to Earth to observe undersea wonders, and are rescued by a ship fittingly named the *S. S. Méliès*. The tremendous popu-larity of this video, MTV's 1996 Video of the Year, indicates just how permanently the images of Méliès's film have been etched upon popular culture, proving that the one-hundredth anniversary of *Le Voyage dans la Lune* is indeed worth celebrating.

# SECTOR GENERAL: THE NEXT GENERATION?

From one perspective, it is entirely appropriate to have a James White Award for short fiction, since White was unquestionably a expert at the form: the early Sector General books that made him popular were assemblages of novelettes, and later novels written for book publication, like *The Galactic Gourmet* (1996) and *Mind Changer* (1998), characteristically took the form of a novella preceded by several vignettes.

Yet White's special talent for short fiction has not been widely acknowledged; instead, his Sector General series gave him the reputation, in the words of blurbmeisters, as "the master of medical science fiction." It is hard to recall another author who so thoroughly dominated a subgenre: in the 1940s and 1950s, there were many science fiction stories about future physicians, including series from L. Ron Hubbard, Murray Leinster, and Joseph A. Winter, M.D., but by the 1960s, White's superior product—a good-natured blend of likable physicians, a huge and variegated space hospital, and a plethora of imaginatively exotic aliens afflicted by strange maladies—had driven away all rivals. Major writers made no effort to compete with White, and minor authors who launched their own series involving space doctors, like Edward Llewellyn, Susan R. Mathews, Jody Lynn Nye, and Sharon Webb, never got anywhere, which is why you haven't heard of their heroes.

Given his triumphs in the area, then, readers unfamiliar with the James White Award might assume it was designed to recognize writers who were best carrying on White's tradition of medical science fiction. And, if such a James White Award had actually been established, there would today be only one strong contender, S. L. Viehl.

\* \* \* \*

For the record, Viehl insists on her website that she had never heard of White until reviewers began comparing her novels to his work, yet the timing of her emergence inevitably suggests a conscious effort to fill the gap left by his absence. In 1999, White died, and the final Sector General novel, *Double Contact*, was published. In January, 2000, Viehl's *StarDoc* appeared, the first in a series of four novels to date featuring, like the Sector General series, a dedicated doctor in a spacefaring future society filled with colorful aliens. Further, while no smoking guns prove Viehl's testimony was inaccurate, some aspects of *StarDoc* debatably imply some awareness of White: the novel's intelligent bacterial plague is not unlike the menace in White's *Final Diagnosis* (1997), and while White featured a kindly alien physician who resembled a giant fly, *Star-Doc* features a kindly alien physician who resembles a giant spider.

More broadly, *StarDoc* invites analysis as a deliberate attempt to update White, to offer a grittier, more contemporary version of the Sector General series. First, although Viehl's biographical statement is coyly vague about her "medical experience" in "military and civilian trauma centers," she surely has had such experience, since her accounts of emergency-room medicine have an aura of authenticity that White never quite mustered. Other transformations of White's template seem ideal for today's more diverse, and more cynical, society. Instead of that bland white male, Dr. Conway, we have a feisty Native American woman, Dr. Cherijo Grey Veil. Instead of the meticulously well-maintained and lavishly well-equipped Sector Twelve General Hospital, we have a seedy, rundown Free Clinic on a newly colonized planet, where doctors make do with antiquated machinery and inadequate supplies. Instead of a benign space federation doing everything in its power to promptly respond to medical emergencies, we have inefficient bureaucracies that are indifferent or inimical to the efforts of medical personnel.

Viehl also is arguably providing a fuller, more accurate portrait of the medical profession than White. In Sector General stories, doctors came only in various shades of saintliness, from moderate to extreme. In *StarDoc*, although the energetic, idealistic Cherijo would make a perfect addition to the Sector General staff, her father, the brilliant but sinister medical researcher Joseph Grey Veil, provides a sharp contrast; first presented only as a cold, domineering parent, Joseph emerges as a futuristic Frankenstein aggressively seeking to regain control of his "daughter" Cherijo, who is actually a genetically engineered clone created as part of his megalomaniacal plot to father a race of superbeings. In the third StarDoc novel, *Endurance* (2001), we encounter another evil physician, the Mengele-like alien SrrokVar, who delights in torturing patients.

Yet villainous, sadistic doctors, despite their conspicuous absence in Sector General stories, hardly represent an innovation in science fiction; Viehl more strikingly includes characters who are simply lousy doctors, going through the motions while unconcerned about whether they are misdiagnosing a patient or providing the wrong treatment. One of Cherijo's colleagues in *StarDoc* is an indolent half-alien who almost kills one patient and takes naps while sick people urgently need assistance; the fourth StarDoc novel, *Shockball* (2001) features a slacker she met in medical school who profits by selling addictive drugs instead of effective medication to poor patients. One could say that in contrast to White, Viehl is confronting all aspects of contemporary medicine—the good, the bad, and the ugly.

In *StarDoc*, Cherijo adjusts to her clinic, makes some interesting friends, and stops a devastating planetary plague which unfortunately kills her new husband, the blue-skinned alien Kao Torin. It is a pleasant, involving novel that seems a promising start to a new series of medical adventures in the Sector General tradition. However, what happens in later StarDoc novels raises serious questions about Viehl's status as White's successor, and about the future of medical science fiction in general.

* * * *

For Cherijo, it turns out, is not simply a skillful surgeon, but also a marvel of future medicine—blessed with remarkably rapid healing powers that provide virtual immortality—and an experiment that Joseph has been unable to duplicate. To get this valuable creation back to his laboratory, Joseph stops kidding around with stern parental messages and arranges to have Cherijo declared "non-sentient" because she is a clone, legally making her his property, and further offers such a huge reward for her capture that innumerable scoundrels are soon hot on her trail. In the second *StarDoc* novel, *Beyond Varallan* (2000), the focus of attention resultingly begins shifting away from Cherijo's efforts to cure the sick to Cherijo's efforts to avoid death or imprisonment. Embraced by the extended clan of her late husband and welcomed aboard their starship, she endeavors to work as a shipboard physician while periodically having her clinic battered by missile attacks or suffering assaults from a mysterious murderer lurking on board.

By the time we get to *Endurance*, Cherijo's increasingly violent and illogical adventures are recalling the Perils of Pauline. Seized by loathsome reptilian aliens, the Hsktskt, Cherijo is officially enslaved and taken to a prison colony, where various contrivances lead her through cycles of alternately heading the prison clinic, spending days in solitary confinement, and being tortured by SrrokVar.

However, it is in the fourth novel, *Shockball*, that her story begins to provoke unintentional giggles. Captured by Joseph, Cherijo and her second husband, telepathic linguist Duncan Reever, are taken to Earth and imprisoned in his impregnable, state-of-the-art home/fortress/laboratory, from which they are promptly abducted by unknown allies. (Later, after Cherijo voluntarily *returns* to the laboratory to seek medical help for her husband, they are *again* effortlessly snatched from this stronghold within one day.) They join a tribe of Native Americans who secretly carry on their traditional lifestyle in underground caverns; but every week, some of these surreptitious savages travel to the surface to be part of a famous professional shockball team, playing that vicious and popular game to hordes of enthusiastic spectators on their way to a world championship game before they slip back into their unknown underground world with no questions asked. Cherijo has been kidnapped because tribal leader and team owner Rico needs a doctor to help conceal the fact that some players are illegal, half-alien hybrids, although how their alien nature would go unnoticed even with medical tomfoolery, and why he chose the world's most conspicuous fugitive for the task instead of bribing some down-and-out doctor, remain unexplained. When the team needs another player, Cherijo's husband is dragooned into uniform and, despite having displayed no previous signs of athletic abilities or knowledge of the game, he immediately becomes the team's new star player, without anyone observing that he is the husband of the world's most conspicuous fugitive. Don't even ask how the five-foot-high Cherijo ends up on the playing field disguised as one of Duncan's muscular male teammates during the climactic game, and did I mention that Rico is also Cherijo's hitherto-unknown brother, which is why he keeps trying to kill her? In the face of such absurdities, even the strongest of wills cannot suspend disbelief.

Even more disturbing than these novels' senselessness are their sadomasochistic elements. It is not simply that Cherijo is more than a little accident-prone, constantly suffering bumps, bruises, and burns that cause her considerable pain, or that she is occasionally brutalized by malevolent experimenters, but rather that she is regularly attacked by men who are close to her, even men whom she loves, whose assaults are implausibly excused after the fact. In *StarDoc*, she is abruptly raped by future husband Duncan—his behavior later revealed as a response to mental commands from the sentient disease controlling his body, although by the end of the rape she was starting to enjoy it anyway. In *Beyond Varallan*, the brother of her late husband undertakes to shield her from harm while at times losing his temper and hurling her across the room—his behavior eventually attributed to drugs slipped into his diet by the shipboard murderer. In *Endurance*, Duncan suddenly appears in the uniform of a Hsktskt officer, revealed as a former friend of those cruel aliens now welcomed into their hierarchy, and in his new role personally wields the laser that painfully burns the mark of a slave into her arm—his behavior excused when Cherijo learns he has also been clandestinely working to free some Hsktskt slaves. In *Shockball*, Rico regularly attacks his sister, once throwing her off a cliff—his behavior finally depicted as a result of syphilis-induced insanity. Viehl can offer all the justifications she likes, but the deep structure of her heroine's life is all too apparent: Cherijo hangs around with men who like to beat her up, and she keeps coming back for more.

Perhaps this can be defended as another aspect of Viehl's expanded commentary on contemporary medicine, an argument that medicine is supremely a discipline of pain, in which doctors regularly inflict pain and have pain inflicted upon them, and thus a discipline naturally attractive to sadists and masochists. However, I suspect that this violence against women stems from a commentary on medicine of a different kind: namely, Viehl's lack of confidence in medical science fiction as a subgenre.

Unlike readers of White's generation, she evidently believes, modern readers won't be satisfied with leisurely-paced stories of human and alien doctors who calmly ingest synthetic steaks and spaghetti in the hospital cafeteria while discussing the mysterious ailment of the porpoise-like alien on level sixteen; instead, they require a doctor who is simultaneously a capable surgeon, invulnerable warrior, and human target, a doctor who must hurriedly squeeze in her operations between bloody fistfights and desperate escapes with occasional pauses for graphic sexual encounters. And who is to say she is incorrect? With four novels in print and a fifth on the way, her StarDoc series has already lasted longer than any other rival to Sector General, suggesting that Viehl may have indeed improved upon White's formula. Then again, White's stately procession of medical mysteries kept his series alive for four decades, and enjoyed its greatest success in the 1990s, whereas Viehl's hyperactive shenanigans, if continued at their current pace, will likely exhaust both their author and their readers well before the year 2040.

\* \* \* \*

At the moment, Cherijo's career seems at a crossroads; *Shockball* ends with the murder of the menacing Joseph, and Cherijo, her husband, and new daughter are returning to space to see old friends and voyage to the homeworld of the alien woman who raised her. Perhaps this means she will be settling into a more sedate existence resembling Dr. Conway's, her life centered more on doctoring than on derring-do as she awaits the shocking-to-all-but-attentive-readers revelation that she is not merely a clone, but a half-alien to boot. But she may simply be resting up before another round of mayhem and melodrama, and if her life ever gets too serene, the purportedly deceased Joseph may again rear his repulsive head. (Science fiction readers should *never* be entirely sure about the permanent death of a character with a demonstrated ability to clone himself.)

While Viehl's fans await news of Cherijo's coming exploits, however, I must confess that I still prefer the old Sector General series to the updated version, and I currently look forward to reading the two Sector General books I haven't gotten around to yet—*Ambulance Ship* (1979) and *Code Blue: Emergency* (1987)—far more than I look forward to reading another StarDoc novel.

# WHY SCIENCE FICTION FEARS THE FUTURE

When science fiction writers address the general public, they magnificently create. When they address each other, they magnificently complain.

Over the years, I have listened in on some gripe sessions, and jeremiads regarding the woeful plight of the working science fiction writer regularly surface in professional publications. The horrific particulars inspiring the protests vary, but the overview is always the same.

Once upon a time, wise and considerate editors, committed to the highest ideals of science fiction, sought out and nurtured the most talented young writers, caring little about their early profitability as they allowed them to enhance their skills and molded them into polished, productive, and esteemed pillars of the genre. Contracts were fair and relationships were genial, as authors, agents, editors, and publishers all worked cooperatively for their mutual benefit.

Today, however, a plague has descended upon the publishing industry. Soulless accountants who know nothing about science fiction rule the roost, and sales figures are the sole determinants of success; regardless of your book's quality, if not enough copies sell, you are exiled from the industry, forever barred from offering your suspect wares to the public. Instead of being encouraged to create masterpieces, writers are pressured to fritter away their talents on formulaic regurgitations of popular television programs or novelizations of computer games. Advances are down, contracts are canceled on a moment's notice, double-dealings are endemic, and profiteers continually conspire to reduce the income and stature of writers in new and even more outrageous fashions. Things are bad, and they are getting worse and worse all the time.

In response to these laments, there are only two things to say: this picture is largely accurate, and there is nothing anyone can do about it.

\* \* \* \*

With apologies to Peter Graham, who opined that "The golden age of science fiction is twelve," one might offer this general advice to science fiction writers:

The golden age of being a science fiction writer is twelve years before you started your career.

Deal with it.

Instead of constantly complaining, writers might pause to feel blessed, since they are living in somebody's else golden age. It's sad but true: pondering a devastating e-mail message or reading some shocking news in a trade publication, a writer today might justifiably think that this is the final blow, this is the last straw; in terms of any sort of respect or dignity in the profession of writing, this field has absolutely hit rock bottom. Yet if today's writer endures a while longer, the day will surely come when some neophyte tells her, "But you had it easy—you were writing back in 2002," or "Gee, I wish things could be like they were back in 2002." I'm not kidding; the historical record, which I have some experience in examining, demonstrates that writers in the 1960s waxed nostalgic about the 1950s, writers in the 1970s waxed nostalgic about the 1960s, and so on, consistently maintaining the pattern of discerning a veritable writer's paradise a decade or so in the past. Again, the lyrics keep changing—remember when you could make a living by publishing stories in the magazines? remember when publishers maintained a backlist? remember when there wasn't any internet piracy?—but the song remains the same.

This is not, as some would-be rescuers of science fiction would have it, a problem caused by an influx of stupid and duplicitous figures into the publishing industry, a state of affairs readily corrected by installing smart and honest people, like those making these complaints, in positions of authority. To be sure, there are simpletons and scoundrels aplenty in publishing, but it is not Pollyannish to note that companies rarely stay in business long without displaying, at least sporadically, a modicum of intelligence and integrity. And these traits remain in evidence more in publishing than in other provinces of the entertainment industry, such as those producing films and rock music.

* * * *

The problem facing publishers is basic and intractable. First, in the last fifty years, there has been an astounding, exponential increase in the numbers of genuinely talented and committed science fiction authors. Second, during that time, there has been substantially less than an exponential increase in the numbers of devoted science fiction readers. Publishers cannot afford to publish all the writers who deserve to be published, because there aren't enough customers to purchase their books. They require some system to weed out writers so that they only publish enough books to meet the demand.

The tool they have chosen for this task is the bottom line: you sell enough books, and you publish another one; you don't sell enough books, and you're out of luck. Some find this shortsighted; don't publishers understand that they need to give authors time to find their voices, to build an audience of loyal readers, in order to develop dependable brand names for their books? Don't they see they are setting themselves up for future disaster, when established stars fade away and they have cultivated no suitable replacements? Yet today, the answer is no, publishers *don't* need to give new authors time to grow, because gifted writers are like buses— there's always another one coming along. Publishers can afford to keep throwing talent away because new talent is always available; they can keep tossing new writers onto bookstore shelves until they hit upon a winner. Publishers in the 1980s didn't need to squander resources on a bunch of promising unknowns, hoping one might eventually become the next William Gibson; they just kept trying out new models, and sure enough, there materialized Neal Stephenson.

I'm not saying the system is fair. Of course, books can have disappointing sales for reasons that have nothing to do with their quality, such as terrible timing, abominable cover art, non-existent promotion, and flawed distribution, and writers can expound at length on how they have been victimized by all of the above and more. But publishers don't require a fair system—they require a functioning system. And going by the bottom line functions perfectly well as a selection process.

To be frank, I even suspect that this new, much-criticized system might have a few advantages over the old, much-idealized system, inasmuch as people forget that all those lucky writers being nurtured by paternal publishers were not necessarily the best and the brightest. I was once on the panel with a noted writer when the question on the floor was how to find an agent; he replied that he had found an agent while playing a game of poker with some New York professionals who happened to be his friends. Today, at least, promising writers find it easier to get their foot in the door without being part of the old boys' network, even if their tenure inside the threshold is frustratingly brief.

\* \* \* \*

One shouldn't trivialize the trauma that many writers are experiencing. Rejection hurts, and rejection after a period of apparent success hurts even more. Here you are, with a few published novels under your belt; you're thinking about future projects, new directions you might move in, new challenges you might undertake; and you're suddenly told that you have officially been branded Box Office Poison and you'll never publish another novel as long as you live. That's depressing news, it's happened to talented friends of mine, and it's more than a darn shame; it's a special sort of all-encompassing, aching pain, a sense that someone has irrevocably lost something precious, the feeling powerfully conveyed by a tearful Marlon Brando in *On the Waterfront* (1954): "I coulda been a contender."

Yet there are consolations to be had for washed-up science fiction novelists. With a reputation of sorts, you can still publish stories in magazines and anthologies; you can submit books to small presses; you can swallow your pride and accept assignments to write *Buffy the Vampire Slayer* books or Young Adult novels; you can try relaunching your career in another genre or under a pseudonym. Even if such prospects are unpalatable and unworkable, you still live with the knowledge that your books remain on the shelves of thousands of libraries and personal collections, that they are forever enshrined in Bill Contento's meticulous bibliographies. For the rest of your life, you can attend science fiction conventions, serve on panels, enjoy being in the spotlight again, and talk to people who remember your work—"Oh yeah, you wrote the *StarRat* novels."

I also think it inappropriate to draw too much public attention to the sufferings of writers. People want the clown to make them laugh; they don't want to hear about the clown's personal problems. People want science fiction writers to entertain and inspire them, not to demand their sympathy. Barry N. Malzberg once published a novel, *Herovit's World* (1973) about how miserable it was to be a science fiction writer, and while I personally think it was his best novel—sparkling, hilarious, and deeply unsettling—it did not seem to do much for his career.

I bring this topic up in *Interzone* only because it may be relevant to another complaint about science fiction more directly important to readers.

\* \* \* \*

Science fiction, this other lament goes, was once an uplifting, forward-looking literature that expressed a strong belief in the power of individuals to shape and control their futures, a confidence that humanity could eventually overcome its problems and achieve a glorious destiny in the stars. It was a literature of expansive energy and boundless possibilities. Today, however, science fiction has largely lost these desirable qualities; its most admired and most discussed stories seem cramped and gloomy, pessimistic fables of helpless people crushed by oppressive conditions or barely surviving, with happiness to be found only in revisiting or contemplating past glories. Judith Berman's "Science Fiction without the Future" (2001) offered an unusually well-documented discussion of how frequently contemporary science fiction stories are grounded in nostalgia for the past rather than hopes for the future, but charges that science fiction somehow isn't what it used to be have a long history, dating back—interestingly—at least to the 1960s, the same time when writers started bemoaning the sorry states of their career.

Allow me to advance a general, explanatory hypothesis: that the evolving essence, the *zeitgeist*, of any form of literature will always be directly related to its economic and social status at the time. If yesterday's spy thrillers have grown into today's grander, global technothrillers, that is because the field has garnered more respect and increasing sales; if contemporary poetry seems anemic, insular, and self-involved, that is because its audience and market share have precipitously dwindled. In the case of science fiction, prior to the 1960s, writers could accurately see themselves as boats in a rising tide, contributors to a field of literature constantly expanding in terms of income and influence, attracting more and more dedicated readers. Payment rates kept climbing, new markets (the slick magazines, hardcover and paperback books, films, television, comic books) kept opening up, everything seemed to be getting better and better. In such a milieu, it was only natural to write science fiction stories about confident, capable heroes creating marvelous new inventions, improving society, and conquering the universe; in a real sense, such narratives were metaphors for what the field of science fiction itself was accomplishing.

By the 1960s, however, the Big Crunch had begun: the magazine market dramatically and permanently shrank, book publishers reduced production, and film, television, and comics were becoming closed shops uninterested in recruiting print authors. For the first time, many writers and editors found themselves making less money instead of more money. And what happened next? The cynical, downbeat New Wave, uncoincidentally championed by a magazine perpetually on the verge of economic extinction. Since that era, while the science fiction market did start expanding again and generating more income, most of the money wasn't going into the pockets of writers, as a fortunate wealthy few were far outnumbered by others of equal talents being driven out of the game or forced into serfdom.

And that must have an impact on the stories being written. When you're a science fiction writer struggling to survive on an unexpectedly miserly advance who has just heard that the production run of your next novel has been slashed, probably guaranteeing lousy sales and a decision to cancel the rest of your four-book contract, it's hard to come up with boundlessly optimistic sagas of triumphant humanity in a technologically advanced future. Rather, as you feel yourself being shoved out of publishing your own major novels into less lucrative netherworlds of shared-world anthologies, small presses, and franchised-universe products, you are much more likely to produce depressing tales of poor schnooks destroyed by the system or nostalgic fantasies focused on the Good Old Days.

So, for those seeking the sorts of youthfully energetic and heartening stories that once characterized science fiction, the only advice may be to start playing video and computer games, where such narrative qualities are to be found in excess. After all, the creators of these games, unlike today's science fiction writers, are infused with the comforting knowledge that they are part of a field with a glorious future.

# THE HISTORY OF HEINLEIN'S FUTURE

If recruited to join a panel at a science fiction convention on Robert A. Heinlein's predictions in the article entitled "Where To?" or "Pandora's Box," a logical person would find any convenient copy—say, a paperback edition of *Expanded Universe: The New Worlds of Robert A. Heinlein* (1980)—and bring it along. One member of such a panel at the 2002 Westercon did precisely that. But the panel organizers also invited someone with a Ph.D. in English literature, and such persons may approach their assignments differently.

I knew that, unusually for a piece of Heinlein's nonfiction, the article had been published five times and that, unusually for anything by Heinlein, it had twice undergone major revisions. Its publishing history was apparently epitomized in the ragged amalgam of three versions in *Expanded Universe*, but I wanted to look at the original documents.

Soon, at the J. Lloyd Eaton Collection of Science Fiction and Fantasy Literature at the University of California, Riverside, I was examining its first appearance in the February, 1952 issue of *Galaxy*, its republication in Martin Greenberg's 1955 anthology *All About the Future*, the first revision in the 1966 collection *The Worlds of Robert A. Heinlein*, the "preview" appearance of the second revision in the Summer, 1980 issue of *Destinies*, and the official debut of the second revision in *Expanded Universe* later that year. The last two versions are identical, but the others interestingly diverge, in ways both announced and unannounced. Thus, I found a story to tell, one that conveys something about Robert A. Heinlein's character and relationships with editors, but also offers lessons about the perils of authorial prophecy.

First, a textual issue to address: in 1966, Heinlein announced he was including the article in its original "unchanged" form, yet there are numerous differences between that text and the one that first appeared in *Galaxy*. As will be discussed, the differences can be logically attributed to *Galaxy* editor H. L. Gold, so one assumes Heinlein was republishing in 1966 the version he had written in 1950. Therefore, the text embedded in the 1966 version qualifies as the "original" text, while the 1952 article is the second, "corrupted" text—a sequence of dates perfectly suited to an author who delighted in time travel paradoxes. (Note: parenthetical page numbers for quotations from the four major versions will be prefaced by the dates "1966," for the 1950 version not published until 1966 and the additions made in 1966; "1952"; "1955"; and "1980.")

\* \* \* \*

*1950.* Of course, Robert A. Heinlein was not foolish enough to spontaneously sit down and start typing some predictions for no particular reason; as he notes in passages added to the 1966 version, science fiction writers are in the business of entertainment, not prophecy. However, in the late 1940s, Heinlein was struggling to break into as many new markets as possible, and when *Cosmopolitan* approached him about writing an article about life in the year 2000, he wasn't going to turn them down.

The assignment posed a dilemma for Heinlein: should he tell the presumably unadventurous female readers of *Cosmopolitan* what he *really* thought the future would be like, in all its catastrophic, mind-blowing glory, or should he provide a bland, domestic vision of tomorrow more suitable for housewives—a 1939 New York World's Fair exhibit of "the Kitchen of the Future" in prose? In a September 24, 1949 letter to his agent, Lurton Blasingame, Heinlein ponders the problem: "If *Cosmopolitan* thinks my record of accomplished predictions is good enough to warrant it, then… I'll make some serious predictions that will make their hair stand on end. If they want to play safe, I'll do an Inquiring Reporter job and we'll limit it to what the specialists are willing to say" (*Grumbles from the Grave* 150). Evidently getting no signals as to what *Cosmopolitan* preferred, he decided to play it safe and took both approaches, offering first an introductory narrative describing a mildly futuristic home of 2000, then a scattershot list of bolder prophecies representing his genuine expectations.

As usually occurs when one tries to please everyone, the resulting article qualifies as a mistake, destined to please no one: readers anxious to be transported to exotic tomorrows must endure dull portrayals of advanced household appliances before disappointingly underdeveloped glimpses of more exciting futures, while readers who were perfectly content in the kitchen of the future's "Mrs. Middleclass" are rudely chastised for embracing such "*timid* prophecy" (1966 13, 18) before Heinlein shifts gears. Another sign of its mixed messages was the inappropriate title he chose, "Pandora's Box," which would suggest a generally gloomy prognosis ending with a burst of optimism; yet the actual article is precisely the opposite, a mostly cheery picture of future life that lurches into the gloom-and-doom, how-to-survive-the-coming-apocalypse tone of mid-1940s Heinlein in the final paragraphs. If Heinlein had chosen one strategy and run with it, *Cosmopolitan* may have accepted the result;

but they wisely rejected this self-consuming artifact, this prophecy that deconstructs itself.

\* \* \* \*

*1952.* So, Heinlein's article fell into the hands of Gold, the editor notorious for rewriting authors' prose to deadening, disastrous effect. Yet this impression is supported almost entirely by complaints from offended writers—including Heinlein himself, who described Gold as a "copy messer-upper" (*Grumbles* 163) after observing his handiwork on *The Puppet Masters* (1951) and extracted a promise from Gold to henceforth leave Heinlein's prose "inviolate" (*Grumbles* 165). But writers can be unduly sensitive about editorial alterations (hello, David and Paul!). In the case of "Where To?," we have copies of a text Before Gold and After Gold, enabling us to judge the merits of his editing for ourselves.

One can garner evidence that Gold, charmingly labeled a "run-of-the-mill hack" (*Grumbles* 163) by Heinlein, indeed had a tin ear for prose style. Even after infuriating his prize contributor, Gold could not resist making minor changes: Heinlein's "when you have sniffed at her for not doing so" (1966 14) became "when you have *disapproved of her not doing so*" (1952 14), and Heinlein's "they offer us hope in every other field" (1966 22) becomes "they offer *impetus to* every other field" (1952 21). Gold also had the irksome habit of adding unnecessary explanations and qualifications, weighing down Heinlein's crisp declarations with pedestrian clutter. Consider these Heinlein predictions, with Gold's additions italicized:

> 1. Interplanetary travel is waiting at your front door—C.O.D. It's yours when you pay for it, *which the government is doing at least on an experimental basis.* (1952 19)
>
> 5. In fifteen years the housing shortage will be solved by a "breakthrough" into new technology which will make every house now standing as obsolete as privies. *The housing* [intervening passage inserted by printing error] *shortage will get worse until then.* (1952 19)
>
> 20. Fish and yeast will become our principle sources of proteins. Beef will be a luxury; lamb and mutton will disappear, *because sheep destroy grazing land.* (1952 20)

Does anyone find these additions salutary? But my favorite example of Gold's inept tinkering has to be:

> Intelligent life *of some sort* will be found on Mars. (1952 19)

This addition is presumably designed to cover Heinlein's bet in case, say, the equivalents of chimpanzees are discovered on Mars.

There was also one act of outrageous editorial interference: to Heinlein's list of "things we *won't* get soon, if ever" (1966 21), Gold adds an item of his own:

*Control of telepathy and other E.S.P. phenomena.* (1952 20)

Gold is working in a dig at editorial competitor John W. Campbell, Jr., then vigorously promoting "psi" powers in every issue of *Astounding Science Fiction*; yet doing so by adding language to another writer's article (particularly one who was reasonably open-minded regarding the prospects of harnessing psychic powers) seems beyond the pale.

Still, there were virtues in Gold's rendering of Heinlein. Considering the predominantly male readership of *Galaxy*, he properly edits passages too clearly aimed at female readers, removing the sentence where the reader is referenced as "Duchess" (1966 17) and revising a paragraph about the desire of "a woman" (1966 15) for an improved appearance to consistently refer to "a man or a woman" (1952 15). One also develops an appreciation for his blue pencil when it is simply used to cross sentences out. Heinlein's concluding paragraphs, as he desperately seeks a cohesive ending to this incohesive article, are all over the map—earnest, flippant, despairing, chipper—and Gold shrewdly omits some of the most discordant sentences.

When Heinlein attempts to get serious about the chances for future war, it hardly helps to exclaim parenthetically, "It might even end with a war with Mars, God save the mark!" (1966 24). When Heinlein waxes poetic about the stormy days ahead, he falls flat: "Today the clouds obscure the sky and the wind that overturns the world is sighing in the distance" (1966 24). When Heinlein seeks to belatedly justify his title, he struggles to achieve eloquence: "The last thing to come fluttering out of Pandora's box was hope—without which men die" (1966 24). Gold deleted these sentences, and even if he was primarily trying to keep the article from bleeding on to another page, their absence is welcome.

Further, Heinlein ends the article abruptly: "Long after the first star ship leaves for parts unknown, there will still be outhouses in upstate New York, there will still be steers in Texas, and—no doubt—the English will still stop for tea" (1966 24-25). I can't speak for every reader, but this doesn't sound much like a conclusion to me. Gold recognizes the problem and adds a final, two-word paragraph: "Stick around" (1952 22)—not a scintillating conclusion, but better than no conclusions at all.

Overall, Gold may not be much of a writer, but considered as an *editor*—someone who shortens and shapes others' prose—he does pretty well with a flawed piece of writing. Purists will scream, but given the choice of which version of the article to republish, I'd choose Gold's version every time.

\* \* \* \*

*1955.* When "Where To?" reappeared in *All about the Future*, it didn't change much—editors of anthologies rarely change much—except for a word added here and punctuation altered there. Yet one thing is worth mentioning. *Galaxy* accidentally inverted two passages at the start of Heinlein's list, so the text jumps from the word "wonder" in the middle of his original introductory "axiom"—"A 'nine-day wonder' is taken as a matter of course on the tenth day" (1966 page number)—to the middle of the second prediction—"of disease is revising relations" (1952 18-19)—and continues until, in the middle of the fifth prediction, the first axiom resumes. Since Gold ended the fifth item with "The housing shortage will get worse until then," the result was to accidentally create the sentence, "The housing is taken as a matter of course on the tenth day" (1952 19). Yet readers can see something is amiss with the text and figure out what went wrong. In the 1955 version, the problem of the juxtaposed passages is entirely corrected—except the new sentence is retained to conclude the fifth item (20), with no surrounding material to suggest an error has occurred.

Thus, a new prediction has been inadvertently but unambiguously placed in Heinlein's mouth, that a new system of house-building will enable a person to order a new house and obtain it ten days later—precisely the sort of revolutionary "breakthrough" in mass-produced housing that he had in mind.

\* \* \* \*

*1966.* In 1965, realizing he had enough reasonably good uncollected stories for one more collection, Heinlein was planning *The Worlds of Robert A. Heinlein* with Donald A. Wollheim of Ace Books, who requested an updated version of "Where To?" Still attentive to editorial requests at this stage in his career, Heinlein agreed, but recognized that the original article was essentially beyond repair. Instead, he opted to republish his manuscript in its original form—on the stated grounds that he did not wish to "conceal my bloopers" (1966 12)—and surrounded it with new passages contextualizing and revisiting his original predictions. Also, by mentioning all of the stories in the collection during his introductory remarks, the expanded piece could do double-duty as the introduction.

Still angry about Gold's justifiable decision to retitle the article "Where To?", Heinlein revives "Pandora's Box" as the lengthened version's title and defiantly begins and ends the wraparound material with new references to Pandora's Box, though it is still dysfunctional as a unifying theme. After discussing predictions in relation to his stories, he segues into the original article, explaining that "a science fiction writer should avoid marihuana, prophecy, and time payments—but I was tempted by a soft rustle" (1966 12). (Of paper money? Of the skirts of *Cosmopolitan*'s female readers?) Later, he adds endnotes to 13 of the original 19 predictions as well as some final remarks, including his famous declaration that "Man...is mean, ornery, cantankerous, illogical, emotional—and amazingly hard to kill" (1966 30).

Heinlein's new comments are generally calm, if sometimes grouchy, but an ominous note emerges when he explains why a prediction of new house-building techniques proved incorrect: "I underestimated (through wishful thinking) the power of human stupidity—a fault fatal to prophecy" (1966 27). It is as if Heinlein was adding, after the fact, a qualification to the original predictions: "these things will come true *if people are as intelligent and enlightened as I am*." But genuine prophecy must take into account human resistance to change, economic realities, and similar factors, and inaccurate prognosticators cannot explain away their failures by complaining that citizens simply weren't farsighted and judicious enough to do what they should have done.

The larger problem is that the premise underlying the original article—that one properly extrapolates the future of humanity as a rising parabola leading to ever-accelerating scientific and social progress—isn't valid. Throughout history, the curves of human advancement have unpredictably risen, flattened, and fallen, and if we haven't quite maintained the pace of the first half of the twentieth century, that doesn't necessarily mean that humanity has suddenly fallen into ignorance, irresponsibility, and depravity. But I anticipate the argument that emerges more clearly in the 1980 version of Heinlein's article.

\* \* \* \*

*1980.* By the late 1970s, there was a new editor at Ace Books, Jim Baen, eager to assemble a new, larger version of *The Worlds of Robert A. Heinlein*. Far from seeking to edit Heinlein's prose, Baen wanted as much of it as he could possibly get—so much so that he recorded long phone conversations with the Great Man and transcribed the results to serve as lengthy introductions and afterwords to pieces in the collection. The equally voluminous additions to "Pandora's Box," however, seem more a product of Heinlein's typewriter than his voice.

Readers are again assured that the language of "Where To?" was reproduced exactly as originally written, and one would assume the material added for "Pandora's Box" was also reproduced exactly as written. But it wasn't, though most changes involve trivial matters of spelling, punctuation, and capitalization. Language referring to times of composition, potentially confusing in a piece combining prose from three different eras, is reworked for clarity; an awkward 1950 phrase—"nor is the pool chill" (1966 15)—is revised to "and the pool is not chilly" (1980 319); a 1966 sentence praising Frank Herbert's *Dune* (1965) is removed.

A few changes, however, interestingly reflect a punctilious concern for the niceties of English grammar. A rhetorical flourish from 1950—"there will be no security anywhere, save what you dig out of your own inner spirit" (1966 24)—is revised to the more formal "save *that which* you dig out" (1980 350). "Just," often criticized as a superfluous, slangy qualifier, is removed from the 1966 comment, "I'll hedge number eighteen just a little" (1966 28). A parenthetical "hopefully!" in 1966 (26), improperly used to mean "I hope," is changed to "I hope!" (1980 329). Elsewhere in *Expanded Universe*, Heinlein offers a lengthy condemnation of the appalling writing skills of students at the University of California; he can hardly allow himself to be observed writing in any manner not sanctioned by the highest authorities.

More conspicuous, of course, are huge chunks of new prose preceded by "1980" and, unlike the 1965 additions, shoved right into the middle of the article (where the 1965 additions are also relocated). (There is also an added "poem," entitled "Where To?" [315], combining lines about the sparrow building a nest in the spout with heavy-handed complaints about building inspectors.) This time, Heinlein adds commentaries to all 19 predictions, and if anyone is keeping score, Heinlein seems to be gloating about 4 or 5 predictions that were coming true while feeling a need to explain why he has not been vindicated in other cases. (In 2002, the scoring would be more generous—7 out of 19 correct.) With these lengthy interruptions, sometimes several pages in length, the limited charm of the original article is all but dissipated.

In an especially annoying passage, Heinlein addresses the problem of humanity's failure to explore the solar system as he projected. This is ridiculous, he asserts; why, all we need is a spaceship with constant acceleration, and we could travel anywhere in the solar system in weeks, if not days. This is an accurate but not especially helpful observation, given the technological and economic difficulties of constructing such spaceships—not unlike saying, "If scientists would just figure out how to make pixie dust, we could all fly to Mars without spaceships." Yet it remains a suggestive observation that an advocate of space exploration might defensibly present.

Yet Heinlein is not content to merely present the observation. He orders readers to pick up their calculators; he tells them what formulas to employ and which figures to insert; he insists that they punch out the calculations *themselves*, to be persuaded *beyond any doubt* that Heinlein is correct; and in case they make any mistakes, he provides the answers in a later section of the book. Heinlein has become the person we all wish to avoid at parties, who corners victims and browbeats them on some point until they meekly acknowledge he is completely correct.

Reading such diatribes, it becomes painfully clear why writers should not try to predict the future:

1. You will probably be dead wrong;

2. You will then feel obliged to explain why you were wrong; and

3. Given the choice of saying either "I was stupid" or "The whole world was stupid," you are lamentably likely to opt for the latter explanation, which is questionable and unpersuasive but less destructive to your ego.

That is, acknowledging our largely suspended conquest of space, Heinlein theoretically might have said, "I predicted that in 2000 couples would stroll along the beach watching the first interstellar starship leave Earth orbit; J. G. Ballard predicted that in 2000 couples would stroll along the beach staring at rusting remnants of abandoned rockets; and I must admit that I was wrong and Ballard was right." But it would be difficult to say such things, and it's only to be expected that Heinlein would instead argue that our unforeseen lack of progress is an anomaly created by political idiocy and bureaucratic short-sightedness.

* * * *

There is another lesson here for professional writers: do not always write what editors ask you to write, and do not always publish what you have written. Tempted by *Cosmopolitan*, Heinlein devoted considerable time to researching and writing an article he knew that he shouldn't have attempted, and on two later occasions he devoted considerable time to efforts to revise and improve the defective product of his labors—time he might have spent writing new stories more worthy of analysis. Clearly, Heinlein would have been better off if he had never written "Where To?," or if he had never published it. Every time he bothered with it, he lost his way, straying from his strengths into profitless fidgeting.

Now, as the world begins the process of deciding which Heinlein works to remember and which ones to forget, "Where To?"/"Pandora's Box" is manifestly destined for the latter list, to be read only by future scholars with an obsessive interest in the minutiae of twentieth-century science fiction. And that is the only prediction of the future that I care to make.

# THE END OF SCIENCE FICTION'S CHILDHOOD

To judge by some recent e-mail messages, some people out there seem to believe that I am an expert on children's science fiction.

I suppose this is not entirely irrational; after all, I wrote a book entitled *Science Fiction, Children's Literature, and Popular Culture* (2000) and co-edited a book entitled *Nursery Realms: Children in the Worlds of Science Fiction, Fantasy, and Horror* (1999). Further research would uncover other publications on topics related to children's science fiction, including an essay entitled "The Genre That Evolved: On Science Fiction as Children's Literature." Confronted with such evidence, it seems, I would be obliged to confess to some degree of knowledgeability in this area.

Even if tempted by egoboo or filthy lucre to do precisely that, however, I cannot honestly portray myself as an expert on children's science fiction. At best, I might admit to some awareness of what children's science fiction *used to be*, but not what it *is*.

\* \* \* \*

A note on terminology: books for younger readers are commonly divided into three categories for three age groups: "picture books," for ages 0-through-5, featuring elaborate illustrations with captions to be read aloud by adults; "middle school books," for ages 6-through-10, combining lengthier texts for developmental readers with copious illustrations; and "young adult books," for ages 11-through-15, short novels with occasional illustrations. When speaking of "children's science fiction," I will be primarily thinking about science fiction for young adults, the category usually receiving the most attention.

The reason for my chronologically limited knowledge of children's science fiction might be stated this way: when it emerged as a distinct publishing label in the 1950s and 1960s, children's science fiction was primarily a subcategory of science fiction, so I became familiar with it as a science fiction reader and scholar. Today, children's science fiction is primarily a subcategory of children's literature, and hence it rarely comes to my attention.

This shift in classification can be deduced by observing the ways that libraries—American libraries at least—once shelved, and now shelf, their fiction. In the 1950s and 1960s, there was almost invariably a science fiction section—albeit a small one—where children's science fiction was shelved alongside adult science fiction. In one place, young readers could find Robert A. Heinlein's juvenile *Red Planet* (1949) and his adult collection *Revolt in 2100* (1953) right next to each other. Today, libraries put children's science fiction in their children's section, intermingled with other children's books, so that juvenile science fiction and adult science fiction are far apart. Similar patterns of organization are found in the other place where today's youth find their reading material, the chain bookstores.

The old system made sense, given where children's science fiction used to come from. Entering the 1950s, the publishers of children's literature faced a predicament: they had become aware of the existence of science fiction, they recognized there was a young audience clamoring for it, but they didn't really understand what it was, and the authors they usually relied on weren't prepared to tackle this new form of writing. So, publishers had to approach adult science fiction writers and hire them to write for younger readers. Heinlein famously produced a series of juveniles for an editor at Scribner's who was alternately baffled and appalled by his products but obliged to publish them due to their tremendous sales. The Winston juveniles recruited noted authors like Poul Anderson, Arthur C. Clarke, Lester del Rey, Chad Oliver, Jack Vance, and Donald A. Wollheim. Andre Norton proved popular with both younger and older readers for her numerous science fiction juveniles. Isaac Asimov, transparently disguised as "Paul French," chronicled the exploits of heroic Lucky Starr, while Wollheim related the adventures of young astronaut Mike Mars.

However, while science fiction writers were regularly employed to write for children in the 1950s and early 1960s, the market soon shriveled, for various reasons. The children of the Baby Boom were maturing into rebellious hippies, and not as many children were coming along to replace them, resulting in a general contraction of the children's market. Science fiction authors had unwisely focused too much on near-future stories about the conquest of space that were rapidly overtaken by events; once Yuri Gagarin and John Glenn had actually orbited the Earth, it was hard to muster enthusiasm for fictional accounts of Mike Mars or Tom Swift, Jr. doing the same thing. Moreover, even younger readers, absorbing NASA propaganda about the experienced test pilots with the Right Stuff serving as astronauts, could realistically discern that plucky teenagers with good connections were not going to play a role in exploring space. (To this day, the only person within shouting distance of adolescence even considered as astronaut material, boy band singer Lance Bass, had been asked to fork over 20 million dollars for the privilege.) As one illustration of the overall shrinkage in the market, the bibliography of Karen Sands and Marietta Frank's *Back in the Spaceship Again: Juvenile Science Fiction Series Since 1945* (1999) reveals that the numbers of new science fiction series, plentiful in the 1950s, plummeted in the 1960s and 1970s.

The major problem, however, was that American publishers of children's literature in the 1960s confronted dilemmas far graver than devising ways to maintain the viability of the children's science fiction market. Having perfected formulas for safe, palatable stories that celebrated white maleness and the absolute perfection of all things American, they now struggled to generate new forms of fiction that responded to the newly voiced concerns of women and minority groups, new forms of fiction that would take a more jaundiced look at America's past and present. The entire field of children's literature needed to be revamped, reworked, and updated to match the sensibilities of a revolutionary new era, and with those important tasks at hand, publishers allowed the field of children's science fiction to stagnate.

During that decade, though, science fiction was becoming more prominent in the media of film and television, and the burgeoning popularity of *Star Trek* reruns in the 1970s, followed by the astounding success of *Star Wars* (1977), alerted publishers to the fact that there were vast new profits to be made in children's science fiction. But this time, there was no need to make phone calls to veteran science fiction writers. The new generation of children's writers already knew what science fiction was, having watched *Star Trek* and *Star Wars*. Correctly or not, they felt perfectly well prepared to write science fiction, if that was what their publishers wanted. So, instead of importing science fiction writers, children's literature began to develop its own—writers like Bruce Coville, H. M. Hoover, William Sleator, Alfred Slote, and others that adult science fiction readers may have never heard of.

I read several of their books as part of my catholic research into the literature of space stations, and I found some were very good, while others were less estimable. To a seasoned science fiction reader, however, they seemed bland mixtures of familiar tropes that provided colorful new backgrounds for timeless tales of teenage angst. They recalled S. E. Hinton more than Robert A. Heinlein, and hence they appeared to be a form of science fiction beyond my expertise.

* * * *

Described in this fashion, the decoupling of science fiction and children's literature can be attributed to a series of unrelated events—demographic shifts, poor authorial decision-making, and significant social changes. But one can also describe this development as a story of abandonment.

Up to this point, I have been ignoring the fact that, well before publishers like Scribner's and Winston transformed children's science fiction into a recognized category of hardcover literature, there were innumerable science fiction books and stories aimed at younger readers—like the Frank Reade, Jr. dime novels, the Great Marvel series, the original Tom Swift series, and Carl Claudy's stories for *American Boy* magazine—even if these were rarely welcomed into libraries. More broadly, many science fiction works ostensibly for adult readers were increasingly being aimed at adolescents. Jules Verne's novels were viciously bowdlerized in translation to eliminate his politics and satire, leaving only exciting adventures for the young. The pulp magazines where science fiction achieved its generic identity quickly abandoned editorial pretensions of a broad audience and frankly targeted precocious boys with devices ranging from offers of science kits for subscribers to covers featuring buxom beauties in brass brassières. "Adult" science fiction writers could easily adapt to writing children's science fiction in the 1950s, one might argue, because they had in a sense always been writing for children.

Things began to change in the 1950s, when H. L. Gold's first editorial for *Galaxy* magazine was entitled "For Adults Only" and another new magazine, Anthony Boucher and J. Francis McComas's *The Magazine of Fantasy and Science Fiction*, deliberately set out to publish science fiction that was mature, respectable literature. Science fiction now wished to be taken seriously, and to many that meant that science fiction needed to sever its connections to children and write exclusively and conspicuously for adults. The New Wave of the 1960s took this goal even more seriously, as writers produced works featuring graphic sex, four-letter words, convoluted experimental prose, and other devices designed to exclude young readers as a matter of definition.

There was nothing to *prevent* science fiction writers in the 1960s and thereafter from continuing to write for children, even if the market was contracting and publishers were less receptive, and a few of them did—as evidenced by Ben Bova's Exiles trilogy in the early 1970s and by striking juveniles from Richard A. Lupoff and Vonda N. McIntyre in the early 1980s. But most writers simply weren't interested. While Heinlein could have continued to write and profit from juveniles like *Podkayne of Mars* (1963), he didn't want to; he preferred to focus on producing books that were longer, more experimental, and more adult.

The works of other major writers, while variegated in their approaches, reflected similar ambitions.

Thus, in its aggressive pursuit of adult readers, science fiction had effectively abandoned the children's market. When there developed a renewed interest in children's science fiction, then, publishers found it not only possible, but even necessary, to recruit an entirely new cadre of writers to produce it. And, if these writers weren't exactly attentive to the traditional principles and priorities underlying science fiction, that was only to be expected.

* * * *

By the 1990s, a number of factors—the visible profitability of the children's market, the ongoing vicissitudes of the adult market, the perceived aging of the science fiction readership—inspired some to lament the genre's longstanding neglect of the young and to take corrective action. They resolved to undo the past, to again recruit science fiction writers to write for children and provide young readers with the best talent available, to effectively produce Winston juveniles for a new generation. Tor Books created the Jupiter Novels for younger readers, with six books by Charles Sheffield, Jerry Pournelle, and James P. Hogan, while Avon Books launched David Brin's Out of Time series, with three novels by Roger McBride Allen, Sheila Finch, and Nancy Kress. While these particular series were evidently unsuccessful, with no new items appearing in recent years, Tor has soldiered on with additional juveniles by David Gerrold and John Barnes, though these also appear to be garnering little attention and disappointing sales.

To explain why any sorts of science fiction books fail to find an audience, one can always call in the usual suspects—inept marketing, inadequate promotion, poor distribution, and the like. Realistically, however, the cited initiatives were probably doomed from the start, even under the best of circumstances. Decades ago, when the genre of science fiction was young, it could naturally appeal to the young without deliberate effort, because its then-dominant themes of space travel, fabulous new inventions, and unlimited progress were by their very nature exciting, youthful dreams. Today, with its sense of confidence in those old dreams all but shattered, the genre can only hesitantly seek to compete against legions of professional children's writers vastly more experienced in appealing to the young. In the face of their slick confections about alien teachers and Young Jedi Knights, it seems obvious in retrospect that recycled 1950s juveniles about troubled teens in space, like James P. Hogan's *Outward Bound* (1999), weren't going to achieve massive popularity. Still, struggling writers of all varieties often seek refuge in replicating the patterns of previous successes, and this should inspire sympathy more than reprobation. Sheffield's and Brin's hearts were in the right place, even if their products seemed a bit stale.

Anyone can articulate what is needed: fresh, imaginative, vigorous science fiction for younger readers that will relegate the formulaic fodder of the children's science fiction industry to the remainder tables and recruit hordes of new fans to the genre. But whether the old dog of science fiction can teach itself such new tricks remains an open question, and this aging non-expert on early children's science fiction can offer no suggestions.

# RULES FOR ROBOTS: VERSION 1.0

In the Holy Bible of science fiction, Olaf Stapledon's novel *Star Maker* (1930) is the Book of Revelation, Robert A. Heinlein's song "The Green Hills of Earth" (1947) is the Twenty-Third Psalm, and Isaac Asimov's Three Laws of Robotics are the Ten Commandments.

Given our peculiar fascination with *laws*—which are continually reexamined and reinterpreted in light of new contexts and situations—Asimov's Laws have predictably received a disproportionate amount of attention, both inside and outside the science fiction community. In later stories by Asimov himself, authorized sequels to his works, and unofficial homages, the Laws have been examined, played with, and expanded. Experts in robotics have published articles on possible applications of the Laws to the creation of artificial intelligence. Discussions of the Three Laws permeate the internet.

Despite evidence of great interest, no one to my knowledge has examined how the Three Laws gradually achieved their final form—their legislative history, as it were—perhaps because no one realized they had ever been different. For in all publications of Asimov's robot stories and novels since 1950, the wording of the Three Laws has always been precisely the same, replicating the version presented as the frontispiece of the first edition of Asimov's first collection of robot stories, *I, Robot* (1950):

> 1. A robot may not injure a human being, or, through inaction, allow a human being to come to harm.
>
> 2. A robot must obey the orders given it by human beings except where such orders would conflict with the First Law.
>
> 3. A robot must protect its own existence as long as such protection does not conflict with the First or Second Law. ([7])

However, in the pages of *Astounding Science-Fiction* where eight of the stories in *I, Robot* originally appeared, one finds Asimov expressing the Laws in various ways, in passages that were removed and replaced with the canonical text when the stories were revised for book publication. True, these provisional versions are not strikingly dissimilar, but they cumulatively provide an illuminating paper trail of the issues in contents and phrasing that Asimov faced in developing precisely the right language to express the Laws.

* * * *

For the first text of the Laws of Robotics, unavailable in *Astounding*, we must rely upon the after-the-fact testimony of the only person who heard them enunciated.

On December 23, 1940, Asimov visited John W. Campbell, Jr., editor of *Astounding*, to discuss his idea for a story about a mind-reading robot, later written and published as "Liar!" (1941). During that conversation, as Asimov reported in *In Memory Yet Green*, Campbell commented,

> "Look, Asimov, in working this out, you have to realize that there are three rules that robots have to follow. In the first place, they can't do any harm to human beings; in the second place, they have to obey orders without doing harm; in the third, they have to protect themselves without doing harm or proving disobedient." (286)

They weren't elegantly phrased, but that was never Campbell's forté. The question is: if the Laws first came out of Campbell's mouth, did he invent them? Since Asimov probably had already developed the key idea of "Liar!"—a robot disobeying orders to tell the truth in order to avoid hurting people's feelings—he might legitimately take credit for at least envisioning the first two Laws. However, nothing in "Liar!" or the robot stories before it—"Robbie" (1939) and "Reason" (1941)—contain any intimation of the Third Law, which thus can be attributed exclusively to Campbell. From one perspective, this is merely paradoxical: the young, insecure Asimov focused entirely on imposing human values and priorities on his subservient population of robots, while the older, overbearing Campbell was giving robots some backbone by granting them a drive for self-preservation.

On the other hand, one might criticize the mindset that led Campbell to concoct the Third Law. After all, if one considers western civilization's major code of behavior, the Ten Commandments, in the context of Asimov's Laws, the first five Commandments relate to the essence of the Second Law, obedience—to either God (worship no other gods, make no graven images, do not take the Lord's name in vain, keep the Sabbath) or one's parents (honor your father and mother). The other Commandments relate to the essence of the First Law, altruism (do not kill, commit adultery, steal, lie, or covet what your neighbor has). There is nothing in the Ten Commandments about a moral imperative to protect your own ass, yet Campbell elevates this selfish concern to almost the same level as altruism and obedience. (In Campbell's defense, though, one might argue that robots require this Law, lacking a biological instinct for self-preservation, or that writers require this Law, to better generate conflicts between robots and humans.)

\* \* \* \*

The First Law was introduced in a conversation between robot psychologist Dr. Susan Calvin and two colleagues in "Liar!":

> She faced them and spoke wearily. "You know the fundamental law impressed upon the positronic brains of all robots, of course."
> The other two nodded together. "Certainly," said Bogert. "On no conditions is a human being to be injured in any way, even when such injury is directly ordered by another human."
> "How nicely put," sneered Calvin. (53)

This rendering of the First Law is in the passive voice ("not to be injured," "is ordered"), a stylistic infelicity common to novice writers and certainly a weak way to communicate the idea. But at this stage, the exact language of the Law was not important, as indicated by Calvin's reply that it was "nicely put." Here, Asimov envisions the Law as an instruction, symbolically embedded in robot brains, that is not equivalent to any particular sequence of English words; one might express that Law in any fashion that comes to mind. Only later will the Laws take the form of specific language in the *Handbook of Robotics* that is memorized and recited by all roboticists. Imbuing the Laws with such *gravitas* demanded a sense of self-confidence that the young Asimov did not yet possess.

\* \* \* \*

The "three fundamental Rules of Robotics—the three rules that are built most deeply into a robot's positronic brain" debuted in their entirety in the fourth robot story, "Runaround" (*Astounding*, March, 1942), during a conversation between Gregory Powell and Mike Donovan, Asimov's traveling robot overseers:

> "One: a robot may not injure a human being under any conditions—and, as a corollary, must not permit a human being to be injured because of inaction on his part."
> "Right!"

"Two," continued Powell, "a robot must follow all orders given by qualified human beings as long as they do not conflict with Rule 1."

"Right!"

"Three: a robot must protect his own existence, as long as that does not conflict with Rules 1 and 2." (100)

This is close to the final version, with certain exceptions. At this moment, Asimov prefers to think of these principles only as "Rules," created by individuals to control games, perhaps because he does not yet feel comfortable about proclaiming grander and more imposing "Laws," created by governments to control nations. The term "corollary" too overtly communicates his advanced education in mathematics and science. He thoughtlessly genders the robot as male, then grammatically permissible, but creating a loophole for a homicidal female-gendered robot who could let humans die because it would not constitute "inaction on *his* part." And note that the Second Law demands obedience only to *qualified* human beings, without clarifying precisely what qualifies humans to command robots. This problematic stipulation would eventually be dropped, engendering worries in later stories about powerful robots controlled by four-year-olds or lunatics.

* * * *

The next robot story, "Catch That Rabbit" (*Astounding*, February, 1944), only offers another version of "the First Law of Robotics: that a robot may not injure a human being or, through inaction, allow a human being to be injured" (165). The story additionally contains the first reference to the "Handbook of Robotics" (160) later established as the official source of the Laws.

In "Escape" (first published as "Paradoxical Escape," *Astounding*, August, 1945), all three of "the Robotic Laws" make their second appearance, though Asimov endeavors to express them as tersely as possible:

Robertson slurred them out rapidly. "One: A robot may not, by action, or through inaction, harm a human being. Two: A robot must obey orders given by authorized human personnel, except where this would conflict with Rule One. Three: A robot must protect its own existence except where this would conflict with Rules One and Two." (81)

The concise rewording doesn't really work for the First Law—how might a robot actively "harm" "through inaction"?—but Asimov has at least settled upon "it" as the proper pronoun for robots, and the Second Law's revised phrase "authorized human personnel" is a tad more precise, implying that some sort of employment "authorizes" humans to control robots.

* * * *

By the time one gets to "Evidence" (*Astounding*, September, 1946), "the three Rules of Robotics" are being described as "the famous bold print on page one of the 'Handbook of Robotics'" (129), and Asimov is visibly striving to encapsulate them in a tightly structured and dignified fashion:

> [Calvin] spoke them carefully, clearly ....
> "Rule One: A robot may not harm, nor, by inaction, cause to be harmed, any human being.
> "Rule Two: A robot must obey all orders given it by authorized personnel, except where these would conflict with Rule One.
> "Rule Three: A robot must preserve its own safety, except where that would conflict with Rules One and Two." (129)

He is still fumbling the ball in striving for a nice rhetorical balance in the two parts of the First Law (this is also a story about Asimov's evolving skills as a prose stylist); the omission of "human" from the Second Law might raise concerns (are all "personnel" necessarily persons?); and broadening the Third Law to prioritize "safety," rather than "existence," would potentially lead to robots unable to leave their homes and cross the street because of the minuscule but genuine threat to their "safety" such a move would create. Wisely, Asimov would quickly revert to "existence."

What is more intriguing about "Evidence" is that Asimov is not merely using his Laws to generate clever stories; he is visibly *thinking* about his Laws. Calvin comments, for example, that "if you stop to think of it, the three Rules of robotics are the essential guiding principles of a good many of the world's ethical systems" (129), suggesting Asimov's understanding that his Laws, far from innovative, are better regarded as adaptations of widely accepted moral values. He is further discovering inherent complications in the First Law, fittingly emerging in connection with the first Asimov robot who is also a lawyer.

A district attorney is suspected (correctly) of being a robot, but the question arises: how could a robot oversee a system that necessarily injures certain humans—accused criminals—by imprisoning or even killing them? In response, Calvin describes a robot who must kill a single person to save the lives of several people; it is in the position "of having broken Rule One to adhere to Rule One in a higher sense .... He protects the greater number and thus adheres to Rule One at maximum poten-[t]ial" (130). Similarly, if the robot attorney knows that his work is beneficial to large numbers of law-abiding citizens, he can justify actions that harm a few lawbreakers. This sense of a First Law "in a higher sense" or "at maximum potential" will eventually coalesce into the Zeroth Law of Asimov's *Robots and Empire* (1985): "the prevention of harm to human beings in groups and to humanity as a whole comes before the prevention of harm to any specific individual" (463).

\* \* \* \*

"Little Lost Robot" (*Astounding*, March, 1947) offers the First Law in its almost definitive form—"*No robot may harm a human being, or through inaction, allow a human being to come to harm*"—though the negative seems misplaced: "No robot may harm" as opposed to "A robot may not harm" (114). The story also demonstrates that the second part of the Law, seemingly a legalistic afterthought, is actually the more powerful injunction. When, as in this story, robots are built with only a truncated version of the Law—"*No robot may harm a human being*" (114)—the danger is created, as Calvin explains, that a robot could let go of a heavy object, watch it fall and crush a human, and argue that the force of gravity, not the robot, did the harm.

In the story, Asimov offers only succinct summations of the other two Laws: "the Second Law of obedience" and "the Third Law of self-preservation" accompany "the First Law of human safety" (124). Perhaps, as Asimov's reputation and stature were growing, he now felt comfortable referring to his principles as "Laws" and, recognizing that they were becoming familiar to the readers of *Astounding*, he no longer thought it necessary to state them in full every time.

The last robot story in *I, Robot*, "The Evitable Conflict" (*Astounding*, June, 1950), appeared only months before the book, so one would expect to find canonical versions of the Laws. Surprisingly, Asimov is still toying with his language: "the First Law of Robotics" is rendered here as "No robot may harm a human being; nor, through inaction, may he allow one to come to harm" (51). "The Second Law is as follows: 'All robots must obey the orders of all qualified human beings as long as these orders do not conflict with the First Law.' The Third Law states: 'All robots must protect their own existence as long as such protection does not conflict with the First and Second Laws'" (53).

Notice, throughout this history, that the First Law has been most frequently mentioned, and most frequently tinkered with. Understandably, this is the Law that people are most attentive to, because it is the Law that protects their own asses. In revisiting it this time, unfortunately, Asimov has been not only clumsy, but ungrammatical; since the "he" of the second part must refer back to "No robot," the second phrase translates to "no robot may not allow one to come to harm," a double negative meaning that any robot must allow a human to come to harm. In establishing Laws for beings that now include lawyers, such sloppiness in language is inexcusable. Also, the robot has somehow become a "he" again, a problem Asimov presumably recognized and immediately addressed by violating parallel structure and shifting to plural forms ("robots...their") for the Second and Third Laws.

More significantly, when Calvin describes the actions of the advanced robot intelligences known as the Machines who "work not for any single human being, but for all humanity," Asimov has her develop and articulate a preliminary version of the Zeroth Law: "No Machine may harm Humanity; nor, through inaction, may he allow Humanity to come to harm" (67). In retrospect, then, no one should have been surprised by the official unveiling of the Zeroth Law in *Robots and Empire*.

* * * *

In settling upon the canonical language introduced in *I, Robot*, and making one later addition, did Asimov achieve a perfect version of the Laws? Almost, I would say. At the level of copyediting, my personal preferences, to maximize the parallelism and aura of logical precision, would be to have the First Law use "harm" twice instead of "injure"; to change the "where" in the Second Law to "when"; and to revise the Third Law to more closely mimic the Second: "except when such protection would conflict with the First or Second Law." More globally, I might mention potential conflicts involving the Third Law that are parallel to the conflicts Calvin discerned in the First Law: it would seem desirable for a robot to sacrifice its own existence to preserve the existence of forty robots, but the Third Law as written would not permit such self-sacrifice. Perhaps the Third Law could be subdivided to prioritize the existence of robots in groups or robotry as a whole over the existence of individual robots ....

But this game can go on and on, as web-surfing will reveal, leading to more and more refinements and expansions of the Laws that eventually seem frivolous and finicky. We might be better advised to embrace the Laws as Asimov left them to us, for he worked harder than people realize to whip them into shape—and in light of their lengthy tenure and continuing prominence, one cannot say that his efforts were wasted.

# WHO DIDN'T KILL HORROR

The genres of science fiction, fantasy, and horror, unlike the genre of detective fiction, rarely focus on the process of solving a murder. Perhaps that is why people in the field are not very good at it.

The homicide under investigation here is the much-discussed "death of horror" that occurred in the 1990s: a robust, expanding category of literature abruptly and precipitously shrank in dimensions and almost vanished from sight. Publishers dropped their horror lines, bookstores removed their horror sections, magazines and small presses collapsed, and major authors couldn't get their novels into print. Battered survivors of the holocaust surveyed the scene of the crime and began to search for the perpetrators. And likely suspects were not difficult to find: terrible writers and opportunistic publishers.

Robert Weinberg, in *Horror of the 20th Century* (2000), outlines what became the standard theory of the crime:

> When horror sold well, too many companies took sales figures as evidence that anything published with the word horror in the title would sell .... Bookstore racks were filled with tasteless, poorly written horror novels that should never have been printed .... Mediocre books squeezed the good novels off the shelves and when customers stopped buying the mediocre novels, there was nothing left to sell. Horror fiction wasn't killed in the mid-1990s. The field committed suicide. (243)

In a 2002 interview cited by Paula Guran in her article for Locus Online, "Tribal Stand," Dan Simmons became one of many to echo the same argument:

> Horror solved its ghetto problem through the simple act of destroying its own genre—greedy publishers, sloppy editors and lazy writers producing so much junk and in such quantities that "Gresham's Law" kicked into effect. The bad drove out the good. Then the whole genre imploded.

It seems a plausible solution to the mystery, and one envisions the good horror writers, in the role of upstanding police inspectors, slipping the handcuffs on the accused criminals—bad writers and their partners in crime, bad publishers. However, like other snap judgments rendered in the opening pages of detective stories, there is something suspicious about the whole scenario, providing an opening for a more astute detective to probe deeper and poke some holes in the official theory.

* * * *

One might explain doubts about the theory's validity in this fashion. If you accuse someone of committing a crime, you are necessarily asserting that the same person could have prevented the crime; if Colonel Mustard killed the victim in the ballroom with the candlestick, he could have kept the victim alive by declining to wield the candlestick in that locale. If talentless writers and unscrupulous publishers killed horror, they could have kept it alive by doing something differently.

So, how could horror have been saved? All across America, incompetent writers should have said to themselves, "Well, I can see that writers might make lot of money by writing horror, but honestly, the horror I'm writing or could write isn't very good. So, to ensure the long-term survival of the genre, I must resolve to stay away from horror and instead exercise my meager talents in fields where there is less money to be made."

And all across America, avaricious publishers should have said to themselves, "Well, I can see that publishers might make a lot of money by publishing horror, but honestly, the stuff I have on hand or could attract isn't very good. So, to ensure the long-term survival of the genre, I must resolve to not publish horror and instead publish other forms of fiction which are less likely to be profitable."

The only question to ask is: and on what planet were these decisions supposed to have occurred?

The "crime" said to have been committed here is a normal, natural response to a common situation. *Of course*, when a genre becomes successful, hordes of inept writers will rush into the field in search of income; *of course*, when a genre becomes successful, hordes of publishers will flood the market with whatever examples of the genre they can lay their hands on, no matter how inferior they are. To rail against the people who do these things is silly; it is railing against the entire capitalist system, railing against human nature itself.

And such a normal, natural response to a common situation *cannot*, simply cannot, destroy a literary genre. If it could, then every literary genre that ever garnered popularity would be swiftly driven to extinction. And this hasn't occurred.

Consider some precedents. In the 1950s, the noteworthy success of a new publishing category, science fiction, led undiscriminating publishers to put out novels by some pretty bad writers—works like Stanley Mullen's *Kinsmen of the Dragon* (1951), Jerry Sohl's *Point Ultimate* (1955), and Allen A. Adler's *Mach 1: A Story of Planet Ionus* (1957)—that are remembered today only because Damon Knight so delightfully eviscerated them in reviews reprinted in his *In Search of Wonder* (1956). In the 1970s, the newly prominent and profitable genre of heroic fantasy again engendered innumerable atrocities, such as the various trilogies and Robert E. Howard pastiches churned out by Andrew J. Offutt that are now read only by people who are paid to read them (as I was when I was commissioned to epitomize Offutt's career for a reference book). Please note, however, that these execrable effluences did not kill science fiction, and they did not kill fantasy; the markets may have contracted a bit after the booms, as markets invariably do, but both genres endured their Invasions from Mediocrity and have retained a wide audience.

There is no "Gresham's Law" of literature; bad novels do not drive out the good ones; the appearance of many awful books in a genre cannot destroy that genre. It can be proven by example after example.

We reach the moment in the story where the astute detective confronts the less-than-astute police inspector and announces that the accused persons could not have committed the crime—there were no bullets in their guns! Lousy writers and imprudent publishers did not have the ability to kill horror. One might properly criticize them for many reasons, but they are not, they cannot be, guilty of this particular crime.

\* \* \* \*

So, if armies of inept writers and stupid publishers didn't kill horror, who is actually the criminal here? I was afraid you were going to ask that question, and I've already confessed to representing a field that isn't especially adept in solving crimes. So, I might respond to the question by taking refuge in two explanations rarely found in detective fiction but often invoked in official death certificates: "unknown causes" and "natural causes."

Unknown causes? The factors that govern the popularity of literary genres are multifarious and, despite abundant research on the part of publishers and others, still poorly understood. The phenomenon involves so many variables as to be governed by chaos theory and hence may be beyond rational explanation. Certain types of writing sometimes sell very well and sometimes sell poorly; the fluctuations may be mild, and they may be extreme. One might confront the issue of "who killed horror?" simply by stating that during the 1980s, for some unknowable reason, horror became successful, and during the 1990s, for some unknowable reason, horror suddenly became unsuccessful.

Still, in forensic medicine and in literary criticism, "unknown causes" is always the last resort. We are the pattern-seeking animals, and we don't wish to concede that certain situations resist the imposition of explanatory patterns.

We are left, then, with the possibility of "natural causes." Literary genres can die naturally, even at an early age, if they are not properly nourished and supported. There is nothing inevitable in the growth of a child to robust adulthood, and nothing inevitable in the growth of a fledgling genre into a fixture of the publishing scene. For a time, horror writers may have been victimized by a sense of entitlement: science fiction got big in the 1950s, fantasy got big in the 1970s, and now, in the 1990s, it was manifestly horror's turn. So to correspond to the Science Fiction and Fantasy Writers of America, you establish the Horror Writers of America, and to correspond to the World Science Fiction Conventions and World Fantasy Conventions, you establish the World Horror Conventions, and you await your destined elevation to a coequal status.

But it takes hard work to keep a genre vibrant and expanding; in book publishing, there's a particular need for dynamic, insightful editors who can attract good works, package them well, and articulate their virtues in introductions and promotional material. The growth of science fiction in the 1950s owed much to editors like Donald A. Wollheim and Ian and Betty Ballantine, just as the growth of fantasy in the 1970s owed much to editors like Lin Carter and Judy-Lynn del Rey. Who were the heroic editors of horror? Names like Charles L. Grant and Ellen Datlow come to mind, but perhaps they lacked the frenzied fanaticism, the single-minded devotion to a genre, that distinguished their science fiction and fantasy predecessors.

Still, this line of thought leads back to reckless allegations, with editors now accused not of improvident overproduction but of lazy or inadequate promotion; and, quite possibly, not even the most herculean of labors could have kept the patient alive.

Continuing to consider natural causes, we are driven to dark and disturbing suppositions. Perhaps, there is something about the genre of horror that is inherently contrary to modern sensibilities. Perhaps, horror is a form of narrative, like westerns, pirate stories, and jungle adventures, that is by its nature becoming outdated, a problem that cannot be solved by superficial transformations to accommodate contemporary sensibilities—such as putting vampires on motorcycles or maximizing the gross-out factor. Perhaps, with certain exceptions, horror is a genre that fewer and fewer contemporary readers will appreciate, and its short-lived popularity was only a bizarre aberration, a fad comparable to hula hoops and pet rocks that could not endure. Perhaps, therefore, it was only natural that horror died in the 1990s, and it was an event that could not have been avoided or postponed by suppressing its weaker practitioners or developing more judicious publication strategies.

* * * *

It is never pleasant to ponder the possibility that one's favorite category of literature, the genre one has devoted a lifetime to, might be destined to shrink and fade away. I have entertained such speculations about science fiction: since its growth was fueled largely by a mono-myth of humanity conquering space which has now been invalidated, its writers may now be left to hopelessly present the tired old dream to unresponsive audiences or to squander their talents in crafting alternate histories and other frivolities. Commentators on fantasy can similarly wax pessimistic regarding the long-term prospects of a genre constantly on the verge of trapping itself in the stultifying cul-de-sac of Tolkien pastiches. And yet, envisioning the imminent demise of one's genre can be stimulating and productive, as it might inspire writers to do some soul-searching, envision new avenues, push the envelopes, forge into virgin territories. Certainly, the much-heralded "revival" of hard science fiction stems from writers who are scouring the technical journals looking for some experimental finding or new theory that might inspire stories fundamentally different from the stories that science fiction has been telling for decades; certainly, authors like China Miéville are visibly searching for new approaches to fantasy. Thoughtful lamentations about the impending demise of a literary genre, paradoxically, might bring new life to the form.

Horror, it seems, is working hard to avoid this sort of reflective introspection, preferring instead to deal with its problems by finger-pointing and name-calling. Guran's essay for Locus Online was spectacularly venomous in labeling the past and present horror writers not meeting her high standards as "hacks," "bottom-feeders," "lemmings," "wannabes," and "mud-whiners." Perhaps there is something about these people that is genuinely irritable; I cannot say, having had little exposure to their fiction and their commentaries. But to return to the point made earlier, bad writers cannot kill, cannot even damage, a form of writing. To say that they can is to assign them too much power, to elevate them to a level of significance that they do not deserve, to feed the inflated egos that Guran so passionately complains about. Further, while people who find themselves in troubling times may find it comforting to locate and castigate alleged villains, such activities serve only to slander innocent people and avoid productive engagement with the real sources of the problem.

So, in confronting what happened to horror, we arrive at a conclusion rarely observed in the literature of detective fiction: the detective eliminates all the obvious suspects and announces to the interested parties, "Something much more complicated than a simple murder is going on here, so we must launch a thoroughgoing investigation of the various factors that might have contributed to the victim's death." In sum, determining who—if anybody—killed horror does not demand the services of police officers or detectives to find a perpetrator; instead, it requires a doctor of forensic medicine who is prepared to conduct an extensive autopsy and diligently search for the true cause or causes of death. On the basis of my cursory examinations, such a figure in the field of horror has not yet emerged.

# IN SEARCH OF DISMAL SCIENCE FICTION

Many Americans today are preoccupied with matters of economics. The governments of their states face massive budget deficits and, unlike the federal government, they are legally required to maintain balanced budgets. So, there will have to be either large tax increases or (as is more probable) huge cuts in government expenditures. In California, gloomy contingency plans are being prepared to lay off large numbers of government employees, including the faculty and staff of its public colleges and universities. My own day job is reasonably secure, but some friends and colleagues may not be so lucky.

What does this have to do with science fiction? Not very much at all—and therein lies the problem.

\* \* \* \*

In ancient times, humans were very much controlled by natural cycles. First there were droughts, then floods; first hot spells, then cold spells. People could do little more than enjoy the good times and endure the bad times as best they could. Indeed, despite the learned analyses of historians regarding the reasons why various civilizations rose and fell, plausible arguments have been advanced that such developments can largely be attributed to the climate: cultures thrive when the weather is favorable and decline when it is adverse.

Gradually, people have devised numerous ways to cope with these cyclical changes—dams, irrigation channels, new methods of food storage, warmer clothing, better shelters, wiser management of resources. A desire to be protected against adverse environmental conditions has been a powerful engine driving scientific progress, and science fiction has contributed its own suggested improvements, ranging from the ubiquitous glass domes shielding futuristic cities from the elements to the precise control of Earth's weather described in Theodore L. Thomas's classic story "The Weather Man" (1962). And humanity can claim some success in immunizing itself against the effects of Earth's constantly changing climate; disastrous weather conditions of both short and long duration continue to occur, but victims suffer much less than their ancestors did.

However, with the rise of civilization came the market economy and a new sort of cyclical change—economic booms and busts, heady prosperity followed by crushing depression. And though there have also been noteworthy initiatives to support citizens during lean periods, humanity in general still seems much less capable of ameliorating the effects of economic uncertainty. This is paradoxical, for no other discipline has been so obsessively dedicated to crafting mechanisms to predict the future in order to anticipate and deal with economic problems. Yet within the subdiscipline of econometrics, it remains the case that complex mathematical models capable of providing accurate projections about 60% of the time are viewed as tremendous successes, even though results only slighter better than a coin toss are unlikely to be helpful for planning purposes. This explains why even the smartest and most experienced economic experts are regularly surprised by sudden downturns, like those now occurring throughout America. One might assume that the literature of science fiction, another field concerned with the future, would be contributing its own ideas about effective new ways to control the economy, just as it has contributed ideas about effective new ways to control the weather.

In actuality, while the separate tradition of utopian fiction often dealt in detail with the perfected economies of ideal societies, science fiction stories have rarely touched upon economic issues. Of course, there are exceptions; one can locate economic debates, and ideas about posited economic innovations, in the works of authors like Robert A. Heinlein, Poul Anderson, and Frederik Pohl. But the only author who made economics his special interest was Mack Reynolds, who frequently described alternate economic systems on alien worlds or in the future, as in his two sequels to Edward Bellamy's *Looking Backward*, *Looking Backward from the Year 2000* (1973) and *Equality in the Year 2000* (1977). And in his late novel *Trojan Orbit* (1985), completed by Dean Ing, Reynolds presented a devastating critique of plans to construct massive space habitats, based largely on economic arguments.

But overall, science fiction has ignored economics. As support for this claim, one might turn to Brian Stableford's threadbare essay on "Economics" in Peter Nicholls's 1979 *The Science Fiction Encyclopedia*, since all this knowledgeable commentator can find to discuss is some utopias, several stories from the pulps, and the aforementioned four authors. The minimally revised version for John Clute and Nicholls's 1993 *The Encyclopedia of Science Fiction* adds only some comments about recent libertarian science fiction, though its concerns tend to be more political than economic. And in a 2003 essay, Gregory Benford notes in passing that "economics is seldom treated well in sf" ("Stephen Baxter's *Riding the Rock* in Context" 13).

As Reynolds demonstrates, economics might represent a rich, and largely unexplored, field for science fiction writers. And if, as Hugo Gernsback once argued, the imaginative scientific concepts introduced in science fiction might serve as constructive stimuli for scientists and inventors, the imaginative economic concepts introduced in science fiction might similarly be of practical value to today's economic theorists and policymakers, such as the California bureaucrats and politicians now struggling to cope with an unexpected budgetary shortfall.

\* \* \* \*

Unfortunately, instead of examining economics, science fiction more typically seeks to *erase* economics. In the future, many stories suggest, it won't be an issue at all; soaring scientific progress will, in effect, eliminate economics as an aspect of human society, since new technologies will make it so cheap to produce goods that anything resembling a market economy will no longer be necessary. Such expectations have long been associated with projections of the future; some may recall, for example, that according to the original advocates of nuclear power plants, nuclear energy would be so inexpensive that companies would not bother to meter its use. Pohl even wrote a story, "The Midas Plague" (1954), predicting that ongoing advances in technology would create such a problem of cheap overproduction that poorer citizens would be forced to engage in constant unwanted consumption in order to avoid disruptive surpluses.

This contempt for economics as a sort of temporary expedient to cope with our currently inadequate methods of production then became a cornerstone of the future world of *Star Trek*. As one ground rule for the original series, Gene Roddenberry stipulated that no citizen of the Federations of Planets would ever use money for anything; all necessary food and material goods could be instantly created by convenient "synthesizers" at no cost to anyone. Economics was entirely eliminated from future societies, except on certain backward planets, like the world visited in the episode "A Piece of the Action" (1968). This underlying principle was made explicit in the film *Star Trek IV: The Voyage Home* (1986), which included this humorous exchange when Captain Kirk is unable to pay for dinner in a twentieth-century restaurant:

> Gillian Taylor: Don't tell me you don't use money in the
> 23rd Century.
> Captain Kirk: Well, we don't.

Later, Roddenberry developed a kinder, gentler future for the successor series *Star Trek: The Next Generation*, and having resolved to eliminate all violence along with other infelicities like alcohol consumption and swearing, he knew he could not employ as regular opponents the vicious Klingons and Romulans. Instead, he created new, nonviolent villains, the Ferengi, who caused problems for the Federation because they were maniacally avaricious. People concerned with monetary matters in Roddenberry's universe, then, were flatly defined as evil.

In this respect, as in many others, *Star Trek* has exerted a strong influence on all forms of science fiction, which now seem to routinely posit future universes of widespread space travel where there are either no economic issues at all or implausible replications of economic arrangements from Earth's past (trade agreements, piracy, colonialism, embargoes, etc.). Even as the so-called "hard science fiction revival" has brought a wealth of striking new scientific ideas into the genre, the economics of science fiction has largely remained nonexistent or archaic.

* * * *

This neglect of economics may be understandable, even inevitable. After all, economics is termed "the dismal science" because it is so often perceived as dull, and writers may indeed find it difficult to construct involving narratives hinging upon economic issues. Even *Star Trek: The Next Generation* was obliged to marginalize the subdued Ferengi and attract audiences with new, more violent and aggressive enemies like the Borg and the Cardassians. Reynolds may have made economics a central concern of his science fiction, but he would also be high on anyone's list of "talented writers who never garnered the attention they deserved," perhaps due to his attention to economics. In a genre offering readers sagas of bizarre alien creatures and exciting space battles, a story about a radical new sort of market economy might be box-office poison. Still, it all seems rather unfortunate.

Proponents of human space travel (a topic I will otherwise *not* address at this time, for reasons you may understand) routinely base their arguments on the idea that it is the basic nature of human beings to explore. As eloquently explained by Carl Sagan in *Pale Blue Dot*,

> We were wanderers from the beginning .... For 99.9 percent of the time since our species came to be, we were hunters and foragers, wanderers on the savannahs and the steppes .... Even after 400 generations in villages and cities, we haven't forgotten. The open road still softly calls, like a nearly forgotten song of childhood. We invest far-off places with a certain romance. The

appeal, I suspect, has been meticulously crafted by natural selection as an essential element in our survival. (xi-xii)

Yet, as I have argued before, I don't believe this is true. For "99.9 percent of the tenure of humans on Earth," in fact, people have pretty much been content to stay exactly where they are. They travel far from home only when there is some pressing reason to do so, such as an absence of food in their former environment. In other words, humans tend to travel long distances only when they face what could be termed *economic* problems.

One can maintain, on the basis of better evidence, that it is in the basic nature of human beings to *acquire*. In every place and at every time, humans always work their way up Abraham Maslow's hierarchy of needs, seeking before anything else to obtain material goods to ensure their own health and safety. In that respect economics, far more than exploration, would best define the human condition.

And, as a by-the-way, this would certainly seem true of science fiction fans themselves. How many devoted readers of science fiction regularly spend their time climbing mountains, traveling to remote destinations, and venturing into untamed wildernesses? Vanishingly few, I'm afraid. Instead, they hold regular jobs, earn a decent living, and obsessively collect science fiction books, magazines, and memorabilia, often to the point of filling entire rooms of their houses with such materials. (Does this sound familiar to anyone?) When I think of the typical science fiction reader, someone like Sir Edmund Hillary climbing Mount Everest simply doesn't come to mind; instead, I think of that wonderful man, the late Bruce Pelz, who was perfectly content to accept early retirement, start a small book-selling business to earn a little extra income, and otherwise carry on accumulating the world's largest collection of science fiction fanzines and related materials. Within the context of their own genre, science fiction fans visibly delight in the microeconomics of acquiring, trading, buying, and selling goods, making it strange that the stories at the center of these bustling activities so often seem indifferent, or even hostile, to matters of business at both the microeconomic and macroeconomic levels.

In other words, science fiction fans may *talk* like Captain Kirk, saying that humans must "explore strange new worlds" and "to boldly go where no man has gone before," but they *act* more like the Ferengi, devoting all their spare energies to genre-related commerce. Unlike Roddenberry, I hasten to add, I don't see anything wrong with this at all. Indeed, instead of dismissing beings like the Ferengi as scoundrels or clowns, science fiction might profitably muster a more intense and sympathetic attentiveness to economic behaviors, instead of condemning such endeavors or wishing they would all go away.

Science fiction, Brian W. Aldiss once suggested, might be defined as a "search for a definition of man and his status in the universe" (*Billion Year Spree* 8). Considered as such, it would be appropriate for science fiction to abandon the notion that the economic activities of humanity represent some sort of primitive, atavistic behavior, sure to be swept away by new scientific discoveries which will render such business obsolete. Instead, science fiction might embrace the realization that economics is in fact a basic element of human life, and likely to be a basic element in alien life; then, it might begin to explore strange new economies and boldly go where no economist has gone before. For people suffering through hard times, such dismal science fiction might prove surprisingly interesting.

# WHY SCIENCE FICTION (THANK GOODNESS!) STILL DOESN'T GET ANY RESPECT

Two years ago, at a science fiction conference in Hong Kong, several speakers bemoaned the low status of the newly conspicuous genre of science fiction in China. We heard that Chinese colleges and universities were resisting the inclusion of science fiction in their literature classes, that Chinese science fiction stories were never considered for major literary awards, that Chinese science fiction writers found it difficult to secure financial support, and that Chinese science fiction novels were rarely reviewed in the mainstream press.

We were told, in other words, that Chinese science fiction was not getting any respect.

Still, the speakers seemed hopeful that they could soon persuade their literary colleagues to abandon their narrow-minded attitudes and embrace science fiction. Based on the American experience, however, I can discern no reason for such optimism. Today, over half a century after "science fiction" first emerged as an integral part of American popular culture, a preponderance of prominent voices continue to maintain that all science fiction is basically garbage.

One recent example: in the May 18, 2003 issue of *The New York Times Book Review*, one Sven Birkerts begins a review of Margaret Atwood's *Oryx and Crake* with these remarks: "I am going to stick my neck out and just say it: science fiction will never be Literature with a capital 'L,' and this is because it inevitably proceeds from premise rather than character. It sacrifices moral and psychological nuance in favor of more conceptual matters, and elevates scenario over sensibility." While magnanimously willing to concede that there are "Probably" some "exceptions to my categorical pronouncement," Birkerts concludes that there are not "enough of them to overturn it" (12). When this nonsense was shared with members of the fictionmags listserv, one prominent science fiction writer responded that he found it all very depressing.

But why? Such learned "pronouncements" may be surprising and unsettling to Chinese science fiction writers, but they should be old news to American science fiction writers, having regularly appeared for over fifty years. They were silly and wrong in the 1950s, and they are silly and wrong now, but that has never prevented most members of the literary elite from clinging to these risible opinions, all evidence to the contrary. Could any American really entertain the plausible expectation that the recent emergence of yet another generation of science fiction writers with indisputable talent, and the recent publications of yet another set of science fiction novels of indisputable literary merit, would finally cause these people to change their minds?

\* \* \* \*

Part of the problem, I think, is an imperfect recognition of what is really involved in showing respect to forms of literature. People typically regard the gestures that define such respect to writers—like favorable reviews in major literary periodicals like *The New York Times Book Review*, prestigious awards, invitations to give speeches or readings at literature conferences, foundation grants to work on new projects, books assigned in college literature classes, or appointments as visiting professors of creative writing—as matters of *recognition*: the nabobs of literature are constantly on the lookout for works of superior literature, and eager to bestow all due praise on its exemplars. So, it is consequently baffling why they so consistently overlook or belittle science fiction, despite its increasingly obvious virtues.

However, these gestures are actually best construed as means of *financial support*. In some cases, money is overtly transferred to the writer, as with grants, honorariums for conference appearances, or salaried faculty positions; in other cases, money may be an indirect result, since the honor of a glowing review in a respected journal or a story chosen for a "Year's Best" anthology will increase a writer's chance to obtain financial benefits. Virtually all of the writers now esteemed by experts in literature with a capital L, even those rare success stories like Atwood who no longer need the cash, underwent an apprenticeship of humble dependence upon such largess. And if the sought-after "respect" from the literary establishment is viewed in these crude terms—as money given to needy writers or formerly needy writers—the persistent exclusion of science fiction becomes more understandable.

Charitable people like to give money to the people who need it the most. The common perception is that science fiction writers earn a reasonable income from their work and hence aren't particularly in need of money. The common perception is that poets, and writers of similarly uncommercial prose, do not earn a reasonable income from their work and hence may be desperately in need of money. Granted, such perceptions are not entirely accurate: there are more than enough science fiction writers bitterly complaining about harsh marketplace conditions and inadequate compensation, and there are probably some poets out there who manage to cobble together a fairly respectable income from various sources. But it is probably fair enough to say that a major American science fiction writer will almost invariably make much more money than an American poet of comparable stature. A couple of years ago, for instance, a distinguished American poet named Alan Shapiro won the Kingsley Tufts Award, the most lucrative prize for poetry in the world; when interviewed about how the award would change his life, Shapiro remarked that he could now finally afford to purchase his own home. Somehow, I suspect that modern winners of major science fiction awards were already in a position to purchase their own homes if they had chosen to do so.

So, when science fiction writers complain that their work isn't receiving the respect it deserves, they are—fairly or not—greeted with the same scorn that people in tuxedos and evening gowns would receive if they drove up to the Salvation Army in a limousine and asked for a free meal. Why do *you*, Mr. or Ms. Science Fiction Writer, want reviews in *The New York Times Book Review*, foundation grants, Pulitzer Prizes, or stories in *The Best American Short Stories 2003? You* are already earning a decent income as a writer; the people we typically honor are rarely so fortunate. Literary snobs may not articulate, or even be fully aware of, this impulse to reward those most in need of rewards that guides their thinking, but it's a matter of human nature: give food to a starving man, and you see heartwarming gratitude in his eyes; give food to a sated glutton, and you are greeted with disheartening indifference.

Closely linked to financial considerations in the bestowing of literary respect, of course, is the influence of the old boys'—today, the old girls' and old boys'—network. Aspiring young writers are trained in Creative Writing classes to produce certain sorts of highly esteemed but unpopular writing; the more talented and energetic of these publish widely but unprofitably in little magazines that pay in copies, garnering some attention in the right circles; after receiving more and more recognition from the people that matter, they work their way up to positions as book reviewers, literary advisers to the Ford Foundation, members of the National Book Awards committee, and so on; and they naturally single out writers like themselves for their prizes and honors, just as they were once singled out by other writers like themselves. This explains why even the most successful of literary writers will continue to receive awards and recognition, even when they are in a position to disdain them, or even when their works have visibly deteriorated in quality.

So, if earning literary respect is simply a matter of evidencing genuine poverty and working one's way into an incestuous subculture, why have science fiction writers been so spectacularly unsuccessful in learning how to play the game? Many science fiction writers, as noted, can persuasively present themselves as impoverished, and they usually have the necessary social skills to make an impression on the literary set.

The problem is that, at least during the mandatory period of apprenticeship, it requires massive amounts of groveling to obtain the benefits of literary respect, and science fiction writers, even if they aren't rolling in dough at the moment, may find it quite difficult to grovel. Unlike poets and playwrights, they are members of a profession where it is commonplace to earn a decent living from one's craft, and only a certain type of personality can happily endure a career of begging—and, make no mistake about it, writers essentially without an audience, trying to survive by means of influential friends, part-time teaching jobs, and grants, are necessarily involved in a career of begging. In my experience, science fiction writers generally aren't very good at it.

* * * *

Consider, for example, a university planning to hold a writer's conference that has enough funds to attract a well-known writer (typically, money to cover the writer's airfare, meals, and lodging, along with a modest honorarium, perhaps somewhere between $500 and $1000). Let's say that the committee's choice has come down to two finalists: a major poet, like Alan Shapiro, and a major science fiction writer, like Gregory Benford. They will choose Shapiro every time.

Why? In the first place, when you invite someone to attend an event, you want to do so with a reasonable expectation that the person you approach will say yes. With a major poet, this is virtually guaranteed: you are offering him a free vacation and the equivalent of two weeks' salary, which he will eagerly claim. The only time he might say no would be in the extremely improbable case that he had already been offered a better deal to visit another university at the same time.

The major science fiction writer, however, is more likely to decline. The money and the travel will probably not be important to him. If the conference sounds interesting, if it happens to be taking place in a city that he would like to visit for other reasons, if he doesn't have anything better to do, he may agree to attend; but there is an equal probability that he will turn down the offer, forcing the committee to look for another candidate.

Further, the two types of writers will behave differently at a university conference. The poet will attend every single speech, every single reading, and every single panel, maintaining a fixed facial expression of eager attentiveness at every moment. At the opening reception, he will happily stand for hours listening to some graduate student expounding her idiotic theory of poetry, nodding thoughtfully and periodically interjecting some comment to communicate that he is really listening to her. He is very eager to be invited to another conference, or to be invited back to this conference, and who knows? That wretched writer whose reading he politely sits through may two years later be in charge of his own conference; that graduate student at the reception may serve as the student representative on the committee that plans next year's conference. That is why, in every respect, the poet will strive to be an absolutely perfect guest; beggars always do.

The science fiction writer, however, will not be an absolutely perfect guest. Oh, he will perform every duty that he is being paid to perform, showing up promptly for every event he is supposed to participate in. But when he isn't on the program, he might wander away to do something else he'd rather be doing. He will not be unfailingly polite and agreeable; confronted with a graduate student's idiotic theory, he might tell her quite bluntly that she's an idiot and then walk out of the reception to meet some old friends for dinner and drinks. Unlike a major poet, a major science fiction writer will feel no obligation to grovel, and he may leave the conference having made more enemies than friends. And he won't care—because, unlike the poet, he is already making good money from his writing career or expects to do so in the future; he doesn't need the crumbs being tossed out by universities and foundations.

\* \* \* \*

So, when will science fiction finally receive the literary respect that so many feel it deserves? It will happen when science fiction loses most of its audience; when science fiction is no longer profitable, even for the most prolific or the very best of writers; when all science fiction writers will necessarily get down on their knees in hopes of receiving whatever boons they can from the literary establishment in order to stay alive. And once they assume that position, science fiction writers will finally be perceived as persons worthy of literary approbation.

Or, in other words, science fiction will finally receive respect when it is dying.

Thus, we should view the shameful disrespect long accorded to science fiction as a tremendously gratifying compliment to the genre's continuing vitality and broad popular appeal. For unlike poetry and the other forms of literature with a capital L which garner all of that *respect*, science fiction has *readers*.

Why on Earth should it instead want respect?

# FELLOW TRAVELLERS: JULES VERNE AND J. G. BALLARD (WITH DAVID PRINGLE)

(Note: in 1997, as his contribution to the program of the combined Science Fiction Research Association/J. Lloyd Eaton Conference held in Long Beach, California, David Pringle provided a piece entitled "Time-Travellers in Global Space: On Similarities Between Jules Verne and J. G. Ballard (Notes for an Unwritten Essay)," discussing points of similarity between the authors in the form of a numbered list. I wanted to publish it in the conference anthology *Space and Beyond: The Frontier Theme in Science Fiction* (2000), but its scholarly (and stuffy) peer reviewer objected that the piece wasn't a "real" essay, and I was forced to remove it. Never forgetting this gem, I recently relocated Pringle's list and with his permission refashioned its observations to better resemble a "real" essay, also adding a few examples and comments of my own to his original argument. In what follows, to distribute credit and blame where it is due, the introductory and concluding passages are mostly Westfahl's, while the body of the essay is mostly Pringle's.)

They were born at almost the same point in their respective centuries—in 1828 and in 1930—and both men grew up during tumultuous times of wars and revolutions, displaying streaks of independence and rebelliousness. After flirtations with more respectable professions, in business and medicine, they began writing in their twenties, emerged as popular novelists in their thirties, and continued writing and publishing until, in their seventies, they extended their careers into a second century. Today, both men are widely celebrated for their provocative contributions to science fiction.

But the preceding accounts would appear to exhaust all possible points of similarity between Jules Verne and J. G. Ballard.

For, according to standard judgments, Verne and Ballard represent almost complete opposites. Verne, the technophilic optimist, provides expansive adventures about bold explorers venturing into unknown realms; Ballard, the technophobic pessimist, offers brooding meditations involving passive victims of natural and man-made disasters. However, standard judgments aren't always correct, and one can readily argue that, in fact, these two writers display some surprising similarities.

* * * *

In the first place, both Verne and Ballard are commonly classified as science fiction writers, yet both wrote substantial amounts of mainstream fiction, or—more precisely—works which hover problematically between science fiction and mainstream fiction. At the same time, their entire oeuvres *cohere*: their works are always distinctively "Vernian" and "Ballardian." In this respect, they strongly contrast with other writers who have written both science fiction and mainstream fiction, such as H. G. Wells or Brian W. Aldiss, since they tend to write *either* science fiction *or* mainstream fiction (usually social comedy); however, in their varied writings there is little of the problematic overlap between the two modes that characterizes Verne and Ballard.

In addition, Verne and Ballard wrote science fiction (or mainstream fiction) of a broadly similar kind: after early flirtations with futuristic fiction (Verne's long-suppressed *Paris in the Twentieth Century* [1994], Ballard's "Vermilion Sands" stories), their stories are usually set in the present, not the future, and they eschew what some science fiction critics have called *radical exteriority*, in that they do not describe aliens or alien societies. Both writers are more concerned with depictions of their present worlds, sometimes through the distorting lens of science fiction, than with any attempt to envision *other* societies, whether on distant planets, in the far future, or in parallel worlds. Thus, both Verne and Ballard aggressively choose to avoid most of the devices and conventions of science fiction that figure so prominently in the works of other writers like Wells and Aldiss.

Both writers further show a tendency towards what one might call the *metaphorical* rather than the *literal* use of science fiction devices. Both Verne's *Journey to the Center of the Earth* (1864) and Ballard's *The Drowned World* (1962) can be seen as symbolic or metaphorical tales of time travel into the deep past. True, in neither case does the act of time travel "really happen" in the course of the narrative; yet in each case, one can maintain, such imaginative travel into the geo-biological past is what the novel is actually *about*.

Verne and Ballard both can be said to employ in their prose—or at least to strive for—a kind of "poetry of science" characterized by their frequent descriptions of landscapes, their rhapsodies that utilize scientific and technical terms, and an occasional tendency to climax in a kind of visionary mysticism. The objects of their attention are often ruins. This is how Verne describes Nemo and Aronnax's discovery of the underwater Atlantis in *Twenty Thousand Leagues under the Sea* (1870):

> And, in fact, there beneath my eyes, ruined, crumbled and destroyed, lay a town with its roofs caved in, its temples falling down, its arches out of place and its columns lying on the ground. In all these fragments one could see the solid proportions of a kind of Tuscan architecture. Further on there were the remains of a giant aqueduct; here lay an encrusted mound of some Acropolis, with the floating forms of a Parthenon; there the remains of a dock, as if from some antique port that had once sheltered merchant ships and triremes of war at the shore of an extinct sea; yet further on, long lines of crumbling walls and deserted streets. (256)

Compare this passage to Ballard's descriptions of the abandoned Super-fortress in "The Terminal Beach" (1964):

> On either side, sometimes shaded by the few palms that had gained a precarious purchase in the cracked cement, were roadways, camera towers and isolated blockhouses, together forming a continuous concrete cap upon the island, a functional megalithic architecture as gray and minatory, and apparently as ancient (in its projection into, and from, the future) as any of Assyria and Babylon .... Once, he entered a small street of metal shacks, containing a cafeteria, recreation rooms, and shower stalls. A wrecked jukebox lay half-buried in the sand behind the cafeteria, its selection of records still in their rack. (62-64)

As another one of their similarities, Verne and Ballard can be regarded as "global writers" in a way that few others have been, setting their stories all over the world. Admittedly, this is more obvious in the case of Verne (the first truly global novelist, which explains why he is the most widely translated of all fiction writers), but Ballard follows suit, if a little less obviously, as demonstrated by the African settings of *The Crystal World* (1966) and *The Day of Creation* (1987), the Chinese setting of *Empire of the Sun* (1984), the implied Canadian setting of *The Drought* (1965), and the French setting of *Super-Cannes* (2000). Both, then, are in a real sense *anti-parochial* writers; they exude no nationalistic biases, as opposed to, say, the aura of Britishness that permeates Wells's works or the aggressive Americanism of Robert A. Heinlein.

Both authors are *ironists*—a fact often not appreciated in the case of Verne, largely due to poor English-language translations which destroy his ironic tone, dumbing him down to the level of the "boys' book." In "Jules Verne: The Last Happy Utopianist," critic Marc Angenot provides a telling example: in the standard English translation of *The Mysterious Island* (1874), with reference to the suppression of the 1857 Indian Mutiny, Verne is made to say: "Civilization never recedes. The law of necessity ever forces it onwards" (cited in "Jules Verne" 32). What Verne actually wrote, according to Angenot's literal translation, is: "Right, once again, had succumbed in the face of might. But civilization never recedes, and it seems that it borrows all its rights from necessity" ("Jules Verne" 27). The last sentence strikes us as a chilling irony—worthy of Ballard, in fact. (This is one reason why it is not entirely accurate to label Verne as an "optimist" and Ballard as a "pessimist": on a deeper level than at first meets the eye, there is plenty of "pessimism" in Verne, just as one finds an equal amount of "optimism" in Ballard.)

Examining their many stories, one can detect all sorts of similarities in the subjects they address, and the sorts of stories they choose to tell. Both writers are obsessed with the conventions of the desert-island story or Robinsonade—Verne in *The Mysterious Island, The School for Crusoes* (1882), and many other works; Ballard in "The Terminal Beach," *Concrete Island* (1974), *Rushing to Paradise* (1994), and elsewhere. No doubt reflecting their unsettled upbringings—Verne's attempt to run away from home by stowing away on a ship, Ballard's youthful experiences in a prisoner-of-war camp—both frequently employ the motif of the "orphan," or the youngster alone. Both writers display a satirical fascination with the United States of America: Verne in *From the Earth to the Moon* (1865) and its sequels, Ballard in *Hello America* (1981), *The Atrocity Exhibition* (1970), and various short stories. Verne and Ballard share a certain fascination with machines—Verne's many tales of amazing new vehicles, Ballard's *Crash* (1973)—and images of flight abound in the works of both authors.

\* \* \* \*

Finally, though debatably, both authors stood out from their contemporaries in their stunningly prescient priorities. Most novelists in Verne's day were fascinated by the rise of urban civilization and the resulting social problems that afflicted all classes of society; depending on their tastes, they wrote stories about mansions and drawing rooms, or factories and slums.

To Verne, however, the developments that most merited attention were the present and future advances in transportation and communication that were leading humans into new realms and bringing all the peoples of the world into contact with each other; in contrast, examining the new challenges and difficulties of life in the big city seemed a sterile, petty enterprise. This is one reason why readers of the twentieth and twenty-first centuries, living in the technologically-transformed and unified world that Verne provided intimations of, have remained interested in Verne's stories, while all but the very best of the chroniclers of Victorian urban society have been forgotten.

Ballard entered the field of science fiction at a time when most authors, on both sides of the Atlantic, had embraced the notion that humanity's future lay in outer space; they uniformly predicted that people would rapidly progress beyond the planet Earth, establishing colonies on the Moon and other planets and eventually embarking on interstellar flights. The best and brightest humans would enthusiastically abandon Earth to join in this great adventure, leaving the planet to decline into decadence and unimportance. While the New Wave of the 1960s briefly threatened the hegemony of this monomyth, it came back with a vengeance in the 1970s and thereafter, fueled by the popularity of the *Star Trek* and *Star Wars* franchises.

Almost uniquely, Ballard foresaw that the American and Russian space programs would actually have little impact on humanity's future, that their rockets and the grandiose plans linked to them would someday be abandoned. Oblivious to dreams of outer space, he resolutely focused his attention on what he termed "The only truly alien planet," Earth ("Which Way to Inner Space?" 117), and the troubled lives of the people who would remain forced to reside there. Today, with a manned space program that hasn't ventured beyond near-Earth orbit in thirty years—and sometimes doesn't even do that very well—it is becoming increasingly apparent that human efforts to conquer the universe are indefinitely stalled at the very first stage, demanding renewed attentiveness to the future prospects of human life on Earth, not in space. And, as Heinleinesque sagas of space adventure and *Star Trek* novels increasingly seem more like diverting fantasies than realistic projections of our future, Ballard's down-to-earth dramas may, like Verne's novels, remain more interesting to future readers than what will seem in retrospect the myopically space-oriented stories of his contemporaries.

This brings us to what might be regarded as these writers' most important similarities: they were leaders, not followers. They both studied the worlds around them, reached their own conclusions, and stubbornly produced their own sorts of stories, oblivious to changing fashions. If Verne seems less bold than Ballard, that may simply reflect his willingness to be restrained by conservative publisher Jules Hetzel, while

Ballard had no comparable figure to dampen the extremes of his creative impulses. Still, something unique and valuable shines through in both of their bodies of work, as others have repeatedly recognized. There is no need to describe how Verne inspired countless imitators; and virtually every writer of the New Wave, and key science fiction writers of every subsequent generation, have cited Ballard as a major influence.

There are prices to pay, of course, when a writer strays from the crowd and follows his own path. Neither writer has really received the critical respect he deserves: Verne to this day is looked down upon as *déclassé* by most French critics, and Ballard has faced the disdain of both mainstream critics who disparage "science fiction writers" and science fiction critics who dislike what they perceive as his unseemly passivity and pessimism. And writers who ignore generic conventions and effectively develop their own personal genres can themselves fall victim to the generic conventions they create, so that there were times in both Verne's and Ballard's careers when they were accused of becoming monotonous, offering only new variations on familiar themes. Still, writers can be forgiven for occasionally being repetitive if we determine that they have also been *right*—and that certainly seems to be true in the cases of Jules Verne and J. G. Ballard.

# THE ODDS AGAINST TOMORROW, OR, HOW I SPENT MY SUMMER VACATION

I recently discussed a time when my wife, observing me hard at work (as always) on the computer, said, "You need more fun in your life." I immediately responded, "I *hate* having fun!" It's true: I have come to regard the leisure activities cherished by most people—movies, concerts, sports, vacations, long conversations with friends—only as annoyances, keeping me away from productive labor. And when circumstances force me into such situations, I struggle to find some aspect of the experience to study and reflect upon, so as to garner tangible rewards from ephemeral pleasures.

This summer, my family insisted on vacationing in Laughlin, Nevada, a resort community that offers cheap food, lodging, and entertainment to attract gamblers, and hence functions as an economical getaway for persons like myself and my wife who never gamble. Yet I found myself unable to relax by soaking in the spa or watching the shows; instead, I was examining my surroundings, taking notes, analyzing data.

\* \* \* \*

When staying at Harrah's Resort and Casino in Laughlin, or any Nevada hotel for that matter, one necessarily spends a lot of time looking at gambling machines, since hotels are cunningly designed to require all guests to walk past them. Once, these were "slot machines," devices containing three wheels covered with symbols sent randomly spinning by the pull of a handle, the hoped-for outcome being that the wheels would stop with three symbols aligned and trigger floods of coins. Today, one still pulls a handle, but the spinning wheels are virtual, images on a television screen, and video technology has generated new varieties of machines, such as video poker machines.

Many machines have only utilitarian decor; video poker machines are usually labeled only with textual descriptions. Other machines have names and illuminated illustrations referencing the money one might earn, like a machine named "Strike It Rich" depicting huge piles of coins. Some more creatively feature anthropomorphic animals gazing alluringly at potential customers, their big eyes promising instant wealth in exchange for a quarter. There are machines with pictures of knights, cowboys, and hard-boiled detectives. Others are based on board games, television game shows, films, and television programs.

When I saw a gambling machine entitled "Creature from the Black Lagoon," with a picture of the classic Gill Man, I figured out something worthwhile to do: I would determine how many gambling machines were based on science fiction and fantasy, and what titles and themes they had. Others have written about science fiction and fantasy video games and computer games; I would become the first to write about science fiction and fantasy gambling machines.

So, I walked through Harrah's and recorded the names and quantities of all machines related to science fiction or fantasy. I found 12 types of machines, and a total of 59 machines, that matched my parameters. The detailed results:

### Science Fiction Gambling Machines (4 types, 15 machines)

"Austin Powers"—2 machines

"Boom!" (picture of rocketship, background of stars)—5 machines

"Creature from the Black Lagoon"—4 machines

"Little Green Men" (picture of green alien on flying saucer)—4 machines

### Fantasy Gambling Machines (8 types, 44 machines)

"The Addams Family"—1 machine

"Break the Spell" (picture of wizard with magic wand)—5 machines

"Dragon Treasure"—3 machines

"Enchanted Unicorn"—5 machines

"Frog Prince"—10 machines

"I Dream of Jeannie"—10 machines

"Leprechaun's Gold"—6 machines

"The Munsters"—4 machines

I could have inflated the figures for fantasy machines by including the aforementioned machines featuring pigs in overalls, chickens dressed as male strippers ("Chickendales"), and so on, but I restricted myself to machines foregrounding the characters and tropes of genre fantasy. Other casinos undoubtedly included additional types of science fiction and fantasy machines that I was overlooking, like the "Jekyll and Hyde" machine I glimpsed at another hotel, but I had obtained a representative sampling of the machines along these lines now available.

Of course, the numbers meant nothing in themselves without comparing them to the numbers of other types of machines. I needed the total number of gambling machines in Harrah's, information that proved surprisingly difficult to obtain. Three employees professed to have no idea how many machines there were, and the one who ventured a guess offered a number—around 700 or 800—that I knew was much too low. Perhaps hotels don't want guests to know just how many one-armed bandits they deploy. So, instead of interrogating Harrah's workers, I decided the best way to determine the total number of machines was to count all of them myself.

Well, I thought, it sure beats lounging around the pool or enjoying a nice cold beer at the bar.

I walked through the entire gambling area twice, counting each and every machine. The first time, my total was 1187; the second time, it was 1188. Concluding that my tally was reasonably accurate, I chose the figure of 1188 (not that using 1187 would make any difference).

The statistics: the percentage of machines with science fiction themes was 1.3%; the percentage of machines with fantasy themes was 3.7%; the total percentage of machines with science fiction or fantasy themes was 5.0%. If one removes from consideration the machines arguably linked more to comedy than to science fiction and fantasy ("Austin Powers," "The Addams Family," "I Dream of Jeannie," "The Munsters"), the total percentage plummets to 3.5%.

The contrast with this era's other form of interactive electronic entertainment—video games and computer games—could not be stronger. Though many games are based on sports, car racing, World War II, and the like, it seems obvious, even without statistical proof, that a majority of today's games involve science fiction or fantasy. Yet the genres apparently figure in only a tiny fraction of today's gambling machines. The virtual invisibility of science fiction, which I will now focus on, is especially striking.

* * * *

What does this all mean? Perhaps, nothing. Video games and computer games appeal primarily to the young, who grew up in a mediascape dominated by science fiction. Gambling machines appeal primarily to the old, who grew up when the genre was less prominent and may be less enamored of its icons. People who play video games and computer games only want to have fun. People who play gambling machines may be driven by desperate greed, so glitzy science fiction imagery may be the last thing they care to think about—engendering a preference for unadorned machines that announce in a businesslike manner what they are and how much money they provide. Owners of major science fiction franchises like *Superman* and *Star Trek* happily license characters to wholesome video games and computer games, but they may resist allowing their family-friendly heroes to be tainted by association with the unsavory business of gambling. There are numerous ways to explain why manufacturers create relatively few science fiction gambling machines, and why the machines they do create remain relatively uncommon.

Still, something significant may be at work here. Not all science fiction fans are young; not all gamblers are old. Given the pervasiveness of science fiction in other media, one would naturally expect more machines along the lines of "Martian Millions," "Asteroid of Gold," and "Mission to Moneyworld." And if superstars of science fiction like Superman or Captain Kirk aren't available, the owners of Flash Gordon and Buck Rogers surely wouldn't mind profiting from their moribund franchises with a gambling machine or two.

To explain my research findings, I offer a working hypothesis: people who like science fiction generally don't like gambling, and people who like gambling generally don't like science fiction. Hence, gambling machines with science fiction themes don't make a lot of sense (or a lot of cents).

The basis of science fiction, the argument would proceed, is extrapolation, examining the course of past and present events in order to extend the curve into the future and make plausible predictions. Implicit in the process is a belief that the world can be explained and understood to provide a basis for rational forecasting and decision-making. To earn money, then, a science fiction reader would study various investments and choose one with a track record promising generous returns.

The basis of gambling, however, is the different belief that the world is essentially chaotic, inexplicable, and unpredictable. What happens tomorrow depends purely on chance. To earn money, a gambler logically relies entirely on luck, since nothing else can be relied on; and while some forms of gambling like blackjack or poker do involve skills that can be mastered to improve results, gambling machines involve no skills, only luck, and hence appeal to persons happy to depend only on luck. Science fiction readers would not be attracted to such methods of making money, and people so attracted would not enjoy science fiction.

\* \* \* \*

To explore this idea, I asked members of the fictionmags listserv if they knew about any science fiction writers or fans with a gambling problem. Now, a question about alcohol or drug problems would have engendered a tidal wave of responses; but only three people responded to my query about gambling addiction with mildly worded comments about a few people who possibly liked gambling too much. (One message suggested that highly intelligent science fiction devotees would generally know too much about probability to succumb to gambling; however, knowledge of unfortunate consequences has never kept highly intelligent people away from alcohol, drugs, and other addictions.)

In any event, the attitudes of the science fiction community may be best expressed in its literature, not its behavior, so I looked at some relevant texts. Gambling at best is viewed as a risky but survivable diversion, as in Fritz Leiber's "Gonna Roll the Bones" (1967), and space casinos are occasionally colorful settings for adventure novels like Mack Reynolds's *Satellite City* (1975) and Ron Goulart's *Everybody Comes to Cosmo's* (1988). More scathing is Harlan Ellison's "Pretty Maggie Moneyeyes" (1967), wherein a down-and-out gambler in Las Vegas, after realizing "what is wrong and immoral and deadly about Vegas, about legalized gambling, about setting the traps all baited and open in front of the average human" (127), dies when his soul is sucked into a slot machine already occupied by another of its victims.

However, a more interesting and intellectual argument against gambling emerges in Philip K. Dick's *Solar Lottery* (1955), depicting a future government based entirely on luck: depending on random twists of a bottle, any citizen at any time might be anointed the new Quizmaster, master of the solar system. (To some, this might seem as good a way as any to choose leaders, and one scholar even proposed selecting legislators with a lottery, to achieve a representative body of citizens to make decisions.) A further element of chance is that while anyone opposed to a Quizmaster can hire trained assassins, the Quizmaster is guarded by telepaths who can detect and foil any assassin following a plan; hence, "You can't have a strategy against telepaths; you have to act randomly. You have to not know what you're going to do next" (76).

While at times the novel halfheartedly defends this form of government, both Dick and his major characters despise it, making the novel a dystopia. The system is portrayed as a regrettable consequence of "The disintegration of the social and economic system":

> people lost faith in natural law itself. Nothing seemed stable or fixed; the universe was a sliding flux .... the very concept of cause and effect died out. People lost faith in the belief that they could control their environment; all that remained was probable sequence: good odds in a universe of random chance. (20)

And Dick's deposed Quizmaster complains that "we're all a bunch of superstitious fools .... We're all dependent on random chance; we're losing control because we can't plan" (59).

While relying on luck is thus viewed as undesirable, Dick further discredits such a strategy by having characters subvert the randomness to be influenced by their careful planning. The twists of the bottle turn out to be not entirely unpredictable; the new Quizmaster gained his position by secretly altering the bottle so it would display bias in his favor. The deposed Quizmaster plans to assassinate his successor with a robot alternately possessed by the minds of twenty-four individuals in remote locations who randomly rotate being in command, making it impossible for telepaths to focus on and follow one individual mind. However, the process turns out to be not truly random; one person is secretly controlling who is in charge of the robot to ensure that someone he dislikes will commit the murder and be killed himself. And just as individuals introduce causality to these previously random events, the novel concludes with another new Quizmaster implicitly determined to openly reintroduce causality to the flawed government he now oversees.

Members of the science fiction community do not want to embrace a "universe of random chance"; rather, they want to believe in "cause and effect." They wish to "plan," and to see the predictable results of such plans. Confronted with apparent randomness, they seek to discern or impose a pattern. They aren't interested in gambling.

* * * *

The irony here is that modern physics increasingly endorses the notion that God in fact plays dice with the universe, that there are chaotic systems where future events are utterly unpredictable. Relying on extrapolation may be futile; the future of individuals, and humanity in general, may be purely a matter of chance, so investors may be wise to put their money into gambling machines and hope for the best. But science fiction writers and readers, like many scientists, remain Newtonians at heart, believing in a clockwork universe amenable to logical explanation and confident prediction, and are disinclined to leave everything up to Lady Luck.

Thus, though constantly enticed to put coins into machines that might provide a fortune in return, I instead chose to work in a place for play, to find an interesting pattern in its chaos of flashing lights and ringing bells, and to develop from my work an article that would, I could reasonably predict, be published to earn the modest rewards of a little recognition and a few pounds. Instead of gambling, in other words, I went for the sure thing.

# SURPRISING SCI-FI SOUL BROTHERS, PART TWO: ROBERT A. HEINLEIN AND PHILIP K. DICK

While we're on the subject of seemingly disparate science fiction authors who actually share significant similarities, let's talk about Robert A. Heinlein and Philip K. Dick.

Of course, one can readily epitomize the ways in which these authors are significantly different. Certainly, the characters that most interest them stand at opposite ends of the social spectrum. In a 2003 speech that was published as "Science Fiction Is the Simplest Thing," I contrasted the celebrated Heinlein Hero, a self-defined superior man, with Clifford D. Simak's typical protagonist, the Simak Hero, a self-defined ordinary man. To cover all classes of future society, one could add to the picture the less uniform but still distinguishable Dick Hero, a self-defined less-than-ordinary man. As Karl Marx would sum things up, Heinlein identifies with the aristocracy, Simak with the bourgeoisie, and Dick with the proletariat. More prosaically, the Heinlein Hero owns the office building; the Simak Hero runs a nice little shop on its ground level; and the Dick Hero sweeps his floors every night.

On a personal note, if the Heinlein Hero, as I discussed, represented what I wanted to be, and the Simak Hero represented what I probably really was, the Dick Hero represented what I was desperately afraid of someday becoming—weak, uninformed, powerless, utterly at the mercy of everyone and everything around him. And this explains why, as a youth, I read Heinlein and Simak voraciously, but relatively little Dick. After all, a young man might find it stimulating to spend some time with his personal dreams, and he might find it reassuring to also spend some time with his personal reality, but why would he want to spend some time with his personal nightmares?

Further, given their sympathies with those at opposite ends of the social spectrum, it is not surprising that the polarizing changes in America during the 1960s moved Heinlein and Dick to opposite ends of the political spectrum. Heinlein, horrified by the counterculture and everything it represented, hardened into a bitter reactionary, eventually endorsing, in

*To Sail Beyond the Sunset* (1987), a longed-for President Patton's policy of shooting drug dealers on sight. Dick embraced the counterculture, freely experimented with drugs, and announced a fervent admiration for young Americans and their liberal, liberating philosophies. For that reason, when commentators discuss the time when Heinlein happily purchased a new typewriter for a temporarily down-and-out Dick, this is presented as evidence of Heinlein's amazingly generous spirit, his willingness to help individuals in need even if they were people he otherwise had reason to abhor.

I respectfully disagree. I think that Heinlein gave Dick a typewriter because he could recognize a soul brother when he saw one. And I would argue that, when one considers the qualities that made those writers great, the qualities that distinguish the wondrous novels and stories written in the first two decades of their careers, one must conclude that they are, in fundamental ways, exactly the same sort of writers.

\* \* \* \*

First, Heinlein and Dick are both *adventurous* writers. In their classic years (for Heinlein, the 1940s and 1950s; for Dick, the 1950s and 1960s), both writers were perfectly willing to begin writing a story without knowing how it would end—or, if they did have some plan for how it would proceed, they were perfectly willing to abandon or alter those plans if writing the story led to unanticipated dead ends or intriguing new possibilities. Inevitably, this is a risky policy, like walking on a tightrope, that may well lead to spectacular disasters like Heinlein's *Tunnel in the Sky* (1955) and Dick's *The Crack in Space* (1966); but the same policy also allowed them to generate masterpieces like Heinlein's *Double Star* (1956) and Dick's *Do Androids Dream of Electric Sheep?* (1968).

Second, Heinlein and Dick are both *impatient* writers. Not knowing while they were writing exactly where their stories were going, they were just as eager as their readers to find out how the stories were going to turn out. One detects in their novels a palpable aura of nervous energy, a strong desire to avoid wasting time, to keep things moving, to get somewhere, anywhere, as fast as possible. Not surprisingly, their novels are often shorter than the norm, as Heinlein and Dick found themselves careening into a conclusion a bit earlier than they had expected. I estimate, for example, that two other outstanding works, Heinlein's *The Door into Summer* (1956, 1957) and Dick's *Galactic Pot-Healer* (1969), barely exceed 60,000 words in length. Again, this attitude is not without perils—both Heinlein's *Methuselah's Children* (1941, 1958) and Dick's *Eye in the Sky* (1957) seem to move faster and faster, to less and less effect, until they abruptly collapse and die—but even such lesser novels have their fair share of memorable moments.

Third, Heinlein and Dick are both *confident* writers. They may not know where they are going, and they may be proceeding with reckless haste, but they are absolutely sure that, wherever their stories may go and whatever they may happen to feel like saying, their readers will always be entertained by the results. These writers are not afraid to interrupt their narratives with, say, a detailed technical description of a spacesuit, as in Heinlein's *Have Space Suit—Will Travel* (1958), or a lengthy philosophical discussion about the human condition, as in Dick's *Galactic Pot-Healer*, because they correctly believe that, due to their reliably adroit writing, readers will find such passages just as involving as fistfights or dramatic escapes. Despite their occasional difficulties in attempting to venture beyond the genre, Heinlein and Dick woke up every morning knowing that they were consistently capable of selling material to science fiction markets and were consistently capable of pleasing a wide range of science fiction readers.

* * * *

As I list these three basic qualities, it will be noted that I am making no effort to describe or defend what happened to Heinlein in the 1960s, or what happened to Dick in the 1970s. Generally speaking, while retaining their sense of self-confidence, I would suggest that they grew a little less adventurous, and that they entirely lost their youthful sense of impatience. Instead, they became more and more willing to ramble on at length about whatever topics they were interested in at the moment, resulting in Heinlein's tedious pontifications about every issue in sight and Dick's extensive philosophical and theological musings, material found in ponderous works that surely will not age as well as their earlier novels.

I will also confess that I am not precisely sure how to *document* that this is the way that Heinlein and Dick approached their writing, and I am aware of certain after-the-fact discussions by the authors that might support a rather different picture of their writing strategies—not that I necessarily trust what writers say about their own writing. Still, signs of a more deliberate writing style in some cases does seem to exist: it was recently announced, for instance, that Spider Robinson has been hired to write what will be touted as a "new Heinlein novel," based on Heinlein's purportedly detailed outline for a novel he never wrote. This is less than exciting news; for even if such a detailed outline exists, I cannot believe that it truly represents, or will allow Robinson to recapture, the genius of Heinlein typing away every morning, churning out his daily quota of words, hurrying his story along. I am finally not precisely sure what specific features in a text one could point to as clear evidence of authorial adventurousness, impatience, and confidence, or how one might train young scholars to identify those features in the works of various writers.

All I can say is that, when I am reading science fiction, I can somehow recognize these features, and I can somehow recognize the absence of those features. And this explains why I am not always fond of certain contemporary science fiction writers, even when they are widely extolled and winners of numerous awards.

\* \* \* \*

Consider, as one example, Dan Simmons. I will freely concede that, if one prepared a list of the characteristics of superior writers, and carefully applied those criteria to Heinlein, Dick, and Simmons, inevitably Simmons would qualify as the best writer of the three. I further acknowledge that, on two previous occasions, I found myself contractually obliged to praise Simmons, and that I contrived to find a way to do so without lapsing into blatant insincerity. Still, despite his impressive and indisputable writing skills, I am generally bored by Simmons's works, and I will never again pick up one of his novels unless there is money to be made by doing so.

Why is this true? The answer lies in the list. In the first place, Simmons is a supremely unadventurous writer. It is obvious that every one of his novels has been carefully planned, chapter by chapter, scene by scene, and that Simmons always adheres to the script he has previously prepared.

Second, Simmons is an infinitely patient writer. He will linger on each moment of his narrative for as long as it takes to provide every evocative detail and wring every conceivable idea and emotion out of it before plodding on to do the same with the next moment.

Finally, Simmons is a desperately insecure writer. Every aspect of his novels seems designed to please this or that segment of the science fiction audience. One gets the feeling that Simmons is not writing the kind of story he really wants to write, sure that readers will like the results, but rather is writing the kind of story that he fervently hopes (but does not really know) will make his readers happy. When I read Simmons, I find myself paying attention not to each new development in his story, but to the wheels that turned in Simmons's brain as he planned each new development. Let's see, he thinks as he prepares his chapter outline: some sophisticated readers like literary references, so I will toss in a bunch of them here; next, for the more plebeian readers, I will provide a thrilling space battle; then, for the more romantically inclined, I will put in a tender love scene; and so on and so on—everything meticulously calculated, painstakingly and skillfully rendered, and utterly lacking in genuine passion or conviction.

Sorry, but instead of a new Simmons novel, I would rather reread Heinlein's *Orphans of the Sky* (1941, 1963) or Dick's *Clans of the Alphane Moon* (1964). Both have any number of rough edges and missteps along the way, but they are living, breathing stories, bubbling with enthusiasm and excitement, and they stand in sharp contrast to the polished, sterile artifacts crafted by Simmons.

\* \* \* \*

Others might articulate their fondness for Heinlein and Dick in other ways, but one other similarity between the authors is inarguable: both writers enjoyed success during their lifetimes, and even greater success after their deaths. Virtually all of their novels and collections have remained in print, and their unpublished manuscripts have all been unearthed and brought to the marketplace (except, in Heinlein's case, when he chose to expressly forbid the publication of certain materials). Their papers have found permanent homes in respectable university libraries—the Heinlein Archives are at the University of California, Santa Cruz, and Dick's materials are at California State University, Fullerton. Hollywood executives, belatedly recognizing the unique talents of these writers, have optioned dozens of Heinlein and Dick stories, and several have already made their way to the screen. Although scholars have displayed much more interest in Dick than in Heinlein—probably because of the unpalatable politics of Heinlein's later years—both authors retain their prominent positions in the syllabuses of science fiction classes and the articles published in science fiction journals. And whenever science fiction writers venture into unknown regions of space, or probe deeply into the human psyche and its tenuous relationship to reality, they reflect the powerful influence of Robert A. Heinlein and Philip K. Dick in the visible substance of their works if not in the less visible methods of their composition. Still, as with any performers who walked on a tightrope, theirs is a hard act to follow.

# BIG THEMES, OBSCURED BY SMALL SCREENS, OR, SPACE OPERA VERSUS SOAP OPERA

In her entry on the television series *FlashForward* (2009-2010) for the online Encyclopedia of Science Fiction, Abigail Nussbaum echoes the complaint made by virtually every commentator on the series: that it was doomed to failure primarily because of its unsympathetic protagonist Mark Benford, who Nussbaum fumes was "a self-righteous, heedless bore not at all brought to life by Joseph Fiennes's stiff, blank performance." Perhaps she meant to say "boor," but it remains evident that she, like the other commentators, was not exactly enamored of the character.

As it happens, she is discussing one of the few recent television series that I can speak knowledgeably about; for having decided to review the series for the website Locus Online, I diligently watched every single episode and reported my impressions in three reviews—of its first episode ("A Glimpse at the Future"), the first half of its season ("Searching for Tomorrow"), and its final episodes ("Tomorrow Numbly Dies"). And, unlike everyone else who has written about the series, I never really noticed that Benford was an unlikable jerk.

In light of the critical consensus, this might seem a damning admission of extreme inattentiveness, so I should immediately add that, in fact, I never really developed any fondness for Benford or any interest in all of his contrived problems; thus, had I been asked, I would have agreed that the character was not particularly appealing. But Benford struck me as unremarkable in this regard because I never really developed a fondness for *any* of the series' characters or an interest in *any* of their contrived problems. Benford, in other words, appeared to be essentially similar to all of the other characters in the series—melodramatic "bores" or "boors," each and every one of them.

Benford's repulsiveness struck the other commentators as more noteworthy because contemporary television programs are almost invariably focused on their characters—due to the fact that producers believe, no doubt correctly, that shows become popular primarily because audiences begin to bond with their characters and keep tuning in to learn more about them. I am not a typical television viewer because, like most science fiction readers of a certain age, I am attracted to narratives primarily because of their stimulating ideas, not their appealing characters, and I had resolved to regularly watch *FlashForward* solely because of the intriguing prediction at the heart of its source material, Robert J. Sawyer's novel *Flashforward* (1999): the development of a replicable scientific process that provides people with brief glimpses of their future. And after enduring episode after episode that focused on pointless action and personal traumas, I was heartened to notice, as I explained in my final review, that the series was belatedly becoming more genuinely science-fictional than the novel in beginning to develop a future world wherein these "flashforwards" would become standard features of their societies, permanently altering and influencing people's lives in the manner of all scientific innovations in the real world (unlike the novel, where the process is abandoned after a second effort is perceived to have no effects— although it actually does). Conversely, I couldn't care less about whether Benford would start drinking again, whether his friend would be able to reconnect with his purportedly dead daughter in Afghanistan, or any of the other interpersonal dramas that were foregrounded in most episodes.

\* \* \* \*

Over the years, I would argue, science fiction television has grown less and less worthwhile because it has become more and more like television. The science fiction series I watched as a child were manifestly *not* character-driven; a few, like the anthology series *The Twilight Zone* (1959-1964) and *The Outer Limits* (1963-1965), didn't even have any regular characters, unless one counts narrators Rod Serling and "the Control Voice." Even the original *Star Trek* series (1966-1969), while at times focusing on the personal relationships of Captain Kirk, Mister Spock, and Doctor McCoy, generally offered stories that did foreground some intriguing future possibilities: a world where individuals can escape unpleasant realities to live within a world of comforting illusions ("The Menagerie" [1966]), a look the alien Vulcans' peculiar sexuality and mating practices ("Amok Time" [1967), and a posited race that lives at such an accelerated rate that humans seem motionless to them ("Wink of an Eye" [1968]), to choose one episode from each season.

Yet the series, admittedly, also offered episodes that were little more than soap operas in space, such as "Journey to Babel" (1967) and "Elaan of Troyius" (1968), and this unfortunately became the pattern for the successor series *Star Trek: The Next Generation* (1987-1994). Whereas Kirk and company had generally visited previously unexplored worlds and often encountered new phenomena, the universe of the second series seemed to be crowded with planets and races that humans were already familiar with, and the episodes tended to involve matters like trade disputes, diplomatic intrigues, and interpersonal crises involving crew members and visitors. This was even more the case in the third, and dullest, of the *Star Trek* series, *Star Trek: Deep Space Nine* (1993-1999), which routinely addressed such fascinating scientific issues as: what are those nasty Cardassians up to now? What is Quark's latest duplicitous scheme? What's going on with those wild and crazy Bajoran priests? This was soap opera raised to the nth degree. (Yes, I know, some commentators have described this as the best *Star Trek* series, yet this only goes to show that there is no accounting for taste.)

*Star Trek: Voyager* (1995-2001) and *Star Trek: Enterprise* (2001-2005) in part reversed this trend to again feature a less populated universe offering challenges other than relating to other people (or aliens that resembled people), which did result in an occasionally interesting episode, but I long remained unable to muster any interest in watching episodes of *Star Trek: The Next Generation* or *Star Trek: Deep Space Nine*. Then, one day, I surprisingly stumbled upon an episode of *Star Trek: The Next Generation* that seemingly contradicted my dismal assessment of those series.

As I began watching "The Chase" (1993) sometime around the middle of the episode, I immediately recognized that, for once, something actually interesting was going on. Evidence had emerged that an ancient alien race had seeded human-like species throughout the galaxy and left behind some sort of message embedded in the DNA of their scattered progeny. Captain Jean-Luc Picard and the *Enterprise* were engaged in a quest to locate the DNA of one final race, now extinct, that could complete the puzzle and finally reveal the message, an effort complicated by the fact that hostile races were also striving to unravel the same mystery. After a tense confrontation with the Romulans and Cardassians on the sought-after planet, Picard and Dr. Beverly Crusher locate the missing DNA fragment and generate a recorded message from a member of the extinct race, who explains that they had sought to create a number of humanoid races throughout the galaxy to alleviate the loneliness of their early universe and expresses the hope that their progeny will someday communicate with each other and develop harmonious relationships.

Here, it seemed, was a singular episode of *Star Trek: The Next Generation* that seemed fully and satisfyingly science-fictional: it provided a somewhat reasonable explanation for *Star Trek*'s bizarre future universe of aliens who had emerged on planets separated by many light years yet were nonetheless not only humanlike in appearance but capable of interbreeding with humans; it offered a noteworthy scientific speculation about how an advanced race might contrive leave a message that would endure for countless millennia (due to the reliable replication of DNA molecules); and except for frissons of threatened violence between the competing species, it was wasting no time on hackneyed personal squabbles. Having discovered an episode of *Star Trek: The Next Generation* that was actually worth watching, I kept checking the television guides so that I could someday see the entire episode. Yet when I finally managed to do so, I was vastly disappointed.

What I learned was that the genuinely involving story I experienced had been preceded by an inane personal drama. For the episode begins when Picard is visited by his former archaeology professor, Richard Galen, who berates his former student yet again for his foolish decision to abandon archaeology, a field where he had shown so much promise, for a career as a Starfleet officer; and he insists that Picard must now resign from his position in order to assist him in a mysterious new research project of immeasurable importance. When Picard, quite understandably, refuses to do so, Galen storms off to work by himself; he is promptly attacked and injured, and by the time the *Enterprise* reaches his spacecraft, he is dying. Then, after he dies, Picard examines the research materials he left behind, gradually figures out that his old professor was seeking scattered fragments of alien DNA in order to assemble some sort of ancient message, and resolves to solve the mystery himself. That is about the moment when I tuned in for the first time.

It is impossible to understate just how idiotic these preliminary developments are. In the first place, each and every year, thousands of undergraduate students who display great talent in one field choose to pursue a career in another field, and their professors calmly accept those decisions, wisely recognizing that students themselves are best able to choose their own careers and understanding that their disciplines will always keep attracting a sufficient number of qualified graduate students even if some students with great potential make different choices. For heaven's sake, when my daughter was at college, one of her mathematics professors urged her to seek a doctoral degree in mathematics, but when told that she was instead planning to go to law school, the professor didn't scream at my daughter that she was ruining her life by failing to pursue a career in mathematics. Instead, she wished her the best of luck and carried on with her career without pestering her again.

In the second place, if seasoned scholars are ever in need of assistance, they will look for a person who possesses the appropriate credentials—another professor with a doctoral degree, or an advanced graduate student. They would never for a moment think about recruiting a former undergraduate student, no matter how brilliant he or she was, because such an individual, lacking the necessary advanced training, would be utterly useless to them.

All of Galen's actions, then, are impossibly stupid. As a comparable situation, imagine that President Barack Obama, sometime during his second term in office, had been visited by his old chemistry professor from Princeton, who yelled at him for foolishly abandoning chemistry to go to law school and demanded that he immediately resign the Presidency in order to assist with an important new experiment. Does anything about this scenario sound plausible to you?

Why, then, one must ask, would authors Ronald D. Moore and Joe Menosky precede their unusually worthwhile story with this ridiculous preamble? One cannot discount the possibility that it was simply a matter of killing time, since the story of tracking down the DNA and obtaining the message evidently proved insufficient to fill the forty-eight minutes or so that every episode must occupy. Yet by the time they had reached the series' sixth season (when "The Chase" was filmed), writers had perfected many different ways to kill time during episodes, one favorite device being a subplot involving the personal travails of the self-involved android Data. There were any number of strategies that the writers might have employed to extend the story of "The Chase" to the necessary length; why did they create the character of a former professor who briefly seeks Picard's purportedly valuable assistance?

The sad conclusion one must reach is this: the plot of "The Chase," from the perspective of the series' producers, was inadequate because it lacked a *personal* angle. One could not have Picard and his crew searching for pieces of an alien puzzle purely as a matter of *intellectual curiosity*; no, their audiences couldn't possibly relate to *that*. Instead, some character had to be provided with a *personal* motive to make the quest seem plausible and resonant for viewers. Thus, Picard would undertake to solve the mystery of humanity's origins solely in order to perform a final service for a beloved professor whom he had previously disappointed, and in that way he would make amends for his perceived misdeeds. And that would make his quest truly *meaningful*.

This sad theory is confirmed by Larry Nemecek's *The Star Trek: The Next Generation Companion* (1995), which notes that "what finally sold [producers Rick] Berman and [Michael] Piller on the idea" for the episode "was the addition of the emotional stakes for Picard with his mentor's death" (243), as the character of Galen was introduced to replace a Vulcan scientist with no previous ties to Picard. Another book quotes co-writer Moore reporting Piller's original problem with the episode: "There wasn't enough character. He felt there wasn't a strong

Picard drive for why he would do this" (cited in *Captains' Logs* 276). Apparently, therefore, the series now needed to revise its series' iconic introductory oath, acknowledging that the "continuing mission" of the *Enterprise* was now "to explore strange, new worlds; to seek out new life, and new civilizations; to boldly go where no one has gone before… but only if the captain has a compelling personal reason for doing so."

Needless to say, this prologue to the episode functioned to fiercely trivialize the pursuit of fascinating new knowledge that had first appeared, based on my partial viewing, to drive the episode. But as is almost invariably the case in television science fiction, the story ultimately had to be about *people*, not about *ideas*, because, after all, what could possibly be more important in a vast and incomprehensible universe than the daily concerns of a few typical people? That is why *FlashForward* devoted virtually all of its energies to developing its characters and exploring their personal issues, and why it became a series, like virtually all contemporary science fiction series, with very little to interest the traditional science fiction reader.

* * * *

So, what is the answer for people who originally became devoted to science fiction because it pondered exciting new ideas and mind-expanding future possibilities? If television programs, now devoted to retelling conventional dramas in novel settings, are not providing that peculiar sort of intellectual thrill, one might expect a commentator to suggest that people turn off their sets and spend their time reading science fiction books and stories. Unfortunately, however, if such a call inspired individuals to visit the science fiction section of a bookstore or library, they would largely be greeted by shelf after shelf of science fiction television in the forms of books: in many cases, the books are literally adaptations of television series like *Star Trek* or *Doctor Who*, with all the flaws of their source material, and in other cases, the books will be devoted to stories that are very much like television, featuring recurring heroes like Honor Harrington or Miles Vorkosigan adventuring in a future universe that seems very much like the present, except for all of those spaceships and exotic aliens. Thus, just as I have largely given up watching science fiction television, I also spend very little time reading recent science fiction novels.

Instead, I am increasingly choosing to escape from a disturbing present by escaping into the past—a strategy outlined in another innovative episode of the original *Star Trek*, "All Our Yesterdays" (1969) and Clifford D. Simak's *Our Children's Children* (1974), wherein residents of doomed planets seek refuge by time-traveling into past eras. So I continue to read a lot of older science fiction, rediscovering cherished works by authors like Arthur C. Clarke and Philip K. Dick or experiencing for the first time some of their less renowned works. Perhaps that is simply what one would expect an old man to do, but it is entirely rational to prefer the past to the present if the past is actually better than the present, and I would objectively argue that that is generally true in the case of science fiction. And so, after completing this column, I will be happily rereading Dick's *Galactic Pot-Healer* (1969), a novel that is surely most interesting and worthwhile than the vast majority of science fiction novels published today.

# WORKS CITED

Aldiss, Brian W. *Billion Year Spree: The True History of Science Fiction*. 1973. New York: Schocken Books, 1974.

——, with David Wingrove. *Trillion Year Spree: The History of Science Fiction*. New York: Atheneum, 1986.

——, Brian Stableford, and Edward James. "On 'On the True History of Science Fiction.'" *Foundation: The Review of Science Fiction*, No. 47 (Winter/Spring, 1990), 28-33.

"All Our Yesterdays." *Star Trek*. New York: NBC-TV, March 14, 1969.

"Amok Time." *Star Trek*. New York: NBC-TV, September 15, 1967.

Anderson, Poul. *The High Crusade*. 1960. New York: McFadden Books, 1964.

Angenot, Marc. "Jules Verne: The Last Happy Utopianist." *Science Fiction: A Critical Guide*. Edited by Patrick Parrinder. London and New York: Longman, 1979, 18-33.

Ashley, Mike. Letter. *Interzone*, No. 128 (February, 1998), 5, 30.

Asimov, Isaac. "Catch That Rabbit." *Astounding Science-Fiction*, 32 (February, 1944), 159-178.

——. "Escape." (As "Paradoxical Escape") *Astounding Science-Fiction*, 35 (August, 1945), 79-98.

——. "Evidence." *Astounding Science-Fiction*, 38 (September, 1946), 121-140.

——. The Evitable Conflict." *Astounding Science-Fiction*, 45 (June, 1950), 48-68.

——. *I, Robot*. New York: Gnome Press, 1950.

——. *In Memory Yet Green: The Autobiography of Isaac Asimov, 1920-1954*. Garden City, New York: Doubleday, 1979.

——. "Liar!" *Astounding Science Fiction*, 27 (May, 1941), 43-55.

——. "Little Lost Robot." *Astounding Science-Fiction*, 39 (March, 1947), 111-132.

——. *Robots and Empire*. 1985. New York: Del Rey/Ballantine Books, 1986.

———. "Runaround." *Astounding Science-Fiction*, 29 (March, 1942), 94-103.

Ballard, J. G. "The Terminal Beach." 1964. *Chronopolis*. By J. G. Ballard. 1971. New York: Berkley Books, 1972, 59-82.

———. "Which Way to Inner Space?" "Guest Editorial." *New Worlds*, 40 (May, 1962), 2-3, 116-118.

Benford, Gregory. *Deep Time: How Humanity Communicates Across Millennia*. New York: Avon Books, 1999.

———. "Stephen Baxter's *Riding the Rock* in Context." *The New York Review of Science Fiction*, No. 175 (March, 2003), 13.

Berman, Judith. "Science Fiction without the Future." *The New York Review of Science Fiction*, No. 153 (May 2001), 1, 6-8.

"The Best of Both Worlds." *Star Trek: The Next Generation*. Syndicated: Paramount, June 18, 1990, and September 24, 1990.

Birkerts, Sven. Review of *Oryx and Crake* by Margaret Atwood. *New York Times Book Review*, May 18, 2003, 12.

Bleiler, Everett F., with Richard Bleiler. *Science-Fiction: The Gernsback Years*. Kent, Ohio: Kent State University Press, 1998.

Campbell, John W., Jr. "Non-Escape Literature." 1959. *Collected Editorials from Analog*. Selected by Harry Harrison. Garden City: Doubleday, 1966), 227-231.

Card, Orson Scott. *Pastwatch: The Redemption of Christopher Columbus*. New York: Tor Books, 1996.

"The Chase." *Star Trek: The Next Generation*. Syndicated: April 26, 1993.

Clute, John. "Books Reviewed: Been Bondage." *Interzone*, No. 126 (December, 1997), 52-55.

———. Comments in "Mantra, Tantra, and Specklebang." *Ansible*, No. 118 (May, 1997). At news.ansible.uk/a118.html .

*The Day the Earth Stood Still*. Twentieth-Century Fox, 1951.

Dick, Philip K. *Solar Lottery*. New York: Ace Books, 1955.

Egan, Greg. Letter. *Interzone*, No. 130 (April, 1998), 2.

"Elaan of Troyius." *Star Trek*. New York: NBC-TV, December 20, 1968.

Ellison, Harlan. "Pretty Maggie Moneyeyes." 1967. *I Have No Mouth & I Must Scream*. By Harlan Ellison. 1967. New York: Ace Books, 1983, 123-152.

Forster, C. M. "The Machine Stops." 1909. *The Wesleyan Anthology of Science Fiction*. Edited by Arthur B. Evans, Istvan Csicsery-Ronay, Jr., Joan Gordon, Veronica Hollinger,

Rob Latham, and Carol McGuirk. Middletown, Connecticut: Wesleyan University Press, 2010, 50-78.

Franklin, H. Bruce. *Robert A. Heinlein: America as Science Fiction*. Oxford and New York: Oxford University Press, 1980.

Gernsback, Hugo. "The Science Fiction League." *Wonder Stories*, 5 (May, 1934), 1061-1065.

———. "Science Wonder Stories." *Science Wonder Stories*, 1 (June, 1929), 5.

"Gernsback, the Amazing." *Time*, 43 (January 3, 1944), 40, 42.

"Greetings, Electronitwits!" *Newsweek*, 23 (January 3, 1944), 54, 56.

Gross, Edward, and Mark A. Altman. *Captains' Logs: The Unauthorized Complete Trek Voyages*. Boston: Little, Brown, 1995.

Guran, Paula. "Tribal Stand." Locus Online website, posted on September 9, 2002. At http://www.locusmag.com/2002/Commentary/Guran09_Standard.html .

Heinlein, Robert A. *Grumbles from the Grave*. Edited by Virginia Heinlein. New York: Del Rey/Ballantine, 1989.

———. "Introduction: Pandora's Box." *The Worlds of Robert A. Heinlein*. New York: Ace Books, 1966, 7-31. Revised and updated version of "Where To?"

———. "Ordeal in Space." 1948. *The Past Through Tomorrow: "Future History" Stories*. New York: G. P. Putnam's Sons, 1967, 281-293.

———. "Pandora's Box." *Expanded Universe: The New Worlds of Robert A. Heinlein*. New York: Ace Book, 1980, 309-353. Further revised and further updated version of "Where To?" and "Introduction: Pandora's Box." Listed in the Table of Contents as two separate articles: "Pandora's Box" (309-315) and "Where To?" (316-353), the later treated as a subsection of "Introduction: Pandora's Box" in its 1966 publication.

———. "Where To?" *Galaxy*, 3 (February, 1952), 13-22. Republished, as "Where To?," as one of two "Introductions" in *All About the Future*. Edited by Martin Greenberg. New York: Gnome Press, 1955, 13-23.

"Journey to Babel." *Star Trek*. New York: NBC-TV, November 17, 1967.

"The Menagerie." *Star Trek*. New York: NBC-TV, November 17 and November 24, 1966.

Miller, Jack, writer. Will Ely, artist. "The Secret of Mount Olympus. *Rip Hunter...Time Master*, No. 11 (November-December, 1962).

Morressy, John. *The Mansions of Space*. New York: Ace Books, 1983.

Nemecek, Larry. *The Star Trek: The Next Generation Companion*. Revised Edition. New York: Pocket Books, 1995.

Nicholls, Peter. "Big Dumb Objects and Cosmic Enigmas: The Love Affair Between Space Fiction and the Trancendental." *Space and Beyond: The Frontier Theme in Science Fiction*. Edited by Gary Westfahl. Westport, Connecticut: Greenwood Press, 2000, 11-23.

Nussbaum, Abigail. "Flashforward." The Encyclopedia of Science Fiction. Edited by John Clute, David Langford, Peter Nicholls and Graham Sleight. Gollancz website, posted on December 21, 2011. At http://www.sf-encyclopedia.com/entry/flashforward .

"A Piece of the Action." *Star Trek*. New York: NBC-TV, January 12, 1968.

Pohl, Frederik. *The Way the Future Was: A Memoir*. New York: Del Rey/Ballantine Books, 1978.

Pringle, David. "Time-Travellers in Global Space: On Similarities Between Jules Verne and J. G. Ballard (Notes for an Unwritten Essay)." Worlds Enough and Time: Exploring the Space-Time Continuum of Science Fiction and Fantasy. Program of the 1997 Science Fiction Research Association/J. Lloyd Eaton Conference, Long Beach, California. Edited by Gary Westfahl. Privately printed, 1997, [6–7].

Putnam, Robert D. "Bowling Alone: America's Declining Social Capital." *Journey of Democracy*, 6:1 (1995), 65-78.

Robinson, Kim Stanley. *Blue Mars*. 1996. New York: Bantam Spectra, 1997.

Rood, Robert T., and James S. Trefil. *Are We Alone?: The Possibility of Extraterrestrial Civilizations*. New York: Scribner's, 1981.

Ryman, Geoff. "Family, or, The Nativity and Flight into Egypt Considered as Episodes of *I Love Lucy*." *Interzone*, No. 127 (January, 1998), 34-50.

Sagan, Carl. *The Cosmic Connection: An Extraterrestrial Perspective*. Garden City, New York: Doubleday, 1973.

——. *Pale Blue Dot: A Vision of the Human Future in Space*. New York: Random House, 1994.

———, F. D. Drake, Ann Druyan, Timothy Ferris, John Lomberg, and Linda Salzman Sagan. *Murmurs of Earth: The Voyager Interstellar Record*. New York: Random House, 1978.

Sands, Karen, and Marietta Frank. *Back in the Spaceship Again: Juvenile Science Fiction Series Since 1945*. Westport, Connecticut: Greenwood Press, 1999.

Schweitzer, Darrell. Letter. *Interzone*, No. 131 (May, 1998), 4-5.

Stableford, Brian. "Creators of Science Fiction, 10: Hugo Gernsback." *Interzone*, No. 126 (December, 1997), 47-50.

———. Review of *Meeting in Infinity* by John Kessel. *Foundation: The Review of Science Fiction*, No. 56 (Autumn, 1992), 124-128.

*Star Trek IV: The Voyage Home*. Paramount, 1986.

Sterling, Bruce. "Preface." *Mirrorshades: The Cyberpunk Anthology. Edited by Bruce Sterling*. 1986. New York: Ace Books, 1988, ix-xvi.

"Turnabout Intruder." *Star Trek*. New York: NBC-TV, June 3, 1969.

Verne, Jules. *Twenty Thousand Leagues under the Sea*. 1870. Translated by Anthony Bonner. New York: Bantam Books, 1962.

Viehl, S. L. *Beyond Varallan*. New York: Roc Books, 2000.

———. *Endurance*. New York: Roc Books, 2001.

———. *Shockball*. New York: Roc Books, 2001.

———. *StarDoc*. New York: Roc Books, 2000.

Weinberg, Robert. *Horror of the 20th Century: An Illustrated History*. Portland, Oregon: Collectors Press, 2000.

Westfahl, Gary. "America's Dumbest Columnist, Or, The Remarking Moron." *Interzone,* No. 161 (November, 2000), 55–56.

———. "The Anthology on the Edge of Forever." *Interzone*, No. 159 (September, 2000), 47–48.

———. "Big Dumb Opticals: Film Considered as the Motion Pyramid." *Interzone*, No. 150 (December, 1999), 52–53.

———. "Celebrating a Century of Science Fiction Columns with *A Trip to the Moon*." *Interzone*, No. 176 (February, 2002), 47–48.

———. "A Christmas Cavil, or, It's a Plunderful Life." *Interzone*, No. 151 (January, 2000), 48–49.

———. "Claremont, California: Notes from the Home Front." *Interzone*, No. 174 (December, 2001), 52–53.

———. "Cremators of Science Fiction, 1 and 2: Brian Stableford and John Clute." *Interzone*, No. 130 (April, 1998), 51–53.

Revised and republished as "Cremators of Science Fiction: Brian
Stableford and John Clute on Hugo Gernsback and His
Legacy" in *Hugo Gernsback and the Century of Science
Fiction*. By Gary Westfahl. Jefferson, North Carolina:
McFarland Publishers, 2007, 7-16.

——. "Did Alien Astronauts Make the Shroud of Turin?" *Interzone,*
No. 136 (October, 1998), 50–51.

——. "The End of Science Fiction's Childhood." *Interzone*, No.
184 (November/December, 2002), 49–51.

——. "The Genre That Evolved: On Science Fiction as Children's
Literature." *Foundation: The Review of Science Fiction*, No.
62 (Winter, 1994/1995), 70–75.

——. "A Glimpse at the Future: A First Look at *FlashForward*."
Locus Online website, posted on September 26, 2009. At
http://www.locusmag.com/Reviews/2009/09/glimpse-of-
future-first-look-at.html .

——. "Going Where Lots of People Have Gone Before, or, The
Novels Science Fiction Readers Don't See." *Interzone*, No.
170 (August, 2001), 54–55.

——. "Greyer Lensmen, Or Looking Backward in Anger."
*Interzone*, No. 129 (March, 1998), 40–43.

——. "The History of Heinlein's Future." *Interzone,* No. 182
(September, 2002), 53–55.

——. "In Search of Dismal Science Fiction." *Interzone*, No. 189
(May/June, 2003), 55–56.

——. "Janeways and Thaneways: The Better Half, and Worse Half,
of Science-Fiction Television." *Interzone*, No. 140 (February,
1999), 31–33.

——. "Martians Old and New, Still Standing Over Us." *Interzone*,
No. 168 (June, 2001), 57–58.

——. "A Modem Utopia, Or, Why Allison's Boring Daddy Hopes
the Machine Doesn't Stop." *Interzone,* No. 149 (November,
1999), 53–54.

——. "The Nine Billion Names of Fantasy…and an Encyclopedia
of Other Concerns." *Interzone*, No. 142 (April, 1999), 52–53.

——. "The Odds Against Tomorrow, or, How I Spent My Summer
Vacation." *Interzone*, No. 193 (Spring, 2004), 29–31.

——. "On the True History of Science Fiction." *Foundation: The
Review of Science Fiction*, No. 47 (Winter/Spring, 1990),
5–27.

——. "Pastwonder: The Redemption of Orson Scott Card."
*Interzone*, No. 144 (June, 1999), 50–52.

——. "Point and Cringe: A Non-Innovative, Non-Interactive Column." *Interzone*, No. 131 (May, 1998), 52–53.

——. "Poul Anderson and the Human Crusade." *Interzone*, No. 173 (November, 2001), 46–47.

——. "Prehistory Lessons." *Interzone*, No. 157 (July, 2000), 49–50. Title given on Contents page as "On Prehistory Lessons."

——. "Reading Mars: Changing Images of Mars in Twentieth-Century Science Fiction." *The New York Review of Science Fiction*, 13 (December, 2000), 1, 8–13.

——. "Robert A. Heinlein's *2001: A Space Odyssey*." *Interzone*, No. 163 (January, 2001), 54–55.

——. "Rules for Robots: Version 1.0." *Interzone,* No. 185 (January, 2003), 53–55.

——. "Science Fiction Is the Simplest Thing." *Foundation: The International Review of Science Fiction*, No. 89 (Autumn, 2003), 5–12.

——. "'Scuse Me While I Kiss the Sky: An Open Letter to a Young Science Fiction Scholar." *Interzone*, No. 147 (September, 1999), 53–54.

——. "Searching for Tomorrow: A Second Look at *FlashForward*." Locus Online website, posted on March 14, 2010. At http://www.locusmag.com/Reviews/2010/03/searching-for-tomorrow-second-look-at.html .

——. "Sector General: The Next Generation?" *Interzone*, No. 179 (May, 2002), 52–54.

——. "The Sky Is Appalling, Or, Go to Bed, Jeremy, An Asteroid Isn't Going to Land on Our House Tonight." *Interzone,* No. 134 (August, 1998), 45–46.

——. "The Sound of the City…and the Call of the Cosmos." *Interzone*, No. 153 (March, 2000), 48–50.

——. "Surprising Sci-Fi Soul Brothers: Robert A. Heinlein and Philip K. Dick." Locus Online website, posted on March 1, 2005. At http://www.locusmag.com/2005/Features/03_Westfahl_RAH_PKD.html .

——. "Talking to Aliens—and to Ourselves." *Interzone*, No. 164 (February, 2001), 55–57.

——. "The Three Most Important Reasons Why Gary Westfahl Doesn't Compile Science Fiction Lists." *Interzone*, No. 166 (April, 2001), 46–47.

"Tomorrow Numbly Dies: A Final Look at *FlashForward*." Locus Online website, posted on May 30, 2010. At http://www.

locusmag.com/Reviews/2010/05/tomorrow-numbly-dies-a-final-look-at-flashforward/ .

——. "Unlucky Starr and the Omission of Venus." *Interzone*, No. 138 (December, 1998), 51–52.

——. "What Is a Science Fiction Magazine? (And Why on Earth Are They Still Around?)" *Interzone*, No. 155 (May, 2000), 38–39.

——. "Who *Didn't* Kill Horror." *Interzone*, No. 188 (April, 2003), 50–51.

——. "Why Science Fiction Fears the Future." *Interzone*, No. 180 (June/July, 2002), 54–55.

——. "Why Science Fiction (Thank Goodness!) Still Doesn't Get Any Respect." *Interzone*, No. 190 (July/August, 2003), 55–56.

——. "Why the Stars Are Silent: The Decline and Fall of the Science Fiction Monomyth (and, Incidentally, the Human Race)." *Interzone*, No. 128 (February, 1998), 43–46.

——, and David Pringle. "Fellow Travelers: Jules Verne and J. G. Ballard." *Interzone*, No. 191 (September, 2003), 55–57.

"Who Mourns for Adonais?" *Star Trek*. New York: NBC-TV, September 22, 1967.

"Wink of an Eye." *Star Trek*. New York: NBC-TV, November 29,, 1968.

Wollheim, Donald A. "That Moon Plaque." *Men on the Moon*. Edited by Donald A. Wollheim. Revised edition. New York: Ace Books, 1969, 146-147.

——. *The Universe Makers: Science Fiction Today*. New York: Harper, 1971.

www.ingramcontent.com/pod-product-compliance
Lightning Source LLC
Chambersburg PA
CBHW032210030726
47494CB00020B/946